FILTHY DARK

THE FIVE POINTS' COLLECTION: THREE

SERENA AKEROYD

D1713385

DEDICATION

To Christine, Cynthia, Jennifer, Anne-Susann, Gem, Amber, and Jemma.
For your help, support, and most importantly, friendship.
<3

PLAYLIST

IF YOU'D LIKE to hear a curated soundtrack, with songs that are featured in the book, as well as songs that inspired it, then here's the link:

https://open.spotify.com/playlist/3JeKrEAH4jqVvv1cEwmewp

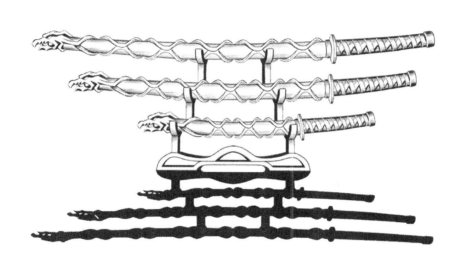

WARNING

AT SOME POINT in this book, you *will* come across terminology you won't appreciate.

And I certainly don't.

But many people, especially of Aidan Sr.'s generation, do agree with it. It's a disgraceful standpoint, however, I'm of Seamus's ilk. If we don't open a dialogue, how do we get people to understand that hate is hate?

I make this warning only so you're aware that I AM 100% anti-homophobia, and a full believer that love is love *is* love. So, don't hate on me for raising a topic of conversation, one that might take place around any dining table around the world, and drawing light on it.

With kids like Seamus around, maybe, just maybe, we can make the next generation more understanding.

With that being said, much love to *you*. <3

BRENNAN

SEVENTEEN YEARS AGO

HUNCHING my shoulders against the cold, I watched my breath mist out in front of me. It was either that or head into the convenience store opposite and grab some cigs, which I couldn't do.

Ma'd already threatened to lop off my head if she caught me stinking of smoke, and while I wasn't averse to a clipped ear, what with being twenty-three, I didn't give much of a shit anymore. My wrist was fucked, thanks to how many times Da had broken it, and I'd been shot at twice. I could cope with her pulling on my ear like it was stuck on with Velcro. Dealing with Mariska's repugnance, however, was another matter entirely.

Her man smoked. Heavy duty Cubans were his poison of choice, and whenever she smelled them on me because Da had a habit too, it always took her twice as long to get into it.

I needed to get off like a junkie needed a fix, so getting some smokes was only going to delay what my body craved.

Her.

It had been a motherfucker of a day. We'd lost two men in a stupid goddamn raid with the Haitians, which I could easily see triggering a war as they weren't bowing to my father's will like he was used to. The waste of life as well as the futility of our work just made me wonder what the fuck I was doing all this for.

It wasn't for Mariska.

She'd never leave her husband. I didn't blame her either. It wasn't like she was married to some shoe salesman. You married into the Bratva and you didn't get out. Not outside of a body bag. And when you were the Pakhan's woman, death was a kind fate.

Leaning back against the wall, I felt the bricks dig into my bones, but I was used to being uncomfortable, so I just stared straight ahead, patient as ever until, in my periphery, I saw about four or five kids running toward the store.

They had tights over their heads and were packing heat. The sight of them told me exactly what was about to go down, but I made no move to get involved. This was our territory, so technically, I should offer to help, especially since the convenience store paid us protection money.

Instead, I watched curiously.

Especially when one of the kids, in a pair of retro-ed Air Jordan XIIs, caught my eye.

My brother had just bought a pair of them, and they stuck out like a sore thumb. Not only had they been on a shortlist, so they were rare as fuck, but the white and red design caught my attention—Declan's.

I scanned the guy, registered his height and weight, and knew it was likely, even if the fact he was jacking convenience stores blew my mind.

I'd warned Da that the crew he was hanging around with was no good. That Cillian Donahue gave me bad vibes, and that Jonny kid? He was messed up. Had weird-ass eyes that were the opposite of trustworthy. But my fucked up father insisted they were what Declan needed. "They'll make a man out of him," he'd told me the last time I raised the subject with him.

When the gang surged in and surged out, my initial impression was they did a great job. It was practically pro—no screaming, and at a moment where the number of patrons was low so there were fewer risks of casualties... this wasn't their first time.

As I scraped a hand across my jaw, I watched as they headed out, triumphantly holding their winnings, before they rushed into the darkness.

I had no idea what kind of game Declan was pulling, but I wasn't a snitch. We all got into shit, it was how we grew, how we figured out if our crew had our backs or not... it was an important life lesson.

While my mind ticked away as I wondered how deeply into this shit Dec was, a car pulled up.

Recognizing the Porsche, I slipped away from the wall, stooped my shoulders, and kept my face in my hood as I headed to the vehicle. Ducking into the car, I kept my gaze straight ahead. I didn't even turn to greet Mariska, just rested a hand on her leg as a silent 'hello' as she revved the engine and we got the hell out of there.

Declan wasn't the only one getting lucky tonight.

ONE

AELA

NOW

HAVE your eyes ever met someone's across a crowded room?

Have you ever looked into that person's eyes, and somehow known you were theirs?

That they were yours?

I was fifteen when that happened to me.

It wasn't the first and only time it happened either. It kept on happening, only with the same guy. Over and over and over, it occurred.

Our eyes would connect, and it was like the sun would peep out from behind the clouds on a dull day.

I knew it sounded like nonsense, but it actually wasn't.

Every time my gaze was captured by Declan O'Donnelly's, I knew we were meant to be together.

That was what made things so awkward.

I wasn't his.

He wasn't mine.

He was my best friend's.

And that was only the start of all the trouble.

My father had been low down on the totem pole in the Five Points' Mob for most of my life, meaning I'd been pretty much a nonentity. Only when he'd been promoted had I started attending a decent school, and that was where I met Deirdre.

She was the kind of girl who knew everyone and everything, and somehow, she'd taken me under her wing when I arrived at St. Mary's Middle School for Girls.

Nearly twenty years later, I still wasn't sure if that was the best thing that had ever happened to me or the worst.

Deirdre had been kind and sweet to me. Enough so that I hadn't realized what a manipulative bitch she was until I was nearly seventeen.

You read that right—for nearly six years, the cow managed to pull the wool over my eyes. But I didn't do what I did to get back at her.

No, back then I'd been too innocent to be so conniving.

I'd appreciated her friendship when I'd suddenly gone from a regular, run-of-the-mill PS162 school to a private Catholic middle school.

When St. Mary's had been forcibly closed due to—and this always amused the hell out of me—abuse because the nuns used to get whippy with it when you were really bad, we'd had to go to St. John's High School.

A *mixed* private high school.

For girls who'd only been surrounded by other girls all their school life, it had been groundbreaking. For me, it was just normal. Still, I'd been allowed to meet Deirdre's Declan for the first time ever, and when we *had* met?

That was when the whole world crashed and burned to a halt.

All this time later, as I sat beside his hospital bed, I still couldn't believe how powerful that moment had been.

I was an artist now. A mom. I wasn't some dopey kid who had her head in the clouds, her hands covered in paint—although they still were most of the time—and her will easily molded to what others wanted.

With the power of time, a reputation that had been hard-won, and after coming to terms with being a single mom, I was still mind blown by that connection.

I created art in many mediums, had worked in studios around the world, picking up techniques and teaching them, my mind was a hive of creativity... but no matter what I did, I couldn't replicate that sensation.

It was like a lightning bolt between the eyes. It was so strong, it should have killed me, but it didn't. It almost zapped my heart, but hearts were a little supernatural in their ability to regenerate themselves—over time.

Or so I'd thought.

Watching over the man I'd grown to hate, a hate that would always be founded with a seed of love, was proof of that.

I'd thought that was it for me. I was one and done. Guys were a pain in the ass that I had no time for. The only dude I wanted around was my kid. He took up every second of my non-working time, every ounce of my energy. But it took one look at Declan for me to know it was all bullshit. Lies I told myself to make it easier to live without the love of my life.

That was why it was a punch in the gut for him to have almost died.

My hands itched with the need to draw him, to take in the majesty of his face. A hard jaw, a stubborn firm slash for a mouth, eyes that were usually narrowed with distrust. He had a dark face, one built with features that were perfect for his choice of career. Somehow, though it was hardened, it was utterly perfect to me.

So wonderfully complex to draw.

There was a play of light and shadow on his brow, furrowed lines between them too. Either side of his eyes, there were squint lines, making him so much more interesting than he'd been as a boy.

Pitch black stubble made him look even tougher, and while his hair was a tousled mess and should have made him look less hardcore, it didn't. So much so, I wanted him to open his eyes because that would reveal the only softness to his nature. A softness I'd lost any and all rights to access a long time ago—his soul.

Mournfully, I blew out a breath, then jerked when the door opened and my gaze clashed with Brennan's.

I liked Brennan, but unfortunately when I looked at him, we didn't have the same sparks.

I wished we did.

I wished I could be with him.

He was insane, like all the O'Donnelly sons—you couldn't not be when spawned from Aidan Sr.'s seed—but he was the most grounded, I thought.

When I looked at him, I felt calm, felt like my brain wasn't whirring with a mixture of panic.

But I didn't want to paint him, and that was indicative of my feelings for him. Or the lack of them, I guessed.

So I smiled at him weakly as he rasped, "What are you doing here?"

I shrugged. "I don't know."

His brow furrowed. "Hmm." That was all he said, almost making me snort.

Brennan was a man of few words, that was for damn sure.

I pressed my head to the side of the armchair, just resting it for a second.

I wanted, badly, to walk away. I knew when he woke up again, he'd discover the truth and call me chickenshit, but I didn't want to be there when he learned he was a father.

Maybe I should be the one to tell him, but I didn't think I could.

I'd spent so long running, so many years hiding, that I just couldn't do it.

Brennan shook his head at me like he knew what I was thinking. "You need to get out of here, Aela."

I gulped. "I know I do."

"The doctors say they're drawing him out of the coma. When he wakes up, we'll be telling him the truth. You need to bring the kid down here."

"You mean your nephew?" I snapped, irritated by his dismissal of my pride and joy as just a 'kid.'

Brennan wafted a hand. "You know what I mean."

I gritted my teeth. "He's the best O'Donnelly out there," I told him.

"Course he is. He hasn't been tainted by us yet," Brennan rumbled, and his words had me flinching inside.

Because they were true.

And in his eyes, I knew he was being candid and earnest, and it killed me.

For a second, my heart pounded, and the sensation of being trapped was so all-consuming that I wasn't sure what to do.

I'd done the right thing. I'd helped someone in need, but I should have stayed out of it, and now my boy was going to pay the price for that.

Suddenly feeling like I had a melon lodged in my throat, I stared at him and I saw sympathy etched in his features.

Sympathy.

I closed my eyes, clenching them tightly because I couldn't cope with that look.

"Don't even think about running," he warned me, but it wasn't really a warning, it was more of a gentle reminder.

My mouth tightened. "You think I don't know the drill?"

"You forgot it once upon a time," he rasped, making me flinch.

"Because I had sense."

"No, you'd have had sense to stay gone," he told me, and again, his honesty hit me square in the gut. "You always were good people though, Aela. I'll have your back if ever the time comes where you need it."

I gaped at him, unable to believe he handed me that offer.

Everyone knew it was the O'Donnellys against the world. Against the universe. And truth was, they needed to be so tight-knit. They were the head of the Five Points, the one and only Irish Mob family in the tristate area because, long ago, Aidan O'Donnelly Sr. had taken over every other piece of the puzzle and consolidated it, establishing himself as king of the hill a long time before I was born.

As a result, they were the most powerful family on the East Coast. The billionaires and one-percenters thought they were powerful, but that was nothing compared to the clout the O'Donnellys had.

I'd been born revering them like they were the second coming of Jesus though.

The O'Donnellys, for all they were headed by a psychopath, were good leaders. Everyone respected them, loved them even. It was rare to get a traitor in the midst, and not only because Aidan would cut you like a motherfucker either, but because they earned it.

They treated the commoners like they treated the lieutenants—sure, the pay was less, but the respect wasn't. And for people who did the running, who were the most likely to be tossed in jail or prison for the crap they did for the family, respect meant everything.

Feeling tired, I got to my feet because I didn't want to be dealing with any of this now. I just... I didn't even know what I was doing here.

I should have been running far and wide across the Atlantic, but there was no stone I knew the family would leave unturned now that I was in the picture.

Now that Seamus was in the picture.

My jaw clenched and I started to walk toward the door, toward Brennan.

When his hand reached out to grab my arm, and he turned me to face him, I looked up at him and muttered, "I'll probably need your help in the upcoming weeks. You might regret offering me the olive branch." Especially when I thought about the futile argument we'd had this evening, just before Declan had gone off like Mad Max and had come back shot.

What a waste of goddamn energy that had been.

Life, I realized, and not for the first time, was so short. Too short to waste on harsh words and bitter regrets.

He shrugged. "You think I'm frightened of Dec, *laoch*?" His lips twitched, and he revealed the slightest of smiles that, along with his Gaelic endearment, would melt any woman's heart.

Just not mine.

Mine belonged to the bastard on the bed.

The bastard who'd almost *died* on the bed. Twice.

When I'd learned he'd been shot, I'd been unable to stay away. For years, I'd pushed distance between us, uncaring what he did or what happened to him, just living with survival instincts in mind.

But the second I'd known he might be dying?

I'd had no alternative but to come and see for myself.

Thanks to a few misspoken words when I thought the love of my life, the father of my son, was about to leave this world forever, my kid's future was in jeopardy. I'd hate myself for it if I hadn't been traumatized by the sight of Declan as a bunch of surgeons, in this illegal hospital, gathered around him and started to cut his chest wide open.

No one should have to see that.

No one.

"I don't think you're scared of anyone, Brennan," I told him carefully, well aware that was true.

Some might say I was still a dreamer, unrealistic, but I knew how to read people. More than when I was a kid.

I knew what Brennan was and wondered if he knew it too.

He was Aidan Sr. reincarnate.

The thought made a shiver rush down my spine, because that meant he was a psychopath, but Brennan had a self-awareness that was very uncomfortable, and made his kindness all the more perplexing and my trust in him all the more concerning and bewildering.

When Eoghan, Declan's younger brother, had discovered I'd been hiding a son from the family, he'd gone apeshit.

Brennan?

He'd dealt with me—there was that word again—*kindly.*

I gulped, and whispered, "Will you do everything in your power to protect my boy?"

He patted my shoulder. "He's *our* boy," he corrected me, making me shudder. "And you know we will. You should go get him. Bring him here. Not for Declan. We don't want the boy to see his da like this for the first meeting, but the family will want to get to know him."

My stomach twisted, turning sour at the prospect. "I-I have responsibilities up there."

He shrugged once more, and I knew he was about to dismiss a decade's worth of hard work as if it was nothing. "You know they mean shit now."

I gritted my teeth with fury. "I'm a professor at the Rhode Island School of Art, Brennan. Do you know how difficult it was to obtain that position? Do you know what I had to sacrifice—"

He snorted. "Use that argument on Declan, and I'm pretty sure he'll blow his top." Another pat. All the more discomforting. "Your life's been in New York ever since you got pregnant. You've just been procrastinating."

I wanted to wail that I had a life, that I had plans that had nothing to do with the many and various crimes the family committed. That that wasn't my future anymore.

But when I looked at him, I knew what I was seeing.

The stonewalling that would make it so that if I didn't do as I was told, Seamus would be taken from me.

Was it weak to concede defeat?

Or strong to accept it? Because for my boy, I'd kill. And in this world, those words held real-life consequences.

I bit my lip, grinding my teeth hard as I shoved away from him, and when I walked toward the door, he called out softly, so softly that I felt the threat worse than if he'd pressed a knife to my throat. "Don't think to run, Aela. If you do, the consequences will be a thousand times worse."

The statement, and that he'd felt he had to repeat the warning, had me shoving the Velcro-ed sheets that acted as a doorway open, dashing out of the freaky clinic I was sitting in, and running to the bathroom so I could puke my guts out.

The place was beyond weird.

Situated in the middle of a warehouse, clear, see-through plastic had been rigged up to create a sterile space within a space.

Inside, there were two hospital beds surrounded by all the equipment you'd expect in an ER or ICU.

That was the clout the O'Donnellys had.

They didn't need access to hospitals, they had their own. Anywhere, any time. With a team of nurses and doctors and surgeons on hand who'd jump to help, it was all the more disconcerting to be in the web again.

To know the spider was closing in on me, and I was the one stupid enough to come traipsing inside.

When my knees were aching, my body trembling as the aftereffects of fear, stress, and anxiety hit me, I leaned back and away from the toilet, pushing the lever so it flushed.

As I watched my meager stomach contents disappear down the drain, I tried to get my thoughts in order.

Obeying didn't come easily to me.

I was known for my anarchist art, known for my feelings on the current government, and my anti-populist stances. It was all well-represented in my work, for God's sake, and my art was internationally renowned.

I'd created pieces for bigwigs. Made works of art for billionaires and corporate sharks, even a few Saudi princes.

Why?

Because I bled them for all they were worth, for every inch they'd given me to have a piece of Aela O'Neill in their homes, and that money? I gave it back to the people.

I was a modern-day Robin Hood for a reason.

I knew what it was like to be controlled, to be under someone's thumb, and I did my best to protect anyone else from that fate.

Of course, there was no one here to help me now.

My Maid Marian was a dude lying on a hospital bed who'd loathe me the second he opened his eyes, and who'd treat me like crap.

But my fate was entwined with his.

I should have known it would bring us back together—sometimes, wishful thinking just never got you far enough away.

I clambered to my feet, and I washed my hands and face with the soap provided. It cut through a day and night's worth of grease, but I still needed a shower badly.

Blowing out a breath as I looked in the mirror, taking in the black curls, the blue streaks that were my rebellion, the elfin face that was too weak, and the eyes that were exhausted, I shook my head and pushed myself away from the spotted mirror and the chipped sink and headed on out.

Was I surprised when a couple of goons appeared at my side?

Maybe I was.

Maybe I wasn't.

I'd thought Brennan was giving me a semblance of control, making it look like I had a say in this, even though I didn't.

The goons?

Proof otherwise. Proof that I wasn't to be trusted.

Pretty smart of them.

When I cast both men a look, I saw Eoghan in the background, Dec's younger brother, eying me.

And I knew.

He'd sent the goons.

I gritted my teeth. I was grateful that Aidan Sr. and Lena O'Donnelly weren't here anymore. After the old man had slapped Brennan for speaking up, for telling the old man to calm down because he was freaking the staff out with his wild temper, I was grateful that they'd gone to Finn O'Grady's apartment to get some rest. Only having to deal with my babysitters was a boon, but I still ignored Eoghan and stormed out into the street.

There was nowhere to go, nowhere to run, but I had to make sure Seamus was prepared for the future that was coming our way.

Unfortunately for me, he was a teenager.

And teenagers were like mini mafiosos without the murdering power.

FML.

DECLAN

"YOU'RE SHITTING ME."

It wasn't a question. It was a statement.

A statement because I knew Brennan was joking. He had to be, didn't he?

Of course, there was massive concern over the fact that he was the one imparting this news to me.

After all, Brennan rarely joked.

It wasn't that he was somber, it was that he saw the world a little differently. There was nothing wrong with that considering the world we lived in was a shower of shit, but still, he wasn't easily amused.

And he'd never laugh or joke about the fact that I had a son out there.

A son I'd fathered with Aela O'Neill.

My throat tightened at the memories of her. She'd been the one who got away. The one I'd loved. Who I'd *let* get away.

At the time, a part of me had been relieved when she'd gone, so there'd been no blame. No recriminations. I'd even thought she was smart to leave the city.

A lot of people underestimated her, but never me.

She was a little ditzy because her mind was usually in a sketchpad, cooking up various things for her projects, but anyone who failed to see how smart she was deserved to be in the outer circle.

She'd been one of the best people I'd known.

Until shit had gone wrong. Until my past had come crawling up my butt and I'd had to let go of the best thing that had ever happened to me.

"How?

Brennan scowled at me. "How?"

Because I knew why he was scowling, I rolled my eyes even though that hurt, and ground out, "I don't need a talk on the birds and the bees, Bren. I'm just talking out loud."

"Oh." He shrugged. "You were boning her on the side for a while. You were dumb back then. Not too hard to figure it out."

I narrowed my eyes at him. "Fuck off, you never knew that."

His lips twisted slightly. "I know everything about the family."

That had me complaining, "When you and Eoghan say crap like that, it's creepy as fuck."

"Maybe, but you should be grateful. At least I know the stuff that would make our enemies come if they got their hands on our weaknesses."

"You didn't know about my son though, did you?" I wasn't smug about that, because I wished I'd known about him too, but Brennan could be an arrogant shithead sometimes.

He wriggled his shoulders. "I can be forgiven for that. When you were busy boning Catholic schoolgirls—"

"I was a Catholic schoolboy at the time," I groused. "So don't make me out to be a pervert—"

"I was working full-time, and you know I had to work hard to make the docks ours."

I rolled my eyes. "Overachiever."

His lips twisted. "You're taking this better than I thought."

"Probably the drugs. They're wearing off," I replied honestly, staring around the hospital ward that was something from a nightmare.

Or an episode of *The Blacklist*.

I'd only woken up in one of these joints once before, and I had to say, I hated it.

We drew out the big guns when someone was badly injured, *illegally*, and waking up like this was just horrendous and something I wouldn't wish on an enemy. Being in the middle of a black space in a bright area that was covered up in plastic sheeting made me feel like the kid in *E.T.*, when the house was all excluded.

Fuck, I'd hated that movie, and that goddamn alien still visited me in my dreams.

Reaching up to rub my eyes, I muttered, "The drugs make everything bearable, I guess."

Brennan snorted. "Don't get any ideas. We've already got one junkie in the family."

I grunted. "Aidan ain't no junkie."

"You're a fool if you don't think he is. Just because he isn't shooting up and doesn't have track marks all over his body doesn't mean he isn't an addict. We're pussyfooting around him—"

I raised a hand. "I can't deal with this right now."

Brennan winced. "Sorry, bro."

"No. It's okay. We need to do something about him, you're right. But I just got my ass handed to me. You need to remember that."

He pursed his lips. "You were reckless."

"Maybe."

As one of the lieutenants of the Five Points' Mob, I often got my hands dirty. Brennan too. It was part of the job, part of the life.

We were high-ranking—the highest because our father trusted no one more than he trusted his boys—but we were still involved with integral parts of the puzzle, even though in most families like ours, the heirs were untouchable, rarely getting involved in wet work.

Things had devolved a few nights ago. Aela O'Neill—a blast from the past if ever there was one—had been visited by an MC Prez's daughter.

The kid had discovered that her partner had been kidnapped by the *Famiglia*, and the Italian cunts were going to kill him unless we helped rescue him.

While we sure as fuck were no white knights, the Hell's Rebels MC was renowned for the quality and their level of production of ghost guns—a type of weapon that had no serial number on them, so they couldn't be traced.

When we'd cut a deal, we'd gone in and saved the fucker, but I'd gotten shot up in the process. I knew for a fact that we'd lost another of our men too.

A sad day.

And even worse, my body hurt like a fucker.

In my own way, I was used to pain though. We all were. Knife fights, gun fights, fist fights—they were par for the course.

That was my life, and I didn't want—

My jaw clenched.

I shouldn't think about that crap.

Couldn't.

Because if I did, I'd do something stupid. I'd be kind or something. I'd think of the son I didn't know existed and not of the family, and family was everything.

It was all.

That was our creed. Something that had been drilled into us for a lifetime.

But with that creed came the realization that if I didn't protect the boy who I'd never known about, he'd be in danger too.

"What's that look on your face?"

Brennan's question had me blinking at him. "Huh? Nothing."

He narrowed his eyes at me. "What's going on with you, Dec? I thought you'd be wicked pissed. That's why I made sure to tell you on my own. Didn't want you upsetting Ma."

I scowled. "Why do you always think I'm going to upset Ma?"

His lips twitched. "Because you usually do."

"Now you're just pissing me off," I growled.

"That's what I do best." His sage tone had me huffing, before he said, "I thought you'd be furious."

I wasn't.

That was the kicker.

I wasn't furious, and I knew I should be.

I had a son.

And family was everything.

I should have been there for him, should have helped him grow, should have helped form him into the man he was going to be some day.

Instead, I'd had no input, but I got it.

I did.

And I was almost sad for the kid, because now?

He was going to be introduced into the life, and it wasn't a good life.

I could admit that to myself.

I could admit it when I'd never thought a damn thing about what I did for a living before, because what I did was just the way of it.

As natural as night following day.

O'Donnellys worked for the family.

That was it.

How it worked.

Like clockwork.

My da had worked for his father, and his brothers had done the same—not that they were as smart as us, of course. But still. We'd turned the fam around, gotten us out of the penny-ante shit, and turned us into a corporation.

But that didn't take away from the bones of what we were.

And I wasn't sure if I wanted a kid of mine doing that, being involved in this crap.

The dilemma had me wondering if Finn, one of our family friends and the Points' money man, was feeling the same way about his kid.

His wife had just had a baby, well, a while back, and I had to wonder if he thought about his son doing the shit we did.

"You're not angry."

The simple statement had me blinking at the opening in the ward. It was odd because it was a make-shift door with plastic sheets that were Velcroed together, so the sound of the ripping should have dragged me from my thoughts. It hadn't.

Maybe the drugs *were* dulling everything.

I stared at my brother, Eoghan, and shook my head. "I will be. Just give me time."

But he didn't smirk at me.

He just stared at me.

Christ.

Brennan and Eoghan always saw too much.

I felt like a petri dish with the way they were both gawking at me, and I scowled at them. "What do you want me to do? Go full out Hulk on you?"

Brennan shrugged. "I think that was what I anticipated."

"Did the doctors say he woke up too early?" Eoghan asked Brennan, pissing me off that they were talking around me, not to me.

I heaved an irritated breath. "Look, I'm tired. I need to rest."

I didn't.

I felt wide awake.

I was definitely more mellow than I should be, definitely a lot more chilled about this situation... yeah, had to be the drugs.

Eoghan grunted. "Stay awake for a little bit longer. Ma's on her way. She was shitting herself."

"Not literally, I hope," I rumbled, trying to tease and failing.

Brennan and Eoghan didn't crack a smile—serious fuckers. "Jesus, where's Conor? At least he'll laugh at my crappy jokes."

"He's asleep in the waiting room. We're all exhausted because we've been here for two goddamn days watching over you."

My mouth turned down. "Yeah. I get it."

"No. I don't think you do," Brennan retorted.

I gritted my teeth before I muttered, "Move the pillows out from behind my head. This position hurts."

Eoghan moved toward me and helped shuffle out the two pillows a nurse had stacked under my shoulders when I'd woken up and found Brennan sitting at my bedside.

The instant relief was enough to make me sigh heavily. I allowed myself to rock back and let my muscles settle.

"I'm just going to rest my eyes," I mumbled, suddenly needing the peace of sleep and a spare moment to stop the buzzing in my head that had nothing to do with almost being shot, blood loss, drugs, or the aftereffects of emergency surgery.

A low hum of conversation came next, and I heard the Velcro softly open and close as they left me to the nightmare ward.

I rocked my head to the side, saw the partition between me and the other guy, Ink, the man we'd gone in to save, and saw he was out cold.

Then again, he'd been tortured. I figured it probably wasn't the first time, judging by all the scars I could see on the parts of his body that weren't covered up with tape, gauze, and wires, but still, torture always took it out of a person.

I pursed my lips, rolled my head up to the ceiling where those godawful surgical lights were blaring onto me, and even though it hurt, I reached up and covered my eyes with my forearm.

I needed to reassimilate things. Needed to figure out what the hell I was thinking and feeling.

I was a father.

I had a son.

That changed everything.

I just didn't know how yet.

TWO

AELA

BEFORE

IN MY PLAID skirt with its box pleats, a crisp linen shirt, and a heavy jacket, I felt more than just stupid. I looked it too. My squeaky leather shoes had these tiny tassels on them, for God's sake. Throw in the knee socks, and I looked like a character from some weird show.

I wasn't used to wearing a uniform. Back before Dad's promotion, I'd just worn regular clothes at my regular school. Then I'd had to move to St. Mary's Middle School for Girls, and we were now being shunted off to St. John's High. St. Mary's had been bad enough with its ankle-length skirts, but, and I knew this was horrendous, it hadn't mattered at St. Mary's.

I was just one girl among a thousand.

St. John's was a different matter entirely.

It was mixed.

Boys were going to see me wearing this getup.

Somehow that was more nauseating than anything else, and I didn't consider myself a vain person. My friend Deirdre, on the other hand, was totally vain, but the only reason she wasn't bitching about the uniform and the fact that we looked like some creepy uncle's 'favorite' niece was because of Declan.

Declan Shmeclan. I'd be glad to meet him at long last just because she went on about him so damn much.

Honestly, it was boring. Like, it never stopped.

Declan this and Declan that.

You'd think he was Brad Pitt with the way she could wax poetically about him. Sister Sarah would have fainted with glee if she'd shown as much imagination in English class, that was for damn sure.

I was pretty certain that Declan was either going to be the most handsome guy the world had ever seen or the most blah. The fact that our other friends had met him and seemed to agree with her told me I was in for a treat, even if it was only on the eyes.

"Stand up straight," Mom chided me, as she shoved me against the wall beside the door.

With Dad's promotion, we'd moved to a better building, but though that move had been two years ago, I still missed the old place. The wall beside the front door had little pencil marks measuring how tall I'd grown, and it was a ritual for us to take my first day of school pictures here.

We were making new rituals in the apartment, but it wasn't the same.

Not much was.

Dad had never been that important in the Five Points, and he still wasn't, but ever since he'd moved up a level, he just wasn't around as much, and he hadn't been around a lot before. If I missed him, I couldn't even imagine what Mom felt. It was no wonder she was taking more and more of her happy pills. Of course, the more she took of them, the less happy she was. Go figure, huh?

I gave her a false smile because she looked so proud to see me dressed in this outfit, and I straightened my shoulders as she held her breath for a second, then hovered her finger over the button. In a snap, a Polaroid was spitting out a little photo, and she wafted it in the air, beaming at it then at me.

"You look beautiful," she told me with a grin, dumping the picture on the hall table before bustling over and hugging me tight.

She gave the best hugs.

Always.

I squeezed her back, loving the way she almost always smelled of vanilla cookies, and wished I was just going to a regular school. Sure, I had friends now, and those friends had been hard earned, but I'd still prefer my old PS.

She kissed my temple and murmured, "You're going to knock 'em dead."

"I doubt it," I grumbled. The only thing unusual about me wasn't something the sisters at St. Mary's had appreciated. I had a good eye for color. That was it. Everything else about me was just average, but I was okay with that.

"You will. Chin up, sweetheart." Another kiss to my temple. "Now, come on. The bus will be here soon."

Twenty minutes later, I was sitting beside Deirdre on the bus as she primped and preened in a mirror.

I wasn't sure how often she had to confess about being vain, but I knew the sisters had removed her compact mirror more times than they'd chided me for my inability to concentrate.

"I can't wait to see him," she was saying, excitement making her voice breathy.

I shot her a look. "You saw him yesterday, didn't you?"

We weren't high enough in the ranks to have attended the end of summer BBQ the O'Donnellys held at their compound, but we all knew about it. And everyone who couldn't attend wished like hell they could.

"Well, yeah, but it wasn't enough." She released a dreamy sigh. "I'm so lucky he's mine."

Wanting to gag, but managing not to, I just hummed. I still wasn't sure why I was friends with Deirdre. She and I weren't alike, but I was grateful to her because she'd taken me under her wing my first day at St. Mary's and had brought me into her circle.

Sometimes I thought it was for the same reason a bride always made her bridesmaids wear shitty dresses—to make herself look better—but I was still happy not to be on my own. She tended to search me out too, sitting next to me and choosing to talk with me rather than the others, though she'd known them a lot longer than she had me and their families were similarly ranked.

Last year, we'd learned about the caste system in India, and I'd realized that was how life was in the Irish Mob. You stuck to your caste, you didn't move from it, you didn't leave it ever, and you worked among it too. Unless you were promoted, and those promotions happened for a reason.

Dad had never said why he'd gone from being a run-of-the-mill gofer, a simple runner who ducked and dove for the Points, to a crew man who answered to a captain, and I'd never ask.

I didn't want to know.

Our good fortune was paid for by the blood of others.

Sometimes, I thought I was the only one who saw that.

In the distance, St. John's loomed up ahead.

It was an old building, looking like something from an architecture magazine, because it resembled a cathedral in my opinion, with its towering turrets, endless rows of windows, and craggy walls that had gargoyles on them—gargoyles I knew I'd be studying and drawing later tonight. It took up an entire block, and in space poor Manhattan, that was really saying something.

As Deirdre carried on talking about Declan—her favorite subject and potentially the reason why she liked sitting next to me, because I let her talk for hours on end about him—I stared at the high school and tried not to be nervous.

I hated new beginnings.

I hated change.

By the time we were halfway through the day, I was still feeling on edge, nervous, but a little better because with the morning done, I only had a couple of hours before I could get the hell out of this uniform. The box pleats bunched up under my butt, making it uncomfortable to sit on, especially because Mom had used a whole freakin' bottle of starch on it. And the shoes pinched.

Badly.

Grunting as I took a seat at the cafeteria table opposite Deirdre, I muttered, "Anyone else hate this uniform?"

It wasn't the first complaint, but because we'd all been dealing with it for half the day, it stirred an argument because Kylie insisted plaid did better things for her butt than the old skirt at St. Mary's had.

As I pondered how plaid could do anything for a butt, I saw him.

I didn't have to know his name to recognize who he was.

What he was.

An O'Donnelly.

He wore the same crappy uniform as us, but he somehow managed to look like a man instead of a boy in it. The guys wore gray pants with a faint pinstripe, a white shirt, matching shoes, and a larger blazer with a long plaid tie. The tie he'd loosened, and he'd unfastened the top button of his shirt. In his hand he held his blazer, and it was all bunched up in a way that told me he didn't give a shit if he wrecked it, and that money didn't matter because if I'd done that and had to buy a new one, Mom would have had a fit.

But the uniform wasn't what made the man, because I was most definitely looking at a man. He was surrounded by boys with fuzz on their lip, for God's sake, weeny kids, where he was a mile ahead of them.

Was it Conor? I knew he was the eldest O'Donnelly at school. Eoghan was a couple of years below me, so this could be Declan.

Deirdre's Declan?

She'd never shown me a picture, but God, no wonder she could talk about him for days.

He was beautiful.

I wanted, so badly, to draw him.

To capture his face in ink, in pencil, in charcoal, in paint. Oils first, then acrylics. I'd even try watercolor, just to see if I could match the color of his skin that was like gold but not. Black Irish. Everything about him screamed it.

Blacker than black hair, rich blue eyes.

Damn.

Just, damn.

I licked my lips, aware I was staring and unable to stop myself. He was so much more than I'd anticipated, like a rock star had come storming into the cafeteria rather than another student.

And I knew I wasn't the only one who felt that way.

Conversation hadn't stopped, but it had definitely toned down. People were watching him, watching his crew, and a weird feeling hit my stomach, something that made me feel hot and shivery as I saw how he commanded the place without even trying.

His gaze darted around the room, and when he found Deirdre, whose back was to him, and who was deep in the middle of a conversation about how the knee socks made her ankles look fat, I expected him to smile—or do something that indicated he liked her.

If anything, his mouth pulled taut, his eyes pinched, and a strange kind of... *no.* That couldn't be.

His features twisted slightly, marring his beauty, before one of his friends caught his attention and his focus broke as he replied.

Then, after he had, and he grinned at whatever they'd been talking about, he turned back to Deirdre.

I sucked in a breath.

He looked at her like he hated her.

Then he looked at me, and I knew why.

Like any predator, he'd scented prey, and my reaction had drawn his eyes to me.

Only, when he looked at *me*, it was the exact opposite of hatred that flashed over his face. He looked startled. Surprised. He even halted in his tracks, which had his buddies bumping into him, which forced him to carry on moving. His nostrils flared for a split second before he managed to get his features under control.

By that time, I ducked my head and focused on my lunch.

As I stared at the baby carrots I'd been dunking in ranch, my mind raced a mile a minute.

What had just happened?

Why had he looked at Deirdre like he hated her, then looked at me as if he didn't?

Feeling overheated and sweaty—neither of which was pleasant in my polyester uniform—I forced my lungs to calm, my heart to slow down. Then he approached my table, and all hell broke loose.

I thought I was going to burn to a pile of ash on the seat, especially when he put his hand on the table and leaned on it.

His body was beside me, his heat so close that the ash thing could still happen, and his scent? Sweet baby Jesus. I'd never smelled anything like it.

It was like heat and man and musk and mint and citrus.

Who smelled like that when they were a teenager? Shouldn't he reek of Axe?

I licked my lips, well aware that, though he was beside me, he didn't look at me again. His focus was on Deirdre, and his voice? Unpleasant.

Oh, not his actual voice. That was deep and husky. Again, making me wonder if he'd had to stay back a grade or something because he was so *old*. He felt so much more mature than anyone else.

Aware I was sweating like I'd been in P.E. all morning, I hunched my shoulders as I recognized that the inherent dislike I'd seen on his face when he'd looked at Deirdre was totally present in his tone too.

She didn't notice. Her cheeks turned bright pink, her eyes glittered, and she stared at him like he was a trophy she coveted.

Maybe he was.

She liked to think of herself as the leader of our little gang, so being tied to Declan upped her position not only among her friends, but in the entirety of the Points.

If she could keep hold of him, tight and fast, and get him to an altar... that would change her whole future.

The thought left me shaken for some stupid reason. I had no idea why the thought of Deirdre marrying Declan like he was some kind of cash cow put me on edge, but it did.

It was done in our world all the time.

Advantageous matches were the norm.

I bit my lip as I reached for my Diet Coke, but unfortunately for me, my movement came at the same time Declan snapped, "You need to stop fucking around, Deirdre. Either you can go, or you can't—"

While I was used to Dad huffing and puffing, the hatred in Declan's voice had me stunned. I knocked over my can, and immediately went to right it, but his hand was there, catching it.

His fingers brushed mine.

And it was like something from a book.

The sparks shot through me, making the tiny hairs on the back of my neck stand on end.

I gulped as he gritted out, "You should be more careful." But his tone was different.

Softer.

Peeping up at him, I shot him a shy and apologetic glance. "Sorry."

"Don't be." His eyes lingered on mine, and I felt the laser-like brand as if I'd just had LASIK.

In my peripheral vision, I saw Deirdre puff up like a pissed off peacock and immediately ducked my head and stared at my tray.

Conversation started up again, and his deep, rumbly voice carried on, but even though everything just muddled on its way, nothing was the same.

Nothing at all.

And I had no idea why.

THREE

AELA

NOW

WHEN SEAMUS'S head popped up at the door opening, I grinned at him.

He'd just turned fourteen, and while he was a precocious pain in my ass because he was a teenager, and he'd been overridden with hormones that made him a jerk, he was mine.

I was proud of him.

I mean, I'd known that before this whole shitstorm, but to be honest, I felt it even more so now.

I'd done this.

On my own.

I'd not only helped give birth to this wonderful kid with zero support system, but he was smart, well-rounded, and a good boy. He worked hard, was conscientious, and he gave a fuck.

Yeah, that was probably what mattered the most to me.

He gave a fuck about things that a lot of kids his age might not have cared about.

He was the one who sorted out our recycling, for Christ's sake. He was the one who was planning on joining a walk next month to protest some Congress ruling that was rolling back ocean conservation.

I'd made this boy what he was, and I had to have faith that his father wouldn't ruin fourteen years of tutelage.

"Mom!" he declared, his face lighting up with happiness now that I was home.

Of course, it was quashed a second later when he realized he was fourteen and he shouldn't be happy to see his mom—it wasn't cool.

But I'd take that one second of joy.

We were close, Shay and me. Even if testosterone was putting a wall between us that I wouldn't be able to breach until he was back to being normal.

After the last few days I'd had, I needed a hug from my main man, so with him on his feet, I didn't even give a shit that he backed away from me like I had pus-ridden sores on my face, like I was a frickin' zombie. I just grabbed him, tackled him into a bear hug, and when he let me, when the struggle wasn't too bad, I smiled into his hair, because he wanted this too.

"Missed you, butt face."

I felt him snicker. "I inherited the butt face from you."

I grinned. "That's why you're so purty."

He scoffed at that, and I let him, just enjoying the hug, enjoying the way his arms were so tight around me—

Fuck.

Was this going to ruin our relationship?

I'd never hidden who his father was from him. What was the point? Along the way, he'd ask, he'd find out, so I'd been candid with him. Just like I was about everything.

He wanted to know about sex at nine, so I told him. Not graphic things, nothing like that. I just explained it, and I did so in a way that wasn't embarrassing because I wanted him to know that he could come to me about anything.

He was a curious kid, and he'd asked questions, just like he did about everything. I fostered that need to grow, and we were solid as a result. Sure, he was getting more secretive and his bedroom door remained glued shut for reasons I thought were penis related, but what went down with him and his sock and hand were his own issues.

So long as I didn't have to clean the socks.

Still, even though he was a little gross, and smelled a bit sweaty after a day at school, he was my boy.

Mine.

Not Declan's.

Even though he was a teeny-weeny bit.

When he started to wriggle in my arms, I grinned and let him go, only after I'd kissed his temple and told him, "You need a shower, stinky."

He wrinkled his nose. "This is the smell of honest, hard-earned sweat."

I arched a brow at him. "What did you do?"

He raised his arm and did a bicep curl. He was still pretty small, but he'd been working out to try to get onto the football team. So far, he was on the squad, just not in the position he wanted to be in.

Something to do with him being too light to be a linebacker, or some crap like that.

I knew the basics of football for his sake, but the minutiae? Not even motherly love could make me embrace that particular game.

My son was a conservationist jock.

I'd done that.

I'd created the next hybrid.

Lips twitching at the thought, I listened in as he explained, "I worked in the garden."

My brows rose at that, and I peered out of the kitchen window and into the yard I'd just passed. It was dark, though, and I couldn't see anything in the meager light.

He huffed. "You'll see in the morning."

I grinned at him. "Should I be excited?"

"Only that we have a lawn now. It was just behind ten tons of crap."

I sniffed. "I considered it a work of art."

"You just hate mowing—"

"You bet your ass I do." I leaned back against the counter. "You been a good kid for Caro?"

He shrugged. "Pretty much."

Taking him at his word, I nodded. "Thanks, Shay. I know it was last minute—"

He heaved a sigh. "I'm not a kid, Mom. I don't need you to explain why you had to go away on business." He rolled his eyes.

I wanted to sob and smile at the same time because he looked so grown up at that moment, it was heartbreaking.

Worse than that, he looked like Declan.

I mean, I'd have been a dumbass if I hadn't seen the likeness between my boy and his father over the years. With Declan's face imprinted on my retinas, a face I saw before I closed my eyes at night, and the first one I saw in the morning? That routinely made an appearance in my art?

You could bet your way to the bank that I thought about their similarities.

But it rammed it all home harder as I took him in now.

In four years' time, he'd be eighteen.

He'd wanted to go to Harvard. Wanted to be a lawyer, for Christ's sake. Wanted to change legislation from the inside out—get into politics even.

It blew my mind, but that was his goal.

He even had a five-year plan.

And now, here I was, about to wreck everything for him.

Did I do it now? Rip it off like it was a Band-Aid? Or should I let him think everything was normal, that nothing had changed?

Which was the greater kindness?

Before I could say a word, he scowled at me, then I realized it wasn't at me, but something behind me.

He darted forward, past the whitewashed table that was shabby chic and a project we'd worked on together, and toward me. When he jerked me back, pushing me behind him, the motion not only stunned me, but it made me want to cry again.

Such a good kid.

"What is it?" I demanded, as tension soared through me. I peered at the window, trying to see what he had.

"I saw a shadow—"

A knock sounded at the door, making us both jump. I moved past him, heading to answer it as I called out, "Who is it?"

I wanted to groan when the voice called back, "It's Rogan, Ms. O'Neill. Just wanted to assure you that the property is secured."

Wincing, I muttered, "Thank you."

The goons were more than just watching over me and making sure I obeyed... they were protecting us.

Protecting us because, as I'd learned on the ride home, the Irish were at war with the Italians, for fuck's sake.

I hadn't just brought chaos into my life, I'd brought *war.*

A war that was going to impact Seamus.

Fuck.

"We'll be out in the car until you're ready to return to the city."

"I have a lot to pack," I argued, tensing up at being bossed around.

"No. We have our orders. You're to pack the bare minimum, then we'll be returning to organize and put your things into storage."

My mouth dropped open at the heavy-handed bullshit Eoghan was pulling, but then...

I scrubbed a hand over my face, unable to hide from the truth, even as I loathed being told what to do.

I'd been around for the war with the Colombians and the Haitians. Daddy had almost died, and Uncle Freddie *had* lost his life in a knife fight.

War was brutal.

It took no prisoners, not in this kind of battle anyway. Or, at least, if prisoners were taken, they were tortured and killed. No Geneva Convention or any number of Amnesty International rulings protected the Five Points' men from being torn to shreds.

Hell, and I'd just brought my son into this universe.

What had I been thinking? Why hadn't I just told Amaryllis to get gone when she'd seen my tattoo?

When I thought back to how this had all begun, I wanted to cry because it was so preventable. I'd been so stupid to get involved, and now Seamus was at risk.

But when a student had come to me, eying the tattoo, the tag, on my wrist like it was a lifeline from God himself? What was I supposed to do? Tell her to fuck off? Especially when she broke down, when she started sobbing in my classroom, telling me things about her boyfriend who'd just been kidnapped—using names I remembered. Phrases that I'd worked hard to eradicate from my brain by becoming as mainstream as possible.

Sure, I might have blue-tinted hair, and I might come across as a rebel for Sally across the road, but I was a suburban mom. I drove a minivan, for God's sake. I wasn't supposed to be getting involved with mafia wars anymore.

I'd striven long and hard to make a life for myself, a life for Seamus that was free from prejudice and free from violence. But one girl's tears, her helplessness, the outpouring of love I'd heard in her voice for her man, had unraveled everything I'd spent years building. I'd been unable to say no. To back off. I'd pulled contacts I hadn't talked to in years all to get her help.

And this was my thanks.

Jesus, it really didn't pay to be kind, did it?

When Seamus asked, "Mom, what's going on?" I bit my bottom lip, wanting to gnaw the damn thing off. Hell, that would be less painful than what I was currently going through, because admitting the truth to him was going to feel like I was taking a bullet to the belly.

And having taken one of those before, I knew exactly how painful it was.

Ironically enough, that had been by accident. Proof, I guessed, that violence was everywhere. Whether you were in the world I'd been raised in or not.

When the goon trudged off, evidently assuming I was pissed and that expecting an answer was dumb, I twisted around and whispered, "I-I..." I gulped, staring into eyes that were a bright blue, just like his father's.

Everything about him was a mini Declan, so much so that it was painful to behold. At the same time, I'd never been so damn proud of him. When

Declan saw him, he was going to shit a brick because it had to be like looking in a mirror, and since he was a handsome fecker, he'd passed on all the good genes.

There was barely any of me in Seamus's face. That was why I called him 'butt face'. Because he had a butt chin too, and that was literally my stamp on him. Great thing to pass on, huh?

"Mom? What is it?" His voice broke, and he winced. He hated how his voice kept changing, and I knew he was going to be even madder when he faced his father with a squeaky voice.

I blew out a breath, decided to stop being a chickenshit, and rasped, "It's about your dad."

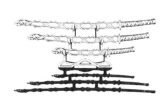

DECLAN
BEFORE

"YOU NEED to start pulling your weight more, kid."

It was so hard not to roll my eyes, but knowing I'd get a backhander was the only reason I restrained myself.

Pull my weight?

I'd like to know how I could do more than I already was.

"Leave the boy alone," Ma snapped, her gaze drifting over me. "He's already got a lot going on with school."

"School? School?" Da pshawed. "What the fuck will school do for him?"

"How many times have I told you not. To. Swear. At. The. Table?" she roared, slamming to her feet and smacking her hands against the table, making the cutlery and battalion of plates and dishes rattle, as the pair of them locked eyes and practically snarled at each other.

Ma was the only person, and I meant, *the only person,* who would ever get through to Da. It was impressive, considering she was tiny, but it always made me feel like a jerk that I needed my mother to back me up.

I was sixteen, for fuck's sake.

Sixteen.

I shouldn't need a woman to get someone off my back, but Da had it in for me. Some days more than others, and today was worse than usual.

I had a bitch for a girlfriend who dangled me around her pinkie, teachers who wanted homework in even though I barely had time to attend school, never mind everything else, and then Da wanting more. Always wanting fucking more.

The only good thing was that Deirdre was terrified of me.

Sure, she liked to pretend that she wasn't, but she was.

She was well aware that she had a lion by the tail and, as such, she knew to tread carefully. What she had on me could end me. Family or not, *son* or not, Da wouldn't stand for it if he knew what she did. So while, *technically,* she had all the power in our relationship, she was still scared.

Rightly so.

"Are you even listening?" Da snarled, jerking my attention back to him.

I cut him a look. "I'm listening," I rasped, shoulders hunched, head ducked down.

Unfortunately for me, the whole family was sitting around the table today. It figured Da would choose this moment to outright humiliate me. Aidan Jr. and Finn were here, with two giggling girlfriends at their sides—not that they were giggling now—and Brennan, though he'd just moved out, was eating with us as well. Conor and Eoghan were choking down food like the pigs they were as usual, but that my older brothers were here to witness this shit just put me in a fouler mood than before.

"I can't make the men respect you," he snapped.

"He's sixteen! What kind of crew *would* respect him?" Ma growled, still on her feet. "You're acting like he's twenty-seven and should be acting as your general. But he isn't. He's still a boy!"

"Still a boy? Aidan, Finn, and Brennan had power at his age. Why do you always defend him? 'Oh, he likes looking at paintings, Aidan, leave the boy be,'" he mocked in a high falsetto. "'What harm is it that he likes to listen to Beethoven?'" he snarled. "I'll tell you what, it's turning him into a feckin' fairy! No one will ever listen to him if they think he's lifting shirts—"

I jumped to my feet at that, and pretty much like Ma had, slapped my hand against the table. "I'm not gay. For the millionth time, I'm not goddamn gay. I've got a bitch, haven't I? I do everything you ask of me, don't I? I do more than my fair share. You've got me running around Hell's Kitchen like your personal lackey, and everyone knows to avoid me because I'm usually the bringer of *your* bad news. If no one respects me, it's because they know I'm your gofer.

"You want me to get power, then give me something to do with power."

He was bristling, but he folded his arms and mocked, "And what, pray tell, would you like to do?"

I scowled at him. "I'm good with numbers. Not the best, granted, but I'm good enough. I'm good at organizing. I'm good at matching things up. I know you're having issues with the warehouses. Let me in there. I'll get things sorted out. Why shove me onto the streets when you know that's not my strength?"

"Because you're my son, and every aspect of the business needs to be your strength."

The injustice in that statement had me gaping at him. "That's bullshit."

He glowered at me. "I beg your pardon?"

"You heard me," I growled. "That's bullshit. The only son who needs to know every aspect of the trade is Aidan. He's your heir. But Finn's good with money, and you shoved him somewhere he can succeed. Brennan's good with his fists, so the girls and gambling are the best fit for him—"

"Aye, you're right," he intoned grimly, then cracking his knuckles, he ground out to Aidan and Finn, "Get your girlfriends out of here." As they got them out of the house, without even questioning his order, Da kept his gaze glued on me. Only when the front door slammed did he rasp, "Finn's never been comfortable with wet work. But he did it. He proved himself. And that's exactly what you're doing. You can't do shit until you've proven yourself to the men.

"You can't pick and choose what you want from this life. I put you where I need you after you've shown the men whom you'll be ruling over that you've gone through the same shit as them. Do you hear me?"

"What more do you fucking want from me?" I screamed, the urge to pull my hair out a real and living desire. "You shoved me into this goddamn world two years ahead of time. I've done everything you asked, and it's still not enough. Tell me what you want and I'll do it!"

I knew I'd pushed it the second I blasphemed, but his speed always surprised me. Before I even finished my sentence, he was around the table and his fist connected with my jaw. As I sprawled on the ground, a position I was too accustomed to for anyone's liking, he spat, "From now on, you'll be with me. Whatever I ask of you, you'll do. It's time you grew up, boy."

When he turned his back on me, I scrambled to my feet and, without a backward's glance at my ma or my brothers, ran out of the room.

Working with Da... *fuck*. I knew what that meant.

My eyes pricked with tears that unmanned me, but I didn't—

I sucked in a breath as I pretty much flew out of the house and headed for my car. When I was behind the wheel, I put my pedal to the metal and got the fuck away from my family. From this fucking world.

Only then, only when I was away from them, did I take a deep breath as Mozart surged from the speakers at a volume I *hoped* would wreck my ears because if it did, then at least I'd be half-deaf when Da told me my first orders.

The urge to scream was real so I went where I always went when I was stressed, when I was scared, when I was lost... the Met Cloisters.

Traffic roared past me, and I didn't notice. Thanks to a freak storm, the Hudson was like ice, the sky gray and grim, matching my mood to perfection, but I didn't notice.

I needed escape.

I needed relief.

Washington Heights was, technically, Russian territory, but I didn't care. I headed there often enough that the staff recognized me, and only when I'd pulled up and had parked, barely remembering to lock the door to my Spider as I headed toward the oppressive building, did I feel like I was in another place.

It was in a park, surrounded by trees, and the actual edifice made me feel like I was in another country. Several parts of the building were from monasteries in France, and the stonework had been transported to the States in the twentieth century. That set the tone for the rest of the museum, and with the integral courtyards from the ancient monasteries and the gothic and medieval artwork, it was like traveling in a time machine.

When I made it inside, I headed to my favorite part—*the* monastery. AKA, The Cuxa Cloisters. It framed a courtyard that was too miserable to sit in thanks to the weather, but that suited my mood to perfection.

I didn't take any notice of the ancient stone arches that a stoic bell tower loomed over, I barely noticed any of it as I leaned against one of those arches and tried not to fucking cry.

Working with Da meant being his fists. So far it was a miracle I'd avoided wet work, but it seemed like my time had come.

Before the year was out, I knew I'd have my first kill under my belt—

"Declan?"

The soft voice, the whisper of my name, broke into my thoughts.

Before I could get angry at having my space invaded, my private place that was free from the Irish Mob's taint because no Westie would be caught dead here, I saw her.

She was like an angel.

A dark-haired one.

Her face was petite, rounded at the chin with the tiniest little indent in the middle, and her cheeks were rosy with the cold. Her eyes were bright with expectation, and her smile was hesitant as she looked at me like she expected me not to know her.

But I did.

I knew her.

I'd seen her with Deirdre, which should have marked her for death, but how could any lover of art mark a woman like this for death?

She was beautiful. She was gothic. She was a muse in the flesh.

Titian would have switched from redheads to brunettes for her.

Aela O'Neill.

Walking salvation and the promise of hell.

I should ignore her, should send her packing, but instead, I rumbled, "Hello, Aela," and took my first steps, without even a blink, into the abyss.

DECLAN
NOW

"YOU HAVE A SON."

My mother's voice was calm. Relatively speaking, anyway. Lena was one of those women who either looked like she was a duck—all serene on the surface, but below it, her flippers were paddling like mad—or she was just so crazy that she didn't get flustered by much.

Having known her for as long as I'd been alive, I figured it was a mixture of both.

To put up with my father, you had to be a little nuts. Let's make that a lot. Aidan O'Donnelly Sr. had a rep the size of New York state, and for a reason... he was insane.

Categorically, undeniably.

He saw the world in a different way too, and God help me, after having been around him my whole life, I knew I had his slant on things as well. All in all, that didn't bode well for me as a parent, did it?

Two nutcases for folks... didn't exactly put me in the major leagues for potential parenting skills.

I mean, I knew Ma and Da would kill for us. But that was part of the problem.

Most parents usually only said that, they didn't think they'd have to act on it. In the life, murder was as much a part of it as having eggs for breakfast.

I scrubbed a hand over my brow, rubbing my eyes which were crusted from sleep, and rolled my head to the side on the pillow. I felt like shit warmed over, which was better than death warmed over, I figured, but not by much.

At least I wasn't in total agony. Not of the physical kind anyway.

When the bed started to move without me doing a thing, I gritted my teeth, and when the new position put me directly in the firing line of my folks? I winced.

Da was there, and he was looming in the corner.

There was an unspoken rule in our household.

Never piss Ma off. If you did? You invoked Da's wrath, and no fucker wanted that. Christ.

Irony being, of course, aside from the psychopathy, he'd been a good father. Hard on me, but I'd needed the direction because it had stopped me from getting killed before I was twenty. I just wasn't sure if I wanted to emulate him.

I looked like him, and while I wasn't the baby of the family, that was Eoghan, I knew Ma tended to give me a bit of leverage, some room for maneuvering she didn't necessarily give to Aidan and Brennan, my older brothers. Conor got more leeway because he was a genius and he was weird with it. Eoghan was the baby, so that justified her trying to coddle him. Me? I was in the middle and should have been ignored. It was a curse and a blessing that I looked like Da, I guessed.

There were shadows under both their eyes, a fatigue that came from fear. There was never denying how much we were loved. Funny how I thought that now, when it'd never have been a blip on my radar before. Not because I'd almost died, because fuck, whenever we left the house, almost dying was a distinct possibility, but because I had a son. She was right.

A son whom I had to somehow help raise.

Care for.

Not get killed.

My jaw worked as I saw their fear for me entwined with a kind of concern I wasn't accustomed to seeing.

From her tone, which had been carefully free of all expression, I'd anticipated her anger. I thought they'd be pissed at me, but they weren't.

In fact, as I tried to read Ma's expression and then Da's, I realized they were both keeping things on the down low.

Was that a positive or a negative?

I had no way of knowing until I answered their question.

"Looks like it," I muttered, staring at my feet, which were peeping through the standard-issue hospital blanket—it was half paper, half cotton, and with all those tiny holes in it.

Christ, I was looking forward to going home to get a real bed that didn't come with a remote.

"Looks like it? You didn't know?"

I scowled at Da, pissed he'd think that. His eyes were concerned, I saw, as he stepped toward me. I didn't want to say trouble was brewing in them, more like he was worried. For who though? Me? The kid?

Shrugging set off a tidal wave of aches in my body. "I didn't know."

"I told you he wouldn't have kept the lad from us, Lena," Da cooed, and I watched, confused, as Ma's shoulders sagged like that was the best news she'd heard all year.

"You thought I'd kept a kid from you?" I muttered, mostly bewildered, but a little pissed off too. After all, who the fuck did they think I was?

Family was everything.

Jesus.

That was the first rule, wasn't it? The first of a million, granted, but that was at the top of the agenda.

"I wasn't sure," she rasped, and when her eyes started to gleam with tears, I groaned.

"Ah, hell, Ma. Don't cry."

Brennan was right. I did somehow upset her more than most of my brothers, and I didn't have a clue why. It wasn't like I was particularly bad—bad in our world was relative—or that I pulled stunts to break her heart, but it didn't stop her from getting weepy over me.

I was used to it, but even so, it pissed me off because the last thing I wanted was her to get upset and for Da to blame those tears on me.

We had a working theory as a family that every tear Ma shed, Da would go out and kill some of our enemies to that exact number.

Sure, sounded lofty and romantic, impossible even. Only it wasn't.

Da was just that much of a psycho.

I pinched the bridge of my nose, and muttered, "You know how things ended with Deirdre, Ma."

"I do."

When Da didn't give me shit for swearing in front of her, I figured getting shot came with some perks. "Well then, you know that what happened with Aela was—"

"Was that why Deirdre was down at the docks that day? Following you around? Because she thought you were cheating on her...and she was right."

I was well aware that it made me a dick, but I shrugged. "She shouldn't have been there."

Ma frowned at me, her hands pleating a handkerchief on her lap.

The weirdest thing about my family?

We all looked like the Kennedys. I didn't mean we shared facial features. I meant that we looked like a political dynasty. Here I was, in the middle of a makeshift ER/ICU unit in a warehouse probably in Queens, but Ma looked like Jackie O with her pearls and neatly coiffed hair. She even wore a pencil skirt and had a blouse tucked into her trim waist. She wore makeup, perfectly applied, and could have graced any magazine with ease.

As for Da, his suits were expensive, and it showed. The pair of them looked after themselves, and though they were nearly seventy, they didn't really look it. Da had let his hair go gray, but Ma hadn't. She was still a redhead, just with more silver sparkles shining through.

So as I looked at them, seeing how picture perfect they both were, I had to shake my head because here I was, talking about a girlfriend who'd been murdered.

A girlfriend who I was glad had died.

A woman who my entire family thought I loved and had mourned for over a decade.

I pursed my lips, wondering what I could even say to explain all this because there wasn't much to say anymore. I'd thought that part of my life was over and done with, and I'd been mostly happy about that.

Except for one thing.

One not so small thing.

Aela O'Neill.

Was it fate that brought her back into my life?

Fate or just God laughing at me?

Maybe a bit of both considering what I did for a living.

My jaw worked as I said, "Aela was a good girl."

I'd admit that whatever I thought I was going to say? It definitely wasn't that.

I knew they hadn't expected it either, because their shoulders straightened and they jerked back like I'd slapped them.

Couldn't blame them.

Aela had denied us access to my kid and to their grandson for, what? Fourteen years? Was that how old the kid would be? Maybe fifteen? I blew out a breath.

I had a fourteen-year-old son.

What the actual fuck?

As much as it surprised me, the fact was that in my entire lifetime, there'd only been one woman I could ever see carrying my baby.

Aela O'Neill.

So maybe fate really was with me, because I'd never, ever, have allowed my father to trap me into marriage like he'd done with Eoghan. I didn't give a fuck that Inessa was good people, that I thought she'd make my brother really happy. No one could make the decision over who'd be my bride because I'd already gone through that years ago. Not that they knew that, but Deirdre had been my fiancée because I'd had no choice *but* to tie myself to her. I hadn't wanted her. I sure as fuck hadn't needed her in my life. I'd put up with her and dealt with her because I had no alternative. I'd made the best of a bad situation, and I'd done it well.

Until I'd met Aela.

I sucked in a breath and I murmured, "When you meet her, I don't want you giving her any shit."

Da scowled at me, his shoulders hitching up by his ears as his temper started to soar. "You watch your feckin' mouth, boy."

I gritted my teeth at the Irish in his voice. The fucker had never even set foot on a plane, never mind visited the homeland, so where the Irish came from was beyond me.

Still, I glared at him. "I won't. I'm in a hospital bed, and I've just learned that I have a son, a son with the only woman I ever loved, and somehow, she's come into my life again. You won't make her life miserable, either of you, because if you do—" I swallowed, suddenly feeling like I had a chasm edging at my feet, one that was either going to swallow me whole or throw me out the other side like it was a black hole.

"If you do, what, son?" Ma asked softly, her head tipped to the side, her shock clear, but her voice was modulated because she was good at hiding her emotions, at tempering them.

"You'll never get to know your grandchild."

Silence fell at my words, at my declaration.

The aftermath was like I'd just unpacked the notch from a hand grenade. Time was ticking away, just waiting on the grenade to explode, and I felt my heartbeat starting to pound, my pulse starting to soar—something that made itself known on the monitors.

I was pretty sure I'd never been so stressed in all my life, then Da scoffed, "You can't be serious?"

Shooting him a look, I dipped my chin. "I am. Deadly."

"I'm confused," Ma whispered. "I thought you loved Deirdre—"

"I hated her," I snapped, but before I could say another word, the doctors came rushing in, and they started to shoo my folks out of the ward.

Neither of them wanted to go, but when my chest started to scream blue bloody murder, and sweat dripped from my pores, drenching me?

I knew something wasn't right with my body.

Maybe before, I'd have just gone with the flow. I'd have just let shit lie, because if it was my time to go, it was my time to go.

But things were different now.

I had a son.

And there was Aela.

With or without me, she was coming into the life again. No way would my da let her get away with not bringing Seamus into the fold. She needed me.

More than she could ever know.

So when the doctors started slapping a ton of crap on me, talking in loud, rushed voices as they started prepping gear I didn't understand and squirting meds across the room as they prepped shots, I grabbed the guy I thought was the head honcho by the wrist.

He squealed in surprise at my firm hold, but it took more than a cardiac arrest to take me down. So when I drew him to me, my eyes were fixed on his as I ordered, "You fix me. You fix me or my father will make your entire family pay for it."

It wasn't a fair command, but I'd gone past the point of fairness.

Fairness had left the building.

Aela and my son needed me, and now was not my time to die.

FOUR

AELA

"SEAMUS?" I called out, as I hauled a bag from my room and dumped it in the hall.

The trouble with packing up all my stuff was that there was a lot of it.

I mean, I knew that. I had to pack everything sporadically anyway when we moved, because we moved a lot.

Intentionally.

I never liked to stay in one place longer than necessary. Sometimes, I'd stay only long enough to do a course or to teach one. Sometimes, it was for as long as it took to craft a particular project. But Rhode Island? I'd gotten soft.

I'd been stupid.

Instead of changing scenery a few years ago, I'd stayed here because Seamus had said he was sick of moving, so I'd gotten a job teaching at one of the best art schools in the world. I'd loved my role there, loved my position and the way I could create and help propagate more creations in the seeds I helped sow in students.

So I'd stuck around, let us get some roots, and I'd seen how Seamus had flourished. It figured he'd be like his da in that. His father who'd never lived anywhere other than Hell's Kitchen. His father who practically thought New York was an island all of its own.

I'd monitored him over the years. I'd been compelled to.

Not only to make sure that we were under the radar, but also because it was a sick, bittersweet need to check in. To see what he was doing. To make sure the life hadn't killed him.

Even while I'd run, far and wide from him, I'd never stopped caring.

Couldn't stop.

This kind of love didn't just die. Didn't just burn away.

It stayed there, pretty much like the Olympic goddamn flame—

"Mom?"

Seamus's voice was a little squeaky, but I was getting used to that. He had zits on his chin that he moaned over in the mirror too, and when I said he stank at the end of every day? I wasn't joking.

Hormones weren't only a bitch for him.

"What is it?" I called, moving toward his voice because he sounded a little on edge.

Sure, he was randomly squeaky, but at moments of high pressure, it stayed that way.

As I trudged down the hall, with its tribal red and white rug that I'd picked up on a job in Dubai, where Seamus and I had lived with a Bedouin tribe for three months, I stared at all the trinkets I'd picked up over the years.

I couldn't take everything with me even if I wanted to.

And want I did.

These things were my past. Each item had a memory.

Like the massive seashell on the stand from when Seamus and I had gone out to collect sea glass in Devon over in the UK. Then there was the wooden mask from the Zulu tribe we'd interacted with when Seamus was about four.

He didn't remember it, but I did. They'd painted him up like he was one of their own and he'd run around, wild and free, more wild and free than most kids could ever imagine.

He'd had more opportunities with my career than any boy could hope for. Had seen things, done things, lived more in his fourteen years than most did in a lifetime.

I had to believe—

No, I hadn't done wrong by him.

I hadn't.

I refused to believe I had.

So when I found him standing by the window, peering out into the yard in the dark, I wondered what he was doing.

We were vigilant by nature. I had two alarm systems that worked simultaneously, and I had two guns. One that went in my nightstand, and one that I stored in a cupboard on the wall in the hallway.

Seamus knew about that one.

He also knew that I'd kill him if he took it out and used it.

Guns were supposed to be stored in a safe place, locked away and secured. And this one most definitely wasn't. But Seamus was a good shot too. He knew how to lock and load a pistol, knew how to clean a weapon and strip it down—because with his heritage, I had to train him. I had to make sure he knew what he was doing, just in case *this* ever happened.

Just in case we were back in the life.

I bit my lip, on edge to see that he had the gun in his hand, and rasped, "What are you doing with that, son? And why are you in the dark?"

He cut me a look over his shoulder, and at that moment, it was more than just a similarity to Declan.

It was like I was looking at him that first day I'd met him.

Fuck.

They'd been similar ages, only Declan had been lucky. He'd somehow turned into a jock from a teen rom-com movie. Not a zit in sight, and I don't remember his voice ever squeaking once.

I was pretty sure it had, and maybe he'd used foundation, or maybe his hormones were controlled to the extent where he never even had to worry about zits because he had them under his domination.

Either way, aside from the few differences, it took me back to my youth seeing him standing there. One occasion, I could easily remember Declan getting a gun out of nowhere and using it to protect Deirdre and me. I'd been so shocked that, to be honest, I couldn't even remember why he had to get his weapon out. What I *did* remember?

Being jealous.

After Declan had kept us safe, she'd clung to him like a limpet, making an octopus look like she had fewer arms as she stuck to his side, all arms and legs around him, tangled up in him.

Me? I'd been out in the cold.

All while over her shoulder, he'd stared at me with the deepest look. A look that still made my skin heat, my blood rush. God, I could remember that so well. The way my adolescent body, one filled with urges I'd never experienced before, had responded to his, to that fire.

I'd been too young to know what that felt like, and yet, I was one of the lucky ones.

Even if Declan was my end, even if it brought me back into a fold I wanted nothing to do with, I could never regret knowing what those emotions felt like.

I considered it my superpower.

Nothing could ever replicate the magnitude of what I'd felt, so I never looked for it. I just had a few hookups, discreet so it would never inflict an 'uncle' on Seamus, and I'd even messed around with some clients while I was working on projects for them.

Why not?

I was young, free, and single. I could do whatever the hell I wanted with my body, but I never wanted my heart to be engaged again.

Why would I?

It was the sweetest torture. The most devastating torment.

Love was pain.

Love was pure.

It hurt.

If it was done right.

And because I'd experienced that so young, I knew what it felt like, knew that it wasn't for me anymore and that I didn't have to go out there and find something to replicate it. You couldn't replicate the un-replicable, and to be honest, I had no desire to ever find myself feeling like I'd once felt. It was an insidious weakness, and I hated being weak.

I liked being strong.

I'd taught my son that too. I'd taught him to be independent, resilient, but seeing him armed with an intent to use the weapon I'd instructed him with set my nerves on edge.

"Look at the car on the street."

Scowling, I stepped forward. His tone had me hugging the wall, moving over to him on the other side of the window so I could peer out. His gaze was intent, his concentration absolute—so absolute, in fact, that I wished he could be that dedicated to his frickin' math homework so I didn't get any bullshit from his teacher. I peered out onto the street, trying to see what he was seeing.

We lived in the city, but it was a good part of town. I hated driving, hated commuting even more so I made sure that, wherever we lived, it was near where I worked. I only had to walk a few blocks to hit the college campus, which made this neighborhood incredibly expensive, but I could afford it.

I'd long since stopped caring about how much things cost, and only instilled a sense of value in objects so that Seamus wouldn't grow up to be a precocious spoiled brat.

He didn't know how wealthy I was, wouldn't until the day I died and he inherited everything, but that was for another time, another place.

The street was neat, manicured in a way that I didn't like but dealt with. Everything was perfect. And when I said everything, I meant it. The roads wouldn't dare get potholes, the houses were all flawlessly painted, not even needing a second coat of paint on them. Driveways were cobbled or tiled or paved without a single weed sticking out from between the cracks.

It was the kind of street where not even the lightbulb on a streetlamp would flicker. And if it did? The city would have someone out within the day to make sure it was replaced.

So what he saw—

Then, I just happened to catch a glimpse of the BMW.

It was black. Dark.

And in the shadows.

There weren't many on this street because there were a lot of street-lamps, but he'd parked kind of catty-corner, in a way that made him difficult to see from a certain angle.

Our angle.

I cut Seamus a look, then rasped, "Give me the gun, baby."

He shook his head, but his hands were shaking. "No," he squeaked. "I have to keep us safe."

Reaching over, I pressed a hand to his shoulder and murmured, "You know how good a shot I am. I'll protect us."

His shoulders quaked, and I could feel his fear from over here. It tinged the air with pungent teenage sweat, and it made me want to hug him, wrap him in my arms, and tell him that I'd protect him until kingdom come, that he never needed to worry.

But there was definitely somebody watching us.

Somebody that wasn't affiliated with the Points, because I knew how the Points worked.

Outside our door, they were in a massive SUV. If Eoghan had asked for a detail to follow that SUV, it would have been a matching tank, not a sleek sedan that wasn't even pointed in our direction. That was hiding in plain sight.

The Five Points were blunt objects. Hammers, not scalpels.

I could feel sweat trickle down my brow as I accepted that, somehow, somewhere, we'd become involved in something we had nothing to do with.

Cupping Seamus's shoulder tighter, I implored, "Please, sweetheart, give me the gun."

"I saw him leave the car," he whispered, his hands shaking around the weapon. "He was heading for the SUV."

Something in his voice had me staring at him. "What did you see?"

He gulped. "Someone was shot." His mouth worked as he twisted to look at me. "The man who came to the door, I-I think he's dead."

I gritted my teeth and tried not to panic.

But who the hell was I kidding?

Fuck!

I reached up and tried to think what the fuck I should do. Then my cellphone buzzed, making both of us jump. It wasn't so much of an issue for me, but with my trigger-happy son at my side, it rattled us both when he knocked the muzzle into the windowpane.

Thankfully, it was quiet enough for it not to have caused an issue, but I whispered, "Be careful, Seamus."

He nodded. "Sorry." I could see the fuzz on his top lip, where he was starting to get a bit of a mustache, was beginning to gleam with sweat.

I reached for my cell and peered at the screen as I tried to cover it so the gleam didn't reflect in the window. Because I couldn't see who was calling, I just hit the green button and raised it to my ear. "Hello?" I whispered, half terrified it would be whoever had just killed our guards.

"Aela? It's Brennan—"

"Brennan! Thank fuck! Someone shot our guards."

Silence fell on the line, but it barely lasted fifteen seconds before he growled, "Stay on the phone. I'm going to get the cops over there."

The cops?

My eyes flared wide. "You're calling the cops?" *Was this a parallel universe?*

"Of course," he rumbled, but though he sounded furious, he also sounded calm. Like this was just another day at the office for him, which, of course, it was.

I gulped.

What had I done? Bringing Seamus into this world? I was the one who needed shooting.

Turning my back on the window for a second, I pushed my spine into the wall as I closed my eyes, trying not to think about the clusterfuck going down around me.

Then, realizing it was stupid to leave my son watching over the scene, I twisted around and carried on scanning the front yard.

I didn't see anyone, and peering into the car didn't give me much hope either. So I put the phone on speaker, turned the sound down so it was barely audible, and focused on the street.

"They were both killed?"

Seamus squeaked out, "There were three men in the SUV."

"Three?" Brennan rasped, but his voice was different, tempered.

He knew who he was talking to.

"Yes. Three," Seamus confirmed, and it was stupid, but I was proud that he sounded so sure of himself. Sure, he was squeaking, but that didn't matter, did it?

"Seamus?"

"Yes. I'm Seamus," he replied.

"I'm your Uncle Brennan. I promise, when this is all over, it won't happen again."

Seamus was quiet for only a second before he whispered, "Why is it happening at all?"

A sigh sounded down the line. "I don't know, but I promise you I'll find out. Now, you said there were three men in the SUV?"

"This afternoon I was doing yard work, and I saw this strange car down the road. No one drives BMWs around here—"

I winced because while it was true, it made it sound like we were living in a ghetto. This was one of the priciest neighborhoods in the area, but it was liberal to its core. Everyone drove Teslas and hybrid vehicles, for God's sake.

"So I watched because I heard the rumble of the engine."

My brow puckered at his attention to detail, which rarely came into use when he was forgetting to do things like pick up the laundry in his room or when I asked him to not leave dirty dishes in the sink.

Kids.

Heaving a sigh and deciding this was not the time to wonder why my son had the wherewithal to notice details in a crisis but was incapable of focus on a regular basis, I tuned back into the conversation, grateful he'd noticed anything at all.

"It pulled up into a position that I also considered odd, because it was parked on the Mandelson's drive, and they're on vacation, and I've been keeping my eye on it ever since. When I was packing up, I happened to see someone get out of that car, walk over to the SUV Mom said belonged to—well, you—"

"And you as well, Seamus. You're an O'Donnelly now."

Was now really the moment to throw that in there?

I didn't say a word, but my irritation flared.

"I'm an O'Neill," Seamus corrected, his own anger stunning me, as well as the vehemence in his voice.

Maybe it took Brennan aback too, because he didn't get mad, didn't even say a word. Just let Seamus continue.

"There was a shot fired, I heard it, then the guy who rode with us got out of the SUV and walked back with the shooter. Rogan, I think that's his name... he didn't get out. I think, I mean, well... that has to mean he's dead, right?"

My brows rose at that, and I felt a little winded. "Seamus, you need to think very carefully about what you just said there," I murmured. "You mean to tell me that one of the Five Points' men got out of the vehicle and went over to the other car?"

"Kind of. They didn't go back to the car on the Mandelson's drive. They disappeared."

All my ideals about the Five Points came crashing down around me, because as far as I knew, traitors weren't exactly cosseted with gems and riches. You fucked with the O'Donnellys and they more than fucked with you.

"You have a traitor in your midst, and you brought them with us," I growled, fury and terror whittling down my voice until I was almost whispering in my outrage.

"The cops are on their way," Brennan replied smoothly, and once again, I recognized just how like his father he was.

It took a psychopath to register another's terror and to sound as if we were talking through our takeout order for a Friday night.

I closed my eyes, praying that the cops would make it here fast, but I knew, from my past experience, that luck was rarely on my side.

And that was only confirmed when I heard the tinkling sound of glass breaking.

My heart almost stopped at that, and when I turned to Seamus and I saw the outright terror in his eyes, I wanted to weep.

I'd done this.

Me.

I'd hurt my boy, I'd made him look like this.

I sucked in a breath, determined that if anything happened to him, I'd rather die, so I grabbed him by the back of his shirt and started hauling him toward my bedroom. He began to struggle, but that whole 'a woman can pick up a car if it means saving her child' stuff was, I realized, true.

One hundred percent true.

I didn't care that he was like a brawling cat that was trying to scratch and hiss at me. I just needed to make sure he was out of here and in a safe place.

Dragging him back down the corridor to my bedroom, I was grateful for the thickly woven rug that dampened our footsteps. My door was wide open because I had a thing about never closing them, much to Seamus's horror, because I'd inadvertently flashed him a few times, and I didn't stop hauling him in until we were in my room.

"You stay there," I snarled at him, shoving him into the cupboard that acted as a safe room. "You stay small, and you stay in the corner. You have your gun aimed at the door, and if anyone opens it, you shoot. You shoot straight in the chest, remember like I taught you? Bang in the middle of the torso. But don't waste bullets," I hissed at him. "They're not going to kill you, Seamus. You're too valuable." The words annihilated me, but it was vital he was aware of that. "You're an O'Donnelly, and that means you're too important. So they won't kill you, but they will incapacitate you. You make sure that doesn't happen. The cops will be here soon, and once they are, your uncle will be here next."

He gulped. "Not my father?"

"No, sweetheart. Remember, he's in the hospital. He's too sick right now." I hadn't told him about the extent of Declan's injuries, had just said he was resting up in a clinic. Now I regretted that because it figured Seamus would paint a pretty picture of his father, and instead of Declan being the one to come storming in to the rescue, it would be Brennan.

Of course, it wouldn't actually be any O'Donnelly. It would be me. I'd be the one who made sure that no one hurt my son.

The thought had me grinding my teeth as I rasped, "Here's my cell. Stay on the line with your uncle."

"No," Brennan replied, his tone modulated. "I want to talk with you."

I narrowed my eyes, but I wasn't about to argue, not when I had things to do. I triggered the security alert on the alarmed door, then turned to Seamus and whispered, "Remember the code?" His swift nod had me continuing, "You make sure you fire calmly. Methodically. Don't waste bullets. But do not—do you hear me?—allow yourself to be moved to another location. They shouldn't break through the door, but do as I say, okay?"

Seamus nodded, and because he registered my tone, the severity of it, his face turned from pure white with fear to a staunch resolve that told me he was ready for whatever might come his way.

Of course, that might involve listening to me being shot or...

I blew out a breath.

Raped.

Fuck.

I sent up a quick prayer to a God I'd stopped believing in a long time ago, promising, 'I promise I'll attend church again if you just make sure Seamus doesn't have to hear that.'

When there was no answer, no miracle that made things better, I just heaved a sigh, closed the closet door that was part of a safe room I'd had installed before we moved in, and heard the locks click into place.

Rushing around the bed, I turned off the speaker and put the phone to my ear even as I opened the nightstand drawer to pull out a revolver.

It dwarfed my hand, and looked a little ridiculous in my grasp, but it could look stupid all the way to the bank. I didn't give a damn so long as the fucker worked.

"How long until the cops get here, Brennan?"

"They're saying four minutes ETA."

I gulped. "A lot can happen in four minutes."

"You'll be fine," he told me, his tone almost soothing.

In a previous life, Brennan had either been Sigmund Freud or a hypnotist. I wasn't sure which.

I checked that the gun was loaded—even though I knew it was—and when I found it packed with ammo, I sucked in a breath and settled myself at the side of the bed, my back to the nightstand, my arm on the mattress for support.

With my butt on the ground, I listened to the reassuring sound of Brennan breathing—slow and deep, no panic to it. No rush. And I forced my heart to stop pounding, forced myself to calm down and to emulate his breathing.

"You did good, Aela. You taught him well."

"Had to. He's one of you even if I tried to protect him from all this. Would be like sending a baby chick into a fox's den and expecting him not to get bitten."

Brennan's snort said it all. "Maybe, but I never expected you to instruct him the way you did. You did good."

Because I didn't live for any man's approval, I said nothing and just rolled my eyes. I was a mom, for God's sake. What did he expect me to do? Leave my baby unprotected?

Of course, I apparently had. Somehow my security system had been bypassed. That was a half a million down the drain, but more than that, Seamus wasn't safe.

God help me.

Tuning my ear into the silence of the house, I had to wonder if I was overreacting, if I'd even heard the glass breaking, the sound reminiscent of someone messing with the back door to gain access to the handle. If it *had* happened, why hadn't that tripped the alarm? I didn't get it. Unless...

I'd set the alarm, hadn't I?

In the mayhem, had I forgotten?

Christ, I couldn't remember.

And when I couldn't hear a single footstep, didn't hear a squeak that indicated where they were, it merely made me question if I'd heard right in the first place, but then I figured that it would make sense for there to be no noise. After all, if the carpets I had down in all the rooms protected us from making random sounds, why wouldn't it help our intruders?

A gentle hushing noise, so soft that I almost missed it, and would have if Brennan's breathing hadn't calmed me down, ricocheted outside in the hall.

I tensed, preparing myself for anything, and when the door opened, gliding inward, panic filled me because my senses hadn't failed me, but I forced myself to calm down as the door carried on moving inward gently, as if the person was trying to make sure that the hinges didn't squeak. I waited until a shadow hovered in the open space, then I sucked in a breath, aimed my gun, and fired.

The explosion triggered the intruder's weapon, but even though I heard the whistle of the bullet, it missed.

Mine didn't.

His yelp of agony was quickly hushed up, but I heard the bastard drop to his knees. The thump was heavy, heavy enough for me to feel the vibration through the rug under my butt.

I waited, watching, not wanting to give away my location, so I stared into the darkness, pierced only by the glow of the streetlamp, and waited for the home invader to make a decision. Was he going to get up, was he going to take another shot?

Behind me, about two feet to the left of my head, the dust and plaster from the dry wall cracked and shifted, sending little plumes of motes into the air. They tickled my nose, making it next to impossible not to sneeze. I drew in a breath, trying to stop it, but nothing would.

The explosive sneeze triggered a gunshot from across the room, but it also gave me a location—he was hiding beside the foot of my bed.

I'd never be able to get a shot at him there.

Of course, Seamus said there were two men, and this was only one of them.

Was the other in the house? Or somewhere in the hall? Just waiting on us to rush out, thinking we were safe, only for us to fall into his clutches?

My heart started roaring again, but even though I could hear the gentle whisper of Brennan's breathing, it wasn't enough this time.

I had two invaders in my home. Two people who maybe wanted me dead, and who, very likely, wanted my son alive to kidnap. I could just imagine what the O'Donnellys would be extorted to pay for his safe keeping.

The only heir to the O'Donnelly throne?

Jesus Christ.

I pinched the bridge of my nose when another sneeze started to build as dust made its way into my sensory receptors. But this time, as my eyelids clamped down with the beginnings of the internal explosion, I blindly pressed my finger to the trigger and pulled.

When the guy yelped again, I tensed, unable to believe that had worked, and figured he'd moved out into the open because he'd been about to take a shot at me. But I still wasn't taking any chances. Waiting for the bastard to make another pop at me, I aimed my gun higher, finding it next to impossible not to carry on firing into the dark, Scarface style, but that would only waste precious ammo, and while I had some of that in the cupboard downstairs, that was exactly the issue.

It was downstairs.

Only the shooter didn't make another move. Had I killed him?

Were we safe?

Grimly, and feeling the sweat beading my brow, making my skin slick with it, as well as the strong scent of body odor from my pits as I went through worse sweats than I'd endured during childbirth, I waited for something, anything...

And I got it.

Sirens.

I wanted to cry. I wanted to whoop and holler with joy.

I was the daughter of a gang member, I'd been raised in the life, had been reared to understand that business was business, and that sometimes, Daddy would come back from work with blood on his fists and bruises on his face, and to accept it as normal.

Regular.

I'd also been taught that the cops were pigs and never to call on them unless I had to.

But here and now?

I'd never been so happy for a bunch of blues to make their way onto my property.

"I can hear them, Aela," Brennan told me, his voice as calm as ever. "Don't move, and be prepared to fight the other guy. Just because the police are there doesn't mean that the other intruder will stop. He's there for a reason, and we both know what happens when you don't follow the boss man's orders—being thrown in jail is a kinder fate."

I gulped, knowing he was exactly right.

My mouth trembled, and even though I was trying to be quiet, fear prompted me to ask, "The *Famiglia*?"

"It's likely. We're at war with them—"

"Rogan told me," I breathed.

I didn't have to see his face to know he was surprised. "He did? Why?"

"I knew him back when I was a kid. We were neighbors, lived next door to each other before my dad's promotion." Not that you'd have known with the formality between us. I wasn't even sure why he'd told me the little he had.

Nostalgia?

And now he was dead.

He had to be, didn't he? Why would he have told me any of that when he fully intended on betraying the family a few hours later?

No, there was no love lost between him and I, but he'd been warning me. The thought of him bleeding out in the SUV had guilt spearing me in the chest, but it was overridden when I heard the sounds of the police rushing into my house, taking over the fight on my behalf.

I kept my Ruger raised though, just waiting for the other guy to come at me, but when he didn't, when I heard footsteps pounding up the stairs, and a, "Ma'am? This is Officer Fellows. It's safe to come out now," I felt like crying.

So, because I felt like it, I allowed myself one weakness after a night of being strong and called back— "On my way down!" –before I placed the gun on the ground, covered my eyes with my hands, and let myself sob, just for a handful of seconds before I had to put on a brave face for Seamus.

FIVE

BRENNAN

SHE WAS CRYING, and the sound pissed me off.

I'd always liked Aela. She was good people, strong, and exactly what my brother had needed in a woman. That bitch Deirdre had been all about the position, the posturing. The family name and the family wealth. I'd known she was a money-grubbing slut, had known she was tangled up with Declan for a reason even if, to this day, I had no idea why they were together because I'd seen Dec's loathing for her every time she stood by his side.

I was surprised the rest of the family hadn't noticed that either, but sometimes I saw things that no one else did, so it didn't come as that much of a shock.

While Deirdre was everything I loathed in a woman, Aela was the exact opposite.

She'd have been my type too, if she didn't have her hooks into Declan, and when I said hooks—I meant it. I'd never seen him go gaga for a chick before, but I got it. Not only had she been beautiful, still was, truth be told, but she was solid, honest, and good. She'd been raised to know that wet work was part of the life. Had been nurtured to accept that the things men did for the family weren't always the nicest, but it was just how it was.

She wouldn't question. She would only accept.

But for all that, she wasn't biddable.

Even back then, I'd seen the spark in her.

I'd actually seen what would trigger a career in art that still took me aback.

A few years ago, I'd seen her in Manhattan, and I'd started keeping tabs on her. Those tabs, however, hadn't enlightened me to the fact that she was a single mom. If they had, I'd have looked into the kid, because how she and Dec had ended things, over a goddamn grave, it wouldn't have surprised me if there'd been a baby. And I'd been right.

Which just proved that I should have listened to my instincts.

Heaving a sigh, I pointed at the screen, put my phone on mute so she couldn't hear me but I could hear her weeping, and I told Conor, "Hack into her security system."

He sniffed. "Bitch, please. I'm already in. What do you want?"

"Eyes on her."

"She's in the bedroom, right?"

"Far as I can tell. Sounded like she activated a safe room though. Maybe she's somewhere else in the house." I'd heard the telltale sound of automatic locks that indicated there was some heavy-duty security in the place, and I'd had Conor on the case ever since.

"Useless as always," he told me, but I ignored him and his snark. He was just pissed I'd woken him up.

We were still at the warehouse, still at Dec's side after he'd given us all a scare and had gone into cardiac arrest. He was okay, stable again, but he was unconscious, and I had this weird feeling that if I left the warehouse, if I took one step off the property, he'd die.

I knew it was stupid, knew it and was pretty ashamed of it.

It felt far too much like superstition for my liking, but even so, if it meant sticking to his side and keeping an eye on my baby brother, I'd do it.

Dec was good people. One of the best of us. Sure, he was just as deep into this shit as we all were, but I loved him. Not because I had to, but because I chose to.

People didn't realize there was a difference, but for someone like me, who didn't love often, who loved seldomly in fact, it was a massive deal.

My thoughts had me glancing at my father. He was snoring away, his head tipped back against the wall with his arm around Ma, who was tucked into his side. Her hair had fallen out of the high bun she usually wore it in to keep her mass of curls out of her face, and she looked exhausted with tear tracks on her cheeks, her face lined from the way she was sleeping.

I loved my ma. By choice.

My da? Not so much.

With them both sleeping, Eoghan and Inessa huddled in one corner napping, and Aidan out front, limping back and forth in front of Declan's ward, scaring the piss out of the doctors on staff, Conor and I were the only ones around who could help Aela and her son.

Our nephew.

Fuck.

I rubbed my chin as, on the screen opposite us, a screen that had been installed earlier today at my insistence and for an occasion such as this— although I'd never anticipated one of our men turning traitor, nor had I expected an attack on Declan's woman and son, I'd just foreseen her running and had wanted eyes on her—a video of the house's layout popped up. Conor's skill never ceased surprising me.

Or terrifying the piss out of me.

For all that, it was pretty much how I imagined it. Aela was a bold woman. A strong one. I didn't think she'd have a white, blank space for a home, and my belief was merely confirmed as I peered into all the rooms where cops were storming through the house, trying to find the second invader I'd warned them about when I'd made the 911 call.

Getting to my feet, I practically tiptoed past my parents, because I wanted them to stay asleep, then I reached the screen, squinting into each room to see where she was.

I could hear her weeping still, and the sobs were heavy enough to tell me she'd be burning out soon after the adrenaline wore off.

She wasn't used to violence, which was both good and bad. Good, because it meant she'd been safe in the years she'd been away from us, but bad because our world *wasn't* safe. Not while we were at war with the Italians, and not, in all honesty, on any day.

There was always danger. Always the threat of violence. It was just how we rolled.

When I found her in a bedroom, I narrowed my eyes on the body on the ground. He was splayed on his back, mouth wide open as he ate dust now that he was dead.

I didn't recognize his face, so that told me he was *Famiglia* because they had a seemingly endless list of goons they could ship out on jobs. *This* was why we were better. We gave a shit about our people.

I saw her tucked against the side of the bed, her shoulders shaking, huddled up small as she came to terms with what had just happened. Knowing her, she wasn't upset by the killing of someone, just by the fear that had struck her hard. Aela was strong. She was born into violence. She knew how things worked. Tonight could have ended a lot differently, which was what she was processing.

Slowly, she rolled herself onto her hands and knees and started toward the foot of the bed, rightfully cautious.

Her reaction prompted me to take her off mute.

"Aela, you don't need to worry. The shooter's dead. Keep me on the line while you're dealing with the cops. I'm recording everything." I shot my brother a look, making sure he started picking up on our conversation. "I want to make sure they deal with you fairly."

I knew she appreciated my calmness, because I saw her face pucker for a second before it flashed clear. There was no irritation at my lack of expression, not like there would be with some people. If anything, I watched her suck in a deep breath before she whispered, "Okay. I-I'll make sure you can hear everything."

She'd changed since she'd left the warehouse earlier today, and was wearing a kind of plaid shirt, one that had a breast pocket. I watched her as she tapped the screen, turned her phone upside down, and slipped it down into the fold. When the sound didn't cut off, I knew she'd put me on speaker, so I made sure to mute mine again as she headed over to the closet.

My heart was in my throat as I waited on the door to open, to see my nephew for the first time.

"Seamus, kiddo, it's me. You can open the door. The cops are here." She tapped it, then the automatic clicks of the locks sounded, and in a blur of motion, someone rushed out of the small room and hurled themselves at her.

When they collided, my mouth tensed as I saw his fear, his need to protect her, and I understood it. I'd been there myself. I knew how that felt.

Sucking in a sharp breath as I watched them hug, I didn't twist around when I felt someone at my side. Someone who was just as affected as I was by what I was seeing.

"They're close," Conor rasped.

"They are." That much was clear.

"We need to make sure Declan doesn't fuck this up."

"I don't think he will," I said softly, and I hoped I was right. His response to the news he was a father had come as a shock, but it hadn't been a devastating blow to him. Not like I'd expected, at any rate.

He'd seemed stunned by the prospect, but he hadn't been angry. If anything, I thought the news had turned him introspective, and that was never a good thing where he was concerned.

He tended to overthink things by nature, and after Ma had left his 'room' sobbing, I got the feeling from the trace of guilt in her eyes that the reason she was sobbing was because of the words they'd shared before he'd gone into cardiac arrest.

Whatever he'd said to her had made her cry. Though that pissed me off, I got it.

I did.

Ma had learned she had a grandson, and she was all for family. Declan had probably been setting shit straight, and I didn't blame him. Sometimes, especially with Ma, that was imperative. She was Da's benchmark, after all. If she accepted something, he would shortly after. Well, where the family was concerned. Not with business.

Rubbing the back of my neck as I stared at mother and son, I watched as she hooked her arm around Seamus's shoulder, then rumbled, "Don't look at the foot of the bed, Shay."

He shuddered, and of course, he looked at the foot of the bed. But she grabbed his chin and ground out, "Listen to me. There might be a time when you're ready to see that stuff, but tonight is not that night. I took care of things. You don't need to see how."

I wanted to tell her that, by fourteen, I'd already killed a few men, but Seamus, *Shay*, wasn't like me, and I was glad for that.

We'd started in the life way too early, Declan younger than any of us thanks to Da's belief he was gay, and that was a rite of passage I hoped we wouldn't pass onto our own kids. I sure as fuck wouldn't be letting any son I had, if I ever had any, roam around learning the ropes at fourteen to make sure we were man enough for the job ahead of us.

I watched as she grabbed his head, tucked his face into her throat, and practically frog-marched him out of the room. He didn't have a chance to see the body on the ground, not one chance, and admiration filled me.

Conor hummed at the sight too. "She's a good mom."

Of course that was a generalization, and since he wasn't the kind to make such sweeping statements, I cut him a look.

"She might be a shit mother."

He shook his head, keeping his eyes glued to the screen. I wasn't sure how he'd done it, but the security system followed her, tracing her every move, meaning that as she walked out into the hall, the camera switched, and the screen followed her path. She walked toward us where, at the top of the stairs, the police were slowly approaching the upper landing.

She called out, "It's me, Officer. I'm Aela O'Neill. I own the property."

Cops surged upward at that, but what I saw surprised me.

There were eight officers, which was unusual enough. I highly doubted the local force sent out eight cops for a regular home invasion, so that was more than sufficient to have my brows rising. But throw in the plain-clothed detectives, two of them, and one a face I recognized?

Huh.

I cut Conor a look. "Caroline Dunbar."

He dipped his chin. "Fuck."

My mouth twisted at his statement. "Fuck about sums it up. What's she doing there?"

That had him rolling his eyes. "She's a Fed. Her jurisdiction is everywhere."

"I know that, dumbass, but she's normally stuck around us. Like flies around shit."

"Ha, flies. More like bees around honey."

I grinned a little at that, but I zoomed in on Caroline's face.

What surprised me more was that Aela recognized her. Her shoulders stiffened at the sight of her, but Seamus only confirmed it with his, "Caro? What are you doing here?"

Cutting Conor a look when he growled, I muttered, "Entrapment."

"The beginnings of. Why the hell would the Feds target Aela? They had to know we weren't aware of Seamus. There are no records of child support payments. Nothing that would indicate there are any links. Anything she knows would be at least, what, fourteen years old?"

"Doesn't mean there aren't some crimes we can't still be tried over, does it?" I arched a brow at him. "Murder doesn't come with a statute of limitations."

"True." He scowled. "What the fuck could Aela know though? Declan wouldn't have kept her in the loop." He shook his head. "I don't know why I'm even asking. I had no idea they were boning anyway. I thought he was stuck on that Deirdre bitch."

"No. I have no idea why he was with Deirdre, but I knew about Aela. He was always useless at hiding things from me."

"Aren't we all?" Conor muttered glumly.

But I didn't even crack a smile at that. "Wonder if it's Deirdre," I mused out loud.

"What about her?"

"Her death? We covered it up, but fuck knows what that bitch has got her claws out for."

Caroline Dunbar was a severe pain in the ass.

She had a habit of turning up out of the blue with random pieces of evidence that she tried to use to bring us down. It never worked. Even if she had a shot of us with a gun in our hand and the bullet flying out of the muzzle before it penetrated someone's chest, it wouldn't matter worth a damn.

We operated like ghosts in this city because everyone was in our pocket.

Didn't matter what department it fell under, didn't matter worth a damn. We were untouchable. But she kept on forgetting it.

It was my turn to growl as Aela asked, "You're a detective?"

Dunbar dipped her chin. "Of a sort. I'm an agent with the FBI. I've been keeping an eye on you."

Ha. *More like surveilling her.*

I could see from the tension in Aela's face, the rigidity of her posture, that she didn't believe that either. She knew a pig always stank, and it didn't matter if it looked like they were on your side or not—they never were.

She did us proud as she demanded, "Why? What do you think I know?"

Seamus, his gaze whipping between the two women, questioned, "Mom? What's going on? Why is Caro here?"

"She's not here to babysit you, butt face," Aela replied calmly, but her gaze was stony as she stared at Dunbar.

"She worked her way in as a babysitter?" Conor hissed. "Well, that's a new low."

He wasn't wrong.

"I'm here to help," Dunbar insisted, her arms spreading wide with entreaty. "There was chatter about you, and I wanted to make sure you were safe."

"You'd only hear the chatter if I was on someone's radar, and if you were trying to keep me safe, then you'd have told me I was on a radar in the first place." Aela's mouth turned down at the corners, but I saw a flash of grief whisper across her features, one that told me she was upset. Not just about what had happened, the safety scare, but also the fact that she'd liked Caro.

Had maybe trusted her?

I got the feeling Aela didn't trust many people with her son. Somehow, and I had no idea how it was possible, but she'd managed to keep Seamus under wraps. Not a single article I'd read about her had included the information that she had a son. Not a single one. And with a rep like hers? That was impossible.

She was an artist, sure, but she wasn't a starving one. If anything, she was rich, and well renowned for her work, to the point where I'd admit I was even proud of everything she'd achieved. But somehow, she'd kept Seamus out of the limelight. I knew that was because of us. The second a picture of him flashed online, it was more likely we'd spot it and spot him. Declan and Seamus's likeness was incredible. There was no doubting his heritage.

She'd evidently paid to keep Seamus safe, what with all the security on hand in the house... so to let Caroline Dunbar into her life, to allow her access to Seamus, I knew she had to be close to the woman.

But that was the trouble with our world. You couldn't trust anyone unless they were family, and even then, that didn't always stick.

Case in point—the police hadn't cornered anyone in the house during their sweep, which meant there was a Five Pointer roaming the streets of Rhode Island right now with a set of crosshairs between the eyes because he'd be dead before tomorrow was out. We'd been betrayed, according to Seamus's observations, and we dealt with traitors swiftly and harshly.

Of course, he wasn't the first traitor in recent times, so maybe we'd need to deal with this one differently. Really ram home the message that the O'Donnellys didn't take mutiny kindly.

"Seamus, why don't you go with the officer and tell them what happened?" Dunbar directed my nephew, but being the smart kid he was, he scowled and shook his head.

"No. I'm not leaving my mom."

Dunbar's mouth tightened, and she looked to Aela for backup. Only, there was none to be had.

The trouble with Caroline Dunbar was that she was persistent. A little like a bulldog. And even though I loved bulldogs, I had to admit, they weren't always the smartest dog in the pound. She'd had the brains to realize that the way to get close to Aela was her son. But she hadn't grasped that if she'd leveraged Seamus's safety, then she'd have figured out a way to get information out of Aela.

By lying to her, getting close, and then letting her figure out the truth of her identity the way she had, she didn't have a snowball's chance in hell of getting a word out of Aela.

Something I was glad for, because I'd have hated to have to kill the love of my brother's life too.

SIX

AELA

I STARED at the woman I'd thought I'd known, a woman I'd come to trust, a woman I *liked*, and regret hit me with a one-two punch.

Even when I thought I was out of the life, I hadn't been.

I'd been as much a part of it as ever before.

Seamus trembled in my hold, and I knew why.

Throughout his life, I'd shared things about his father with him, had never hidden Declan from Shay because I'd never seen the point of it. What I hadn't told him, until today, was the ties his father had.

I never lied to Shay. Ever. I could hedge, fudge the facts some, but this wasn't a lie about who a guy was to me. This wasn't me hiding that we were millionaires when I told him he couldn't have a new PS4 when he'd broken his.

This was life.

Our life.

Declan would sometimes come home with bruises and covered in blood. Seamus would see that. He was a smart boy. He would notice those things and would ask questions.

What was I supposed to say?

Oh, your dad just walked into a bottle of ketchup.

Oh, he's covered in red stuff again? Well, he's into amateur dramatics, and they get a little handy with the red corn syrup.

My kid was no dummy.

Plus, when he realized how rich the family was, their status, a quick

Google search on the O'Donnellys would reveal things... maybe not much, because I knew they worked hard to appear legitimate, but if anyone would find anything, it was Seamus.

He could be like a dog with a bone when he wanted to, and discovering things about his new family would be at the top of his agenda when he had a spare moment to get his thoughts in line. So I'd told him stuff no kid should have to learn, and on that very evening, he learned another aspect of his new world.

Betrayal.

Not just from his own people, but from a cop too.

I'd always tried to train him to be wary around the police. Most parents wouldn't do that. They taught their children that 911 was their salvation, and to respect and uphold the law. I didn't do that. Not just because of my background, but because I didn't like being told what to do by anyone. And *that* was my family background coming into play, nothing to do with the Five Points.

I knew the cops would inveigle their way like cockroaches into a dirty kitchen into any and all aspects of someone's world, pulling nasty stunts and underhanded moves to get close to the person they wanted to stick their knives into...

Case in point here.

Caro and I had been friends. We'd gone for drinks together, for God's sake. We'd even had a dinner party where we were co-hosts! She'd been here the past few days, looking after Seamus while I was out of the house.

Had she been searching my room? Looking for information on the O'Donnellys? Because that was why she was here. Without a shadow of a doubt. She knew who Seamus's father was.

Though I'd been a Five Pointer too, and though I wore the brand on my wrist, my folks were small fry, not big enough to require a sting operation like this, and sting it was because I'd known her for years.

Ever since I'd moved into the neighborhood.

Jesus.

What did they think they'd learn from me? What did they expect me to be able to tell them about the O'Donnellys when the last time I'd seen them was when I was a kid?

I reached up and rubbed my forehead where fatigue and stress were starting to hit me hard. I wanted to sleep, wanted to rest and close my eyes and forget there was a dead body at the foot of my bed. But I couldn't.

One day back in Declan's world and my house of cards was already beginning to crumble.

I pushed past Caro, needing to get away from the stench of death which was littering a bedroom I'd made my own—the first in a decade, because I'd rarely settled down for as long as this in the past.

My mouth crumpled as I nudged them out of the way, and I was, I'd admit, surprised they let me go.

"Why's she here?" Seamus whispered.

"You know why," I murmured, and even though I was well aware Brennan could hear every word I said, I'd done nothing wrong.

I was no threat to the O'Donnellys.

I wasn't an idiot.

The second you ratted them out, the second you did anything to jeopardize business, you were a threat. Something to be eliminated.

And there was nowhere that would keep you safe.

Not WITSEC, not jail or prison.

They were everywhere.

But, truly, I'd never felt the need to get them into trouble. Maybe I knew things I shouldn't. Had overheard a few conversations, picked up on some information that would get them into hot water, but I'd never share it.

Ever.

Not only because I didn't have a death wish, but because I wasn't raised to be a rat.

As we trudged downstairs, Caro, or whoever the fuck she was, trudged with us. I heard her heavy footsteps, and each time she moved, I wanted to twist around and tell her to get the fuck out of my home. But for the moment, that home was a crime scene, and the only people who could help me were two hundred miles away.

They were listening though. Would they send a lawyer over?

Did I even need one?

I'd acted in self-defense, after all, so in regular circumstances, I wouldn't need one, but things were different. Caro's presence here told me that.

Were they going to twist this around? Use it as leverage to get me to spill family secrets?

My mouth tightened at the thought, and when we made it into the living room, I told Seamus, "Don't say a word."

He nodded, but his gaze was wary as he moved over to the other side of the room to sit in one of the armchairs there.

I'd made this place my own too. All light beiges and creams on the walls and in the overlarge sofa and chairs, just so they could showcase the things we'd picked up over the years. The Murano glass decoration that sat atop a simple console table and was the size of a toddler. A full-size print of Aboriginal artwork that was tilted over the fireplace.

The room was a blank, comfortable canvas that highlighted the memories of trips we'd had as a family.

It was a bold choice, considering Seamus was a boy and filth seemed to be magnetically attracted to him, but keeping things beige wasn't too hard when you had a maid service come in twice a week.

Money changed a lot of things.

It was only when I'd had it that I realized as much. But my money was hard earned, and it was mine. Not tied to blood or death or drugs or anything illegal.

I worked hard. My clients paid a high price for my art. People were stupid enough to stalk my agent so they could have a piece of my craziness in their homes—who was I to argue?

Walking over to a copper singing bowl I'd picked up on a trip to Tibet, I started to run the baton around the outer edge. The D flat note started to ring around the room, soaring high as I tried to calm my heart, tried to tone it down. It was hard, because I could feel it fluttering in response to the current stress and the unknown of what was happening, but mostly I was concerned about Seamus.

He wanted to become a lawyer, for Christ's sake. Even though I'd taught him never to trust the pigs, he'd formulated his own response to them, evidently, because he wanted to be integral to the process. I didn't want to think I'd been short-sighted by informing him of the Five Points and their ties to everything illegal, but maybe I had.

Maybe I'd given him too much credit.

Just because I treated him like an adult didn't mean he was one, and if he said anything to Caro about what I'd told him, she'd be on it like white on rice and Brennan would hear every goddamn word of it.

Sure, I could switch off the phone, but if I did that, it would look suspicious. Would look even stranger—

Damn, this was what it felt like to be between a rock and a hard place.

I sucked in a sharp breath as the singing bowl's song soared higher until the baton collided with the rim, and it clicked discordantly as it broke the tune in two.

I let the note die down, let it fade and die as I turned around to face the woman who'd betrayed me.

"Why are you here?"

It didn't take a rocket scientist, but I needed to pinpoint her exact reasons.

She raised her hands. "I'm sorry about the deception, Aela."

"You're sorry?" I repeated a little blankly. "You're sorry that you breached my trust, my confidence, and that you've been, what? Snooping around every time I've asked you to look after my kid? What have you been doing? Looking through my lingerie every time I needed you to help me with Seamus?"

Her mouth tightened. "No. Don't be stupid."

"Stupid?" I huffed. "I don't think I'm the one who's stupid. What are you doing here?" I snapped, my brittle temper shattering around me like a window after someone had pitched a baseball through it.

She squinted at me for a second, then reached up and rubbed her eyes like she was tired. "I was placed here to monitor your activity."

My activity? For a second, I could only gape at her. What the hell had I done to incur any level of curiosity from the Feds?

Before I could implicate myself in something I didn't even know I was implicated in, she muttered, "It came to our attention that select individuals were using your services as a means of laundering money. You were passed around like you were on Yelp, and I was placed here to monitor you and your activities, so we could use that as a means of uncovering further criminal activity."

If I'd been gaping at her before, that was nothing compared to now.

"You're using me to get to other people?"

"Yes."

I narrowed my eyes at her. "Bullshit. Name a client who's been laundering money through their purchases with me."

She pursed her lips. "Donavan Lancaster?"

I hissed out a breath, hating that I had to concede that one. But in all honesty, it didn't mean anything. Everyone knew Lancaster had been into trafficking ever since one of the women he'd tortured, some wife of an MC biker, had come forward to testify against him. The bastard was somewhere in Asia now, apparently, rocking around the continent as he evaded extradition treaties and went on one long vacation.

Prick.

And for the duration of our contract, I'd stayed in his pool house. Seamus had too.

I shuddered at the thought.

My project in New Jersey, a small town called West Orange, was the sight of one of my most adventurous pieces—a ceiling of glass balls that was crafted to represent the solar system. Lancaster had told me I could do whatever I wanted once he'd shown me the space in his living room where he wanted the art collated, and I'd gotten on with the work.

He'd even come onto me, though I'd pushed him aside, something he hadn't liked, but I'd lied and told him I was gay. That was my standard excuse when someone was a prick and couldn't handle rejection, and it worked like a charm—even with psychopaths like Lancaster.

"Who else?" I rasped, wanting to know more names so I could figure out how deeply they'd been looking into my work.

I paid my taxes and toed the line in all ways. They couldn't Capone—hit me up on nonsense charges just to get me inside—me.

Well, they couldn't before I'd shot someone in my bedroom.

But no... Brennan would never let that happen.

Declan wouldn't either, would he? Unless he hated me for keeping Seamus from him.

Earlier today, they'd been drawing him out of the coma, but that didn't mean he was awake and responsive, did it? Maybe he was still in the dark about being a father...?

I sucked in a breath because if he was awake, knew the truth, and *did* hate me, this would be the perfect way to get rid of me, wouldn't it?

To shove me in prison. To never let me have access to my son—

"Mom?"

Seamus's voice cut through the panic. I twisted to look at him and saw he was staring at me oddly, but his gaze was relatively calm considering the crap we were going through together.

I sucked in a breath, turned back to Caro, and demanded, "Which other clients?"

"Gianni Kilhain. Matthew Wright-Smythe."

I frowned at her. "What about them? They're just businessmen."

"They're Lancaster's associates."

Panic flickered through me, but I growled, "I haven't done anything wrong."

"I never said you had. I already told you, you were a means of monitoring criminal activity." She pursed her lips. "Who's the guy on your bedroom floor, Aela?"

"Ms. O'Neill to you," I sniped, twisting around to look at my singing bowl again. "And I have no idea who he is. I just know that he—" My throat tightened. "I believe he took out one of my guards, and then broke into the house."

"One of your guards?" she repeated, and I heard the slight quiver in her voice, the slightest of intonations that told me this went so much deeper than her so-called look into my client list. "Why do you have guards? You didn't have them this morning, Aela."

"Security threat," I told her blandly. "Apparently, I hired them just in damn time too." My mouth tightened, but before I could say another word, there was a tap on my door.

I didn't even have to head out into the hall to let them in, the guy just strode in, his suit expensive, his briefcase even *more* expensive, and the watch on his wrist was more than Caro made in a year as a government stooge.

I looked at it, studied the lawyer on the whole, then smirked at *her*.

Because I knew exactly what he was, and so did Caro from the outrage in her eyes. My lips forged a smile that told her the interview was over now.

For good.

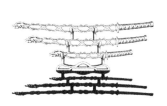

DECLAN

"THEY DID WHAT?" I roared, ignoring the intensity of the heart monitor as it started to practically sing a choral aria as my pulse soared. "They had the Feds on her?"

Brennan scowled at me as he folded his arms over his chest, but it was Conor who replied, "There's no point in getting stressed, Declan. She did well."

She did well?

I almost wanted to wheeze at that, because she shouldn't have to do fucking well.

She hadn't set eyes on me in over a decade, and here she was, a few days in, and she'd been a part of an attack by a *Famiglia* goon, had been betrayed by one of her own, had to kill someone, had the cops in her house, and learned a federal agent had been a mole... what was the cherry on the sundae? Her *not* being arrested?

Fuck.

I scraped a hand over my face as I demanded, "Where is she now?"

"As good as French is, even he couldn't circumvent basic police protocol. She had to stay and be interviewed, give a statement. Seamus too." My entire being tensed at the prospect of my flesh and blood being interviewed by pigs. "Then, the house needed to be bagged and tagged. Her street was a crime scene."

"Rogan's dead," Conor inserted softly.

My eyes flared. "Fuck. You need to go and speak with his ma."

Brennan nodded. "Already did that. I've had Aidan handle the details on the funeral arrangements. Should happen in a few days' time."

"Jesus, what a waste. He was good at what he did."

Conor heaved a sigh. "He was the only guard Ma actually liked. It's going to be tough on her learning that he died."

"This entire situation is going to be hard," Brennan murmured, and the lack of sympathy in his voice wasn't surprising since he rarely had much intonation.

Brennan, more often than not, sounded bored shitless. Like he either couldn't give a fuck or just had zero opinion on anything. Which I knew was bullshit. In recent years, he'd taken a step forward since Aidan Jr., my eldest brother, had been shot, and we'd started going to him with all our problems and not Aid.

He was a smart fucker, wasted on his job on the streets, but you couldn't tell Da shit. He did what he wanted—always had, always would—and because Aidan was the heir and Brennan merely the spare, Da often let Brennan go to waste.

Well, we didn't.

We knew his worth.

"Send them straight to my house."

He arched a brow. "You want them there? I was going to set them up in one of our buildings."

I shook my head. "The second I'm out of here, you know what's going to happen."

"She might not want to marry you," Conor pointed out, ever helpful.

I growled at him. "She won't have much of a choice."

He snorted, then cut Brennan a look. "You can tell he didn't get to meet her, can't you?"

"What's that supposed to mean?" I snarled, when Brennan's smile made an appearance. Sure, it was only a twitch of his lips, but with my elder brother that was pretty much a clown's grin.

"It means she's not exactly the biddable type," Conor answered wryly, as he wrapped his hands around the foot rail and leaned into the bed.

"She never was," I argued, and any idiot who thought otherwise was exactly that—an idiot.

Brennan tipped his head to the side, but he agreed, "No, he's right. She never took much bullshit, even from you, did she?"

I narrowed my eyes on him. "How the fuck do you know that?"

"Big brother has eyes and ears everywhere," Conor intoned, his tone mocking.

"There's more than eyes and ears. Me and Aela were sneaking around—"

"For a year, Dec. Maybe longer," Brennan interjected. "Jesus. And you weren't exactly smart about it. You were lucky no one else picked up on it."

Someone had.

I pursed my lips. "I wasn't as bad at hiding her as you're making out then, was I?"

"You were boning her for a year?" Conor ground out. "What the actual fuck? I thought you were into Deirdre."

My mouth tightened at just the mention of that cunt's name. I scowled down at my blanket-covered feet, hating that I was here, hating that I needed to be here.

I'd take this kind of treatment for a week maximum before I'd go home. I didn't give a fuck about what the doctors said either. I could rest in my own bed, in my own building without needing to be in the center of a goddamn warehouse.

And if my kid was there too?

Even better.

I could get to know him, and he could get to know me. If he wanted to, of course.

A wave of resentment hit me for the first time as I thought about how much I needed to learn, but I decided to shuck it off. That had no place in the here and now. Not yet anyway. Maybe if she was as much of a pain in the ass as Conor was making out, that resentment might come to the fore again, but I was going to try not to let it.

From what Brennan had told me of the night's events, they were close.

If I alienated her, then I'd alienate him, and I was the outsider here. No matter that I might want to break through the walls that were between us, walls she'd put there by lying to me, I had to protect their relationship.

She might not have considered mine with him, but I wasn't about to give her any shit on that score. I mean, I might want to at some point, during my recovery when I was hurting. It might seem like an easy thing to do, but reality sucked because I knew what I'd been like the last time I'd seen her.

Cold. Hard. Mean.

Why would she tell me she was pregnant? Why would she share anything with me?

I was lucky she'd even come to us now. Lucky that I would get to know my son before he was a full-grown man, and even then, that was only happening because Aela had been good people.

That was her problem though. She'd always been good people. Had always given a damn about folk when she should have been selfish, when she should have thought about *numero uno*, because that was how this miserable world worked.

If you didn't think of yourself, you were screwed.

And I was right, because she was.

I ached. Deep inside. Not just from the pain, not just from the stupid heart attack, but from loss.

I'd missed out on so much, so much that I wished I could take out on Deirdre's hide. It was her fault. All of this was. But she was dead, and I could only be grateful for that fact, even if her memory still lingered on with the ten grand payment I had going out every month, which made her a thorn in my side even in death.

In the grand scheme of things, ten grand was nothing. Didn't mean I didn't begrudge it. Getting used to shedding that kind of dough was simple when you earned as much as I did, but when I thought about what I'd lost out on? When I thought about what someone else's greed had driven me to? I knew I could shit a brick.

And because, at the moment, my heart was dicey, rather than give myself another cardiac goddamn arrest, I decided to burst Brennan's bubble.

Because even though he thought he knew everything about the family, even though he prided himself on knowing all.

He didn't know this.

But it was time he did, and it was time my blackmailer died a nasty, painful death. Something that was definitely a long time coming.

SEVEN

CONOR

IF I HAD any more programs running on my laptop, I figured the RAM on it would send it flying into outer space.

It was already throbbing like a motherfucker on my lap, and I might as well have invited the Sahara to come and bake my balls.

Did my brothers give a fuck, though, as they breathed down my neck, trying to get information out of me?

A big fat fucking no.

They didn't give a crap about the fact I probably wouldn't be able to have kids after this clusterfuck.

And it wasn't only my brothers' fault that the future Mrs. Conor O'Donnelly was going to have to visit a sperm bank to get her some baby Conors. Nope, it was that bitch Lodestar.

After the fourteenth round of malware she'd sent my way, I was currently working to disinfect thirty grand's worth of kit, all while I had my brothers harping on at me about hacking into bank accounts.

This petty shit was so below my paygrade, but fuck, what was I supposed to do? Say no? This was for Dec, after all.

"Why's it making that noise?" Brennan asked, peering at my laptop pretty much like it was an alien. Or it was about to do as I'd already said—take off and soar into the stars.

"It's working."

"Harder than you, dipshit," Aidan grumbled.

On the brink of snapping back at him, I cast him a look and watched him rub his thigh. We all knew what that meant. His knee was hurting him like a bitch, which always made us go easier on him.

I was half certain that was the reason the prick had turned into an opiate junkie, because we'd stopped giving him ten tons of hell all the time. When a man was raised with that kind of constant infighting, it had to be a culture shock to lose it.

Huh.

That was a thought.

Maybe I should give that hypothesis a go?

"I'm working plenty hard," I told him softly. "Unlike your junkie ass."

The silence in the waiting room at my declaration was heavy. Hell, it was like I'd let off a fart worthy of a mushroom cloud.

But no one said anything. In fact, no one said shit.

We all knew Aidan had been dropping the ball since the drive-by shooting that had put him in the hospital for months on end, and we'd let him get away with it.

That no one argued with me told me they agreed, but that no one backed me up told me they were too chickenshit to stand with me.

Cowards.

I huffed at the thought, and feeling a little self-righteous, I cast him a look and stared him square in the eye when I saw he was glaring at me.

I didn't even shrug, by no means did I even think of apologizing, even by expression only.

I wasn't sorry.

I loved my brother, but he was being a dick. And he needed to get help. Tiptoeing around the fucker wasn't going to get us anywhere.

Finn, ever the pacifist, not, muttered, "Have you found anything on Aela?"

Shrugging, I said, "I'm in her bank account."

"You are? Why the fuck didn't you say?" Brennan grumbled, and I glowered at him.

"Because I'm in, doesn't mean I don't have to figure out her incoming and outgoing payments. Jesus, I know I'm smart, but I'm not a computer." I rolled my eyes at their expectations, and while I usually lived up to them, I wasn't AI.

Yet.

Grousing at him under my breath, I ignored the weighted stares of the five people who I cared most about in the world.

I loved Ma and Da, but these were my brothers. We'd been raised together, cured together like the finest Iberian ham—my favorite—and they were the only people I could stand for more than a few hours.

They were pains in my asses, but that worked both ways. I figured they felt the same because, in the grand scheme of things, none of us had that many friends. We all hung out together, and then did our own lone wolf shit before coming back to the clan.

Of course, that was normal considering we were at the top of the tree. It wasn't like there were many people we could shoot the shit with when everyone in our vicinity was under us and, therefore, not to be trusted with everything we knew.

I sniffed at the thought, but my sniff turned into a curse when the antivirus program I'd created especially for Lodestar's bullshit had an alarm pinging through the waiting room.

We were sitting in the warehouse where Declan was being treated, and I'd been working on his messed up life ever since he'd told us he had a blackmailer.

Not only did I have to find that fucker, I also had to work out if Aela O'Neill was some kind of Mafia stooge, and then I had to deal with this Lodestar bullshit.

I'd come across the hacker when she'd managed to break my code and had penetrated Eoghan's security system on his apartment. It had caused a real shitstorm for him with his new wife, because Lodestar, being a cunt, had tripped his phone too and had sent his mistress a text.

When he and Inessa, his new wife, had walked into the apartment, the slut had been waiting, legs spread, for Eoghan to 'service' her. Leticia was dead now, on my orders—the slut had known what she was doing so I felt no guilt. But Lodestar?

A bona fide bitch, and while I might otherwise be impressed by her abilities, mostly she was a burr under my skin. A mosquito dancing around my ears while I tried to sleep at night.

Of course, as irritating as mosquitos were, they were also one of the top killers in the world... Lodestar was dangerous. That made her all the more fun to play with though. It would also make it even better when I squashed her with my tennis shoe.

"What the hell is that?" Eoghan hissed, rubbing his ear as my laptop carried on sounding the alarm.

Last thing I needed was Lodestar getting into my computer, so I shut shit down, defragged my system, and quickly cleared it. My program had already isolated her presence, and I knew it would be analyzing how she'd jacked into my system, but it was annoying that she kept on managing to do it.

Muttering under my breath as my computer restarted, once it was back online, I quickly logged into Aela's bank account again.

"Okay, so Declan doesn't have to worry about money anymore," was how I started the analysis.

"Huh?" Brennan asked, his brow furrowed when I peeped a look at him.

"She's richer than him," I stated dryly.

Finn, being our money man, got to his feet and wandered over to me. When he saw all the zeros in her account, he whistled under his breath. "Jesus. Wonder if she'd let me play with it. Haven't fucked with the stock exchange in a long while."

"Married life is slowing you down," Eoghan joked, but when the two of them glanced at each other, sharing wide grins, I knew they were happy about that.

And I couldn't blame them.

I didn't want to be tied down. If anything, that was the last thing I wanted, but when I saw Finn with his wife, Aoife, and Eoghan with Inessa? It made me think about things I really didn't need to be thinking about.

Scratching the stubble on my chin as I scanned through her payments, through her income streams, and spotting a few red herrings, I arched a brow and declared, "I don't think she knows she's a patsy, but I figure she is. There are a lot of Fuoco Corp subsidiaries who've paid her for artwork, yet she gets a lot of commissions. It could simply be that one dick in the *Famiglia* happened to see a piece of hers in a friend's house, and his wife decided she wanted an O'Neill in their home too." I shrugged. "No way of correlating—"

"There was enough to warrant an undercover operative being dumped in their lives for years," Brennan pointed out gruffly.

I cast him a look, and even though I was usually blind with this stuff, I wondered if the idiot knew he was halfway to sounding like he had a crush on Aela.

I was pissed that Declan had managed to have a side piece for over a year without me knowing. We were all close, close enough to share intimate details of the women we banged. I knew he and Deirdre hadn't been as close as Ma and Da thought—they'd believed there were wedding bells on the horizon—but Declan had never told me a damn thing about Aela.

And seeing her tat? The brand? That was unusual.

Claiming wasn't something we did at our rank.

"She's loaded," Eoghan drawled from over my shoulder.

That he was impressed was a given. And Finn was too as his eyes scanned over her bank account.

"Jesus," he muttered out of the blue. "Is that how much academies cost?"

"You'd better get Jacob onto a shortlist. I'd hate for him not to be among Manhattan's elite as he grows up," I mocked.

"*We* never were," Aidan pointed out.

"Dragged up," Eoghan joked wryly, even though we'd all gone to Catholic private schools.

Mostly because no way would Da have gotten away with dragging us out of classes the way he had if he didn't have the diocese in his pocket. We'd spent more time out of school with truancy marks on our records once we entered our teen years and became more acquainted with the life.

Even as I thought about that shit, I wondered if Declan knew what Seamus was coming into.

He was a teenager. Ripe for introduction into our world. Did Declan accept that Da was going to be introducing him into the way of things? Was he happy about that?

I wasn't sure if I would be.

There were things we'd all done that I wouldn't wish on any nephew of mine.

Of course, it wasn't my place...

I cut Finn a look, wondering how he felt. He was clearly thinking of sending Jacob to a private school, so did that mean he didn't want his kid to be in the life too?

Pursing my lips at the thought, I decided now wasn't the time for thinking crap like that, and I grumbled, "What else am I looking for? You wanna know how much she spends at Whole Foods?"

Brennan grunted. "No, I just wanted to make sure she was clean."

"Far as I can see she is. All her money is legitimate—from banks that are based in the U.S. So not even any money laundering is really going down either, because the quantities are all high, and they'd be flagged by the IRS.

"She's got herself a good business going on. Jesus, they said crime pays. I never knew art was just as beneficial."

"Why the fuck is she a teacher at a college then?" Aidan rumbled.

I shot him a look. "Maybe it fulfills her?"

He frowned at that, but I got it. Looking for shit that fulfilled us was something that had been whooped out of us as kids.

Dreams and goals were for other people.

We had to work for the family, we had to make the O'Donnellys the most feared clan in the city, and we had to make sure that the Five Points were around for the next generation.

I figured it said a lot about us that we were all in our mid-thirties to early forties and we'd only just started popping out kids. Well, Finn had. Eoghan was the youngest, and his marriage hadn't exactly been his choice, had it? He'd have stayed single if he could, and I wouldn't be surprised if they didn't have kids for a long time because Inessa was practically still jailbait.

"Plus, I've been looking into her movements too," I reasoned slowly. "She traveled a lot while Seamus was young—" Christ, it was hard to believe there was a kid in the family now. "Then, when he turned nine, she started slowing down, still did a lot of traveling though. Probably enough to cause issues with his teachers."

"That's when kids start middle school, isn't it?" Finn asked, his brow puckered.

Eoghan snorted. "No. That's at eleven."

"So long since you were even in school it's a wonder you can remember," I remarked dryly, laughing when he shoved my arm, but his lips were definitely twitching. "Seems like she was starting to put down roots for his benefit," I confirmed.

"With that school, a change of pace, and the look of her house, I don't think any of us can deny that she's done right by the kid," Brennan observed.

I cast him a look. "When Da asks, I'll make sure he knows."

"He's going to be an issue," Finn concurred.

"We need to keep them all apart until Declan's better. Until he can keep a handle on things, because Da is enough to make her run," Brennan warned. "You know how fucked up he gets sometimes, and with almost losing Declan and then learning about Seamus—fuck, it was a cute thing for her to name him after Grandda, but that's only going to mess with his head all the more." He rubbed a hand over his brow, and I could sense his fatigue from all the way over here.

Barely refraining from yawning, I decided I was tired too. It wasn't something I often allowed myself to feel because I had too much shit going on, too many plates to spin to sleep, but as I saw my brother's exhaustion, I allowed myself to feel it as well.

Things had been hectic since Dec had been brought into surgical care here, and it wasn't going to lighten up now that we had family to protect.

From family.

Jesus.

I rubbed my eyes. "Ma's going to be just as bad. She'll want to meet him."

"It's fucked up for Seamus to meet his grandparents before he meets his da," Finn stated, crossing his arms over his chest.

I nodded. "Agreed."

We fell silent, each of us lost to our own thoughts, then Aidan broke it. "I can't believe Hoskins fucked us over like that," he rasped, referencing the fucker who'd sided with an Italian sharpshooter, taken out Rogan, a trusted soldier, and had tried to get to our nephew and brother's woman.

"He's dead now," I pointed out, my tone a tad more gleeful than was appropriate. Especially as the crew we'd shipped after him had been told to be heavy-handed. Messages had to be sent, after all, and they had to make shockwaves reverberate around the Points. "No use overthinking it."

"Always been your trouble," he retorted. "You knock something off your to-do list and that's it. There's a reason he did what he did."

"Money, probably. You know the *Famiglia* pay well. It's the only reason they have any foot soldiers on the streets right now," Finn remarked.

"Conor's right. The cunt is dead, and we have other shit to worry about." Brennan sighed. "Now the threat is contained, I'll go and get Seamus and Aela in the morning. Shit should be wrapped up with the cops by then, and the house will have been processed. If there's a problem, I'll get French on it and make sure everything's tied up neatly. I'll bring them to Declan's, but the folks can't find out about it."

"Only way you can make sure that happens is if you go alone."

Brennan shrugged at Finn's comment. "That was my intention anyway."

I hummed under my breath. "I'll come along for the ride."

It was time to meet this nephew who had the fam in chaos, and as chaos was my forte, I was excited about meeting him. I just hoped the kid wasn't a prick, but I didn't put out much hope because every teen boy at fourteen was one of those.

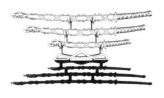

DECLAN

"AELA."

A sharp intake of air was my first clue that she recognized my voice, and to be completely frank, I didn't recognize my fucking voice, so how the hell she did was a miracle.

Still, I wasn't about to question a miracle, not when this entire situation felt very miraculous.

Like I was in the middle of a very lucid dream that I wasn't sure I wanted to wake up from.

The cardiac arrest, the feeling like death warmed over, sure, that could be a nightmare. I'd be very happy to wake up from that and not have to piss in a bag, but the stuff with Aela? With Seamus? I was glad that was happening.

Life changing, and in a way that was positive. In a way that was usually anathema of how lives changed in my world.

"Declan?"

Her voice was husky, shaky, and even though I hadn't spoken to her in years, I was instantly transported back to the days when her voice had been husky and shaky from need, from love, and not just nerves.

I missed those days so fucking badly... more than I knew, more than I thought I did.

"Yeah. It's me." I cleared my throat after I fell silent, and when she didn't say a word, Conor muttered, "My minutes aren't for wasting."

I scowled at him. "You gotta be shitting me. Your minutes aren't for wasting? Get me my own goddamn phone and I'll waste my own minutes. You cheapskate fucker." Millions in the bank and he was whining on about minutes when he had an unlimited fucking plan!

Sniffing, Conor folded his arms across his chest. "Don't know where your phone is."

My eyes narrowed even further, but before I could snap at him to go and find the fucker, which was loaded down with confidential material that we didn't need getting into the wrong hands, a wave of fatigue reminded me that my energy wasn't without limits.

I wasn't supposed to be awake, was supposed to still be in a drug-induced sleep, but I couldn't relax. Something was gnawing at me, keeping me from resting fully.

Aela.

Seamus.

I'd heard my brothers talking. Hushed whispers, discussions about their safety. How the fuck was I supposed to sleep with that going down? *Famiglia* cunts trying to get to my boy? With cops in Seamus's life? Even worse, Feds sniffing around like he was cow shit and Dunbar was one big fucking horsefly?

When I didn't reply to Conor, just glared at him, Aela whispered, "Since when was Conor so thrifty?"

"Always been thrifty," I countered gruffly. "Just on his own dime and not everyone else's. Cheap bastard," I muttered, before I winced as my body ached with just how fatigued I was. Conor snorted, but didn't deny the claim, just reverted his attention to the screen he was working on. In this place, that was about as much privacy as I could hope for. "Aela, in the morning, my brothers will be coming up for you. They'll help bring you to the city."

"Excuse me?" she replied.

I sniffed. "Excuse you? I don't. Excuse you, I mean."

"I have business here," she retorted, her tone snooty. So fucking snooty that, back in the day, I'd have hauled her over my knee and spanked her for it.

Gritting my teeth, I told her, "Business? More important than our kid's safety?"

At my words, she immediately gulped.

"I know about him. Brennan told me."

More silence.

I got it. I couldn't blame her. If I was her and I had to tell me the truth? I'd shit a brick too.

"I did what I thought was best for him."

Her words hit me harder than the bullets had. When they'd sliced into me, tearing through flesh and organs with no regard for what they destroyed, that hurt less than her remark.

But it was also pure Aela.

Pure, 'I won't cower before you' Aela.

She'd been softer back when she was younger. More pliable. But stubborn. So fucking stubborn. I swore, she got my cock harder than three lap dances back to back just with her sass.

Pliable just meant she'd bend and wouldn't break if I put her in a corner, and sometimes, on rare occasions, she'd even come out fighting.

I wondered what a pissed off Aela looked like at thirty-two. I wondered if she looked hotter than she had been back when we were kids.

Closing my eyes at the thought, wanting to savor the memory, I had to admit that I was rocking a boner my heart probably couldn't withstand right about now. Still, her lack of apology, though it gutted me, made me respect her.

She was standing by her decision. I couldn't blame her. Not when a handful of hours after she became a part of my world again, there were some fuckers trying to take her and my kid out.

"Best for him now is to know me, right?"

"Before you die?" she countered, her words filled with a fire that was undeniable.

Just shove a ton of kindling in front of her and she'd be razed to the ground in the flames that were born in that spark of anger.

"I ain't dying."

"No? Almost did last night. Twice."

"All the more reason to get to know me then, isn't it?" I heaved a breath. "Only God knows how long I've got left."

Conor grumbled, "Talk about asking for bad karma."

I ignored him. "I don't have much energy, Aela. But what little I've got, I'm focusing on you. If I could kill the *Famiglia* fucker for you, I would have. I'd slice my own throat before I'd let you and Seamus be in harm's way, and that's exactly why my brothers are coming to get you."

"Since I'm in enough trouble healthwise, the last thing I need is a Cheshire cat grin around my Adam's apple."

I could almost hear her mind ticking away, but the key to breaking her obstinacy?

Logic.

Truth.

Cold reason.

For a creative woman, she was surprisingly rational, but then, if she hadn't been, she'd have driven me crazy—and not in a good way. Back when I was younger, she'd had my cock in a knot. If she'd been illogical and stupid, she'd have just made me want to strangle her.

"Okay," she muttered, even though I knew she wasn't happy about it.

Nerves hit me. "Does he know anything about me?"

She swallowed loud enough for me to hear it. "I never hid you from him."

"Then why did you hide him from me?" I rasped, my voice low, even though I knew the answer.

"I thought you hated me. Thought you'd hate him. And you forget, Declan, I knew you back then. I was well aware how you'd work, how your family *still* works if the photos I saw in the tabloids are anything to go by."

My brow puckered. "Huh?"

I knew I was slurring, even though Conor tapped his watch, telling me to hurry up with it because if Ma caught me on the cellphone, she'd slap me. Bullet wounds to the chest or not.

"I saw Eoghan and Inessa's big day. Nice fancy arrangement, all prettied up for the cameras, but only someone in the life would see a contract behind it."

My jaw ached from how hard I clenched it. "Sometimes, ties have to be cemented."

"And I had no desire to be a tie or to be 'cemented' when I was a kid. Not to a man I thought loved me but looked at me like he thought I was a tramp, not to a man who might have believed I trapped him into marriage."

Her exhausted sigh resonated, because I was equally as tired. Still, I remembered the last time I'd set eyes on her and guilt hit me. "I didn't hate you," I muttered. "I was under a lot of pressure."

"Yeah, because your girlfriend had just been slaughtered," she returned. "Tell me why I'd want to raise a kid in that world, Declan?"

A sweet kind of despair hit me then. Landed straight in my solar plexus.

How was I supposed to answer that?

Because she was right. What woman, in their ever-loving mind, would want to raise a child in this world? It tilted everything on its head. Made me respect her and, crazily, lose some respect for my ma.

"You still there?" she asked warily.

"Yeah. I am." I reached up to rub tired eyes. I wanted to tell her she was right, but I couldn't. There was no escaping the life, merely procrastinating while you were away from it because once you were in it, you never got out.

So because I couldn't tell her she was right, I compounded her words by admitting, "The guy who betrayed Rogan's been handled. You don't have to worry about him."

Conor arched a brow at that, and I knew why too. That wasn't something we shared with the womenfolk.

Certainly not over the phone.

But I needed her to know she was safe.

"That's good to know." She didn't sound like it was, and I guessed, in this situation, 'good' was relative. "Look, you must be tired, and I have to go. If your brothers are coming for me tomorrow, there are things I need to wrap up. Even though the lawyer Brennan sent over has been working miracles, I'm still at the house and they're only just letting us leave."

"What things?" I couldn't stop myself from asking that question, even though I knew she might not answer.

Just the thought of her heading off to a lover's house to say goodbye sent white-hot jealousy roaring through me.

I had no right, and yet every right to feel that way.

Sure, that made no sense, but I was doped up, for fuck's sake. Cut me some goddamn slack.

"Things with work. I need to hand in my resignation." She sighed, and it was poignant enough to tell me she'd miss her job, which made me feel guilty again. "Things with the police. I killed a man, Declan. Christ. That comes with repercussions in the real world."

"You don't live in the real world anymore, Aela. I'll sort it out. Now, you get yourself checked into the Grande. Brennan will pay the tab in the morning—"

"I can pay my own way," she ground out.

"I heard you're a wealthy woman, but that means shit to me. I pay for my woman and my kid."

"Who the hell said I was your woman?" she snarled at me, all fire and venom. "I'm only coming because of the danger—danger *your* family put us in—"

"Me. I said it. You're mine. Always fucking have been, and always fucking will be."

And because I didn't have the energy to go to war, not with a woman who couldn't apologize for keeping my son away from me for fourteen years, with a woman who made me accept she'd been justified in doing that, I put the phone down.

Conor, eying me warily, muttered, "That's one way to get the last word in."

My lips twitched. "Watch and learn, C, watch and learn."

"How did you know about Hoskins?" he asked carefully.

"Heard you all talking. You should have told me. Shouldn't have to eavesdrop in on that conversation."

"You were at death's door, bro. Not the kind of stuff you need to be hearing right now. Not when we got it covered."

"I needed to know they're safe."

"And they are. You should have trusted us. We'd never put them in danger."

"They don't matter to you like they do to me."

"I respectfully disagree. Either way, you shouldn't have told her about Hoskins," he chided. "The phone might be tapped."

"As if you'd ever let that happen. Anyway, you'll understand the rest when you get a woman."

"Already have plenty. All of them dying to get with me."

I snorted, but as the cell tumbled from my hand, before it collided with the bed, I was asleep.

I could rest easy now, knowing she and Seamus were safe. I could sleep. Heal.

Because something told me that when I was back on my feet, she'd give me a run for my money, and hell if that wasn't something to look forward to.

EIGHT

AELA

AFTER DECLAN'S call in the early hours of the morning, where he'd laid down the law, it wasn't a surprise to open the door and find Conor and Brennan there. But welcoming them in felt odd.

Like I was conceding defeat on a battle that had yet to be fought.

Of course, I had enough battles going down around me, so I needed to pick which ones to fight.

My house was a crime scene. There was yellow tape around it, and my bedroom was being processed by forensics, so I'd grabbed all the stuff Seamus and I had been packing with the intention of taking it to New York with us, and had checked us into a hotel instead.

How they'd known about it when I'd specifically gone to a different hotel than the one Declan had named—

Of course.

Conor.

I scowled at him. "Have you hacked into my bank account?"

Even when I was a kid, Declan had regaled me with tales of all the crap Conor pulled with his hacks. I knew, once, he'd almost gotten into NASA, because he was on the hunt for information about Area 51, but before he could get to the good stuff, he'd nearly been caught.

When Aidan Sr. had found out, unlike any other parent in the world, he hadn't chastised Conor. Instead, he'd given him a to-do list of government databases to break into.

I sighed at the thought, inwardly wincing at the bad influences I was introducing into my son's life, but there was nothing to be done about it.

Nothing at all.

I knew I could fight. I knew I could run.

But you couldn't fight the O'Donnellys. And once they knew about you, there was no running either.

Not if I didn't want to die. And I really didn't.

Death was the last thing I wanted, because I totally intended on watching my son grow up and becoming a man. On becoming the person he wanted to be.

I knew what the O'Donnellys were capable of. I knew they were blood-thirsty psychopaths, and I knew they'd come after me with every ounce of their firepower just because of Seamus. So I could fight and almost die, and lose out on a future with him, or I could give in, stay on the inside, make sure I was there for Seamus, and ensure that I had his back to give him some semblance of normalcy.

Maybe I should resent all of this, and I guessed I did—I was only human. But, I'd known this day was coming the second I'd taken off. It had always been there in my future. A kind of D-Day that, with each passing year, hovered in the distance, looming over me like a harbinger of doom.

You couldn't resent the inevitable.

"Of course I did," Conor said, shoving past me to head straight into my hotel room.

Brennan grimaced at me, and muttered, "Conor, you're supposed to ask if you're allowed inside—"

"I'm hungry, and I need a bathroom," Conor grumbled. "I'm not asking for shit."

I rolled my eyes. "Bathroom's on the left," I told him as he moved around the room, evidently scoping the place out.

When he headed for the door I pointed to, a grin of thanks on his face, I moved back to let Brennan inside. He cleared his throat, peered around, cast a look at the unmade bed before making sure that he didn't look me up and down, and stared me straight in the eyes.

He was cute, I'd admit it. Cute in a 'killer' kind of way. I was under no illusion that was what he was, after all.

But my lady boners were all for Declan. Unfortunately for me. Because Brennan didn't look at me like he hated me, and that was so nice. Damn, nice was an understatement.

Of course, Conor hadn't looked like he hated me either.

I frowned at that. Frowned at the lack of disapproval that was coming off them in waves.

"Why the scowl?"

I shrugged at Brennan's question, then muttered, "Just thought you guys would give me a hard time is all."

"No point," he said briskly. "But I'll admit, I want to meet him."

"I can't say the same for him."

"No?" He winced. "Damn."

"You ready to be an uncle?" I teased, surprising myself because nothing was funny about this situation. It was simply that his reaction was pretty sweet.

This hardened criminal really wanted to get to know my kid.

Okay, sweet was *definitely* relative. But better Brennan wanting to get to know Seamus than giving me crap.

Of course, I'd be monitoring how the next few hours would go. If they dissed him, disrespected him in anyway, made a move to belittle him, I didn't give a fuck—I'd find a way to get us out, away from the O'Donnellys. Seamus was cheeky and could backtalk like a pro... if they slapped him, then we were gone.

But his reaction gave me hope, especially as I watched his wince morph into a smirk.

"I was born ready for anything."

Why didn't I find that hard to believe?

I moved over to the interconnecting door and tapped on it. Naturally, Shay didn't wake up.

Rolling my eyes, I knocked again, because he gave me crap about not respecting his privacy if I just walked in, but the little shit could sleep through a nuclear fallout. What was privacy in the face of that?

So I peered inside after I opened the door a sliver, made sure nothing nasty was going down—you never could tell with boys—and when I saw he was a big lump on the bed, taking up far too much room for a fourteen-year-old in the queen size, I muttered, "He's asleep."

Brennan cleared his throat as I closed the door. "Leave him. You guys had a late night."

"You want breakfast?" I inquired, then pointed toward the door Conor was behind and reminded him, "He said he's hungry."

"Is it still breakfast at two in the afternoon?" he asked dryly.

I shrugged. "I just woke up, so it's breakfast for me."

"I could deal with some eggs. Anyway if we don't feed Conor, he'll whine all the way home." Under his breath, he muttered, "Baby."

My lips twitched as I headed toward the phone and picked up the room service menu. I always ate the same thing for breakfast when I was in a hotel, so I tossed it at him and said, "Pick your poison."

He eyed me warily. "Don't feel like dying today."

"Well, if it happens, it has nothing to do with me." Because I got the feeling he thought I was taking this too easily, like I was too accepting and that meant he had to be cautious around me, I decided to drag off his kid gloves straight from the start and explained, "Do you know how long it's been since I last saw Declan? When it all ended, I mean."

He frowned at the change of subject. "No. About fifteen years?"

"Fourteen years, five months, two weeks, and eight days."

That had him blinking. "That's precise."

I nodded. "It is. Because do you know how long I've known this moment would come? Except, instead of you standing here, I figured it would be Dec?"

He cleared his throat. "Fourteen years, five months, two weeks, and seven days?"

"Exactly." I reached up and fiddled with one of my earrings. "And that's why I'm not really upset. Sure, inside I am. I'm all roiled up. I wish there were things I could do, shit I could change, but what's the point? I'm a big believer in embracing what you can't change.

"I gave him fourteen years of normalcy, and you guys are going to break that in the span of a few years." I gulped. "If anything, that's what hurts, but I'll try to keep him on the right path—"

"We're not going to ruin his life, Aela," Brennan countered softly. "Sure, there will be things that will change, but he's about to become a part of the tightest knit family on the East Coast. That has to mean something, doesn't it?"

"Maybe." I didn't argue, because there was no point. Instead, I just said, "Throw that over to him," as Conor stalked out of the bathroom like he was a hungry lion.

"Gimme, gimme, gimme," he growled as he made grabby hands for the menu, and I almost laughed.

Somehow, I had two-fifths of not just the tightest knit family, but the hottest as well.

Aidan Sr. was evident in all their appearances, but their mother was too. Her bone structure combined with Aidan's dark coloring made beautiful babies.

Any woman with these two in her room could let it go to her head, I thought with amusement.

And yes, I was capable of amusement, even though the chains were starting to coil around me.

My life was changing, Seamus's was too, but I was adaptable. I'd had to learn to be.

I'd roll with the punches, metaphorically.

If Declan ever raised a hand to me, that was it. He'd be the one who'd be rolling—into an unmarked frickin' grave. But I had to pray that the boy I'd known couldn't have changed that much. He'd never have hit me. Of course, I'd never have believed he'd dump me the way he had either...

With the phone call from last night resonating in my mind, where he'd told me I'd never stopped being his woman, Conor barged into my thoughts and, like he owned the place, strolled over to the phone and picked it up.

As he placed his order, he looked at me, and I murmured, "Eggs Benedict. Plus get an order of toast and crispy bacon for Seamus."

His eyes glinted with interest at the mention of my kid's name, but he placed his own order. "They said ten minutes."

"Money talks," I commented wryly, as I walked over to the closet, grabbed the bag I'd stuffed in there yesterday, and started sorting through it for something to wear. "I'm going to take a shower."

Neither of them argued, and I'd admit it was weird how unafraid I was around them.

Maybe I should be. Maybe they just weren't giving off those kinds of vibes. Or maybe it was because it hadn't been a week since I'd come under their spotlight and I'd already had to kill a man... That changed things.

Dramatically.

With my stuff in hand, I headed for the bathroom and showered and prepared myself for the day ahead. I knew they were here to deliver us safely back to Manhattan, and I'd admit I was grateful because the O'Donnellys always had a way of making you feel safe.

The ultimate of ironies, of course, because I was only in danger because of my ties to them.

I didn't rush my shower, seeing no point in it. I enjoyed the luxuriously appointed bathroom, indulged in the expensive toiletries, and pampered myself a little. I felt better as I dried off and wrapped my hair in a small towel like a turban. I dressed quickly, then applied some moisturizer before I headed out into the bedroom once more.

There was a room service buffet stand there, and I saw that Conor had already grabbed his and was over by the dining area, chowing down his eggs and bacon like he hadn't eaten in a month. Brennan's and my dishes were still waiting, and so was Seamus's.

It seemed counterintuitive, but I lifted off the cloches until I found the bacon, used the cover on the toast to keep it warm, then let the bacon scent drift through the room.

My kid had a Scooby Doo nose for bacon, and that was one way to get him up.

Brennan eyed the move with a raised brow, but he didn't say a word. Just grabbed his breakfast and mine and moved over to Conor's side.

The table had already been laid with cutlery, a jug of juice, a pot of coffee, and the associated tumblers and mugs, so I poured myself one of each and took a deep sip of OJ before I even thought about eating.

A minute later, the connecting doorknob rattled, and my boy appeared.

He looked a mess, but I couldn't stop the pride that filled me at the sight of him.

His hair was all over the place, he had lines on his cheeks from where the pillow creased his skin, and his eyes were like slits as he peered into the brightness. I was surprised he hadn't grabbed his shades like he usually did, but instead he stepped into the room, then stepped back—not to avoid his uncles who I doubted he'd even seen—but he returned a second later with a cap he pulled low over his eyes. He'd also grabbed a tee but stuck with his boxers and Rick and Morty sock-clad feet.

"Mom, where did I put my sunglasses?"

I snorted. "How would I know?"

He sighed. "You know I can't see first thing in a morning."

"By choice," I retorted, hiding a smile at his dramatics.

Brennan and Conor eyed Seamus like he was a coiled rattlesnake that was waiting to strike. Conor had even stopped eating! They watched him as he wandered over to the trolley and picked up a couple of slices of bacon, all without turning to look at me.

It was quite clear that he didn't have an inkling I was with someone.

I decided not to clue him into that fact, wondering what he'd do when he saw I wasn't alone.

Would he recognize them?

How couldn't he?

When he looked in the mirror in the morning, he had to see the likeness between them all.

He hummed as he chomped down on the bacon, nice and dark like he loved it, then he picked up the cloche and took a slice of dry toast.

"Where's the sauce, Mom?"

"I didn't bring any this time."

His head whipped around. "You always bring sauce!" Then he saw them. And he froze. His cheeks burned hot before blanching, and he took a step back.

Conor tipped his head to the side. "What sauce do you like?"

Seamus bit his lip, then looked to me for backup. Because I'd always give him that, I smiled at him. Gently. Coaxingly. Trying to tell him that everything was okay. That everything *would be* okay too. Not exactly easy after what had gone down in our home, but he trusted me, just like I trusted him. That'd take more than a night to destroy.

Warily, he gulped, then rasped, "It's called HP sauce. Americans never know what it is."

"I know what it is," Brennan rumbled. "Had it when I was over in Ireland." He elbowed Conor. "That stuff that's like A1 sauce but better."

Conor evidently processed that and took a bite of egg and bacon as he did so. Then he hummed. "I remember that stuff. Brown sauce I think you called it?"

"That's the stuff. Seamus likes to have a bacon sandwich with it," I explained.

"Huh," Conor said simply. "Don't they stock it here?"

"I get it online." To Seamus, I asked, "You going to come and sit down and eat with us? There's butter for the toast."

He licked his lips. "I-I guess."

Brennan moved, ever so slightly, and I only noticed because I was aware of him. His shoulders shrank a little and he slipped down in his chair. Conor saw it too, but he didn't look at me askance, just stunned me by doing the same thing.

Then, when Seamus took a seat, I got it. And I wouldn't lie, my heart melted a little bit.

They'd made themselves smaller.

I mean, there was only so much they could do to achieve that, for God's sake. They were both big guys, and Seamus was big for his age too, but I appreciated the gesture. More than they'd ever know, because it gave me hope. Hope that they'd be a good influence and not just a bad one. That they'd be family first, and Irish Mob second where my kid was concerned.

I'd thought they might backhand him for being cheeky, yet here they were, hunkering down to make him more at ease... the relief was real.

Seamus was quiet over breakfast, and I let him get away with it, didn't bother to chivvy him into talking because I wasn't about to force that on him.

What with everything that had happened, it was a wonder he was still functioning. Period. But he was resilient—I'd done that.

I gave myself kudos for it too.

When, an hour later, we'd finished eating and talking about nothing in particular which, somehow, hadn't been as painful as I might have imagined, I told Seamus to pack up his things. He slid off and a little while later, I heard the shower rumble on in his room.

As I gathered my belongings too, I waited for the inquisition, knowing it was coming.

Only, it didn't.

They didn't say a word.

Not until my bags were packed on the bed, and each of them moved over to grab one a piece, did Conor say, "You've got a good kid there, Aela."

Brennan nodded. "He does you proud."

The tears were stupid, but they prickled my eyes anyway. I ducked my head between my shoulders and muttered, "Thanks, guys."

Their approval shouldn't mean anything, but it did.

It really did.

I just had to hope that Seamus's father agreed with them, and knowing him as well as I had back then... I didn't hold out much hope.

AELA
BEFORE

"WHY DO you let him treat you like that?" I whispered in a soft hush, not wanting to upset Mom, but also needing to understand it.

I wanted to think that I'd never let Declan treat me like that, but heck, who was I to judge? I was his side piece. The woman he was cheating on his girlfriend with.

I was lower than the low.

A dog turd.

The betrayal was real, and no matter how many times I thought that, no matter how many times I felt that way and promised myself I'd break it off, he'd look at me with those eyes and I'd fall.

He was lonely.

Alone.

Lost.

This world wasn't his world, but he had no choice. No alternative.

He was stuck in this chaos just like I was. A rook in a game of chess that he didn't want to play.

Inside, I felt sure he was screaming. On the outside, he was cool and calm. He looked like the bruiser his family was making him, but I knew, deep in his soul, he was my sweet Declan.

A man who loved the arts. Who could wander around a museum for hours on end.

I mean, I loved museums. Loved wandering around them too, and my visits always fired me up for when I was home and able to draw or paint, but Declan's appreciation went so much deeper than mine.

It was like he was transported to an alternate world where he wasn't a Five Pointer. Where he was just a man.

Whenever we sneaked away to museums, the only place we were safe from prying eyes because not many people in the Five Points were likely to go there, I'd cling to his hand and walk with him. Past when my legs started to ache and I grew tired, when I wanted to sit and draw, I'd carry on with him, knowing that I, and that time in the museum, was his vacation.

His break from it all.

How could I leave him when he needed me?

When I was his respite?

Because I was.

If the museums fascinated him, I knew I did too. The way he looked at me, it was like an artist who'd found his muse.

But if Declan was an artist, he'd never be allowed to follow it through. I'd tried to encourage him to sketch with me, but he wouldn't. Like it was forbidden fruit or something, he'd eyed the pencil I'd proffered him like it was a snake.

I thought he'd have preferred it if it was.

Within the time we'd been secretly together, he'd begun changing. I knew why too. Even my dad was talking about how good Declan was at getting blood out of a stone, which I knew meant he was acting as Aidan O'Donnelly's fists.

Wet work.

I found it hard to believe that Declan was capable of it.

My soulful lover wasn't born to spill blood. He clung to our private time with a desperation I felt and wished I could ease, but there was no easing his path.

I closed my eyes at the thought, then was jerked back to reality when Mom whispered, "He doesn't mean to hurt me."

Thinking about that, I wondered if she knew what she was saying or if she was aware she was lying to herself.

Maybe she was delusional. She was rattling with how many pills she took, so I didn't see why not.

Carefully, I reached over and patted her hand. It was their sixteenth wedding anniversary, and he was late for the dinner she'd spent hours making.

Just like he always was.

Not just for this meal, but for every other.

She spent hours in the kitchen making him meals to please him, spent hours working out, spent hours making herself look good... to what aim? A disinterested husband who barely knew she, or her daughter, were alive.

Because I didn't want to hurt her, not when he hurt her enough, I got to my feet and leaned over her. Kissing her temple, I murmured, "Happy anniversary, Mom."

She grabbed my hand and pressed it to her cheek. "Thank you, pumpkin."

I wanted to tell her that she could leave him, that he wasn't her reason for being, but what was the point? To her, he was, and I wasn't going to change that.

As much as I loved Declan, I refused to let him mean that much to me. He wasn't my reason for getting up in the morning, and I had physical proof of how that worked. Nothing had been said, but it didn't take much more than a simple calculation to figure out that I was the reason Dad had proposed.

Loaded shotguns in the arms of Declan's father had a habit of making things nice and copacetic, erasing any and all signs of sin.

But the aftermath of that sin, the repercussions, were a different matter entirely. They were something he didn't have to live with, but his men did.

I'd never liked Aidan Sr. Not that I had a say in it or anything. But I'd never liked him, and learning more about him through Declan didn't make me appreciate him any more.

I thought he was a jackass who demoralized his wonderful son, who was turning him into a shitkicker when his soul was made for creation, not destruction.

But that was Declan's path. I knew he felt certain it had been set in stone from the very beginning, and no amount of me telling him otherwise would change what he saw as his future.

I squeezed Mom and muttered, "I love you."

"Love you too, pumpkin." Her fingers tightened around my hand. "You go off and have fun. You're hanging out with Deirdre and the girls, aren't you? Such good people to know, sweetie. Do your father proud."

Wanting to gag because I'd never aspired to make my dad proud, I just hummed and headed out of the kitchen. We had this really archaic way of eating. I would eat in the kitchen, and she and Dad would eat in the dining room together. On the nights he was home, that is.

Just in case he did come home soon, I rushed into my room and changed into a pair of slim-fitting jeans and a tee. I couldn't look too fancy, because it might raise eyebrows, but somehow, with Declan, I always felt fancy. I always felt like I was wearing designer stuff when I was just in regular gear.

I headed out of the apartment with a quick farewell that saw me dipping my head into the kitchen, but when I saw her drinking a large glass of wine, I sighed and disappeared.

All the way downstairs, I wished there was something I could do for her, but my father wasn't an easy man to talk to. If I said that in the past year I'd spoken to him a handful of times, I wasn't exaggerating. So, not only was the opportunity not there, but neither were the words.

He wasn't interested in me, Mom, or our family. He made that abundantly clear whenever he deigned to show up.

As I made it outside, I moved around the corner, and my face lit up when I saw Declan's Spider waiting there. I slipped in as quickly as I could, and when I saw him, I felt my heart start to pound.

He was so beautiful.

I was working on a set of sketches that would never see the light of day because no one would ever be able to know about us, and a set of paintings with him as the subject were bound to catch someone's attention.

"Hey," he murmured, his smile deepening when I beamed at him. He reached over and cupped my chin, sliding his fingers over the crest of my cheekbone with those rough hands that were capable of such violence, yet could be so tender too.

He was a man of many facets, and I wanted to know each and every one of them.

"Hi," I whispered. "Where to today?"

He shrugged. "Got a present for you." He ducked his head a little sheepishly. "Got two, actually."

My eyes twinkled. "Really?"

"Really," he replied, his lips tugging into a grin as he reached behind him for something on the back seat.

When he plopped a little bag on my lap, I eyed it with glee and started to open it. Seeing a box, I laughed, and then laughed some more when I opened it up and found another box. It was long and thin, so not a ring box or an earring box. Maybe a necklace? Although, not with those dimensions.

A little nervous, I stroked my hand over the box and giggled when he asked, "Want me to open it for you?"

His dry question had me shooting him a shy look, then I opened it and my mouth gaped.

"My God, it's beautiful," I breathed, my fingers drifting over the jade hair stick. It had a tiny figurine on the tip, and when I peered at it, I just knew how old it was.

I could literally feel the age on it.

The jade was still as pure, as green, as *regal* as ever, but the carvings in it were soft, smoothed over time like sand on the shore.

"Do you like it?" he asked cautiously.

"I love it," I whispered, beyond touched that he'd give me something like this. I gulped as I picked it up, letting the light hit it, and then I reached up, took my hair out of the ponytail I had it in, and created a loose bun. I slid the hair stick into it, and with stars in my eyes, queried, "How's it look?"

"As gorgeous as you." His hand moved to cup my face again, and like he usually did, he gently angled me this way and that, just like I'd done with the jade hair stick. Positioning me so that the light would hit my face, hit the angles in it, so, like the artist he was, he could appreciate it. "Beautiful."

My smile was shaky. "Thank you."

"Never thank me for the truth," he murmured, his gaze distant, and I wished like hell he was standing behind an easel or with a pen and notepad in his hand, sketching me. He needed that output, needed it more than I did, but I knew he'd never let himself have it.

A tragedy.

"What's my other gift?" I asked, because even though I wasn't greedy, if I didn't change the subject, I'd burst into tears.

He twisted his hand, showing me the tag on his hand. Acuig meant five in Gaelic, and a lot of the gofers had it on some part of their body, which meant almost everyone in the ranks did because you started off as a gofer and worked your way up.

"I want to mark you."

My eyes flared wide in surprise, but I knew why he was doing it, and I knew, immediately, why he'd given me the jade hair pin first.

That was for me.

The tag was for him.

And it was tying me into what I was. What he saw me as. Not what I wanted to be.

I bit my lip and nodded, but my excitement died.

The mark would tell any Five Pointer that I belonged to one of them.

And the lack of a wedding ring?

Declared I was a girlfriend. A mistress.

My jaw clenched at that, and I knew he saw the tears in my eyes because he rasped, "Aela, I love you."

I jerked my head to the side, looking away from him.

I got it. I did.

Some women were for marrying, others were for—

What?

Fucking?

I couldn't label what we had as simply that. I doubted he could either.

I was the only person who knew him. Knew the *real* him.

"Let's get it over with," I whispered, my misery in my tone.

He hesitated for a second, then murmured, "Thank you."

Two words. Not the ones I needed to hear.

Because what hurt the most was the fact that I'd just left my mom, had just promised myself that I wouldn't live for a man, yet here I was, allowing him this power over me.

But Mom and Dad's marriage was proof that being tied together meant nothing. If Dad had a mistress, which I figured he did with how absent he was from the apartment, I knew she got more of him than we ever did.

Somehow, that didn't make me feel better.

As his engine roared to life and we headed to whichever ink parlor he was taking me to, I didn't utter a word.

And neither did he.

NINE

DECLAN

BEFORE

EIGHT WEEKS later

ADRENALINE WAS BURSTING THROUGH ME, making me feel a little light-headed, a lot shaky.

Which, of course, made me feel like a pussy.

This was my first kill. I knew Aidan and Brennan had killed someone when they were a lot younger than this, and I had no real idea why Da had cut me as much slack as he had, but I was grateful for it.

Because I was going to puke.

I knew it.

I was going to shame Da and my brothers by puking over a dead man.

A man who'd betrayed us.

A man who'd deserved to die.

A fucking rat.

I sucked in a shaky breath, gulping when I saw those stars twinkling in the periphery of my vision, but Da slapped me on the back, and muttered, "Well done, son. Hold your gut a little longer, and go and puke back at home."

His compassion stunned me.

Da wasn't exactly known for that. He'd bred us to be tough, bred us to be hard, and that he was cutting me even more slack made me wonder if some alien had popped down and snapped up my father to colonize Saturn or something.

He was certainly extraterrestrial enough to fit in on another planet.

At his words though, I headed out of the warehouse where I'd been told to kill Jimmy D. execution-style, and on shaky feet, I made it out of the massive empty space and into the yard where there were fewer people wandering around.

I wasn't sure how there wasn't blood on me. Why it wasn't soaking into me, into my clothes. Drenching my skin.

When Jimmy's head had exploded the way it had, gore had gone everywhere. I'd thought I'd know what to expect, but I really didn't. I could never have expected the mess. The sheer force as a bullet caved in a man's skull.

I sucked in another breath, but it was too late. I rushed toward a nearby wall and pushed my back into it, trying to keep straight, trying to stop my knees from goddamn knocking.

Feeling like a baby and hating it, I closed my eyes and breathed through the chaos attacking my mind.

Most guys would talk about the first time they got laid, or the first time they got drunk. My brothers often shared war stories. The first time they'd been shot, that they'd killed. But even though I'd listened, and while I'd felt sure I'd learned something from them, I realized I'd learned nothing.

Christ, nothing could have prepared me.

I wanted to puke out my guts, but the one thing that stopped me?

The stupid tune that Aela had set as her personal ringtone on my cell.

My clammy hands found the flip phone I'd shoved into my pocket earlier, and I opened it, rasping, "Babe, I can't talk yet."

"I know it sounds stupid," she muttered, "but I just felt like you needed to hear from me."

Pain speared me at how well this woman knew me, and how little I could give her when she deserved the fucking world. "No way."

"Way." Her laughter was faint. "Stupid, right?"

"Maybe. Maybe not." I licked my lips as I stared up at the floodlights that illuminated the warehouse yard as if it was midday and not almost midnight. "You alone at the apartment?"

"Da's out on business, yeah. Mom took a Valium," she said, her tone shy.

Any other woman, I'd have said she was being coy, but Aela didn't play those games. It was one of the reasons I loved her.

My stomach had stopped protesting the second I'd heard her voice, and the thought of being with her, of being inside her, was a lifeline I couldn't ignore.

"I need you, baby," I told her, my voice low and husky with a desperation I couldn't hide.

"What's wrong, Declan? You sound funny."

"I feel it." My admission came with a sharp sigh. "Can I come over?"

"You know you can," she whispered, making relief rush through me.

I needed her in ways I couldn't even admit to myself, but every time I went to her, I felt like a piece of shit.

I could never be hers, not while Deirdre was alive, and yet, some days, the only thing that got me out of bed was the prospect of seeing Aela. Of her smiling at me, of her kissing me, of her hand in mine, her fingers on my stomach before she reached for my dick.

It wasn't all sex, even if that was a big part of it. I needed her.

I knew she needed me too.

"I'll be there in twenty."

"You're at the warehouse?"

She shouldn't know about that, but one time I'd had her come meet me here while I was on guard duty and we'd had some fun in one of the back offices.

The only time I didn't have that squid fiancée on me like gonorrhea was while I was working, and getting some time alone with Aela was next to impossible but imperative to my mental health.

Yeah, mobsters-in-the-making had mental health issues too—*go figure*.

"You should have told me. I'd have come visited."

The words sent longing through me.

If ever there was a woman who wasn't made for being a side piece, it was her, and though it was crappy of me to treat her that way when she deserved everything I had to give, I was grateful for her.

So grateful.

Somedays, I felt sure she was the only reason I didn't blow my brains out. Just like I'd done to Jimmy D.

Closing my eyes, I rasped, "Tonight wasn't a good night for a visit."

Her voice turned hushed. "Oh."

We both knew what that meant.

Even though Deirdre was the daughter of one of my old man's lieutenants, she didn't seem to understand how shit worked. I wasn't sure why that was or how she couldn't know. Maybe she was just oblivious to it. I knew she was ignorant of the fact I hated her. Of the fact that when I touched her, I hated every second of it. So why would she even notice if crap had gone down, and how would she even monitor it?

I knew she was self-centered. It was one of the many things I loathed about her. And one of the things I loved about Aela was how she was the exact opposite. How she read between the lines and understood the darker days where my soul cringed with what I had to do for my father.

Two women had come into my world, one I hated, one I loved. I was destined to be with both, but not in the way they deserved.

"I'll be there soon," I vowed, and she hummed.

"Can't wait."

I knew she meant it, and my heart skipped a beat with excitement too. She knew why I was coming, and she never turned me away, so that little purr in her voice told me she wanted me as much as I wanted her.

Thank Christ.

Gulping, I disconnected the call before I did something dumb like tell her I loved her again. I tried to do that only when I was emptying my balls in her because I *couldn't* not do that. It always blurted out of me like I had no control over my mouth when I was inside her. Maybe it was a weakness, but she was one big proof of my weakness, and the longer I was with her, the less I cared about that.

Now knowing what I was going to do, and knowing that puking wasn't exactly going to be much of a turn on for her, I managed to keep my stomach contents in my gut, and headed for my car.

When I climbed into the Spider, sinking into it, I locked the doors behind me, and for a second, I rested my head against the headrest. I couldn't go to her wired. I'd be too rough. The last thing I wanted was to scare her away.

So I took a few calming breaths before I started the engine, and then I rolled out of the warehouse parking lot, saluting the men on guard as I headed onto the interstate.

It took barely any time at all to hit her neighborhood. It wasn't the best part of Hell's Kitchen, but neither was it the worst. I didn't have to worry about my car being ransacked—that had nothing to do with people knowing it belonged to me, and that if they damaged it or stole from me, they'd have the O'Donnellys coming after them and their kneecaps—and everything to do with the quality of the area.

I pulled up a block away, because even though it wasn't under threat of being stripped, a Spider still stood out around here where most vehicles were American.

Locking up, I headed down the street toward her building and used the key she'd given me to get in.

When I caught a glimpse of myself in the mirror in the elevator, I grimaced because I was pasty as fuck. Scrubbing a hand over my face didn't do much good, but it confirmed I wasn't walking around covered in blood, so I knew I could go straight to her without showering.

When I was on her floor, I walked to her door, used the key to get in, and then slipped inside. Her bedroom door was open, and the furtive moves always made my heart rush with excitement.

Doing this, having the key to her apartment, moving into her room like it was my right, it all made me feel like this was my home.

Like I was *coming* home to her.

I wanted that, I realized. I wanted that so badly...

Jesus.

I'd never thought I'd want to settle down this young, mostly because my choices were denied to me. Deirdre was forcing my hand every step of the way down the aisle, but she wasn't the one I wanted to settle down with.

When I slipped into Aela's bedroom, I saw she had a nightlight on. The place was still kitted out like she was a kid, which was skeevy as hell for me, but I saw nothing else when she lifted the comforter and revealed her naked body. Barely remembering the need to close the door behind me, I was careful not to make any sudden noises because it might disturb her mother.

Nostrils flaring at the sight of her when I turned back around, my dick hardening to the point of pain, I started to strip out of my clothes. My pants and jacket soon hit the ground, and I almost tore off my shirt, boxers, socks, and shoes in my haste to get naked.

The second I was there, in bed with her, she covered me with the comforter, and I groaned as her silky soft skin collided into me. Her arms slipped around me and her legs cupped my hips as I rolled onto her. My dick settled against her core as I moved atop her, and my mouth came to meet hers.

"Best greeting ever," I rasped against her lips as I started to tease hers into opening.

She was always shy when I kissed her, which was cute when I thought about how she'd greeted me. But it was just one of the many nuances to her nature. Free with herself in some ways, needing me to coax her in others.

Everything I enticed from her was always hard earned and made me feel like Julius Caesar in the aftermath.

With my dick against her heat, it felt criminal to pull back, reach under her bed, and grab the box she kept there for nights when I visited her.

When I fiddled with the lid, managing to open it and grab a condom, she groaned when I ground my cock into her before I passed her the foil packet.

I loved how she eyed that silver wrapper with big, round eyes. She'd been raised uber Catholic. No sex before marriage, no condoms between a man and a wife. I wasn't scared about being caught fucking her or about the condoms because my father, to the Five Points, was more powerful than God himself. Irony being that whole 'no false God' stuff would probably get my da sent to hell faster than all the other atrocities he committed.

Not that I needed to be thinking about him now. Christ, that was one way for my boner to die a swift death.

Because I knew she got a kick out of it, I held onto her hips as I twisted us around so I was flat on my back and she was on top of me. She gnawed on her bottom lip as she settled there, then she sat up, carefully tore the condom wrapper open, and pulled the sheath out of the foil. When she pinched the tip, her breath hitched as she reached for my cock and held it upright. The delicate touch was always enough to make me want to shoot my wad.

I'd been sucked off by pros, handled by women who knew their way around a dick, and nothing got me hotter than Aela's hesitance. Bringing her into the light, awakening her sexuality was the sexiest fucking thing I'd ever experienced in my life.

Bar none.

She rolled the latex down my length, not stopping until I was fully covered.

I dreamed, one day, of taking her without a condom, but I couldn't risk getting her pregnant yet, not until I had her set up somewhere safe. Not when I had to marry that cunt Deirdre.

My jaw worked at the thought, but I focused all my attention on Aela, on the woman who made me happy, on the woman I wanted to possess in every possible way.

She stroked me, a small smile on her lips as she did so. The gesture always amused me because it should have made me feel dirty, like a filthy little secret, but instead, I just felt cherished.

She was exploring all this new stuff that, to me, was old news. We might be the same age, but nothing about sex was new to me. With her, however, it was like I was learning a whole new playbook. Just for her. For us. What we shared.

Her knees spanned my hips as she took me between her hands and carefully slid her way onto me. She was still tight, still so fucking small, but

I gritted my teeth as I let her find her place. She was new to being on top, so I gave her the reins, letting her take things as slow or as fast as she wanted.

I knew that was the one way I could prove to her I loved her. By showing her that. By giving her that.

I never took from Aela. Never stole.

Watching her as she took me in, as she settled herself on me, I clenched my teeth as she rocked upright, then slowly cascaded back on to me. Fuck, it was torture. A long, rigorous descent into madness as I let her have her way with me. The only consolation I gave myself was to grab her by the hips and to hold on tight. My fingers might leave bruises in the morning, but she told me she liked that.

She liked waking up in the morning and seeing proof I'd been here. That it wasn't just a dream.

I didn't like marking her, but that she did fucked with my head so badly.

With her, I could be generous. I wanted to give her everything she wanted. Bites, nibbles, hickeys, bruises, a sore ass, whatever the fuck she wanted, I needed to give her. But I couldn't.

If she showed up at school with a hickey? That fucker of a fiancée of mine would have her nose in our business faster than a fox could get through a hole into a henhouse.

Letting go of her hip, even as I clasped her tighter with my other hand, I reached between us and began to rub her clit. She hissed when I did, and her eyes turned moody, edgy. I loved when that happened. Her pace increased, finally, and she ground down every time I filled her fully. She'd twist her hips a little, making me appreciate the flourish and what it did to her tits, before she reached up and began to grab said tits and squeeze the life out of her nipples.

She liked a side of pain, and that didn't come as a surprise. I knew her father had punished her with a belt as a girl. As much as I wanted to wring his neck over that, she behaved now and wasn't punished often.

The second I graduated, I intended to get a place for us. My house would have Deirdre in it, but my home would be with Aela.

Da would want me to get Deirdre pregnant ASAP, but that wasn't happening.

Ever.

I didn't give a fuck what he said. Didn't give a shit about what the family needed. No way was I spawning anything with Deirdre. My kids were going to be Aela's. No other woman's.

The thought shouldn't have been as much of a turn-on as it was, but it twisted shit in my brain, and within seconds, I twisted *her* around, spinning us about so she was on her back and I was on top of her. I plowed into her, hard and fast, taking what I needed, giving what she wanted.

I was a little rough, but all within the confines of what I knew she could take. The bed started to clang against the wall, but I was too far gone to care. As I shot my wad, she tightened around me, and she gasped her pleasure in my ear. Soft, breathy sounds that had me groaning under my breath, relief easing me down as I escaped in her body.

Slumping over her, my dick cosseted by the tiny pulsations of her pussy, I pushed my face into the pillow beside her. Her hands came up to hold me, her fingers digging slightly into the muscles in my back. She rocked her hips, wiggling around, and I let her, because I knew she was getting comfortable.

If Aela could have her way, we'd sleep like this.

And I was tempted.

Every fucking night I came here, I was tempted.

But I'd already made more noise than was wise. Even though her mom was doped up on sleep meds, I still had to be cautious.

When I could move again—ignoring the insistent urge to fall asleep—I reached for her wrist and pressed a kiss to the Acuig tag I'd had inked there. It was the only claiming I could give her, and while it'd never be enough, it gave me a sense of peace because I knew it'd keep her safe.

After I felt her erratic pulse against my tongue, I rolled off her, and slumped onto my back. She didn't cuddle up against me, just watched me climb out of bed and head over to the connecting bath she shared with her folks.

I didn't switch on the light because I knew my way around here as well as I knew my way around the rest of the place, but when I dragged off the condom, I frowned at the unusual squelch to the sound. When I peered down into the darkness, and saw shit, I switched on the light and hissed under my breath.

The condom was busted.

Fuck.

My mouth tightened, but I took it on the chin. I'd wanted her to have my kids, just not yet. I needed my ring on the cunt's finger and Aela in an apartment, someplace safe.

Brain ticking with a million thoughts as I pondered my next step, I didn't hear the footsteps behind me, didn't even have it in me to jerk in surprise when arms slipped around my waist.

"What are you doing?" she asked softly as she propped her chin on my arm. I knew the second she saw it, because she tensed, then whispered, "Oh."

Yeah.

Oh.

That about summed it up.

TEN

AELA

NOW

DECLAN'S PLACE was nothing like I imagined.

In fact, it was the opposite.

It was... Japanese.

Considering the family was borderline psychotic with their patriotism, both for the motherland and the States, that he'd gone for a very Asian influence clued me into the fact that Declan had opened himself up to the world.

Hell, I bet he even ate ramen on Sundays, not just roasted meat with two veg.

My lips quirked at the thought, even as I took a seat on the futon. Yep, that was the extent to this Japanese fusion Declan had going on.

The dining table was low to the ground, like the same height as a coffee table, and there were unusual dining chairs, which were like office chairs but also low to the ground. They acted as the heads of the table, and large white cushions replaced the regular seats. On the surface, there was a cast iron teapot with little painted teacups on a rush mat.

Beyond, there was a picture window that was revealed when screens were pulled aside on pulleys.

In this side of the room, which was compartmentalized with those translucent screens that were like paper, complete with Asian-style designs on them, there was a low sofa, cuboid and boxy, but comfortable none-theless. A kind of reed-like rug lay on the floor and the coffee table was barely a foot off the ground. Opposite, there was a console table, which was thick, boxy, and dark, gleaming in a way that spoke of expensive Shellac, with a few decorative items on top. Above, there was the only thing I'd expected—a large TV.

What truly interested me in this whole weird *Alice in Wonderland* fugue I had going on were the trinkets on the console.

I'd heard about kintsugi before and had been fascinated by the concept. The Japanese celebrated scars and damage that came in an object's 'life.' They didn't toss them out, instead, they'd painstakingly piece them together again like expensive jigsaw puzzles, and used gold as the glue.

The console table was about nine feet long, and all along the surface there were several such pieces. A few dishes, earthenware and colored pottery, a few vases that I didn't need to be an expert in to know were Ming, and some dishes with Japanese themes—the rolling surf, a bonsai tree, a dragon.

Even as I wondered what that said about Declan, why he chose to celebrate something that was broken, chose to cherish it, I peered at my son who was watching cartoons.

He never watched cartoons.

Said they were too juvenile, too young for him now that he was ancient at fourteen.

Of course, whenever he watched them, I knew it was his way of coping. He had an old head on young shoulders, and the path he wanted to take in this life was equally as turbulent, equally as stressful. If I could, I'd tell him to be an artist, tell him to follow his heart and create, but he wanted to be in law. Wanted to move into politics. Wanted to change the world because it wouldn't change itself.

Even as I feared for him, I was proud of him, and when he did have these moments, when he wandered back a few steps, I just let him. I didn't give him crap about the cartoons, because we had a tendency to tease each other. I didn't even mention them or what might be worrying him enough to watch them.

I just let him be.

Knowing full well that if he wanted to talk, he'd come to me. Which he usually would. Maybe not as soon as I'd like, but he'd come. Eventually.

So I watched over him without being seen, and I was sitting in this uncomfortable living room with a book on my lap when I hated, absolutely *outright* loathed, *Rick and Morty*.

I just didn't get it. But then, I didn't have to.

A long while back, I'd managed to reach that enviable state of motherhood where I could tune out the random stuff he used to watch or listen to.

It had helped get me through *SpongeBob*, *Pokémon*, and TikTok. *Rick and Morty*, however, required ear plugs.

With my focus on the book, my ear plugs working—thank God—I didn't hear any sounds that were out of the ordinary. Only when Shay jerked, jumping to his feet like a gun had fired in the room, did I realize anything was wrong.

I knew it was a testament to my faith in a family that hadn't earned *any* faith at all, that I felt safe.

I even knew he was just overreacting.

The O'Donnellys would let nothing happen to Shay.

They'd let nothing happen to me either.

They'd kill to keep us safe, and to be honest, that was the best kind of security going. I didn't have to worry about alarms or the cops. This was the kind of protection that was priceless.

"It's okay, Shay," I soothed, even as I pulled out the ear plugs and set them in the little carrycase I'd put on the coffee table.

"Who is it? I thought we were alone here."

His nerves bled through the words, and I hated the insecurity, even as I recognized this day had been dawning for a long, long time.

"We are. Someone has probably come to visit." *Sans* ear plugs, I heard the rattle, and knew it came from the kitchen.

That keyed me into the fact it was either staff or... *family.*

I wanted to pull a face, but didn't, because he could misread it and think I was scared too.

I wasn't. Not at all.

That didn't mean I wouldn't prefer the noise to have come from a staff member though. I'd even take a security guard.

As I got to my feet, I moved over to him and pressed a hand to his shoulder. "It's okay, sweetheart," I repeated, smiling at him. What he saw in my eyes must have reassured him because he swallowed, nodded abruptly, then turned to look at the TV.

Knowing that was about as much of a response as I could expect from my kid, I moved toward the noise.

To get there, I had to walk down a small hall made of more of those damn screens, all paper and light. Maybe it was a quirk of mine or his, but I actually hated the light. It was my natural enemy. Most artists adored it. For me, though, I did my best work at night, away from the sun.

This place was like my idea of hell with all the windows and the minutest of coverings over them.

I didn't have anything against Japanese decor, but I had to admit, nothing about it gelled with me or my taste. To be honest, I couldn't believe it fit Declan either. Especially not when I passed an Asian armoire, complete with a carved jade inlay in the doors, or another console with a rack of frickin' katanas on there.

Pretty sure I'd remember if my ex had a Jackie Chan or a Jet Li fetish, I headed for the kitchen and wasn't surprised to encounter Aidan Sr.

Most people were terrified of this man. My father included. As much as he'd respected him, that was nothing compared to how much he'd feared him. But then, a healthy dose of the two kept men in line. Weird as it sounded, I knew that now after being a professor.

Not that I threatened to slice my students' throats if they didn't get their assignments to me on time or anything...

I found, oddly enough, as I stood in the doorway, peering into the only normal room of the house because the weird aesthetic even bled into the bedrooms—except they had functioning doors, windows, curtains, and walls, thank God—that I wasn't scared of him.

I wasn't scared at all.

Leaning against the doorjamb, I watched as my son's grandfather made himself a pot of tea with stuff that was very clearly *not* Japanese. The only thing Asian about it was the name—china. But this was Dresden. I figured Dec kept this around the place for when his parents visited. Just like the Irish teabags he had in the kitchen cupboard. I guessed they were for them too.

"What are you doing here, Mr. O'Donnelly?"

He was fortunate I was feeling polite, or I'd have called him by his given name.

"I'm under orders not to see the boy, but you I can see."

My lips twisted at that. "That's a sin to chalk up to Father Doyle."

His frown was fierce. "What are you talking about?"

"You lied to me."

"I did no such thing."

I shrugged. "Declan, for all his sins, for all his flaws, would never throw me under the bus. I'm pretty sure you'd be 'under orders' to leave me alone too."

"You kept his son from him."

"I did," I agreed, and not for the first time, I felt little guilt over that.

It had happened when Declan had called me, and again now. In theory, I felt bad. I knew keeping father and son apart was heinous, but... And it was a big but, being back here, being around these people... it was a reminder of what I'd taken us away from. If anything, I was glad Shay had had the chance to be normal.

As normal as the kid of a nomadic artist could be, at any rate.

"You feel no shame for that, do you?" he questioned roughly, his hand on the teapot turning white, making me wonder how long the china would withstand such pressure.

"I've not been back in your stratosphere for a week. Declan's been shot, I had to kill a man, my home was invaded, one of your men was murdered on my street, I've had to move houses, and I discovered that a close personal friend is a Fed." I gritted my teeth. "If you think I feel any shame at letting Shay avoid any of that, you're as crazy as they say."

He narrowed his eyes on me, but his hand released its firm pressure on the teapot, and carefully, with a care that told me he was getting himself back under control, he placed it on the counter.

"Who says I'm crazy?"

I smiled at him in earnest this time. "Anyone who's ever met you."

He surprised me by laughing at that. A short, sharp bark, but I had to admit, I'd thought it more likely that he'd scream at me than laugh. "Well, never let it be said you don't speak your mind, Aela."

"I've learned bullshit is futile. Cutting to the chase saves everyone a lot of time. So, feel free, Aidan, to tell me what a piece of crap I am... I've been waiting for it for years." Before he could open his mouth, however, I stated, "Bear in mind that I did whatever I had to in order to protect my son, because that's what mothers do."

"She's right, Aidan."

Lena O'Donnelly.

I cut a look at the other side of the kitchen, and saw she was standing there as poised as ever. I wasn't sure if I'd seen her be anything *but* poised. Even during lockdown, where the women and kids were holed up in a compound for safekeeping, she was rarely rattled. She always looked like a secretary with her pearls and neat skirts, and the only bit of color on her was her hair. The only time I'd seen her dress down was when she cooked in the compound kitchen, but she always changed for dinner.

"That's exactly what mothers do," Lena continued as she ceased wiping her hand on a paper towel.

I looked at the door behind her and winced at the fact that the guards would keep us safe, apart from where their own people were concerned. Evidently, they'd had enough time for her to use the fucking bathroom, and only the fact that Aidan had rattled a dish had given their presence away to Shay, which had alerted me to the danger.

And to be completely frank, that was something I was about to deal with.

Call me brave, call me goddamn crazy, but I just tipped my chin up and said, "If this is going to be where Seamus and I live from now on, I will expect you to respect our privacy."

Aidan's eyes flashed with anger, but Lena's features turned to ice.

"I don't think you have any rights to respect after what you've done—" Aidan started to snarl.

"I protected my son. I'd do it again in a heartbeat. All the while that I kept him safe, you idiots were playing cowboys and Indians, shooting everyone up and getting into a war that, somehow, we were dragged into.

"You ever stop to wonder how a *Famiglia* goon knew where Seamus and I were living? You had a rat. Which put Shay and me in jeopardy. You wanted to meet your grandson so badly you sneaked into his new home. Well, good luck meeting him if he had been in a body bag because of the battles you've brought him into."

Guilt merged with the rage and outrage my declaration triggered. I truly thought Aidan was going to have an aneurysm for how bright pink his face turned, but Lena? If she'd been like ice before, she defrosted.

Tears poured down her cheeks. Her eyes were liquid with her grief.

"You feel like shit now, but how do you think I felt when I had to shove my fourteen-year-old into a safe room I only had in the first place because I knew, someday, your family would find us?" My tone was cold, but I felt it.

I felt frigid as I chose Seamus's welfare over my own.

I tipped my chin up some more, wanting them to know that I wouldn't take their shit.

When I was a kid, I had. I'd listened to these people, or people like them. I'd taken their stupid rules and edicts into full sway, but I wouldn't again. I wouldn't.

I didn't give a shit if Declan married me, didn't give a crap about anyone's respect apart from Seamus's. And the O'Donnellys needed to come to terms with that.

"Now, if you'll see yourselves out. I'd prefer for us to meet again with Declan at my side and Seamus fully apprised of who and what you are to him." I went to turn around, to stalk out of the kitchen and back to the living room that was blasting with cartoon sounds—I had to figure that was the teenage equivalent of ducking your head under the covers because Shay had doubled the volume on the TV—but I stopped.

Paused at Lena's whisper.

"Are you going to take him away?"

"I'm brave but I'm not that brave, Lena. I know full well the reach your family has. I'm not willing to do a damn thing that will compromise my relationship with him. That will make you tear us apart—"

"We'd never do that!" Lena gasped.

I peered at her over my shoulder. "Don't be naive. *You* might never do that, because you're a mother." I cast a derisive glance at Aidan. "He'd do it in a heartbeat. But if you treat my son right, we have no reason to leave."

And with that, I returned to the living room.

Maybe I'd made things a thousand times worse for myself, maybe I'd caused a war within the family, but I needed to lay down the law from the start.

I wasn't a kid anymore. Wasn't an ingenue. I was a woman. A mother. A successful artist. Wealthy in my own right.

I'd consider the conversation a solid check that would lead to a stalemate. And they were odds that I'd never have envisaged having over the O'Donnellys.

DECLAN

WHEN CONOR HELPED me out of the car, I wanted to shove him away. I wanted to get out on my own two feet, because the last thing I wanted was Seamus and Aela to see me acting weak.

Strength was everything in my world.

That was why Conor had blacked out the cameras in my building during the ride into the garage, and my parking area was blockaded by our most trusted men so that no one would see me and think less of me.

If I was weak, someone could try to attack, thinking to hit me when I was down.

The only problem? I *was* weak.

Very weak.

I felt like shit, and if I was in another world, I'd still be in the hospital. But that wasn't going to happen.

I had some downtime coming to me as I recuperated, but the second I was better, I'd be back on the job. Vacation time? Sick pay? Ha. What were they?

So, while I was off, I fully intended on getting to know my son. This was the perfect moment for it, while I had patience and a lot of time on my hands. When he could get to know me without me coming in at two AM with blood on my face after a beatdown, or as I strode in for dinner with the stench of gunpowder still in my nostrils after I'd shown some punk what it felt like to get on the wrong side of the O'Donnelly clan.

"Jesus, you've put on weight."

I scowled at him. "Maybe you need to work on your arms more, pussy," I groused.

Conor sniffed, but Brennan, rounding the car, countered, "It's the ten tons of crap they've been pumping into his system. Plus, you need to work out more."

His grin was sly, wicked, and fast, and Conor frowned at both of us. When I was standing, no longer relying on him for support, I watched him cock his arm up and test his biceps. He couldn't see shit, not through his suit jacket, but it didn't stop him from kissing the muscle.

"Don't listen to them. You're growing nice and big."

"You taking steroids? Or just buying miracle creams?" Brennan asked, but his eyes were twinkling.

One of the family's favorite pastimes, Brennan included, was winding Conor up. Mostly because it was so easy to do. Kid was on cloud cuckoo land. And yeah, I called him Kid when I was two years younger than him.

That was just Conor.

A perpetual teenager with the body of a thirty-four-year-old, the sex drive of a post-pubescent kid, and the mind of a genius.

"Miracle creams," Conor said drolly. "Already got one addict in the family. Don't need another."

Bren scowled. "Stop giving him such a hard time."

"Aidan isn't here so he can't hear me being mean," Conor retorted with a sniff. "The way you all tiptoe around him, it's no wonder the dipshit can't accept what he is and what he's going through."

"Fuck, he's turning into Dr. Phil," I mumbled.

"Well, save the pseudoscience for someone who wants to hear it," Bren groused, shoving Conor in the side.

Deciding a change of subject was necessary, I muttered, "How do I look?"

Conor blinked. "Like you've just been shot, been in surgery, stuck in a ward for a week, and have signed yourself out of the hospital early."

"Gee, thanks. You say the sweetest things to me."

"I'm known for my sugar tongue," Conor remarked, his eyes alight with amusement.

At my expense.

I heaved a sigh. "I know I look as bad as I feel, but still, am I passable?"

Brennan's hand came to my shoulder. "Seamus has never seen you before. He'll just be glad to get to know you."

"Unless he hates you at first sight."

Brennan punched Conor in the arm. "Don't say that, fuckwit."

Scowling, Conor rubbed his arm where Brennan hadn't held his punch and muttered, "Look, I don't know what it is with this family, but we're not in a fairy tale. It's highly likely Seamus isn't going to appreciate having a man around the place.

"Not only is he fourteen—and we all remember what it was like to be fourteen—but he was the man around the house. He isn't used to sharing his mom and he isn't used to being bossed around by guys. And Dec, no matter what you do, you're going to end up bossing him around.

"Statistically, women are far more patient with their children than men. And those are ordinary men. Regular ones. Nothing regular or ordinary about you."

"What the fuck am I? Ground beef?"

He scoffed. "You're a high-ranking mobster. Someone gives you lip, you shoot their kneecaps off—"

"No, Eoghan does that," Brennan interjected wryly, and I shot him a swift smirk because baby bro *had* done that. And recently. It was technically why I was looking like a walking corpse, and why Seamus was about to meet Jack Skellington instead of the Declan of before.

"I know it's going to be a learning curve."

Conor hooted. "More than that."

"Look, someone gives me shit, I don't immediately get my gun out. I'm not going to shoot my kid," I grumbled.

"Reassuring words," Brennan countered with a laugh.

Fucker had laughed more during this conversation than he had in weeks.

I heaved a sigh. "Come on. Neither of you are much use in making me feel better about this situation."

"Didn't realize that was my job," was all Conor said, and I glared at him harder even as Brennan passed me the two canes that I loathed but needed if I was going to walk toward the elevator.

I refused to use a wheelchair, even if it made me a dumbfuck. My heart had been under enough strain, but there was only so low I'd sink. No way in fuck was I about to meet my kid in a wheelchair.

I mean, there was nothing wrong with wheelchairs, and I was all about equal opportunities, but my kid needed to know who I was. What I was.

I wasn't going to lie to him.

Not from the start.

He'd live and he'd learn, and he'd see what he came from so that when the time came and Da pressured him, he could make his own choices. Make his own decisions.

That was important to me, and it was something I'd been thinking about while I lay in that nightmare hospital room, surrounded by cellophane and plastic wrap, beeps every which way, and blinded by a light so sharp I'd had a constant migraine since I woke up.

Da was going to push the issue. By fourteen, we'd all been versed in the life, so Seamus was prime for him to pump, but I wasn't about to have that happen.

As I staggered forward, I ignored Conor and Brennan who were bickering like old hens and headed toward the elevator.

The shiny concrete floor held skid marks from where, over time, I'd driven around the corners too fast, leaving black tire tracks here and there, and the low-level fluorescent light fucked with my head some more. To get to the doors, I had to pass my four sports cars. Vehicles that had once been my pride and joy.

Funny how almost dying changed my perspective. How it made me see through all the crap to what really mattered.

I'd lived life on the edge for so long, and I'd seen nothing wrong with it.

But if I'd died from my own stupidity, Seamus would never get to meet his old man. And even if he didn't want to, even if Conor was right and he hated me on sight, everyone needed to know their roots.

The elevator felt like a thousand miles away, but I made it. Nor was I blind to how my brothers moved behind me, just waiting for me to topple over. They did so in silence, knowing I was grateful, just as they knew how much I needed them for backup.

That was how we worked.

My brothers and I were tight. It was why we were pissed off at Aidan Jr. He was changing dynamics by being all secretive about his habit. Which was why Conor, who liked change the least out of all of us, had started giving him crap.

I didn't blame him, but neither did I think it was wise to piss off a tiger who was limping around half doped up on Oxy.

The second I was in the elevator, the second it was moving, I felt like I could drop to my knees. The gravitational pressure was minimal, but it felt like I had a ten-ton weight on my back.

"Dumbass," Conor muttered, when he carefully raised my arm and hooked it over his shoulder.

I didn't argue, which was probably clue enough as to my status. I just stared up at the moving counter above the doors, and waited, fucking waited, to reach the penthouse.

There was silence in the elevator, like my brothers knew I was focused on standing upright, and when we were one floor from reaching my apartment, without even asking, Conor moved away just in time.

The doors opened.

To nothing.

As I struggled out of the elevator, I heard sounds.

My apartment had been empty since the day I'd moved in. No girlfriend, mistress, or one-night stand had stayed here. Not even my brothers if they'd come over here and gotten drunk.

The sounds were enough to make my heart tick over, simply because I wasn't used to it. But when I heard footsteps, it stopped pounding, and instead took up a shit ton of space in my throat.

He looked like me.

That was my first thought.

He was smaller, leaner, and so youthful that I wasn't sure I'd ever looked as young as him. His eyes were innocent, but they were haunted, and after what he'd been through, after a quiet childhood, I could understand that.

By his age, I'd been to drug dens, strip joints, and had seen men tortured.

The worst thing Seamus had probably done was get into an argument with some kid in class, maybe not pick up his dirty laundry, and get into shit with his mom over back talk.

Fuck, I wanted that for him.

I wanted that for him so much that my mouth worked as I tried to get my thoughts in gear. Tried to figure out what the fuck I should say or do.

He was me. Just miniaturized. With his blacker than black hair, pale skin that gleamed gold in the sun, high cheekbones, narrow blue eyes. Everything about him was me, apart from one thing.

His chin.

I knew that sounded crazy, but it was true nonetheless. His chin was his mom's. I'd kissed that chin enough to know where the little crevice came from.

He stood there looking at me, just as long as I stood there looking at him, and my brothers didn't give me shit over it. If anything, they slipped back into the elevator, and as the doors slid closed, they left me alone with my son.

My boy.

I gritted my teeth as the urge to cry fucking hit me, but before I unmanned myself, before the big, hard ass mobster motherfucker wept like a goddamn baby, I heard the faintest of noises.

For the first time, my gaze moved off my boy's, and I found her.

Watching me.

I remembered her, ironically enough, from just before I'd passed out in the makeshift hospital ward where I'd been patched up. She had blue hair now where before, when she was younger, it had been black as pitch, but the rest of her was the same. Maybe a little older—mostly in her eyes. I could see she'd lived a life. She was no longer my innocent, naive ingenue. She was harder, but that wasn't a bad thing. Not in this world.

Her body had always been banging, but it was better now. Impossibly. Was it weird that I wanted to see her stomach? See if she had stretch marks? Physical proof that she'd held my boy inside her? I wanted to know her, wanted to know every inch of the woman I'd initiated into sex, but more than that, I wanted to know her.

I'd never stopped wanting to know her. To learn her. To be taught everything there was about her.

Her elfin face hadn't changed. It was still delicate, still oddly fragile when I knew she was capable of such strength. Her hair was the same shade of blue as her eyes, and along her earlobes, she had gold studs that I wanted to feel against my lips. Her brows arched high, paving the way for killer bone structure that led down to a butt-indent in her chin. She had a pouty mouth that was made to take my dick, and a stubborn jaw that declared to the world she was obstinate.

Even with all these years apart, I knew *that*.

"Declan," she breathed, and her voice, fuck. Sweet fuck. If my body wasn't hardwired for survival mode, my dick would be at full mast.

Just seeing her, hearing her, breathing in the same fucking air as her—a miracle. Something I never thought I'd have again.

"Aela."

Her eyes shuttered, cutting off those rich sapphire orbs from me, and though there was a lot I wanted to say to her, I was speechless.

Both of them were a rainbow of color, a florid fall of hues that invaded my harmonious living space. I'd controlled every aspect of the decoration, from the colors to the layout, had brought peace into my home because outside these walls, there was no peace for an O'Donnelly.

But they didn't fit in. They weren't peaceful. They brought chaos.

And I'd never been happier for the mayhem that was facing me.

Never been happier in my fucking life.

AELA

"DECLAN!"

Fear hit me the second his knees crumpled, and I could no more stop myself from calling out his name than I could stop myself from rushing over to him, getting to him with just a handful of seconds to spare.

Who helped me get him back on his feet?

My son.

Our son.

He'd darted over just as fast, just as hard. We both lugged him up even though he was fucking heavy, and our panting breaths merged as we managed to heft him on our shoulders and prop him up.

He wasn't deadweight, but he was almost there.

"Where to, Mom?" Seamus rasped, and I knew he couldn't take the weight that much longer.

When Declan didn't speak, I had to assume that he didn't have the strength to. The stubborn ass had come home far too soon, but it didn't take a genius to figure out why.

I was looking at him.

Speaking with him.

"Living room." The bedroom would be wiser, but nothing about this man was wise. I knew, just knew that he wouldn't want to be in bed around Seamus.

He'd want him to think he was the Big. I. Am.

Men. Stupid men and their pride.

But I'd denied him so much of Shay thus far that I couldn't deny him this.

Declan would soon figure out that Shay wasn't like him. Wasn't like any kids he knew from our world.

He wasn't ashamed to feel, wasn't ashamed to be affectionate even if he was going through a phase where it was uncool. I'd done a good job. And no, I wasn't being bigheaded. I'd raised him well, raised him to accept that to be weak, to be vulnerable, wasn't a crime.

Even though I knew that crossed paths with his father's family's ethos.

The pair of us struggled with Declan's deadweight, and for the first time, I appreciated the whacko minimalism because we didn't have to steer around much furniture to reach the futon.

Both of us tried hard not to jolt him as we helped him onto it, and when I tried to rearrange his legs, shaking my head at his stupidity, I muttered, "Shay, turn off the TV, please?"

"Sure." He did as asked, then twisted around to look down at his father. I wasn't altogether surprised when he took a seat on the edge of the low coffee table, his eyes wide as he whispered, "He's still ill, isn't he?"

"Yes."

He cut me a look. "Why isn't he at a hospital then?"

"Because he's pigheaded."

Shay's lips twitched. "Like me?"

"Worse. You get it from him," I said dryly.

"Because you were never stubborn?" Declan rasped, his voice kind of puny. Totally unlike the man I knew.

And, frankly, how I'd pay not to have to hear him.

Declan was a force of nature. Ebullient, strong. Fierce. Ferocious.

He wasn't, and never had been *puny*.

"Nope. Never. Obstinacy isn't one of my virtues," I teased, but I heard the tears in my words, and hid them behind a dry smile I shot my son's way.

He snorted, like predicted, but focused on his father.

The eagerness, the curiosity, neither came as a surprise but I was glad. Really, I was. When I'd told him about having to move, about having to come to Hell's Kitchen, Shay had taken it on the chin. He'd actually taken it better than I'd expected because he was sick of moving around.

One of the major reasons I'd settled in Rhode Island, taken the position as a professor, was because he was tired of being a nomad. He'd even had a tantrum when I'd tried to pick us up and move down to Argentina where Luis Morales, the famous sculptor, was based. He'd wanted to mentor me, and when Luis Morales had you in his contacts, when he asked you if you wanted to study under him, you just didn't say no.

For my kid, I'd said no.

If I'd forced the issue, just packed us up and taken off, of course, I wouldn't be here. Seamus wouldn't be looking at his father like the way he eyed his first GI Joe as a kid.

When I'd stopped fussing around Declan, I took a seat beside Shay, and realized that even though Declan had been relatively quiet, his gaze was fixed firmly on Seamus.

That he was falling in love with our kid came as a relief to me.

I'd never known how he'd take it—if he'd hurl abuse at me, if he'd try to poison Shay against me—but here he was, looking at him like I knew I'd looked at Shay when I'd just given birth. My heart in my eyes, the need to protect this child from everything and anything just as ferocious as the fire I had to create art. Which, back then, in the aftermath of our break up, had been all I lived and breathed for.

That look gave me hope for the future. For the upcoming days.

I swallowed, nerves hitting me when I hadn't been nervous since that day when I'd thought he was going to die. I'd taken all the other punches as they came, accepted Caro's betrayal and the subsequent investigation into my finances and business operations facilitated by the fancy ass lawyer Brennan had hired for me—and had settled into a new home I loathed.

I'd dealt with the matriarch and patriarch of the clan, had stuck my fingers in their face and told them where to go, and I'd begun to come to terms with my new reality, as well as what beckoned. While I was still finding my way, seeing Declan cemented things somehow.

The house no longer felt like a strange hybrid, it was no longer cold and clinical, and I no longer felt like I was an unwanted guest, shoved away here.

With him in the penthouse now, it was like what I'd wanted when we were together. A home. Our home.

"Shay?" I prompted softly when the staring looked set to carry on for a while. And I got it—they were learning each other, but I guessed an introduction was needed. "This is your father, Declan. Declan O'Donnelly."

Seamus surprised me by sticking out his hand, and Declan accepted it, taking it in his callused one and shaking it with a strength that I knew would have Seamus cringing if he wasn't trying to look manly.

"It's a pleasure to meet you, son," Declan rumbled, and when he gulped, his emotions on full display, I'd admit to being stunned.

Maybe it was because he'd been so close to death, maybe it was because he was still weak, but Declan revealed more in that moment than I thought he'd ever revealed to me before.

Unsure what to do with that knowledge, of what to say and how to act, I just sat there, feeling like a third wheel who was somehow pivotal. I figured I was the only thing keeping Shay in place, but I knew Declan wanted to talk to him as well.

Because it was awkward, and because I had to start things off, I decided to be candid. Maybe Declan wouldn't like it, but it was time he learned a few things.

One, I kept very little back from Seamus.

Two, I wasn't the same timid mouse I'd been when I was a kid, when he'd first known me, and when we'd first broken up.

"Seamus, I left your father because of a few misunderstandings and a desire to give you the best I could." Shay twisted to look at me. "You can be angry at me, you can be resentful at your father, but the decisions we both made are in the past. We can't undo them. We can't even rectify them. What we can do is move on from this point.

"We're all here. We're a family. I'm certain there will be a transitional period where things are a little on edge, but you can see your father is sick. He needs rest, some R and R time, and we'll give him that."

Shay nodded, but Declan's confusion was clear. I figured I knew why too, because I couldn't see Aidan Sr. and Lena having this kind of discussion in front of their kid. I couldn't imagine them telling him what I'd just shared with Shay.

I hadn't gone into the gruesome details, hadn't discussed the minutiae behind the breakup and my fleeing the States for Ireland, but he didn't need to know those things. At least not today.

In time, I knew he'd have questions, and I'd give him answers. When he was ready.

Now was not the time for raking up the past. It was for celebrating the future.

It surprised me when Declan seemed to read my mind, because he simply asked, "You like sports, son?"

And that was how I ended up watching a football game.

Even though I hated the sport, I sat through it, wedged at the edge of the sofa by Declan's feet, sandwiched between him and Shay who, for the first time in years, was glued to my side.

It wasn't how I'd expected the day to roll, not with Declan almost collapsing or with the football game, but it was better than a shouting match, that was for damn sure.

It gave me hope that we could make the transition easy on Shay... but then again, hope had always fucked me over in the past.

I just prayed that this time, that wasn't the case.

ELEVEN

DECLAN

THE DAYS after my arrival at home, I slept a lot.

More than I'd like.

I moved from the sofa to the bed and back again, trudging like a zombie from one to another.

As I pulled my best *Walking Dead* impression, an impression that would usually impress only my bonsai tree unless Ma barged her way in with Da at her back blustering over how I made her worry, and a few of my brothers trickling in through the day to make sure I was on the mend, they were there.

Constantly.

Maybe it was stupid of me not to anticipate that, but it came as a severe shock.

What stunned the hell out of me even more?

That I liked it.

She made coffee in the morning.

I woke up, trudged into the living room, and there was a steaming cup there waiting for me.

She wasn't there with the cup, which I'd have preferred, but her presence registered with me.

A little while later, Shay would wander in. He was quiet, not as talkative as I heard him be with his mom when they were in the kitchen together, but he stuck around. We watched cartoons and shit on the box, not really talking all that much until a live game came on and then we argued stats.

Throughout the day, when I wandered out to take a leak, I'd return to find a steaming cup there, a sandwich, and some healthy snacks.

It was such a 'mom' thing to do that it took me a while to recognize that she was mothering me, and the last thing I wanted from Aela O'Neill was to be mothered. Even if, right now, I fucking needed it.

Even my balls ached—and not in a way I was used to—and getting over the surgery, the health issues, as well as adapting to the many drugs I had to take... *no bueno*. Beside every steaming mug? A little dish with pills on it.

Definitely mothered.

Shay didn't think anything of it, which told me he was lucky. It told me she doted on him, and I knew that because as a kid, my ma had doted on me. Sure, that had been offset with my father turning me into a career criminal before my pubes even fully grew out, but hell, from one spoiled kid to another, I got it.

What I also saw?

He appreciated her.

And that made me appreciate him even more.

He was a good kid. A solid one. Respectable.

Everything I wasn't.

Sure, I could hide it right now. I did nothing but zombie walk across my apartment, moving from room to room as the hours of the day and my body required. But when I was back in full working order, things would change. They had to. They couldn't *not*.

I'd used my TV more in the past five days than I had in five years. My office was in whichever warehouse contained the gear I was trafficking, and my cell phone didn't contain apps for fun, but for work.

Every hour of my life was focused on the job. On the family. On making us richer, shoring up our power. That came with blood, sweat, and tears. Preferably, some fucker else's.

"You didn't take your meds."

I cut him a look, surprised he was talking to me. Not only because we were watching cartoons and not sports, but because he'd just woken up. It was twelve PM, he'd been awake twenty or so minutes, and I didn't mind. I was just surprised Aela didn't give him shit about it.

Ma had given us a lot of leeway, but it was either get up with the rooster or have her vacuuming outside our doors to wake us up.

A bitch move, sure, but it saved us from getting our ears clipped by Da.

"They give me an upset stomach," I told him.

He frowned at that, perturbed enough to study me, before he swiveled his focus back to this show he was watching—that I didn't mind—called *The Umbrella Academy*. I figured I was lucky that I got him at the age where he at least didn't want to watch *Dora the* fucking *Explorer*.

If boys even watched that.

Hell, were boys even supposed to watch certain things, and girls too? I knew that new age shit about boys being able to wear pink and girls being allowed to play with toy cars was a 'thing' now... the thought of him wearing pink in front of Da did make me want to laugh though. He'd thought I was gay because I liked classical music and appreciated the arts. If I'd worn pink, his attempts to scare me straight would have transmogrified, worsening a thousandfold.

I reached up and rubbed my eyes, just to hide my reaction in case Shay misunderstood, and thought I was laughing at him or something, when I wasn't. It was the kind of laughter that'd lead to tears.

For all he was young, Seamus had a habit of reading into stuff, was quite perceptive for a kid his age. At fourteen, I'd been concerned about my dick, the pussy I could shove it in, and how fast I could come. In between that, I'd worried about learning the ropes, figuring out how to throat punch someone to death—and never quite managing to do it—and trying to avoid Da's fists. All in all, fourteen had been a good year. Things had gone to shit around twelve months or so later.

He cleared his throat, dragging me from my memories. "Mom will make you a sandwich if you ask."

For someone who hovered around all the time, I rarely saw her. Even if I felt her presence.

"Where is she?"

"The kitchen." His lips twitched. "It's the only room she says is normal."

My brows rose. "What's abnormal about the rest of the place?"

"I mean, I don't care. It's pretty neat. Well, apart from the fact that I keep bumping into shit."

"That's why your shins are all bruised?" I asked, eying his legs which were bare thanks to his basketball shorts.

"Yup."

"You mean she doesn't like the decor?" I queried when he didn't carry on, his focus reverting to the plot on TV.

He watched the shows with the subtitles on, which was strangely addictive. It had annoyed the shit out of me at first, but now I spent more time reading the damn subtitles than watching the show.

And when he switched between Mandarin and Russian? I wasn't sure whether to be impressed or annoyed—annoyed because I couldn't understand those subtitles.

"Nah. It's not her thing. Plus..."

"Plus, what?" I prompted, when he fell silent.

"She likes having all her stuff around her, you know? It's like her collection. She's spent a long time building it up."

"An art collection?"

My boy hummed as he scratched his chest with the remote. He was a little scrawny, but the definition in his arms and chest told me he'd been working out some. From all the football games we watched, I'd learned he'd made it onto his team at his old school, but not in the position he wanted.

I knew that had something to do with a love for the game and a desire for cheerleader pussy.

Not that he'd said as much, but I read between the lines—as well as his blush.

Amusement filtered through me, because I liked this shit. It was like learning a new language or something, trying to figure out what my kid was actually saying without saying it.

I didn't think he was aware of what I picked up on about him without him really telling me that much.

"It's like an art collection, but it's more like the stuff she picked up along the way."

"Along the way where?"

"Here and there," he said, then his grin turned wicked. "Guess how many countries I've visited?"

I smiled. "How many?"

"Forty-eight."

My brows lifted. "Seriously?"

His grin deepened. "Seriously. Mom likes to travel." He crinkled his nose. "She only stopped because of me."

"What do you mean?"

"I got sick of always moving around. I just wanted things to be regular for when I hit high school, you know?" He heaved a sigh, but it didn't flow right. Hitched, somehow, in the middle, in a way that had me studying him until he mumbled, "Just didn't realize that high school was so slow."

"Explain," I demanded.

He arched a brow at my brusque command, but as I chided myself because he wasn't a soldier, but my son, he murmured, "I had a tutor/nanny. Her name was Nina." He smiled. "She was cool. Really smart.

She taught me until I was ready for school, but she taught me too much. It's too easy now, so it's boring."

I hummed. "You're like Conor."

He perked up at that. "I am?"

"Yeah. He was always an overachiever. Got bored all the fuc—" I cleared my throat. "Got bored all the time. Used to get into a lot of crap. Hacked into NASA one time." I tapped my nose. "Don't tell your mom. I told her Conor didn't manage to gain access to it."

Shay's mouth rounded. "Huh? NASA? Like the space agency?"

Laughing, I told him, "Only one space agency in the U.S., isn't there?"

"Well, it depends if you count SpaceX."

"I don't." I winked at him. "Although Conor might have hacked into there by now."

"That's so cool!"

"Is it?" I grunted. "We jerked his chain something fierce for that."

"Why?"

"Because he did it because he could. Little show off."

"How much younger than you is he?"

I shook my head. "He's older. By two years."

"I met Conor. He brought us here. No way he's older than you."

This time, I chuckled freely. "Trust me. Everyone says that."

He eyed my grin a little oddly, his head tipping to the side as he stared at me. "You really love your brothers, don't you?"

"Of course." When he didn't automatically reply, I pressed, "That surprises you?"

"No. I just... I've never really been around a family like that before."

"What do you mean?" I questioned, sitting up slightly. He eyed my grimace knowingly as my body protested the move, and when his gaze cut to the drugs on the table, I heaved a sigh, reached for the water Aela had placed there earlier, and grabbed both.

When I'd taken the meds, his reward was to respond. "The only family I've known isn't like that."

"What family do you know?" He said it like he meant people in particular, not the family of friends.

He hummed, his attention turning to the TV. "My great-grandparents. They used to live in Ireland."

"They moved?"

"No. They're dead now."

"I'm sorry."

"Did you kill them?"

Jesus, this kid had my eyebrows doing the Macarena. "They were murdered?"

"Yes." He cut me another look. "Did you kill them?"

Slowly, feeling like I was out of the loop in more ways than one, I shook my head. "No. I didn't. Why would you think that?"

"Because I know what the O'Donnellys do. You can try to hide everything, but there's always something somewhere."

Warily, I inquired, "Whatever you think you know, you probably don't."

"You're not one of the biggest crime families in the tristate area then?" His smile didn't hit his eyes. "Did Mom ever tell you I'm really good at detecting when people lie?"

"No. She never told me. How did you pick that up?"

"We lived with a circus for a while when she was there taking photos for research. There was a magician, he taught me how to hot read people."

Hearing my teenager talking about 'hot reading' floored me more than if he told me Aela had taken him to a strip joint.

"So, I know when you're lying is all I'm saying."

"Have I lied to you so far?" I asked, curious about his skill level at hot reading. He was a shrewd little shit, so I wouldn't put it past him. And he had a way with game theory that would make Conor a happy bunny if the two of them ever thought about pulling a gambling con.

Yeah, I knew he was fourteen and I was thinking about illegal shit, but hell, that was my world.

We monetized everything.

"You lie about how much you're in pain. Usually every time we ask." His gaze darted over my face. "But I think that's a pride thing. That's it so far."

I hadn't had much to lie about.

His final words were pivotal however.

So far.

I cleared my throat. "Well, you read I didn't kill your great-grandparents then?"

"I did. That doesn't mean someone else didn't."

"Had no reason to kill them," I replied. "I didn't know you existed until your mom came back into my life."

His gaze was intent, and I sensed he wanted to know if that was the truth. He wanted to read whether or not that was a lie.

And I got it.

In his situation, I'd want to know if my father was a deadbeat too.

"Why *did* she come back into your life?"

"I can't talk about that."

His eyes narrowed. "Is it to do with your being injured?"

I grimaced. "Maybe." Deciding we needed a change of topic, I asked, "Did you love your great-grandparents?"

If I'd expected a yes, I didn't get it. He snorted before he let out a hoot. "No. They treated Mom like shit."

"They did?" I asked, annoyed on Aela's behalf. "Why?"

"They were Catholic," was his wry retort. "She was unwed and had a baby. She had no desire to get married, did whatever she wanted whenever she wanted, and it killed them that she was successful at it too. They shamed her for her art, discredited her when they could, but they didn't deserve to die the way they did."

I leaned forward. "How did they die?"

He stuck his finger under his chin, in the soft flesh there that was perfectly shaped to take the muzzle of a gun. I'd shoved one there many a time myself.

"Execution style," I mused, a little taken aback that I was having this conversation with my fourteen-year-old.

I was pretty sure Aela would be pissed if she knew the topic of our discussion, but having made the decision to let the ball lie in Seamus's court, to let him lead the way and figure out how he wanted to get to know me, how he wanted to take this forward, I wasn't about to change the subject and treat him like he was a little kid.

He wasn't.

I knew exactly what boys his age were capable of, and even if he didn't have the experience I had, he was a lot wiser to the world than I'd thought.

"Your mom know you're aware of all this?"

"No."

"How did you find out?"

"You said it yourself. I'm like Conor."

"Christ," I muttered under my breath. "That's exactly what we need."

Pride made his shoulders straighten, and I almost rolled my eyes at the sight.

Instead, I scraped a hand over my face and questioned, "Why would anyone execute a pair of great-grandparents?"

"They were jerks."

"Jerks are rarely slaughtered," I dismissed. "They must have pissed someone off."

"The Garda said it was a home invasion gone wrong." He shrugged. "I don't think that's true."

I contemplated that, contemplated his stance, and asked, "Do you want me to look into it? Is that it?"

"If you want to." His gaze flickered over to me and back to the screen in a flash. "I didn't even like them."

But he'd loved them, otherwise why would he ask for help?

"They treated Mom like shit," he carried on.

"They were good to you though."

"Yeah." He cleared his throat. "Granddad had four brothers. That's how I know how brothers usually act around each other. He hated two of them, one refused to go to the funeral. Then the other two, he was on speaking terms with, but they weren't real friendly."

"We weren't raised that way. We were raised to go to war for one another," I informed him softly. "We give each other crap, but when shit rains on us, we always buckle down and protect the family. It's how we're wired."

"That's intense."

"I guess it is." Softly, I murmured, "I'll ask Brennan. When he was there last, he made some connections in the Garda." Well, he'd coordinated a mutual exchange with the IRA. We shipped them guns, and they acted as our heroin mules. "He'll put some feelers out, so will Conor. Once people know who's asking the questions, they'll soon fold to the pressure."

"Really?"

"Really." But he didn't sound impressed.

"Corruption in action," he muttered.

"Yeah. Everywhere's corrupt, kid."

"I hate that."

"Want to change it?" I shrugged. "Not a bad aim for someone to have."

"Even though that's how you make your money? Through corruption?"

"Corruption eases bureaucratic paths. It doesn't make the money. It just facilitates it."

When his shoulders hunched, I knew he didn't like that answer. "Do you think it's impossible to eradicate?"

"Yes," I replied candidly, but something about the conversation set me on edge.

He wasn't the only person in the room who could hot read another, and I had a helluva lot more experience at it.

His great-grandparents had definitely been executed. He, without a shadow of a doubt, wanted answers. His great-uncles didn't get on with his great-grandfather, and he was genuinely curious about the relationship I had with my brothers, but this line of questioning came from somewhere else.

When I was lying on that hospital bed, my heart attacking itself, my body struggling to survive, I'd made a vow to myself. Hell, I'd made several vows. To let the kid come to know me how he wanted. On his own time. But, also, and more importantly, to let him choose his life path.

Even if that meant getting in Da's face and taking a beating or ten. The old man might not be as strong as he used to be, but that didn't mean he didn't have goons who'd hold us in place.

Eoghan was the recent recipient of that kind of a beatdown. He'd been dithering about marrying Inessa, and Da had made the decision for him.

Something he tended to do frequently—make decisions for *all* of us.

Well, Seamus was mine, and I'd be the one acting as the go-between for grandfather and grandson. First, I had to figure out what was going down here.

It felt like a test.

One I was pretty sure I'd just failed.

"A lot of things are geared toward corruption in this country," I began slowly, trying to get my thoughts together. I hadn't expected any of this kind of chatter today. Fuck, we'd talked sports and cartoons since I'd come home. This was heavy shit, and not something I'd figured a kid his age would even be interested in. "It takes a lot of coordinating to elicit change. That doesn't mean it's impossible. It just takes a lot of good people investing in the future. Improbable, yeah. Impossible...not necessarily."

"Same number of letters."

I smirked. "Smartass." His grin was swift but sheepish. "What I'm trying to say is that if there are enough people out there who want things to be different, then it can be done."

My words had his cocky humor disappearing, and in his eyes, I saw I'd replaced his uncertainty with hope.

Hope was a dangerous thing.

But in my kid, it was the only thing I wanted to cultivate.

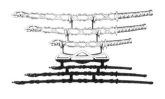

AELA

"YOU DIDN'T HAVE to do that."

One thing I liked about being in the kitchen was the ability to hear everything the two men in my life had to say, all without having to be in there. I wanted Seamus to get to know his father because, whether I wanted it or not, I had no alternative. If we were going to be here, if we were stuck together as a unit, then Seamus needed to understand what and who his father was.

"Of course I did." He tipped his chin up at me, slowly turning his head to the side and switching his focus off his phone and onto me.

I hated how my body responded to having his full attention. There was a time when that was all it would take for me to leap into bed after having stripped. Like I was nothing but his personal sex doll. Only, he'd never made me feel that way.

I'd always felt loved.

Which was the biggest joke of all. Something I'd figured out way too late for my own good.

"You heard the conversation?" he queried, and I dipped my chin.

"That's the beauty of having walls made out of paper, I suppose," I mused, as I strolled into the living room, deciding to get closer to the beast. Closer than I'd come in days.

Call me a chickenshit, or call me busy, but I'd been staying out of his way. Not only so he and Seamus had time together, but also because I...

God.

I didn't like me around Declan.

It had taken the few hours I'd been with him the day he'd come home from that freaky hospital setup to realize that.

Plus, aside from being honest with myself, I also had a lot of things to deal with. The dean at the art school where I worked wasn't happy with me quitting without notice, and I felt really shitty considering I'd been helping a lot of students and was leaving them in the lurch.

Even though Amaryllis had gotten me into this mess, she was one of the pupils I was going to miss. Her art? Incredible. Absolutely astonishing.

I saw true talent in her, and while I was supposed to cultivate it in all my students, sometimes, it was easier said than done. Sometimes, the technical ability was there, but the spark? It wasn't.

I came across a lot of sparkless people, but Amaryllis and a handful of others, like Chloe Downrey, a potter, and James Vance, a sculptor, were three of them.

Then I'd had a few long calls with my new lawyer over my financial records, and the Feds had demanded I turn over all communications with a couple of people who'd once paid me a lot of money to create something for them.

I was cooperating, because I saw no reason not to.

I'd done nothing wrong...

Of course, I'd tell them where to go if I didn't have Seamus. Amazing what having a child did to you. Had you turning against your past, your instincts, your smarts, and doing what was right so that it could be a teachable moment.

"You knew he was aware of his great-grandparents' deaths?"

There was very little love lost between my grandparents and myself. Mostly because I'd grown tired a long time ago of being called a slattern. Still, Seamus was right. They hadn't deserved to die that way.

"I did." My lips twisted as I leaned back on my hands. "Seamus knows most things. He has an uncanny way about him."

"That why you're here now? When he's taking a shower?"

"Yes. As eco-conscious as he is, what he finds to do in the shower is usually long enough to make a three-course meal."

He smiled, even though I knew he didn't want to. "The joys of the fully functioning penis."

My nose crinkled. "I'm well aware of how they work."

"I know you are. I taught you most of what you know," he rumbled, but I saw the flash of anger in his eyes.

Call me stupid, but I couldn't stop myself from rising to the challenge. "What about the way I've lived my life tells you I've been a saint since I left?"

His mouth tightened, but it was a testament, I thought, to how tired he was... he didn't take the bait. "He's idealistic."

"He is. Very. He wants to change things. I'm glad you picked up on that before you broke his heart."

"Would you have let me?"

"I wouldn't have leaped into the conversation to save him. Idealism hurts. And the truth hurts even more. But I know, coming from someone like you, with your background, he'd have responded either way."

"I don't know what you mean," he rasped, a nerve ticking in his jaw.

I tapped my fingers against the table as I let my gaze drift over him. Maybe it was a proprietary glance, maybe it was more of a scan, I'd never be able to say, but what I could say?

"If you'd broken his dreams, he'd have been angry. But he'd have figured out a way to temper the dreams and make them reality. He isn't the kind of kid just to give up without a fight.

"You didn't break his dreams though. You gave him hope. As dangerous as hope is, that you're you, that your background is what it is, it fuels him further."

"He told you what he wants to be when he grows up?"

I laughed, unable to stop myself, and he groaned, knowing full well what my answer was going to be.

"A lawyer. Or a cop, let me guess."

The smile hit my eyes. "You're in luck. A lawyer."

He blew out a breath. "Thank fuck for that. Da's getting on. He's not as young as he used to be. If he found out his grandkid wanted to be a cop, he'd be the one having a heart attack."

Probably.

"I was relieved as well, but I didn't instill blind faith in the police system."

"Smart lass."

I shrugged. "Maybe. We both know what blind faith leads to."

His mouth twisted. "Adoration?"

"Yeah." I caught his eye. "What are we doing here, Declan?"

He didn't act coyly, didn't try to prevaricate. "You know what you're doing here, Aela."

"I can read between the lines, but you have a life that has nothing to do with me anymore. And vice versa. You probably have a girlfriend, maybe even a significant other."

He snorted. "What do you think I am? A legitimate businessman? A significant other—" He hooted out a laugh like that was the funniest shit I could have ever said.

I scowled at him. "If you're not going to take this seriously—"

"I'm taking it seriously. Very seriously. We'll be getting married the second I can stand up to take a leak—"

Nose crinkling at his crudity, I grumbled, "Gross."

"Thought you'd be used to worse with a teenager around the place."

"He's a lot more respectful than you are," I said with a sniff.

"Wouldn't be hard," he agreed.

"What if I don't want to get married?"

"The second you kept Seamus, you knew, someday, you'd end up with my ring on your finger. Don't try to lie to me."

"After Deirdre died, I thought you hated me. I knew it was a possibility, but..."

"But?"

"But you looked at me like I was a piece of shit on your shoes, Declan," I murmured. "Sure, I knew you'd want to marry because of Shay, but I wasn't sure if you'd ever be able to put yourself through it."

He reached up and plucked at his bottom lip, tugging it from his teeth, before fiddling with the soft morsel. Once upon a time, I'd owned him as much as he owned me. If I wanted to bite him there, I could. I would.

Now? He was a stranger. A stranger whose body I knew intimately. Who knew *my* body intimately.

The way he stroked his finger along his bottom lip had my senses stirring in a way they really shouldn't.

Declan was thinner than the last time I'd seen him, he had a white pallor —like he was sick, which he was, and like he was in a lot of pain, which he was—and he was wearing basketball shorts and nothing more. The man I knew existed in expensive leather jackets and jeans that cost a month's rent. If not that, then suits which made a mortgage payment look cheap. And I wasn't going to lie, my art might be all about the anarchy, raging against the machine, but there was no prettier picture than this man in a tailored suit.

Who in God's name needed porn when you had him all gussied up for work?

"If I tell you the truth, you won't believe me."

His words had me scowling at him. "Won't believe you? Maybe you should give me a chance to figure out for myself whether I believe you or not, huh? Jesus, I'm not fifteen anymore, Declan. I have a brain, a rational one. I can think of—"

Before I could continue, my cell phone rang. When Caro's face popped up on the screen, I grimaced. Declan, seeing it, grunted, and held out his hand for my cell.

A little agitatedly, I clutched my phone to my chest and asked, "What are you going to say to her?"

"Only what needs to be said," was his calm reply.

I was a woman who'd been independent from the age of seventeen. Who'd raised a child alone in a family who thought unwed mothers should be sold off to convents to do the goddamn laundry, and their babies should be separated from them to be handed off to 'good', childless, Catholic families in the parish. I'd started a career that had made me millions, was a name to be envied in certain circles.

I did not need a man to look after me.

But the way the O'Donnellys did it, God help me, it twisted me up inside.

They didn't coddle or overshadow. They didn't overwhelm. There was just no shadow of a doubt in their mind that certain things were women's work and other aspects were men's.

Of course, that was going to get fucking irritating over time. I hated being pigeonholed. But damn, right now? With this investigation driving me batshit?

I slowly held out the phone for him to take.

One phone call to a traitorous FBI agent wasn't me giving up my independence.

It was me letting someone who knew these people better than I did take charge.

"She clearly wants to talk, or she'd have hung up by now," he noted, before he connected the call, put it on speaker, and as he raised his hand to his lips in the universal sign for silence, he murmured, "Why, Special Agent Dunbar, what can I do for you?"

The line throbbed with irritation. Seriously. I didn't even know that was possible, but Caro had just proved it was.

"This is Aela O'Neill's phone. I'd like to speak with her, please."

"You won't be talking to my fiancée again, Special Agent," he said cordially, even as a wicked light danced in his eyes when I harrumphed at him.

He knew there'd be hell to pay for that later.

We both knew the marriage certificate was a done deal. There was no getting out of it for either of us. But that didn't mean he could talk about it all blasé. Not without me giving him shit over it.

"Your fiancée?" Her voice cut off on a squeak of surprise, which, in turn, bewildered me. If she was into the O'Donnelly's business as Brennan and Conor had made out on the drive to NYC, well... surely she knew how they rolled?

Kids outside of wedlock just weren't the done thing.

"Yes. We're engaged. Now, I'm sure you're well aware of what that means. As rich as she was before, as powerful, she's coming under the umbrella of my position."

"What position is that, O'Donnelly?" she snarled. "A gangster? A drug lord? A kingpin?"

His lips twisted, but his gaze broke away from mine and he turned to look out the window beyond. "Such a low opinion of me, Dunbar. I mean, what did I ever do to make you think I was anything other than a legitimate businessman?"

"I'll get you one day, you son of a bitch," she sneered.

"No. You won't," he replied, his tone still calm. Declan of before hadn't exactly had a fast burn temper, but he could definitely get riled up in a flash. It'd make sense if this would be one of those moments where his trigger was pulled. "There's nothing to 'get.' I'm a legitimate businessman. I deal in imports and exports—"

"Spare me the BS," she ground out.

"If you can't handle the truth, well, maybe you should rethink your position. Are you truly adept at being a law enforcement agent when enforcing the truth is less important to you than stalking innocent businessmen?"

Her voice turned stony. "My call today has nothing to do with your import/export empire. It's to do with Aela's business ties."

"As you well know, Aela's perfectly innocent of any crime. Our attorneys have apprised us of the situation, and if you continue to call her, I'll consider it harassment and I'll be taking it up with the DA. Now, you've wasted enough of my time, Special Agent. I hope Aela never hears from you again or your career will be on the line."

Before she could reply, he cut the call then passed my cell back to me.

"When have you talked to the attorneys?"

He arched a brow. "I speak with them every day. I'm still dealing with business. I'm just doing it from home rather than in the office."

I shook my head. "How are you supposed to get better if you're not resting?"

"You know what this world is like, Aela," he rasped. "It never stops. Not for any man."

My shoulders slumped, rounding as I dug my elbows onto my knees and asked, "Think she'll give up?"

"She'll have no choice. There's truly no reason for her to continue bothering you. You did nothing wrong. You've been more than courteous in sharing your accounts with them and have answered all their questions.

"She's only digging in because she wants to turn you."

My laughter was harsh. "Turn me? Do I look like a fool?"

His gaze turned somber. "You'd be surprised. There's a wave of it going around. That's two men who've turned on us in the past six months."

"Two?" My brows arched. "That comes as a shock."

"Trust me, no one is more astonished than Da."

"I'll bet." Uneasily, I muttered, "I wouldn't have turned on you. I mean, I don't know enough to be able to."

"There's always some piece of information you can sell, but I know you wouldn't. You're not a sellout, Aela. You never were."

I tipped my chin up. "I'm glad you know that."

"I do."

"You going to tell me what the truth is? What you were talking about before Caroline called?"

His stare was intense when he looked at me, raking me over hot coals with the cocktail of emotions in his eyes.

Many people might say Declan was a cold man, and I'd agree with that. He was dark, so filthy dark that it obscured the truth of his nature.

But to me, *with* me, there was only one point in my life where he'd ever let me see that side of him. Where I'd felt that darkness and had been tainted by it. It had started on the day of Deirdre's funeral. The day my life had begun to turn upside down.

"Would you say that I liked Deirdre?"

I frowned. "No. Not at all. I never understood why you were dating her. I mean, aside from her position. I can imagine you two getting together would have pleased your father."

"You're right. It did. And you're also right—I didn't like her. I fucking hated her." His lips firmed. "Everything about her revolted me. She made my goddamn skin crawl."

"Then why did you stay with her? Why was I your side piece?"

Deirdre had made *his* skin crawl... that was nothing compared to what that word did to me.

Side piece.

God, I hated it. I hated it so fucking much. I hated what it meant, what it represented, and what I'd been. What I'd allowed myself to become. I'd kept the tag as a reminder of what a man could do to me. But really? Declan was the only guy I'd ever debase myself for.

And what that said about me? Jesus, I didn't even know.

"Because I had no choice."

That nonsense answer had me grinding my teeth as I started to get to my feet. "Bullshit," I retorted, but he sat up, caught me behind the knee, and held me there. Gently. With no force, just a reminder of his strength.

Which was amusing considering he was pretty much dragging his tail whenever he stood up.

"You're an O'Donnelly. You always have a choice. It's the people around you who have no say in things."

He winced at that, and it wasn't a minute gesture either. I didn't have to read into his micro-expression to decrypt it. That wince was clear for anyone with eyes to see.

"Maybe, but I didn't, Aela. Not with that cunt. I had no choice. The bitch was blackmailing me, and back then, I couldn't have covered what she threatened to extort out of me."

My head whipped around at that, and I gaped at him. "You can't be serious. *She was blackmailing you?*" I mean, I'd known Deirdre... she was vain, a little ditzy, a lot egotistical.

Shit.

Yeah, I could see her doing that. Being stupid enough to think she could get away with it with her life intact. Of course, she hadn't died for that reason...

His lips tugged into a snarl. "She was. I wouldn't joke about something that still fucks me off so much." He let go of my knee, raised his hand like he was no threat, and said, "I'm still being blackmailed, even though she's dead. The price has changed now though."

"What?" I sputtered, wondering if he'd suddenly started talking Mandarin or something. And to be honest, in my life, that wasn't all that unusual. Seamus would routinely change the shows he watched into other languages for learning purposes. Each and every time it happened, I was always slow to react, wondering if it was my brain or the TV.

"Deirdre had it all planned out. We'd be married the second she hit eighteen." That snarl made another reappearance. "It was the easiest way to keep her silent. The new one, after she died, they're a lot more expensive. Ten grand a month."

"For the past fourteen years?" I gasped.

"Yeah. It adds up, doesn't it?"

"What the hell did she have on you?"

"Plausible deniability... you know what that means, right? Or did you forget that along the way?"

Folding my arms against my chest, I scowled at him. "You can't tell me you're being blackmailed then not tell me why."

He grimaced. "She learned about something she shouldn't have, had photos she shouldn't have, and used them as leverage against me. It was important enough that I obey when I'm not a man to obey anyone." He caught my eye, held it. "That was the reason I was with her. The sole reason."

"When she was dead, you didn't have to—"

"Like I told you, I got a new blackmailer after she died. I knew they could make demands that could put you in jeopardy. I wasn't about to let that happen. It was easier to let you go, to know you were safe, than to deal with you dying because of my past."

Everything about his words should have softened me, but instead, I ground out, "You just paid up? You didn't question who or what or *why?*" Christ, this was like I was talking to a whole different Declan. "You just let me go?"

"Some mistakes will haunt you for the rest of your life," he told me softly. "Deirdre just happened to be able to capitalize on something I'd kill to keep secret. I spend ten grand on my parking garage. It isn't like I can't afford it."

"Thought the whole point of extortion is to get as much out of a victim as possible."

He shrugged. "Maybe whoever it is, is just happy they're getting a nice wad of dough without me wanting to go after their blood. I don't really care. Things haven't changed in all these years, don't see why they'd start now. But... with you and Seamus back, I've recognized that things *have* to change.

"I've set Brennan and Conor onto finding out the identity of my blackmailer. But that's neither here nor there. You don't have to worry about that."

When I stared at him, saw his resolve, I had to shake my head at him. "You can't seriously think that's enough of an explanation for how you treated me?" A breath rattled from between my lips. "You treated me like shit, Declan. To the point where I lied to you. To the point where I felt I had to run away from you."

His jaw worked. "I wouldn't have done that if I didn't think I had no choice."

"Yeah? You need to remember that when your father is sneaking into this goddamn apartment and accusing me of things that are *your* fault." I went to storm off, but he grabbed my hand and didn't let me go when I pulled at his hold on me.

"He's been here?" he rasped.

"Yeah. So has your mother. The guards let them in."

His eyes narrowed into beady slits. "I'll deal with them."

"Good," I replied huskily. "You should. Your words sent me running to people who didn't love me, who made me feel like I was a slut, but it was the only way I knew to keep Shay safe from someone who I thought hated me and would hate him. From this world where the cops are the enemies not friends."

He gritted his teeth. "Help me up?"

I glared at him. "Why?"

"I want to show you something."

"I don't want to see it."

"Tough." He sighed, wiped his other hand over his face, and muttered, "Please?"

What was I supposed to do? Leave him there floundering on the futon?

Although, the day this man *floundered* was the day I had to visit a coffin maker. Declan didn't flounder. He was quiet, pensive, until you knew him. And I'd known him very, very well.

I reached down and helped him up, not used to him needing me in this way, and finding I didn't like it. A man like him was born to be strong. Born to flash society the bird.

It was why he was my soulmate.

Well, before he'd broken everything that made me *me* and ruptured it like he'd slipped a dagger into my gut.

When he was standing, I noticed he didn't pant as much as he did the day before. Not that I'd let him know that I was watching... Did I look like a fool?

The second he thought I had my feet under the table, he'd pull it away from me. The level of hatred he'd aimed my way that day, that had to have been brewing for a long time, so I knew whatever payback he was going to serve up would be a nightmare.

I was the queen of nightmares now though.

I made them my bitch and turned them into masterpieces, because suffering made my art shine that little bit harder.

And that was the tragedy of being an artist.

TWELVE

DECLAN

SHE WAS GOING to hate me.

I didn't blame her. Couldn't, really.

None of this was her fault. It was all mine. All because of pride.

All because of my coveting something.

Two sins, but I lived my life with sins darkening every aspect of it. I didn't care about my immortal soul. Hadn't since she'd walked out of my world.

Pussy.

I let the word flip through my mind, but it didn't anger me. There was no point in getting mad about the truth.

Holding out my hand for her to take, I watched her eye my fingers like they were five snakes skewered onto an orange. With distaste lining her features, she settled her hand on mine, and I barely refrained from rolling my eyes at her response.

Why?

Because, of course, the second we touched, it felt like all the years had melted away. As if we were both way too young to be fooling around, to be getting pregnant.

Her jaw tensed, so I knew she felt the shock as well, but I bypassed it and drew her toward me as we edged out of the way of the coffee table and headed to the door. It was slow going, and she was surprisingly patient. I didn't appreciate being so fucking incapacitated, and I wouldn't stand for it overlong. My body did what I wanted. Simple as that.

I was panting by the time we crossed the hall and made it to my bedroom. Each step I took felt arduous, but as we took a short break, it gave me time to ask her, "You hate the apartment, don't you?"

Her hand snapped up so she could fiddle with one of those sexy studs in her ears. "What made you think that?"

My lips twitched. "You got better at lying over the years."

"Yeah, well, that's how life works, isn't it? Men prefer lies to the truth," she grumbled.

The statement had any amusement dying. "I don't want lies between us, Aela."

"No? You sure about that? Not sure you can handle the truth, Declan."

"Anything you throw at me, I can handle. We're—" I was going to say that we were stuck together. But that implied that I wasn't happy about my status quo.

Any woman who could give you a boner after a cardiac arrest, I figured, was one worth keeping around.

And Aela didn't just make my body hard, she fucked with my head too.

Sex had never been so good as it had been with her. Especially toward the end, when she'd let go of her nerves and had allowed me in all the way.

It had been softer than the sex I was used to now, though, and still some of the best I'd ever had.

In all honesty, I wanted a repeat.

And since we were going to get married, I didn't see why that wasn't doable.

I'd have to woo her. All women needed wooing. But I'd never been playing for such high stakes before. This wasn't even about marriage. Just about playing for keeps. None of the O'Donnellys liked to lose, so I was shitty at it, and where she was concerned, the game had never been more important.

For more reasons than just the fact my son loved her, wanted what was best for her, would defend her like a good boy. He'd turn on me, not her, if I didn't do right by her, and while I didn't need that reasoning to be a decent man, it definitely gave me a kick in the ass.

And the way she looked in a pair of ragged jeans and a cami sure as fuck helped.

Her tits? Banging. One hundred percent. Even better than when she'd been seventeen.

I'd have wolf whistled if I didn't think she'd slap me.

Two or three years ago, she'd been in New York. On my turf. I'd gone to one of her shows. Had tried to catch a glimpse of her but had failed.

I could admit to myself I'd been chickenshit.

I knew what I'd tossed away, knew what I could never get back, and coming face to face with my failure had been shitty, so I'd cut off thoughts of her in my mind.

Seeing her art had made me come to terms with the woman she was today, letting my memories fade away even as I could see the girl in the artist. In the hope and the idealism, in the longing and the anger. I saw a need to rebel against dictates from an oppressive system, I saw a need to clash with anyone who'd try to stop her from doing what she wanted.

Yet, here she was.

Rolling over for the O'Donnellys.

And she'd carry on doing that because she knew what was at stake.

A man had to appreciate a smart woman. Even if those smarts were what would have said smart woman chopping off his dick and serving it to him for supper.

"We'll move into a brownstone I own," I told her gruffly, "if you don't like this place."

She scowled at me. "If you have two buildings here in the city, then I can live in one, and you can live here and we can—"

"What? Split Shay? No fucking way, baby girl. No fucking way. I already missed out on too much of my kid's life, not gonna miss out on anymore." I smiled at her though, fucking proud that she'd try to pull that shit on me.

Maybe I should be angry, but I loved that mouth of hers.

Enough that I didn't just want it around my cock.

She heaved a sigh as we made it into my bedroom, and even though I didn't doubt she'd sneaked a peek in here before I'd returned home, she did some more snooping before I took her to the foot of the bed.

It was a nightmare, honestly. The bed was low to the ground, inset, which made getting out of it and into it hell on earth with my wounds. I wasn't about to ask Shay or her for help, but it was why I spent most of my time on the futon in the living room.

The bedroom was all clean lines, because that was how I needed it. The bed with its simple linens, two shaded *chōchin* lights that were dim, and behind me, a massive tapestry that provided most of the color in the room. It was of an enormous water dragon and had cost me over three hundred thousand to buy at an auction. Of course, if it had been at Sotheby's, it'd have cost six times more…

Over by the window, there was a seating area with a low table and gray cushions that were comfortable for lounging on. I liked to sit there and take my coffee in the morning, watch the world rise with me. But again, every-thing was so goddamn close to the ground that using any of it was impossi-ble. Where a window seat would be, I had a low-level shelf with more priceless artifacts on there than anyone in my family could even register.

I had a problem.

I knew it.

No one else did.

No one but Aela after she saw what I was going to show her.

It had started when I was young. Just small ornaments, little pieces here and there, but it had grown into an obsession.

Over five million dollars' worth of art in the form of ceramics, small antique jade pieces, and even a Ming presentation dish that was over seven hundred years old sat on the shelf in front of the window. Of course, I hadn't paid five mil. Didn't mean it wasn't worth it. Didn't mean it didn't give me a boner when I looked at it.

Well, not at the moment. Only Aela's ass was capable of that right now.

And her tits.

Couldn't forget her tits.

Opposite my bed was where I kept the good stuff.

My jaw worked as I pressed a button on the wall. It was made to look like an AC console, but it was actually the key to opening my safe. She didn't know what I was showing her, didn't know that I'd kill anyone who found this stuff.

Didn't know that, by revealing this to her, I was showing her my trust.

Jail time was nothing to what they'd fling at me if they saw what I had in here.

I cleared my throat, oddly nervous yet excited too, because I knew she'd get it. Before, I didn't think she would. But knowing who she was, what she was, I knew this would thrill her even if she wanted to cut me for it too.

Shooting her a glance, I saw from her scowl she was peeved, but from the way she gnawed on her cheek, I could tell she was nervous too. She gulped when the wall, where the seams were so airtight not even a fucking sniffer dog would be able to sense them, flipped and retracted inwards. Within seconds, a cavity opened up, exposing a silver vault.

Her mouth had rounded into a perfect circle that I remembered stuffing with my dick, and she rasped, "What the fuck, Dec? You turn into Richie goddamn Rich on me?"

My lips twisted. "The Macauley Culkin version? Hell, yeah."

She snorted but folded her arms over her chest. This time, her excite-ment was real.

She knew this level of security was for something hardcore. Something epic.

She wasn't wrong.

The door to the safe was about ten by eight feet. It was made so that once it was open and fully activated, it was like a wall. On nights when I was alone, which I always was because no bitch ever slept here, I'd open it up and stare at my bounty.

I pressed my hand to the sensor, which opened up the initial lock. Then, I pressed my chin to the silver ledge, and let the device scan my retinas. Once that was done, I had to key in a code, and she murmured, "Christ. This is heavy duty, Dec."

I didn't say anything, just took a step back.

There was a buzzing noise as my details were registered, and then a heavy clanking as the doors began to retract, pulling inward before pushing out.

From behind fifteen layers of titanium, that not even a fucking bomb could destroy, three portraits tunneled out on mechanized shelving.

When she took them in, she automatically took a step back.

The two on either side of the central piece were magnificent.

But the one in the middle?

I knew why she flopped backward, not stopping until she was all arms and legs, barreling onto my unmade bed.

"Felt that way the first time I saw it too," I commented.

She gulped, her mouth working still, and I decided to let her take in the glory that, even though its majesty was astronomical, didn't compare to the beauty that had taken my breath away when I was sixteen fucking years old.

Her.

Hobbling over to the door just in case Seamus decided to get his ass out of the shower sometime this century, I closed it, then turned and saw she'd moved with the silence of a stalking panther and was peering at it. So close that her breath was touching the paint.

It was a testament to what I felt for her that I didn't bark at her to back the fuck away.

Behind the safe's walls, for eighteen hours a day, the paintings were in a protected environment. Everything in this room was controlled to protect the oils from the humidity and the temperature. Didn't matter if it was high summer or the dead of winter, it was always seventy degrees Fahrenheit, and the humidity was at a constant fifty-four percent.

Exhausted even though I was excited too, I leaned against the door, then asked her, "You know when I was Seamus's age, I'd been in the Points for two years, don't you?"

When she didn't answer, I knew she was as taken with the pieces as me.

That was to my good fortune.

If she understood, then maybe she'd get why I'd done what I had. Why I allowed myself to be blackmailed.

"It's real." She shook her head a little blindly. "It's actually real."

"Yeah. It is. The others are too." That had her dazedly turning to me, and whispering, "There is no way in fuck that I'm looking at a couple hundred million on the wall, Dec. Please, God, tell me I'm having some kind of psychotic episode."

My lips twitched. "No psychotic episode. You are."

Another gulp. "That's a Van Gogh."

"Sure is."

She raised a hand and covered her face. "And a Flinck."

"Yep."

She peeked at me through her fingers. "And the lost Vermeer."

Because this was what a lady boner *looked* like, I smirked at her. "*The Concert.*"

When I confirmed what she'd already figured out, she twisted to look at the wall and shook her head. Shook it some more. Another time. Then whispered, "I think I have water in my ears."

I said nothing, amused and touched and relieved and excited all at the same time.

She got it.

She fucking got it.

With my back to the door, I continued watching Aela as she jerked back and took in the majesty of my horde. Then, when she finally turned to me, something inside me settled so beautifully, so fucking wondrously, when I saw her eyes.

When I saw her tears.

She hurled herself at me. At first, I thought she was going to hit me, that was how violent her response was, but instead, she sobbed. She huddled into my chest, crying loudly like I'd hit *her*, then she did the damnedest thing.

She leaned up on tiptoe, slipped her hands around my cheeks, and hauled my head down. When our lips collided, she ate at my mouth with the true hunger of someone who understood what she'd looked at. Who knew what it felt like to covet.

Who knew what hunger and need for something insane was.

Her tongue thrust into my mouth, tasting of salt and coffee and mint. She tasted, even more importantly, like mine. Like she'd never been parted from me. Like the last time we kissed was yesterday.

She moaned, her body writhing against mine as she used her hands to guide my head, and even though I was in no state to even be dealing with a boner, never mind this attack, did I look fucking stupid?

This was Aela.

Sweet fuck.

This. Was. Aela.

Her pussy was meant for my dick, for Christ's sake. I didn't know how many cocks had been inside her, but mine was the first to get a taste of that sweet cunt. Me. No fucker else. And I'd be the goddamn last.

The thought sent need surging through me, and when her hips ground into mine, her sweet gasp as she rocked her hips, digging her belly into me, I released a low growl as I pulled back, this time tipping her head up so I could kiss her throat. So I could mark her there.

She arched her neck, letting me have my way, accepting my need like she'd known I never could allow before. I'd marked her tits, her thighs, her stomach. Everywhere but where I wanted.

Now, I had a say in this, and I went on the rampage, sucking hard, not stopping until the love bite would stick around for days in the aftermath, long enough for her to whine about needing to plaster it with foundation every damn day.

Not stopping until I had to slip my thigh between hers, even though it fucked with my balance, so I could let her ride me. Her cunt ground down against my leg, and she rocked there, hard. Heavy. I could feel her heat through the denim of her jeans, making me wish she was wearing yoga pants so I'd feel her sweet cream against my skin because I was in a pair of basketball shorts.

When she moved faster, the pace suddenly surging upward, I moved back to her lips, thrusting my tongue into her mouth this time as I let her reach a peak I'd never anticipated her finding this afternoon.

Not after our discussion.

Her high-pitched moans turned more frantic, more frenetic, until she stiffened, her body on the knife's edge, and she let out a long cry that I swallowed.

As she cascaded back toward the ground, I carried on kissing her, nipping at her lips, tasting her, supping from her, well aware that when she realized what she'd done, she'd pull away. Get defensive. Back off.

I took advantage of the moment, enjoyed the feel of her against my cock, and held her close.

It had been too fucking long since I'd had this. Since I'd even felt anything for a bitch. Aela was the exact opposite though.

She wasn't a slut, a side piece, or a mistress.

She was mine. Born to be fucking mine.

When she pulled back, I almost sighed with disappointment, then she shocked me again by resting her head against my chest and whispering, "I did *not* mean to do that."

My grin was cocky, but she wouldn't know that because she couldn't see it. "I'd never have guessed," I rumbled.

A sigh escaped her. "I needed that."

"*That* I could tell."

I lowered my hands to cup her ass, and deciding to try my luck, I kneaded the cheeks with my fingers, which prompted her to rock her forehead against my pec, before she whispered, "I can't believe I did—"

"Does it matter?" I asked, aware I sounded serious. But fuck, I felt it.

"Yeah. It matters." She blew out a breath then pulled back. "I don't know what came over me."

"Well, technically, it was you who came over me."

My smug statement had her narrowing her eyes at me, and I grinned at her, uncaring that she was a lot stronger than me right now and could totally knee me in the balls.

But her gaze just turned into a thin slit before it danced down my body. When she trained those eyes on my dick, I felt it fucking pulse in time to my heartbeat.

"Shit," she muttered, rubbing a hand over her face. "You're too sick for this," she ground out, glaring at me like this was my fault. She compounded it by pointing her finger at me and prodding the air. "You probably can't even have a boner for like six weeks or something."

"Well, sorry to disappoint, but the second I saw you that first time I was home, and you bent over and I saw your tits, I had a boner. And when I saw your ass in those shorts you wore the other day?" I whistled. "Boner."

She scowled. "You're not supposed to. Everything with the body is six weeks, for fuck's sake. Giving birth, hearts, I bet even surgery—"

Despite myself, I had to snicker. "Trust me, the dick is willing but the body is weak." My snicker turned into a rueful smile. "I want to, you've no fucking idea how much, but I can't. Just standing here is hard on me."

That had her eyes widening again, bigger than when she'd taken in the lost Vermeer, and she instantly hustled to my side and dragged me away from the door and deeper into the room.

When we made it to the bed, she hissed, "This is so impractical."

Because it was exactly that, I didn't argue or get mad at her for dissing my personal taste. I just heaved a sigh, and requested, "Help me down?"

With a lot of grunting, we did it. It was easier than when I did it on my own, but she was glowering at me when I lay back, panting, amid the sheets.

"What?" I groused.

"Cover that up," she retorted, wafting a hand at my nether regions.

I peered down and had to laugh when I saw that the tip of my dick was peeping up above the waistband of my shorts. "Trust me, I had no idea that was even manageable with how painful that was."

A breath gusted from her lungs, and it made the hair that was clinging to her damp forehead budge a little with its strength. But her eyes were glued to my hand and my dick as I tucked the family jewels away.

It was nice to know she was interested. That was for fucking sure.

She folded her arms over her chest, then murmured, "Do you mind if I sit down? I'm still a little..."

When her words drifted off, I told her, "Sure. Be my guest."

I expected her to go to the seating area over by the window, never imagining she'd climb onto the mattress with me. But she did. And I cut her a look, surprised and a lot happy that she'd done that.

The position, however, put her in the direct line of sight of the paintings —exactly why I'd had the room laid out like this—so I didn't take it as much of a compliment. Not when I knew she just wanted the best view of the classical pieces that no one in the general public had seen outside of photographs for at least thirty years.

"How?" she asked simply after five more minutes of just staring at what I found endlessly fascinating.

I'd been staring at these paintings every night before I slept since I'd moved into this place, and I still found it hard to tear my eyes off them.

The only thing that was marginally worth it?

Her.

Watching her come.

Getting to see her unravel in my arms.

I never expected to see that again, so I'd never been able to compare the two, but fuck a duck. Seeing that was a treat worth tens of millions, bar none.

"Did you hear what I asked you earlier?"

She shook her head. "No."

I smiled a little, amazed I could find anything about this conversation amusing. "Didn't think so." I cleared my throat. "Dad was scared I was gay—"

That had her snorting. "You? *Gay?*"

"Yeah." I grinned, appreciating that she knew I was anything but.

Just because I liked the fucking arts, had a seat at the goddamn opera, and enjoyed the ballet, did not mean I was gay.

Of course, in my father's eyes, there was no worse crime.

Rubbing my chin, I muttered, "He shoved me in the Points two years ahead of time because he was scared I was a pussy."

"You never told me you were twelve when you first enlisted!" Her gasp of outrage was purely motherly, and when I saw hell in her eyes, I knew why before she even ground out, "If your mother dares to fucking judge me over anything Seamus does, I'm going to get in her face, because she should have stopped that in its tracks."

Usually, I'd have defended Ma until the end of time, but in this, she was right...

Huh.

Was that why she was always different with me? Guilt? Did she know she should have done better? *Be* a better mom?

There was no point in thinking shit like that, so I sighed. "She thought what she was doing was right at the time."

"It wasn't. I don't give a fuck if Seamus wants to fuck guys, don't give a shit if he gets turned on by cucumbers! So long as it isn't illegal and doesn't hurt someone else, I'm okay with him being who he is."

There was another warning in that.

And I shrugged. "It's a different time."

I genuinely didn't care if he was gay or not either, which, I'd admit, surprised me. I didn't think the kid was, not with the way he eyed some of the cheerleaders in the games we'd been watching, so the point was kind of moot. But I agreed.

"Don't give a shit if it is or isn't," she growled, and seeing her all fired up on our kid's behalf, on the young me's behalf, did something to me.

Fuck if it didn't.

I scratched my jaw, a little uneasy with what I was thinking. Feeling. I hadn't thought talking about this would be so jarring. Not just because of what I'd gone through so young, but because it led to this moment in time.

The way I'd been raised had directly affected the way my son had been raised. It was a parallel I didn't feel like exploring right now.

"I agree," I told her softly. "I won't give you shit over it."

"Good. I should fucking hope not."

When she stopped bristling, when her eyes turned back to being dazed as she looked at my loot, I murmured, "I got into some bad circles because of when I enlisted. Older kids, you know? Da was just grateful that they were putting some sense into me, because after I made friends with them, I stopped doodling and doing the shit he thought made me a pansy."

"Goddamn him," she hissed, then, when her nails dug into the bedding, I watched her calm herself down before she managed to ask, "I thought you hung around with your brothers."

"I did. For a while. But we each had our own cliques. It was expected of us. We ran around some, but we're generals in the Five Points. It's how we pick our army, by who we come up with." I grunted. "Anyway, long story short, I'd been hanging around with guys who were five or six years older than me."

"Christ, you were a baby hanging around with adults?

I winced. "Yeah. Things derailed when I was fifteen, though."

"That was when you started seeing Deirdre, isn't it?"

I shot her a look. "Yeah. Cause and Effect 101."

"Explain," she demanded when I grimaced.

"This kid, Jonny Braden, knew a guy who knew a guy who knew a guy, hooked us up with some guns. Illegal gear, you know? We started doing some stupid shit. Pulling some heists that were definitely not sanctioned by the council. The five of us did it for years. No issue whatsoever.

"Convenience stores here, gas stations there. A couple of pawn shops. Nice pocket money, you know? Then, there was this bigger job. Jewelry store." I whistled. "It was pure luck we didn't get caught. What was even luckier was the haul we grabbed.

"I never thought anything of it, we divvied up the goods the way we usually did, no problem. Then, Jonny starts bitching at this other kid, Paul. Paul was the one who knew our fence—the guy who'd sell our stuff. Jonny starts saying he was bullshitting us on the appraisal, that he was screwing us out of our share." My mind twisted back to that night that had haunted me for decades. "Me and Cillian were just trying to calm shit down, only Paul pulled out his gun, shot Jonny in the fucking head, but not before Jonny whipped his own piece out and hit Paul—right in the fucking gut. One went wide, hitting another one of my crew straight in the chest.

"So, there we were, two kids left, each of us shitting ourselves."

I scrubbed a hand over my face, because this was not my proudest moment, and I didn't know how to carry on. When I turned to look at her, saw she wasn't horrified, it didn't come as a shock. She'd been raised in the life, after all. Her father wasn't supposed to say shit around the dinner table, but fuck, everyone drank a little too much from time to time, didn't they? Said crap they shouldn't?

"What happened?"

"We went to war with the Haitians that year," I mused softly, and watched her as the information clicked.

"You blamed the Haitians for their deaths?"

"I did." I pursed my lips. "I was fifteen and fucking terrified of Da. Too young to be armed, too goddamn naive to be rolling around with guys who were in their twenties, but that's how it works. You know that." I reached up and rubbed the bridge of my nose. "Me and the only other kid who didn't die planted evidence that pointed at the Haitians, and because Da's such a loose cannon, and because they were messing with our gun supply, it was a simple excuse."

"Jesus, that war didn't stop for, what? Another four years?"

Guilt filled me. "Yeah."

"And you never said anything?"

"No. Not until last week. To Brennan and Conor."

"Why?" she whispered, her eyes huge in her face.

"Because it's the source of a threat and it needs stamping out."

"That's what you're being blackmailed over? The cover-up?"

I nodded. "Ask me who the other kid who helped me plant shit on the Haitians was, Aela."

She swallowed, and the sound was so audible, it had me wanting to give her a bottle of water. Only, I was in bed and out for the fucking count. I wasn't moving anywhere.

"Cillian... I know that name," she whispered under her breath. Then it clicked. "Cillian Donahue?"

"Yeah."

Deirdre Donahue's big brother.

"Fuck," she breathed. "He told her?"

"He did." I gritted my teeth. "He fucking told her, because he knew what would happen, knew what she'd do, and he knew I didn't have a fucking choice, the piece of shit."

"Cillian was mean," she whispered, her eyes big in her face. "Really mean."

"He hurt you?" I barked, unable to stop myself, ire flooding me, even though the fucker was dead, at the prospect of her being hurt by that cunt.

"No. Just freaked me out. I never let myself be alone with him, let's put it that way."

"Good," I grunted. "Smart girl." Relief filled me as I muttered, "It isn't my proudest moment, Aela. It's the most shameful thing I've ever goddamn done. It happened, though, and I've been paying ever since. First with that bitch Deirdre, who blackmailed me into being with her. Then with whoever the hell carried on in her place after she died."

"Who could that be? What do they have on you?"

"Photos. Jonny's gun, which would prove that the bullet in Paul was from his weapon, not a Haitian's."

She frowned at me. "Who were you scared of finding out?"

I shrugged. "Da, of course. At that point, jail would have been a fucking vacation. I was miserable, absolutely goddamn miserable until you and I started hooking up. Things derailed even more when Da made me his fists."

Aela simply blinked. "Where did the paintings come from? Why are you showing me them?"

"They're not really related to that night, but with Paul's contact, the fence, these are what I bought, and they're the only beautiful things that came out of my fucking childhood." I winced. "Well, until you and Shay came back into my life."

She didn't react to that, just asked, "You bought them with the money you made?"

"I bought the Van Gogh with the contacts I made from that time," I clarified. "We didn't make enough on the heists to fund something like this, but it was where the habit started. Collecting things, you know?"

Her eyes bugged at me. "*Things?* Declan, these are priceless paintings. Not 'things'."

My grin was as sheepish as my shrug, but it darkened as I murmured, "It's one of the reasons why I had to let that bitch blackmail me. I couldn't stop..." Jaw clenching, I muttered, "Anyway, the guy I bought the *Poppies* from had the Feds chasing after him. He accepted just over four hundred grand. Crazy money. But it set him up in Aruba or someplace."

"It's worth over thirty million dollars. Minimum," she squeaked.

My lips twitched. "I'm Irish. I like a bargain."

That had her heaving a sigh. "This is nuts."

"Sure is," I agreed. "But, and it's a massive but, you have to understand that if I was a cunt to you, I never actually meant to be. When Deirdre died, that fucking morning of the funeral, I got my first demand. Deirdre never asked me for money after she got her own way, but the person who took her place did. I had to scramble to get the ten K they wanted, and they wanted it every fucking month. I wasn't making as much back then as I am now."

"Evidently," she whispered, her gaze back on the paintings. "Every-thing," she mused slowly, "in this place is antique, isn't it? Priceless, too?"

"Most of it."

A breathless sigh escaped her. "My God, Declan."

"I know," I whispered.

"Why did you get involved in those heists?" she queried warily, like she was trying to find the answers to questions she'd long since been waiting to discover.

Maybe she had.

I just took it as a good sign that she was still interested after all this time.

"Because I was stupid, rebelling against Da. The first time, at any rate. I was shitting bricks after it too, but we had a couple of hundred to mess around with, and it was all without Da knowing about it because he tithes everything we earn." That information had her eyes widening. "Then we hit a pawn shop." I whistled under my breath. "See that little jade bottle over there?" I pointed to the window ledge. "That was what started it all."

"The first piece in your collection?" she asked, then she winced. "Declan, you don't have to tell me any of this. You've told me more than I expected—"

"I do," I rasped. "Because, while I don't expect you to walk on hot coals as an apology for keeping Seamus from me, I'm hoping that you want your son to know his father enough to not want him to be in jail." I grimaced. "Or at the bottom of the Hudson."

"Was it wise cluing your brothers in on all this if the reason you've been hiding it for so long is because of your father?" she whispered, her voice husky.

Finding a positive in the fact that she didn't outright leap off the fucking bed and head for her cell phone, I told her wryly, "I was more worried about the blackmailer going to the cops. I stopped being scared of Da when I was seventeen."

"What happened then?"

My jaw worked. "I'd just lost you and stopped giving a shit about most things."

AELA

IF THERE WAS anything he could have said that would blow me away, it was that.

'I'd just lost you and stopped giving a shit about most things.'

I mean, everything about this afternoon blew me away. From the fact he had several lost classics tucked inside his wall, to how I'd rubbed one off on him against the frickin' door.

I mean, the man was ill. *Ill!* I'd ridden him like a damn pony, but...

Inwardly, I sighed.

My trouble was I liked 'naughty'.

I more than liked it.

It was exciting. He'd always excited me. I knew it was weird, knew it was a bit of sickness considering what he did for a living, but I'd never been frightened. The danger junkie in me enjoyed it... Okay, so my morals were questionable.

Without a shadow of a doubt, those classics should be in a museum. I knew that. They belonged to the public. That level of mastery, that joyousness, shouldn't be owned by one person, coveted by one man. It should be in a world-famous collection somewhere...

Only it wasn't.

It was here.

God help me, I wanted to fuck in front of them. I wanted to have him go down on me in front of something so magnificent it just elevated things to a whole other degree.

Not only were they majestic, awe-inspiring, they were stolen. They were *illicit.* They were tucked away, with only him and me knowing the truth.

All three of those things got my juices flowing.

Throw in that this was Declan?

Only the fact he was injured was stopping me from climbing over him like ivy.

I wanted on him worse than poison oak, no lie.

Every issue, every concern, every goddamn circumstance that made this a whole sorry pile of shit, was immediately discarded in the wind.

This was what I'd felt when I was a kid.

And when I'd seen his cock? The only cock that'd ever fit me just *so*. So perfectly that ever since, no one had ever fit right to the point where, over the last year, I'd given up trying. I mean, I'd been no saint, but sometimes a woman just got tired of being gnawed at.

Declan had always savored me. I'd always felt like a feast and he, not a starving man, but a connoisseur.

When he'd gone down on me when I was younger, I'd felt like I was a four-course meal at the Ritz, not an order of burger and goddamn fries at the local fast-food joint.

"Talk to me," he murmured, breaking into my thoughts.

So I did. I said the first thing that came into my mind. "I want to fuck in front of the paintings."

His brows rose. "That can be arranged." His hand snapped out and settled on my cheek. He curved his fingers around it, stroking back and forth along the upper slant, and the sensation sent tingles down my spine.

I was angry for him, angry at him. But everything we were discussing had gone down when he was Seamus's age, and maybe because of that, I couldn't be all that angry. My kid was one of the smartest people I knew, yet he couldn't figure out that putting a red shirt in a white load would turn everything pink.

He was capable of debating current world issues in a way that decimated me into dust, but when it came down to figuring out which way was left and which was right? He had to make an 'L' shape with his left hand.

My kid was clever with a capital 'C'. But he was capable of some monumental feats of stupidity.

Why shouldn't his father have been the same way at the same age?

"I thought you were going to tell me I needed to donate them to a museum."

"Why show me if you thought that was a possibility?" I queried huskily.

"Because I wanted you to know something about me, and that is one of the biggest ways I can show you."

"What did you want me to know?"

"That I'm ruthless, that I'm a pack rat, that I don't share." He released a breath, not a shaky one, if anything, if a breath could be rueful, his was. "If I want something, I go after it. From a young age, I knew what I wanted and when, and it fucked me over because I got what I wanted, but lost you in the process."

"You mustn't have wanted me enough," I said sadly, but I wasn't offended.

We'd been young. So young. *Too* young.

"I did," he countered, with an instantness that was soothing. "It was complicated. Back then, I never imagined you'd take off. I had to worry about Da, had to worry about the Haitians." He sighed. "That goddamn war went on until 2007. It was a clusterfuck. One that fucking Cillian and I perpetrated."

I blinked at that. "Is Cillian the one blackmailing you?"

"No. He died back in '06. In the war with the Haitians."

"Ah, karma's a bitch."

"Yeah, it is. I didn't die, but look what I lost out on because of what we did. You. Seamus. I fucked up. I fucked up badly." He scrubbed his hand over his face, looking so weary that it hit me in the feels.

"Why did you look at me like you hated me that day of her funeral?" I whispered, my eyes on his. He'd answered this once, but I found it hard to accept that he could look at me with such loathing over his ex's coffin. And that had only been the start. After months of him ignoring me, he'd struck the killing blow outside his local pub.

Just thinking back to that night had pain ricocheting inside me worse than a gunshot wound, and the memory of it was a shadow in comparison to the event itself.

"I told you already," he rasped. "Because I'd just gotten my first ransom demand. They were asking for more than I could afford. Which meant I had to get a touch creative. Of course, as I moved up the ranks, things got easier. Now, it's like paying Netflix."

Even though the pain had crucified me before, I had to laugh at that. "You privileged little shit."

"Less of the little," he countered, but his grimace said it all. He hurt too.

Our pasts were mutually painful.

But whatever I could have expected when we got together, it wasn't this.

Could never have been this.

But it felt right.

So right.

And so goddamn good.

His scent was in my nostrils, his heat beside me in a bed that was loaded down with more of him. His beautiful face, a face I'd depicted so many times in my art, was right in front of me. He had scars and nicks that hadn't been there once upon a time, but he was still so fucking beautiful and so dark that it made me feel luminescent.

I was, by no means, a person who was light.

I was just as dark.

Back when I was a kid, less so. But now? Nah.

I didn't mind working with criminals, didn't mind having people buy my art to launder their cash.

The Lancaster family pissed me off because I hadn't realized they were traffickers. The Irish Mob was many things, but they weren't human traffickers. That was dishonorable.

The thought slipped inside me, and I knew, when we got up, I'd be making a call to my broker, asking them to release funds in the amounts of what Lancaster and his apparent associates had paid me, and I'd donate it to a human trafficking charity.

I'd find one, become a goddamn sponsor. I owed the women who'd suffered that much at least. I was a sponsor for over a dozen charities, and I tithed a massive chunk of my income to them, but one more just got added to the list.

"Hey, I lost you," he rumbled, his fingers trailing down to smooth some locks of hair over my ear.

It felt so delicious that shivers rolled down my spine.

"I was just thinking."

"About what?"

I spotted the tension in his eyes, then whispered, "About Caroline Dunbar. She said the Lancasters were involved in trafficking. I'm going to donate my earnings to a charity."

He'd tensed at the mention of Caro's name, not too difficult to fathom why considering our recent conversation, but then he relaxed. "How much does an original Aela O'Neill cost?"

I smiled. "I think you could afford it."

He snickered, and as one, we tilted ourselves to stare at the wall. As silence fell between us, he murmured, "I should have known you'd get it."

"I'm an artist. How couldn't I? I studied these paintings in college, and I taught the artists' techniques in class." I released a shaky exhalation, wondering if I had a strange fetish because I knew I was getting wet again.

Licking my lips, I gritted out, "I've never seen anything more beautiful in all my life. Which is your favorite?"

"That's like asking me which is my favorite ball."

I blinked then, utterly outraged, twisted to glower at him. "You did not just compare *The Concert, Poppy Flowers,* and *Landscape with Obelisk* to your testicles."

His lips curved into a smirk. "I did. Because I can't choose. How can I? It's nothing to do with value, and everything to do with how it makes you feel."

That answer satisfied me more than anything he could have said. "Where did you buy them?"

He tapped his nose. "I have my sources. People know I'm interested in certain things, and they find a way to get in touch with me."

"How?"

Dec stared at me for a second, then his voice was gruff as he growled, "You're wet again, aren't you?"

I gulped then nodded. He released a groan before he slipped his hand between my legs and cupped me through my jeans. A hiss escaped him and I knew he could feel my slickness through the denim.

Rocking my hips, I ground into his fingers, loving that he didn't ask, that he read my cues. I got so fucking sick of men asking me if I liked this or that —I mean, I knew it was sweet and all—but that was never how it had been with Dec.

He just knew.

It was like he'd read all the instructions to my body on day one, and after that, I was tied to him through ecstasy alone.

"I think you should strip."

Somewhere in the apartment, Shay was doing his own thing. Maybe literally, knowing my sex-mad kid. But hell, I couldn't just...

I mean, Dec couldn't either.

Like he knew what I was thinking, he whispered, "Get naked, lock the door, and I'll tell you everything you want to know. I won't move anything but my hand."

Ugh.

The promise in that—sweet Lord.

His fingers rubbed me again, and I knew I'd never felt so empty in my life.

I couldn't have his dick, but his fingers were all mine.

Because I liked the precision of his command, I obeyed.

I wasn't the perfect size two I'd been back when I was with him, but I was proud of my body. I had curves and I wasn't ashamed of them. My tits were bigger, so were my hips, but I had a rocking ass and my legs were nice and toned, my arms too from all the physical work I did.

It was bright out, maybe a little too bright for comfort's sake, but this was Declan. I knew he'd see the stretch marks, the pooch from carrying his son, I knew he'd see the scar from a mugging that had gone wrong, as well as the myriad new flaws because a connoisseur of art would see all those little details.

And I knew he'd love them.

I knew it. Just like I knew my son and he were like identical twins.

Unable to help myself, because I wanted to know the details and I really wanted to come, even though it was insane, I rolled off the stupid bed that was below the ground, goddamn *below* it because it was burrowed into the floor.

I swear, the guy had the best taste in art, but his decorating skills sucked. Grumbling inwardly at the bed, and the fact that somehow, the douche had been rolling in and out of it and again, *somehow*, getting onto his feet, I stripped. Top first, bra next. Followed by my jeans, and then, when I was sure he was looking, I stepped out of my panties.

His clenched jaw had me smirking a little, and satisfied by his reaction, I wandered over to the door and locked it.

Grateful that the bedrooms were the only part of the apartment with walls, I returned and saw he had his hand on his cock. Through his shorts.

Arching a brow at him, I tutted. "Thought you said you'd only move your hand."

"I am."

"It's moving." I watched it bob and sway, a little mesmerized by the sight because I wanted that dick in my mouth more than I could stand.

"Why would I touch my cock when I can touch you?" He arched his brow right back at me. "Get that sweet cunt over here and I'll start behaving."

Oh, God.

Inside, I just melted.

Those were not the words lovers shared, but just like always, his roughness hit me like a lemon meringue pie to the face. Maybe, in the future, I'd prefer a cream pie to the face... but that wasn't for today.

Before, I'd have pretty much danced over there. Maybe have made Usain Bolt's record look like he was a slowpoke. Instead, I did something nuts. I wandered over to the paintings and I looked at them.

There was something glorious about being naked in front of them.

Yes, crazy.

But right, somehow.

"Did you know Richard DeLorenzo used to work on his counterfeits in the nude?"

A smile bobbed on my lips at his words. "Really?"

"Really. Said it made him feel closer to the work. I'm just sitting over here wondering how a decade-long obsession with these paintings is paling in comparison to the sight of your ass." A growl escaped him, and the sound had me twisting around to look at him. When I did, when I saw he was sitting up on one elbow, I did something even crazier.

I took a step back from the wall safe, pressed my hands to the edge where the slots would slide in and out once the mechanized shelves retracted, and bent over. His groan—totally worth it.

Spreading my legs some, I breathed in the scent of oil and paint and years' worth of this masterpiece existing.

Knowing what it was, where it had come from, that Declan had it, I knew I was sopping wet.

I also knew I was weird, but I was happy with my weirdness.

Twisting to look at him, I purred, "That better?"

"Much better. Picture perfect," he replied, and his hand was back on his cock again.

I gulped at the sight, because I had to agree. His cock, his hand around it, much better than even the Vermeer.

My heart stuttered at the thought, and though I teased him by sliding a hand between my legs and rubbing my clit before slipping a finger inside, I watched his eyes darken at the sight.

Declan was masterful in bed. He'd been careful with me, but over the many nights I'd been rutted on by useless lovers, I'd recognized the skill in him.

He'd been preparing me.

From the very start, he'd been giving me what I wanted, teaching me all along what he wanted me to know.

He was dominant in bed. Rough. He'd *owned* me.

I hadn't figured that out until too late though. I hadn't realized that until someone else had fucked me and it had been like eating frozen yogurt with fresh fruit instead of Cherry Garcia.

"One day, I'm going to fuck you like that," he grated out. "And I'm going to take you to my box at the opera, and I'm going to fuck you there, and at the ballet—"

A moan escaped me.

How was my rough lover so deeply into the arts that he had a box at the goddamn opera?

I closed my eyes, unable to look at him, unable to think of anything but my fingers on my pussy.

"If I could get out of this goddamn bed, I'd spank you for taunting me," he rasped, making heat shiver up and down my spine.

"You'd have to catch me first," I whispered, arching up onto tiptoe as pleasure whirred through me. Not just at my caresses, but at his words. Which, to be fair, were far more incendiary. My pussy and my right hand were best friends... His dirty talk had been sorely missed for nearly fifteen years.

That thought made everything hit home though.

What the hell was I doing over here, taunting him, when I could finally have an orgasm that wasn't totally self-administered and that rocked my goddamn world?

Why was I over here when he was way over there?

Because I recognized I was insane, I straightened up, and then he murmured, "Go to the window."

Surprised, my hair whipped my cheeks as I twisted to look at him.

"Go to the window," he repeated calmly. "Look in the last jade box."

I did as he asked, heading for the window seat. Staring out onto Manhattan was heady stuff, especially when I was naked and I had two hundred million dollars' worth of stolen art at my back.

Talk about a sweet 'fuck you' to the city I'd been born and raised in.

I bent over, smiling when he groaned, and let my fingers trail over the jade box. As I tugged it open, I asked, "What's with the jade?" The apartment was Japanese in style. Not Chinese.

"The apartment's Japanese, I know, but I have a thing for most Asian things."

"Why?"

He shrugged. "Don't know. I just love the complicated simplicity of it all. The paradox pleases me."

Well, those were wet dream-inspiring words.

Declan, back when I was young, had been rough around the edges. Never in a million years, without knowing him like I had, would anyone have known he had a fetish for the arts. Of course, he'd been scared of Aidan Sr. back then. Which, I figured, made sense.

It wasn't like the patriarch of the line was in any way normal.

He was insane. If anything, from what I'd seen at the makeshift ER, he'd mellowed out over the years.

Age... the great sanity maker.

I peered down at the box's contents, and seeing a string of beads, I returned the box to its rightful place then moved around to show him what I was holding.

He didn't direct me to put it on, so I didn't, just returned to his side. I knelt down, handed the cold jade beads to him, then watched with wide eyes as he twisted it around, decorating his cock with it.

Instantly, he hissed, but even though the chill had to have affected his ardor, the inferno raging in him seemed to burn me.

I stared at him, wanting so desperately to jack him off. But even though a hand job wasn't as arduous as fucking, I had to reason that it was the act of 'peaking' that wasn't all that good for the heart either.

Having found him now, I didn't want him to die on me.

Even if he was a jackass for all the mistakes he'd made.

I licked my lips at the sight, and asked, "How old is it?"

"Six hundred years old."

The reply had me gasping as I rocked back on my heels. The jade was a pure white, so white that each bead was like frozen milk. There were faint lines in it, but they were faded with age.

"Stolen?"

He smirked. "What do you think?"

That had me swallowing as I whispered, "Don't think it was meant to decorate your dick."

"No? Shame. I think it looks pretty." His grin was wicked. "Don't you?" When he tipped his head to the side, I knew his words were going to be filthy, and I waited on them, waited and wasn't disappointed. "I'm going to come all over these beads one day, and then I'm going to wrap them around your throat and we're going to attend the theater. These things are meant to be worn, but they've been waiting for you. Only you would ever suit them."

I wasn't stupid. I knew, in all the years we'd been separated that if I'd had lovers, he'd had hundreds of them. Even though it was ridiculous to be jealous, I was a little. But something in his tone, combined with the words themselves, told me that no one had ever replaced me.

No one could or would.

"Would you like that, Aela? The beads saturated in cum, touching your skin, making you smell of me all fucking night?"

I let my gaze drift from his dick, which was hard and proud and throbbing with an intensity that I knew wasn't good for his heart. The bright red flesh looked obscene against the milky white jade.

"You're very presumptuous."

"Always was with you," he admitted. "*Mo bhanphrionsa*."

I gritted my teeth at the endearment. "You have no right to call me that."

"Not yet, maybe, but we both know the feelings haven't gone anywhere, Aela. We both know that they never will."

Tipping my chin up, I whispered, "And what are we supposed to do? Just fall in love and live happily ever after?"

He ignored my scoffing sound and asked instead, "Why not?"

Could it be so simple?

Really?

Truly?

"You think you want me now," I argued, "but I won't let you drag Seamus into this world. Not without a fight."

He reared up at that, and stunned the crap out of me by grabbing me by the back of my neck and hauling me down to the bed with him. When his tongue plundered my mouth, I got it.

I got it, and I wanted to weep.

My eyes grew misty as he kissed me in thanks, in gratitude for doing for our son what his mom hadn't done for us.

I didn't blame Magdalena. She was a woman of her generation, a woman tied to a powerful psychopath. What should she have done? Run away? Aidan Sr. would never have let her go.

Declan had let me leave the country.

There was a distinct difference between father and son. But, even so, the apple didn't fall far from the tree. If he'd known I was pregnant, he wouldn't have let me leave. Just like his da.

He fucked my mouth like he couldn't fuck my pussy, and before I knew it, he was on top of me, one knee speared between mine, separating my thighs. His hand was there, his dick with the cold beads at my side, hot and cold scorching my flesh with equal measure. His fingers went to my clit, rubbing me there as he thrust his tongue against mine, not letting up, not stopping until he twisted his hand around and plowed two digits into me.

He caught my sharp cry in his mouth as he ground the heel of his hand against my clit. My head fell back, but he didn't let me go. He moved with me, his other hand urging me to kiss him again. Because I wanted to scream, because I needed to come so badly already, I let him.

The last thing I needed were thoughts of Seamus breaking in on this moment, a moment that was better than every sexual encounter since I'd left him.

He swallowed my whimpers, my moans, taking them into him until I knew he had to be in agony with his own need. But he didn't grab my hand, didn't urge me to touch him.

This was all about me.

All. About. Me.

And it messed with my head in a way he could never have foreseen.

As he let me fly, as he let me soar, he also tethered me to him. He didn't know he did it. But he did. Bindings appeared between us once more. Bindings that had been broken when I'd left and he'd let me.

They weren't as strong as before. Couldn't be. There was too much time between us, too much distance, but with patience, they'd return.

They'd whisper around my heart, around my being, until I knew I wouldn't be able to live without him. Until what I'd gone through as a stupid teenager would pale in comparison. Because I knew what it was like to live without him.

Hell on earth.

And the last thing I wanted was to be thrust back into it, when here, there was a promise of paradise. The only paradise a sinner like me, and like him, would ever be able to reach.

THIRTEEN

DECLAN
BEFORE

I WAS TIRED, and I wanted nothing more than to make my way to Aela's place, but before I could, I had one last errand to make.

The docks, like usual, stank, and because I knew my way around them better than I knew The Cloisters, I knew where I was going with very little light.

I'd picked up a tail somewhere along the way and had taken a few corners to get free of whoever the fuck it was. We were having some beef with the NYPD thanks to the shit going on with the Haitians, so I figured it was an officer, which meant I couldn't wait for them around a corner and beat the crap out of them, just had to lose their asses which wasn't hard.

I'd heard the tap-tap of their feet, but all was quiet now.

This particular dealer liked to do shit in the dark, and when I said dark, I meant it. His warehouse, though small, was usually in the pitch-black until I walked in with the merch and he deigned to put a light on. He only did it, though, because of who I was.

Ah, the lauded O'Donnelly spawn... it was like being a prince in New York.

I'd take being a peasant any day of the fucking week.

As I hefted up the briefcase in my hand, grabbing the handle tighter, my boots thundered down the rain-slick sidewalk before I finally made it to the door. I didn't like this place. It had no gate, no exterior security, but what the fuck was I supposed to do?

He sold to the celebs, and until our supply lines were in order, we needed these fucks to sell our merch. Because it was a big account, worth over two hundred thousand a month, Da sent me or Brennan along.

I tapped on the door, and a minute later, the opening gave way, sliding sideways as I stepped into it. Though I shut it behind me, I never knew whether I'd prefer to lock it or keep it open because this place was decidedly creepy.

Not that I was supposed to admit to shit like that.

The sole illumination in the pitch-black warehouse came from a puddle of light from a single overhead lamp in the center of the space. It put everything else in shadows, and my theory was the dealer was either a vampire or he had a bunch of heavies waiting in the dark to pop my ass if I dared pull a wrong move.

I understood though. I'd be cautious too, even if he had to be insane to think that I'd pull a move on him... Not all dealers were smart. Some sniffed a little too much of their own product than was wise, and I had a feeling from the way Reggie was always hopping up and down like he was a bunny fucking rabbit, he was that garden variety of dealer.

"Yo, my man," Reggie greeted, when I finally made my way to the puddle of light.

There was a crate there, and I placed my briefcase on it before I said, "Hey, Reg, how's it hanging?"

"Business is *gooooood.* You called at just the right time. I ran out last night."

I arched a brow. "Christ, you ran out already?"

"Yeah." He rubbed his fingers together, finally stepping out of the shadows to meet me. We slapped hands together, shook them like we were brothers, then he beamed. "Might need to increase my order. Got a congressman's daughter who likes a little too much blow than is good for her." He jacked his dick. "Sometimes she pays in kind. Just the way I like it."

I smiled at that even though I thought he was a prick, and replied, "Well, you just tell me what extra you need and we'll get it to you."

He rubbed his hands together. "Fuck, I love working with the Westies. So much more organized than those fucking Colombians."

"Couldn't organize a piss up in a brewery, as Da likes to say." I always liked to drop his name because everyone, even this dumbfuck, knew to be terrified of Aidan Sr.

As expected, his smile turned nervous. "Your pop okay, man?"

"He's doing well. Be happy to hear about the increase in your order."

Nerves abated, Reggie grinned at me, but I saw a few beads of sweat appear at his temples. Yeah, that was the power of my father... capable of making grown men sweat.

I was too over Da's hype though. Maybe a long time ago, I'd have felt the pressure as well, now, I was the monster he'd made me.

When I clicked open the briefcase, four two-hundred-and-fifty gram bags of coke gleamed in the lamplight.

Reggie whistled under his breath, reached into his pocket, pulled out some keys, and tore the bag open. When he dipped the tip in there then tasted it, he smacked his lips before he let out a whoop. "That's good shit, man."

"The best," I told him, in full-on sales mode.

Eyes alight with satisfaction, he clicked his fingers, and ordered, "Bring me the money for my main man, Jack."

Jack, like he usually did, appeared from the shadows, but as he did, I heard the faintest of sounds. The slightest creaking of the door as it was pulled open.

All three of us froze and, after shooting each other looks, I knew I needed to own this situation before one of them got trigger-happy, blamed me, and decided to put me down.

"You got someone waiting on me, Reggie?" I ground out, my tone dark. So fucking dark I knew I sounded like my da.

"No, man," he whispered, eyes wide, and I knew I'd shoved the suspicion onto him. "I promise!" Then he grabbed a gun from the back of his jeans, and hollered, "Whoever the fuck that is, get your ass over here now before I send Jack to get you for me."

No answer.

I squinted into the shadows, wondering why the fuck we were in the dark when this was a business deal. Then, before I could grumble too much, the lights blinked on, cluing me into the fact that Reggie did have other men in the warehouse as I'd expected. My eyes strained, but I reached for my gun just as Reggie knocked his elbow into Jack, silently ordering him to make a move.

With the lights on, I saw a fuck ton of crates, the contents of which I'd never know—and from how he kept this place in jet-black darkness whenever I rolled around, I figured Reggie didn't want me to know about their existence either—but when Jack dragged someone out from behind one, and my gaze grazed over Deirdre's scared face, my nostrils flared in surprise.

My tail.

Fuck.

A thousand scenarios flashed before me in the space of ten seconds, but most of them ended up with me dead, and there was no way I was going to die for this cunt.

I saw a chance at freedom, so I dove for it.

"Who the fuck's this?" I snapped, and watched her eyes widen as her skin blanched. "This some fucking Fed or something?" My fingers tightened around my weapon and I turned it on Reggie. His eyes were blown, something I could see now that we were in the full light, and I growled, "Who the fuck is this?"

A squeak escaped Deirdre, and I knew I had a handful of minutes before terror gave way to self-preservation. I'd been on my own for years, working hard to make my place in the family, so very little scared me. But for her? She was cosseted, not just by her family, but my position. By the position I gave her as my future bride.

She was terrified.

I had to take advantage of that.

"I-I don't know, man," Reggie rumbled, before he screamed, "Who the fuck are you?"

Before she could even say a word, Reggie's drugged brain made the leap for her. And for me too.

His gun went off, and a scream escaped Deirdre just as she crumpled to the ground. Death rattle noises slipped from her lips, and I watched as blood blossomed over her heart.

I turned to Reggie, eyebrow cocked high, and murmured, "Good shot."

He blinked a few times, licked his lips, and rasped, "I ain't never seen her in my life, bro. You gotta believe me. I didn't bring her here or nothing."

"Who is she then?"

He shook his head. "I don't know, man. I don't fucking know."

I strode over to her, then, in a role that would see me win a goddamn Oscar if I was an actor, I released a shaky breath. "Sweet fuck."

"What? What is it?" he demanded, grabbing my arm, but I jerked it from his grip.

"It's Deirdre."

"Who the fuck is Deirdre?" he bellowed.

I let out a scream as I dropped to my knees and hauled her dying, soon-to-be corpse into my arms. Rocking her against me like I gave a shit, like I wasn't happy the cunt was dying, I rasped, "My fiancée."

Pulling back so I could watch her take her final breath, I kept my eyes fixed on hers, hoping she saw my satisfaction, my malevolent pleasure in her death because, for the first time since I was a kid, I was free.

And not only did freedom taste mighty fucking fine, it came shaped like Aela O'Neill who, if I had my way, would soon be Aela goddamn O'Donnelly.

FOURTEEN

CAMMIE

NOW

IT SEEMED IMPOSSIBLE TO ME, but Father hadn't changed the safe combination since I'd left.

Maybe if he'd known I knew it by heart, then he'd have changed it, but as it was, I figured there was no better time than now to grab the necklace that Inessa coveted from Mama's collection, one that her husband, Eoghan, had requested I steal for him.

Objects meant nothing to me. I'd given everything up the first time I'd run away from home, heading for New Jersey where I'd heard chatter of a biker who killed men who abused children.

In my father's line of work, as the Pakhan of the Russian Bratva, violent chatter like that was constant, but gossip about such a killer had stayed with me.

When Father had hit me for the last time as I argued about the marriage he was arranging between me and his ancient *Sovietnik*, I'd decided enough was enough and though it seemed crazy and stupid now—because it most definitely was, especially as I was coming home with a broken heart—I'd run to the Satan's Sinners' MC compound and had found the man I'd thought was my soulmate.

But he wasn't.

And here I was, home once more. My father was in the hospital, his knees shattered from a *Famiglia* sniper's bullet. My stepmother was wandering around the house like the queen bee of Slutsville. My youngest sister was afraid to say boo to a goose. My middle sister was married to a Five Pointer.

My heart was broken because Nyx had chosen another. I'd done everything I possibly could to be perfect for him. To fit his particular mold. I'd gone to him a virgin, and that hadn't mattered worth a damn.

Nothing had mattered to Nyx apart from reaping vengeance on his sister's behalf. Apart from the killing of sick pedophiles who deserved to die.

Until Giulia.

Until she'd come along and wrecked my hopes of becoming his woman on a permanent basis.

The only consolation about returning home was seeing how happy Inessa was with her man. That was why I was here, sneaking into my father's safe even though it might mean him chopping off one of my hands for thieving, but it was worth it.

Inessa wanted this. My stepmother didn't deserve to have a piece that belonged to our mother. And my father, as always, was a bastard.

So steal her necklace I would.

I retrieved Mama's jewelry box and pulled it from the safe. Knowing no one would barge in, because this was Father's office and there was no reason, on pain of death, for being here, I took my time.

As I separated the tangled necklaces that were proof my bitch of a stepmother didn't appreciate the fine pieces here, I happened to see a long, thin necklace that didn't belong among the heavily set emeralds and rubies, the fine diamonds and sapphires that had once belonged to a Tsarina.

It was delicate. The chain frail. But I peered at it and recognized it was platinum, so it was expensive in its own small way. Suspended from the center was a tiny star. Each of the five points were dotted with an emerald as green as Mama's eyes.

I rubbed my fingers over it, feeling a connection with the woman I'd lost too many years ago, too soon, and too violently. Tears pricked my eyes, because Mama and I shared the similar fate of falling for the wrong man...

Knowing Father would never remember buying such a simple chain for his Mariska, who was nothing more than a distant memory for him now, I draped it around my neck and tightened the clasp so it hung between my breasts. I realized that it was too long for anything else, which meant it was supposed to be hidden.

The thought had my brows drawing in, but before I could ponder it, I heard a noise in this side of the house. Though most of the men should be in bed, it wasn't like the foot soldiers worked nine-to-five jobs. Gathering the chain Inessa coveted, I tucked it in my pocket, quickly replaced all the chains back into the jewelry box, and shoved it inside the safe.

Closing it up, I moved the painting that covered it back into place and quickly dashed over to the other side of the room.

Moving behind the door, I waited, my heart in my ears, my fingers nervously fingering the star pendant, for someone to come inside, but no one did. The sound of footsteps faded away, and with it, my panic.

I waited another five minutes, staring at an office that had been the headquarters for far too much bloodshed, and slipped out into the hall.

No one caught me.

But then, no one ever did...

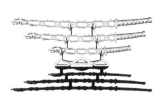

DECLAN

OVER THE NEXT FEW DAYS, I watched her.

And Seamus watched me watch her.

I didn't know if the kid had some kind of radar, but I thought he knew that something had changed between the pair of us.

Was that good or bad?

I guessed it depended on whether he liked me or not. But either way, I had no intention of us not being a family. Hell, we were still young. Maybe we'd have more kids in a couple years' time.

You read that right—that was my thinking.

I was in the future. Flying forward. Thinking shit I didn't have a right to think yet considering Aela was a prickly pain in the ass who had my cock aching like a SOB.

Everything about her got to me.

Every-fucking-thing.

Watching her cook, make coffee for us. Watching her paint, hearing her on the phone. Watching her sigh, following the strokes of her pencil over a notepad.

She was beautiful.

I was a man destined to appreciate the arts, but never fated to have the talents that would let me be a part of that world. To me, she was a masterpiece. A living, breathing one.

For fourteen days, my family left us alone.

Two whole weeks of blissful radio silence unless a Pointer came by with a wad of documents for me to peruse.

With each passing day, I grew stronger. With each passing day, I got reacquainted with Aela's body.

Every night, she'd sneak into my bedroom, and every night, she'd bitch when she had to roll off my futon and scamper back to her own so that it didn't upset Seamus.

Because he was protective, I let him be. I was proud that he was looking after his ma's best interest. Wasn't that what a son should do? But I was waiting for a sign to take things up a notch. Either that, or I was just waiting on the all clear.

My life had changed.

Before, I'd have flipped any doctor the bird if they told me I had to wait to have sex. If I wanted it, I'd have it. But now, I had a son. I had Aela.

I had a future.

I wanted to matter to them. I wanted to be important to them. And I couldn't do that if I was a corpse.

Patience, never my strong suit, was something I was having to learn. Because ever since Seamus had sensed me and his ma were getting closer, he'd pulled back.

It was why Aela had made the suggestion to sneak into my room. She didn't want anything to get in the way of us growing closer, and I appreciated that as much as I appreciated that pussy of hers that was always wet around me, as much as I appreciated her adoration of the artwork on my wall, her understanding of the past. Her acceptance of it.

Because, crazy though it might be, she did accept it.

Maybe she registered I was telling her the truth, because I was.

One hundred percent.

There was no need to lie to her, not now. Not with so much time having passed.

I had a lot of regrets. So did she. That was the biggest win. She'd felt no guilt before, but I could tell she did now when she saw how hard I was trying.

I didn't want her to feel shitty, but that she did meant her opinion of me had changed.

Of course, that would come to an end soon. The second I went back to work. Every day that I grew stronger, healthier, was a day that put me closer to the front line.

A sniff from the other side of the breakfast table, followed by, "Such an asshole," had me blinking in surprise. Seamus was quiet in the morning, but he had his AirPods in and was watching something on his phone.

I was used to it by now. Quite liked it, if I was being honest. Aela ate a yogurt and drank tea then made a to-do list for the day, and I caught up with my emails as I ate the omelet she made for Seamus and me.

Breakfast was quiet. Reflective. Proof that the three of us were meant to be a family because none of us were morning people.

"What is it?" Aela asked, her head tipped to the side.

She didn't mind if he cursed, and though I didn't, I knew I'd have to warn him about Da. Da *would* mind until he was eighteen and then it was a free for all. Except in front of the women.

Christ. That reminded me.

I'd have to take them to church soon. And for the family Sunday roast.

Fuck.

"I still can't believe that prick won."

"Which prick?"

"Alan Davidson. God help us now he's President."

I shrugged. "He's good for business."

"Shit for the environment. I'm the one who's going to have to deal with him destroying the ozone layer," he grumbled. "I'm the one who'll have to live with zero ice caps while he rolls back laws that destroy nature so that fat cats like you can get richer."

My brows rose at the vitriol in that statement, but though I could have grown angry, I didn't. My lips twitched instead, which I knew pissed him off further. "Hate to break it to you, kid, but you're not exactly living like a pauper. With your brand-new iPhone, and your brand new iWatch, and those fancy AirPods, you're as much of a capitalist as anyone. So before you start throwing stones around, acting like I'm the only fat cat in the room, bear in mind that your ma is richer than me."

Aela's nose wrinkled at that, but Seamus's mouth dropped open as he swung around to gape at her. "What?" he boomed.

Didn't take a miracle worker to figure out that Seamus hadn't known that.

She evaded his gaze by blowing on her tea. "Your father's right," she murmured, and her backup was appreciated even if I'd thought she'd take things a different way. "You can't sit and cast judgment on people when you're sitting in a penthouse in one of the most expensive cities in the world. You're privileged, kiddo. But... that doesn't mean you have to be a schmuck about it. You're going to change things, aren't you? Well, you're in a position to do it."

His brow furrowed. "Why didn't you tell me?"

"Because what's in my bank account isn't yours," she said wryly, but she reached over and swiped away the messy locks that had tumbled onto his forehead. "Look, you're about to go to a school where you're going to rub shoulders with the best of the best. You can take that one of two ways. Be a jerk, make no friends, stand out because you're the anarchist. Or you make friends with everyone, get into their pockets, and when you're older" —she tapped her nose— "remember every little thing they did wrong, and use it as leverage to get them on your side."

"That's not honorable."

"Neither is rolling back environmental laws, is it?" She shrugged. "You want to trigger change? Now's the time to do it. You schmooze, and you approach every day in class like it's your first day in court."

"Court's only the beginning," my kid muttered.

"He wants to be a politician," she clarified, "but he thinks becoming a DA is the smartest way to hit the Senate running."

There was amusement in her words as she spoke, and I knew why.

A DA in the family?

Sweet mother of Jesus.

I rubbed a hand over my face, but when I thought about it, when I really calculated how badly that could go awry... I knew I could play it to my advantage.

Da would try to drag Seamus into things soon. He'd try to recruit him. If I hit preemptively, then I could make him see that Seamus was in a unique position to do what Da had been wanting for a long time—get a politician in the ranks.

He wasn't to know that Seamus was an idealist.

Shay, still processing his mom's words, murmured, "You think that will work?"

"What? Schmoozing?"

I snorted. "You mean licking ass."

Aela pulled a face. "Really, Dec?"

"Tell the boy how it is. He wants to get into the world of politics, he needs to get used to the taste of shit."

Seamus groaned. "Ew."

"Yeah. Ew." I wasn't about to treat him like he was five. He wanted to be treated like a man, so I would.

Even if that meant talking about things she didn't approve of.

I shot her a look, saw her disapproval, and smiled at her, before I asked my son, "Do you know what a PAC is?"

He blinked. "Isn't it, like, where you get a group of people together and they donate money for your campaigns and stuff? To get you into seats of power?"

"Yeah. When you meet your grandda, you talk to him about it."

"Why?"

I shrugged. "It interests him." He'd been planning this for years, and didn't he just have the luck of the Irish that Shay was going to fall into his lap?

If he played his cards right, of course.

I'd need to warn him... Wasn't that going to be a barrel of laughs?

Aela returned to her to-do list, I went back to my emails, and Shay carried on grumbling at some political show he was watching on YouTube. I didn't even know kids watched that stuff, but you lived and learned.

When, twenty minutes later, I got an email from Da, I got to my feet and said, "I'm going out today—"

"It's too soon," was Aela's immediate reply, and her concern was the best balm imaginable to the tears in my soul.

"No. I'm fine. I won't push it. I just have to see a few people."

She frowned at me, and silently, I knew she was asking me if I was ready for it. I replied with a nod and a soft smile. "I can't keep the front door locked forever," was all I said, and I did it softly so Shay wouldn't overhear and misinterpret my meaning.

Biting her lip, Aela mumbled, "I don't want to open it."

"I know. It's been really nice, hasn't it? But my folks care, babe. Despite whatever mistakes they make along the way, they really do give a damn. They might be good for him."

"Can you imagine how he'll respond to your father?" She shook her head. "It's a disaster waiting to happen."

"I think it'll be quite funny." I grinned at her. "You're forgetting he'll be on his best behavior."

Her eyes rounded. "You really think?"

"I really think." Casting a look at my grumpy kid, seeing his attention was elsewhere, I stared straight at her, telling her silently what I wanted to do to her. What she made me feel.

When her cheeks started burning, I grinned again, happy that the message had been received. "I'll see you later."

She bit her lip. "If you're going out, then don't be worried if, when you get back, we're not here."

Tension hit me. "There's a war, Aela. You can't just go—"

"Shay needs to get back to school, Dec," she retorted immediately. "He can't stay around here forever. He needs space. He needs a normal routine. He's getting antsy because he's bored. He's not used to having so much free time on his hands."

"I thought he'd like it."

She shrugged. "He isn't like you or me."

"Truants?" I teased, happy when she laughed.

"Yeah. Straight as an arrow. I'm not sure how it happened."

"I am. You did a good job."

Her nose crinkled. "You won't be saying that when he's DA."

I blinked. "Fuck. It's going to happen, isn't it?"

Her lips twisted. "It's messed up enough for it to be a possibility."

"I can hear you, you know," Shay grumbled, making me snort.

Even though we hadn't reached that point yet, I clapped his back, then ran my hand over his hair. If the move stunned him, it stunned me. I hadn't meant to do it, not really. I certainly didn't mean to run my hand over his hair and muss up the messy tumble. But he didn't pull back. Didn't pull away or shove me aside.

If anything, he bit his lip.

I gulped, feeling oddly vulnerable, and when I looked at Aela and saw she'd gone all watery on me, it was weird to accept that she saw it too.

Seamus, even though he had a real attitude right now, *hadn't* rejected me.

And that made me feel like I was on cloud nine.

Before I got ahead of myself, ahead of where Seamus was really at, I headed to my room where I showered, shaved, and got dressed. My usual outfit consisted of jeans, a leather jacket, a tee, and boots because I worked in the warehouse. Brennan and I had the lackey jobs, not because we were dumbfucks, but because we just weren't built for office work, even if a large percentage of our job was administrative.

I ran the trafficking ops, he ran the bookies and loan shark operations, with both of us handling drugs if needs be though it was mostly my scene.

That meant we needed a pair of shit-kickers more than we needed some hand-crafted Italian loafers.

But when it came to meeting Da, we had to change into suits or he'd get pissy. And pissing Aidan Sr. off was never at the top of anyone's agenda. Sure, I'd stopped being scared of him when I was a teenager, but that didn't mean I wanted to deal with his sniping about me looking like a degenerate, so I wore a suit to keep the peace.

I really wanted to head back into the kitchen, kiss Aela farewell and hug her, but I could hear them talking. I was tempted to listen in, especially when I heard Shay prodding his ma for more info on how rich they were, as well as her views on how to schmooze, but I had other things that needed my attention.

Things like a blackmailer who was due to be paid soon. Things like a father who was running out of patience. Things like a war with way too many people ratting us out.

We were used to having moles, but recently, we'd had a handful of men turn to the *Famiglia,* and trust me, a handful was four too many.

As I headed into the elevator, I almost wasn't surprised when I found Conor sitting in it.

Kid was a weird fuck. I didn't even know how long he'd been there, ass on the floor, legs out as he worked on whatever he was working on. With his ability to get comfortable anywhere? He could have been here ten minutes or ten hours.

I scowled at him, demanding, "What the hell's going on?"

He blinked up at me. "Knew you were going out today, thought I'd make sure your security was tuned up." Conor's pride had been pricked when, over the last few years, two people had managed to get through his code. That was the height of hubris.

I didn't doubt that Conor was one of the best hackers around, but he was a cocky shit. Sometimes, he needed to fail to realize he was human too.

"How'd you know I was heading out?"

"Spoke with Da. Knew he was going to email you." The doors closed, and with a flourish of his fingers over the keys, like a concert pianist adding a decorative flair to his performance, he tapped a few more times and then stopped. "Done."

"Everything good?"

"Yep. Yours is tight, and I tuned it up with the next upgrade I've been developing." He squinted at me. "How are you feeling?"

"Tired."

"Not surprising. Takes a lot of time to get over what you went through."

I shrugged. "I'll live."

"Yes, I'm sure you will."

"Found anything out about my blackmailer?"

He hummed. "I have an address."

That had me gaping at him. "You're fucking with me."

"Why would I do that?"

"Why the hell didn't you tell me sooner?"

"Because you were supposed to rest, and I knew you wouldn't if I told you what I learned."

I glowered at him. "What did you learn?"

He smiled at me. "You'll love this... Cillian Donahue isn't dead."

FIFTEEN

DECLAN

"WHAT THE HELL are you talking about? Of course he's dead. I saw him die."

"No, you didn't," Conor retorted, finally getting to his feet and coming to stand. He left his laptop on the floor, stretched, then bent down to grab it before yawning. "He's not dead."

I grunted at his surety, then stormed out of the elevator only to find my brothers there, waiting on me.

Gritting my teeth at the sight of them, then at the sight of the gas guzzling tank that I loathed riding in but knew would fit us all, I grumbled, "What are you doing here?"

Eoghan and Brennan shrugged, exposing bumps at their shoulders that revealed they were carrying. I mean, I was too. But...

Shit.

Had I lost that much weight?

I peered down at the suit which, I had to admit, hung on me where before it had fit like a dream, hiding the bulge of my piece where it was fully visible on their frames. "Crap."

"What is it?" Eoghan asked, his brows furrowed.

"I look like a bag lady."

"I think bag ladies wished they wore custom-tailored suits," Conor replied, carefully replacing his laptop in a carry case that Brennan held out for him.

"You just need to get some weight back on you," Brennan remarked. "You'll look more normal in your usual gear."

True, and I wanted to hug the bastard for knowing exactly where my mind was at.

Conor, as usual, had his head in the clouds.

The last thing I needed was to look like a pussy. We already had enough fucking crosshairs dancing on our chests, we sure as hell didn't need any more. And sometimes, the slightest glimmer of weakness was all it took for some motherfucker to think they could overtake your patch.

Sure, I was an O'Donnelly, and that gave me more protection than most, but there was always some bright spark who started thinking shit they shouldn't.

Case in point Cillian Donahue.

Mind racing as I leaned back against the fender, well aware we weren't going anywhere until Conor's baby was wrapped up tightly in the case he hefted everywhere with him. It was like constantly traveling to the goddamn airport. He couldn't be without his laptop, which meant he had a very expensive pacifier.

"Cillian died," I said unequivocally.

"Did you see him flatline?" Conor queried.

I blinked at him. "No. Why would I have?"

"Then how do you know?"

"We went to his fucking funeral," Eoghan groused, slapping Conor upside the head.

"Was it an open or closed casket?" He wafted a hand. "We go to so frickin' many, I can't remember. Hell, I can't even remember if Rogan's was and that was last week. Jensen's was open though, so I'm not too brain dead yet."

"Christ, I should have been at both," I said guiltily.

"Trust me, you didn't miss anything," Conor replied. "I mean, nothing changes."

"Is it supposed to?" I retorted.

"Well, you've been to one and you've been to them all, is what I'm saying."

"Disrespectful shit," Brennan grumbled. "Jensen took a bullet that could have been lodged in Dec, and Rogan died keeping Shay and Aela safe."

Conor huffed. "I wasn't being disrespectful. I'm very grateful to them. Just don't see why we have to stand around a fucking hole in the ground to show them that respect."

Eoghan, who was like Da, a goddamn eidetic, didactic freak, inter-rupted, "Donahue's was a closed casket ceremony. So was Rogan's."

Conor's smile turned smug and he slapped Eoghan upside the head in retaliation. Eoghan would probably only allow us and Finn to ever do that without trying to do damage to a part of the other man's body.

Everyone knew Eoghan had a fetish for kneecaps.

Well, blowing them out.

His wedding gift to his father-in-law was the reason this war with the Italians had commenced. Of course, it had been a war that had long since been brewing. Sadly, even though I'd been around for three wars, they just kept on coming. Rolling around every five or so years, but never with the big boys.

In New York City, the Russians, Italians, and the Irish ruled the roost. There were spats with the Haitians and the Latinos, but the major players were never a part of the action.

For the Russians and the Irish to be allied against the Italians was unheard of.

We had a real chance of annihilating the scum sucking cunts. Although, they were like fucking cockroaches. Even a nuclear blast wouldn't stop the fuckers from coming back.

"If it was a closed casket," Conor was saying, "then the body could have been swapped."

I had a feeling I knew where he was going with this. Back in 2007, we'd had some issues with a flurry of DEA agents trying to intercept our shipments.

"If they put him in WITSEC," I mused, "then there'd have been a court case. They don't just protect people out of the good of their own heart."

"Might have just run off on his own merit. Might have been scared," Eoghan pointed out.

"Maybe. But remember when the DEA was sniffing around us? Seemed to be one step ahead of us?" I threw down. "It'd fit if he was the one feeding them intel. But there was no court case."

"Could have just turned informant. Never did like that piece of crap," Brennan grumbled.

"Where's he living now?"

"Astoria," Conor told me.

I shook my head. "Why the hell would he run away to Queens?"

Conor blinked. "No. Illinois."

"Illinois, what?" Brennan snapped.

"Astoria, Illinois."

My brothers stilled at Conor's statement, and my lips twitched as I realized they'd come ready and willing to wage war on my blackmailer, who was halfway across the fucking country.

"You could have mentioned it was a different fucking state, Conor," Brennan snarled, his hands balling into fists.

Conor was lucky that Ma had instilled in us a certain appreciation of our brother's brain or he'd have had the crap beaten out of him right then.

"Why the fuck do you think we're here? To go fucking bowling?" Eoghan inserted, scowling at Kid.

"It can't be Cillian," I muttered, breaking into the brewing argument. "He was loyal to the Points."

"Maybe Deirdre's death messed with him."

"He had plans for her," I said, unable to disagree with Brennan. Then, I muttered, "Please tell me that while you were sharing this with Eoghan, Da or Aidan didn't overhear?"

Brennan grumbled, "What the fuck do you take me for?"

"An eejit?" Conor tacked on helpfully, earning himself a glower that would have felled a lesser man.

Conor wasn't lesser. Just a little whacko where reality was concerned.

Eoghan sniffed. "Why the fuck didn't you want me to know?"

"Because you're busy. These two have no goddamn life anyway. You've got Inessa now. I don't want you getting involved with shit that isn't important."

"Not important? Some fucker's been skimming millions off you over the years and you think that ain't important?" Eoghan growled. "I'm the security man. Why the hell wouldn't you keep me in the loop?"

"Bro, I triggered a fucking war," I muttered under my breath, just in case the CCTV cameras were compromised.

"And I didn't? And you didn't have my back? Help me out with getting the right weapon?"

I grimaced. "I appreciate the loyalty, but I didn't break Ma's favorite vase or crash Da's car. I caused a lot of shit."

"So have I. Anyway, back in '06, the Haitians were trigger happy. It was bound to happen," he dismissed.

"You know it makes Da happy when we're at war. Means he can play." Conor's blasé tone had me grunting.

"Well, just because he likes to play with his food doesn't mean I want him to play with me. Even if he didn't give me shit over the war, he'd give me a fuck ton of crap over the lying."

At that, each of my brothers shuffled around like we were teens again.

Aidan Sr. did not deal well with liars.

In fact, people had a tendency to lose extremities if they lied to him.

While I was pretty sure I'd be safe, I didn't feel like dealing with the repercussions of a lie that was older than my son.

"We can keep this from Da," Brennan reassured me, then asked Conor, "Can't we, doofus?"

Conor shrugged. "I don't see why not. He's preoccupied now anyway. If he did find out, your being injured would probably help, and the fact that Seamus is a lost grandchild is bound to take his interest. Of course, there's the strip club and the—"

My heart skipped a beat as I remembered the rituals Da had dragged us through when we were young. "Fuck," I rasped. "I forgot about that shit. Two weeks of relative normalcy and it skipped my mind how insane Da is."

"You forgot about the drug den?" Brennan shook his head, but he was laughing as he did it. "Not sure how you forgot about that."

"Well, apparently Aidan Jr. did considering he's a junkie."

Eoghan sighed. "Conor, you keep on saying that shit, he's going to shoot you."

"Better than shooting up some..."

When his voice petered off, I eyed him. "Shooting up what? He's taking prescription meds, Conor. Not hardcore narcotics."

"Slippery slope," was all he said, but he sniffed too. "Look, you might have all day to shoot the breeze in a parking garage, but I can assure you, I don't."

"I need to speak with Da too," Brennan said. "I'll drive us both there, and I can drop you two off as we go."

When Eoghan and Conor nodded in agreement, I didn't argue because I didn't feel up to driving. This entire conversation was a mess just waiting to hit me between the eyes. I had a feeling Da wouldn't find out, but he didn't need to for trouble to be brewing.

If Cillian wasn't dead, if he was the one behind the blackmail, then I had a nasty feeling he'd have been charging me a hell of a lot more than ten grand a month.

And if someone was pretending to be Cillian, having assumed his identity... well, there was an end game in play, wasn't there?

I rubbed my chin as I hefted myself into the passenger seat. That I looked like a bag of bones and a piece of shit was confirmed when neither of my brothers called shotgun on the seat and settled in the back.

When we took off, the radio raged with some old school Queen of the Stone Age.

Quite fittingly, the song that was blaring out?

'No One Knows.'

Even if it was one of my favorites, I grimaced. When the goddamn playlist agreed with you, things really were up in the air.

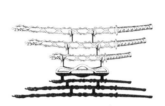

DECLAN
BEFORE

"I'M SO sorry for your loss."

Though I wasn't actually grieving, I'd admit that if I was, hearing that on repeat was going a long way to pissing me off.

I wasn't in the best of moods.

Not because today was the day my bitch of a fiancée was finally being put in the ground, but because I'd been stupid.

Well, not stupid. More hopeful than anything else.

Of course, Deirdre had a failsafe. *Of course, she fucking did.*

Which meant the bones of my ruination were in the air.

A handful of pictures and a goddamn gun were all that lay between me and the fucking noose.

A noose held up by my own father.

Sure, if it fell into the hands of a cop, I'd be fucked, but being fucked might have a happy ending. If Da ever found out about *how* I'd caused a war, then there were no happy endings. There'd be fucking nothing, because I'd be in a body bag before the night was through.

I rubbed a hand over my face, tired of playing a game, tired of looking like I was mourning when I was just glad that cunt was dead.

I'd had five days of feeling like I was flying high, even having to keep my distance from Aela hadn't spoiled my glee, and then boom. Today, in the mail, my nightmare started up again.

Behind me, Deirdre's body was in the ground, we'd dumped soil onto the casket, and I'd spent the past fifteen minutes shaking everyone's hand and wishing I was anywhere else.

I stared at nothing, going through the motions like a robot, until a soft hand slipped into mine.

Jerking to life, my eyes were trapped in Aela's.

Fuck.

I loved her.

I loved her so fucking much.

It was hard to keep my features under control, impossible even. Instead, I forced my entire being into rigidity, knowing that if I didn't, people would figure out that she meant something to me.

Now that Deirdre was dead, I thought we could be together. It was one of the reasons why I'd been floating on cloud nine these past few days, because with that bitch out of the picture, I was free to be with whoever I wanted. But this morning's mail put everything on the backburner.

Until I figured out who the fuck was behind it, I was at a loss. Which pissed me off even more.

She jerked back, making me aware my hand had tightened around hers, and I let go with a wince. Her eyes were big in her elfin face, and though I longed to cup her cheek, to draw her mouth to mine, I didn't. *Couldn't.*

Not yet.

Maybe not ever.

The future had been filled with promise with Deirdre's death.

Now, my end could be nearer than I'd like, and if Da ever found out, which was a distinct possibility because the ten grand the blackmailer wanted was going to be a bitch for me to get together, I'd be dead before I had a chance to really live.

The last thing I wanted was to bring her down with me, and with that as a distinct possibility, I knew I needed to put some distance between us until I figured things out.

Because it killed me, my voice was gruff as I dismissed her and said, "Thank you for your condolences."

The words were nothing, trite, but my tone was clear, and she reacted like I'd shot her. Like my rejection was a killing blow.

I didn't look at her. Couldn't. I had to protect her. Not just from me, but from Da, and from whatever fate rested in front of me. I'd been walking this path for so long that I'd thought I knew my options. But as it stood, I wished Deirdre was alive.

She was the devil I preferred, and I'd acted in haste, but was now repenting in torment.

AELA
BEFORE
Two months after Deirdre's funeral

I'D NEVER UNDERSTOOD JUST how true being sick to your stomach was.

When you were pregnant, hormonal, weighed down with guilt, heart-broken, and terrified—those were emotions that made you truly sick to your stomach.

Wanting to puke all the time and not because of morning sickness, I felt like I was a prisoner inside my own mind.

I hadn't seen Declan in weeks. He wouldn't answer my calls, and he ignored my texts. On the rare occasions I *had* come across him, he'd ignored me, and when he looked through me like I meant nothing, it rammed home my place in his life.

The side piece.

I was tagged and bagged as such, and hoping for more got me nothing. Would never get me anything other than loaded down with a welter of baggage and heartache.

I'd given up on him, I'd admit. It had been two months since the funeral. Two months for him to have gotten over Deirdre's death. I knew that sounded horrible, but he didn't love her. I knew he didn't. He treated her terribly, but then...

Wasn't that how he was treating me?

Had he already shown me his true colors and I'd never even noticed?

I should have seen the signs in his behavior around her, but I'd been a fool. A stupid, naive fool.

I saw that now.

I was getting my just deserts. I'd betrayed my friend for him. I'd been a party to him cheating on her, and in the end, that was what had gotten her killed. Lizzie Bryan had told us in recess that Deirdre had confided in her, told her that she was sure Declan was screwing around on her, and she was going to follow him to learn, once and for all, if he was.

That was why she'd died.

She'd gotten involved with Points' business, and had lost her life as a result.

Her death was on me, on us... No wonder he felt horrible. I did too. I felt evil for having mistreated her that way even if we'd stopped being close friends a long time ago thanks to my growing a spine and refusing to listen to her wax poetical about Declan for hours on end.

But even if he was a bastard, I had to tell him.

I had to.

I couldn't *not* warn him. Could I?

So here I was, outside Flanagan's Bar, waiting for him to come outside.

It had rained at some point, but I still stood here, under a too-flimsy umbrella, waiting on him to leave.

It had been two hours by now, but it was worth it. I deserved the punishment. I deserved it for what we'd done to Deirdre.

Tired, I rested against the streetlamp, then jerked because the second I did, the door opened and out he walked. He was with a few of his crew, and they were laughing and joking. Declan wasn't.

His face was grim.

And it grew grimmer still when he saw me.

His eyes narrowed, and he said something to his crew, and though they shot me curious looks, they went away, their steps clipping against the slick sidewalk as they left me with the man I'd believed was my soulmate.

"What are you doing here?" he demanded, and the scent of whiskey on his breath was so strong I almost stepped back.

It was like a cloud around him.

I'd never known him drink before. What on earth was going on with my sweet, loving Declan?

I reached out to him, went to cup his cheek, but he jerked back like I'd tried to slap him.

"No," he ground out. "No!"

Tears pricked my eyes, but I raised my chin. "What's going on with you? Why won't you answer my calls?"

He hitched a shoulder. "You have no say in my life, Aela. I've had it up to here with people telling me what to do, how high to jump, how far to run. I'll do what I want and I won't be contained. Do you hear me?"

He boomed the last words at me, and because I wasn't used to him shouting at me, I jumped back, stumbling against the streetlamp in surprise.

"What's wrong with you?" I rasped, my fingers turning white as I clung to my umbrella.

"Everything's wrong with me," he snapped. "Is there a point to this?"

"I wanted to talk to you."

"Yeah? Well, I don't want to talk to *you*." He loomed over me. "Didn't you get the message, Aela? When I ignored your hundredth call?"

"No," I breathed. "Apparently I didn't."

He grunted. "Well, do you understand now?"

"Yeah. I do." I tipped my chin up. "I just wanted to reassure you that I'm not pregnant. I handled it."

Something flared in his eyes. I knew *what* as well.

The memory of that night.

It triggered a wildfire that stormed inside him, but he clamped down on it so fiercely that it was like he was made of stone.

"Good."

Then he walked off.

Just walked away.

Without looking back at me. Uncaring that I was wet. That I was standing here, my heart on the sidewalk in front of me.

He left me.

So, I knew I had no choice but to leave him. I wouldn't be the noose around his neck like Mom was to Dad. I'd go away. Far away. I'd raise his baby like I wished *I'd* been raised. Normally. No crime, no violence. Just with love.

Always with love.

Because even though my baby's parents had been torn apart by death and guilt, shame and lies, he'd been created in love. I'd spend the rest of my life making sure he or she knew it too.

SIXTEEN

AELA

NOW

IMPATIENCE MADE it hard when the staff eyed my blue hair and my earrings like I was an alien who'd just crash-landed on Midland Private Academy's private helipad.

The liaison was kind enough, however, and didn't seem to have a stick shoved up her butt as she showed us around. It was just the teachers in every class who stared at my hair that drove me crazy.

Either Seamus didn't notice or he didn't care. His gaze was fixed on things that should probably interest me but didn't. I was more bothered about their terrible art program, but he wasn't an artistic kid even if I tried to drag it out of him to help him express himself better.

He preferred boring things like science labs and large libraries, while I fully accepted that my priorities were unlike any other mother's. I figured few parents were complaining about the lack of a kiln and were more worried about there only being five chemistry labs.

I trudged along behind the pair of them, amused as they discussed things that told me they were on the same wavelength, and which confirmed my darling boy was a nerd.

The school was my idea of hell, but he seemed to like it, and whenever he saw a bodyguard stationed outside a classroom, or inside, it caught his attention.

I could almost see the mental chalkboard in his head scrawling, 'child of important person standing at ten o'clock.' He probably had a running tally, and I wasn't averse to that. Anything to take his mind away from the fact he'd been on the football team back home and would have to try out again.

Of course, 'back home' was relative.

The tour took forever, and while I preferred his old school in Rhode Island, I wasn't about to complain that he seemed to like this campus. Our talk this morning had put some things into perspective for him, even though I wasn't particularly happy about Declan blurting out that I was richer than him.

It wasn't like I'd needed proof to know that Conor had hacked into my accounts.

The lack of security on my finances put me on edge, but it was one of those things. Hackers could get anywhere they wanted. I just had to hope that they'd leave me alone. Unless Conor could put some kind of whacko trapdoor on my account alone, which I wasn't sure Bank of America would be totally happy about. Or maybe Conor had done that already—I *was* family now, wasn't I?

We ended the tour with Shay seeming happier than I'd expected, especially since we were supposed to visit another two schools today. As we left Park Avenue and headed into the city, I prepared myself for a long tedious day, which was what I got. The other tours were just as boring, just as annoying with the reaction to my hair because I had to wonder if these people had ever even heard of Instagram, but Shay's reaction just wasn't as positive. Shame, too, because the second school had a better art program, and the third was closer to the penthouse.

By the end of the final tour, I was ready to go home, and though I wasn't comfortable driving through Manhattan anymore, I didn't have to.

We had two, count 'em *two,* armed guards. George and Liam, although Liam would only be around when Shay was in class.

They'd shown up about a half-hour after Declan had left, and the necessity set my nerves on edge even if it had confirmed something to Seamus that I didn't particularly want confirming.

He was like the kids in the schools he'd just been wandering through.

He needed a guard.

I wasn't sure what was going through my kid's mind, but I didn't like it. I didn't want him getting too cocky for his own good, too big for his britches as my grandma would have said, but toning things down wasn't easy. One semester at the fancy school he liked cost more than a family home, and the penthouse wasn't exactly slumming it.

I'd managed to keep things on the down low before, but he'd been dragged into this world and was coming face to face with the truth of his status.

At fourteen, that was enough to turn my great kid into an egomaniac, so I needed to make sure to bring him down a peg or two.

All throughout the tour, I'd been planning what to do, and my solution was simple.

Remind him of who he was.

What he was.

"Can you take us to the nearest KFC, please?"

The guards, neither of whom I recognized, didn't reply, nor did our driver, which made me wonder if we'd even be heading that way. Were their orders to take me home immediately? I wouldn't argue, even if the constraints would wear on me quickly.

The city had changed a lot since I was last here. Three or so years ago, I'd dared dash back for a gallery opening of old art school friends that I'd helped by holding an exhibition there, and had even had time to hold a workshop or two, but I'd sweated bullets each and every visit.

In my line of work, avoiding NYC was a death knell, so I'd braved it and, miracle of miracles, hadn't been caught.

No, what had trapped me was the tag on my wrist.

Thinking of Amaryllis, my student, who had come to me for help with her partner who'd been kidnapped, I wished we'd been close enough for me to call her, to find out how her partner was doing. But I barely knew her. Barely knew anyone in this life anymore.

Well, except for Declan.

The whirl of the city blurred by, and Seamus, who'd never visited, and who'd often complained and even had a tantrum or two over not being able to come with me on my infrequent trips, was in a stupor as he came to terms with his new home.

In such a short span of time, everything had changed. In more ways than one. I'd gone from thinking that Dec would loathe me, to actually feeling like we might make something work. And I said 'something' because I'd never be the wife he probably thought he wanted.

I'd take a back seat, not take center stage when the macho man act had to come out, but no way was I putting the brakes on my career. No way was I going to stop doing what I loved.

Having figured out a path for myself with Seamus, I saw no reason why a boyfriend or husband would get in the way.

At first, I thought we were being taken on a scenic route, and then when we eventually made it to Hell's Kitchen, I realized what had happened.

They'd taken us around and around in circles, driving from one part of the city to the other depending on whose territory we were in.

Amazing how these things were coming back to me. Amazing how I'd forgotten that a city wasn't just split into blocks and districts and neighborhoods, but into invisible lines that were ruled by no governing body that had been elected by the people and for the people.

There were worlds within worlds here, cities within cities. It was a hard, cruel life, and I was envious of the people who weren't touched by it. But, in the grand scheme of things, few *weren't* touched.

Protection money had to be paid if you owned a business or a restaurant. Drugs were dealt on street corners, bikers passed by on major arterial roads, protecting shipments that were under watch from the FBI. Most people would never come into contact with the Feds, but for us, it was a way of life.

I reached up and fiddled with one of my earrings, and when a KFC came into sight, I didn't even have the option of eating in. We went through the drive-thru.

A little peeved at the lack of choice, even if it was for our security, we placed our orders, grabbed our food, and Seamus tucked in.

It always amazed me how my big kid reverted to his younger self when fast food was on the table. He beamed a grin, the first for a few days, and I had to hold back a smile at the sight of the honey mustard sauce coating his lips like makeup.

I didn't bother cleaning him up—I wasn't that kind of mom. He was only going to get dirty again, so I just let him enjoy his meal and questioned him about his choice of school.

When I knew Midlands would suit him, and that it was what he really wanted for himself, I focused on the streets again, and wouldn't you know it?

Somehow, we'd ended up right outside my old home.

Stuck at a red light, I leaned forward, and while I didn't know the driver or the guards, I knew they'd know the answer to my question.

"Do Mary and Kyle O'Neill still live there?"

One of the men, George, had a wide smile and kind eyes, but he lived on his nerves, always fidgeting, which made his gun rattle against the holster and his belt buckle jiggle. The men wore expensive suits, which told me they weren't just gofers—the lowest of the low—but high-ranking.

In this world, a man guarded his treasures or they were taken from him.

It was strange to think of myself that way, and with anyone else, I'd feel like an object. But Declan had a way about him, a way that made me feel cherished. These past weeks together had only confirmed that.

"The O'Neills still live there, yeah," George answered, and the driver, Jerry, an older guy with a watchful stare, scanned the road like we were in downtown Benghazi.

"Can we stop, please?"

George blinked and Jerry caught my eye in the rearview mirror. "Why, ma'am?"

God, I hated being called 'ma'am.' I was in my early thirties, not ready to settle into my dotage.

Gritting my teeth, I muttered, "They're my parents, and I haven't seen them in years."

What I didn't say was that if my parents' schedule hadn't changed—which I highly doubted because it hadn't altered an inch in the years of my childhood—then Dad would be tucked away in the pub with his cronies and Mom would be alone.

I wanted to see her. It had been too long, not only between visits but for phone calls.

When she'd helped get me to Ireland, she hadn't exactly cast me out, but neither had she defended me, something she'd compounded by never visiting.

As for Dad, I didn't even know if he was aware I had a son, and if he did, I wasn't sure if he would be interested. It wasn't like he was the most fatherly of people.

Of course, things might be different because Seamus was a boy.

Goddammit.

Two sets of grandparents who'd more than likely want him in the life...

How was I going to keep him on the narrow path that, so far, had fired him up? Had made him get out of bed every morning to work hard, train hard, study hard?

A little at a loss, I barely registered when the vehicle slowed, but as I became aware, I directed my kid to, "Stay here."

He arched a brow, but knew not to argue with me when I used that tone. Man, that made me sound like a hard ass, but there were some places I just didn't want him to go.

This was one of them.

I had no idea of what welcome we'd get. No idea if I even wanted to be welcomed.

Coming back home didn't mean a family reunion was going to happen, but the least I could do was visit and see how things were. See if I wanted my kid under the same roof as my folks.

Pursing my lips as George clambered out of the car, while Liam stayed put, I waited on him to open my door for me—this security situation was going to get wearing fast.

As a young kid, the family had never been that important where we'd necessitated such things. We hadn't even been put into lockdown on the Five Points' secret compound until Dad had moved up the ranks some.

George nodded at me, and I sensed he was grateful I wasn't being a pain about this. Inwardly, I felt all the irritation, but it wasn't his fault. He was just doing his job. There was no need for me to be a bitch about it.

I peered up at the building, unsurprised to note it hadn't changed much in my absence. That they were still here told me Dad had peaked, never getting another promotion, and I knew why too. He'd always had a bad temper, one that was exacerbated by the drink.

Old fool.

When I climbed up the steps to the front door, I hit the buzzer to the place that had once been my home and heard her voice. "Yes, who is it?"

She sounded a little dazed—no change there either.

With Dad focused on work and whiskey after the job ended every night, and Mom popping pills to stop herself from feeling anything at all, it was a wonder I'd managed to grow up and be pretty normal.

Of course, normal was relative.

To many, I was the exact opposite of normal. Especially when I was in the middle of a project.

Not even Declan had seen me like that. Only Shay knew what I was like.

The thought had me pursing my lips, wondering how Declan would react, then deciding not to worry about that now, I murmured, "It's me, Mom."

Silence fell. "Aela?" she asked hesitantly.

Did she have some other kids she hadn't seen in over a decade?

Rather than be difficult, I just said, "Yes."

The buzzer sounded, and I knew that meant Dad wasn't home. I was pleased about that. I had no real desire to see him, but Mom was different. I'd like to reconnect.

George pushed the door and stepped in front of me. He placed his hand on his weapon, then peered around here and there, guiding me down to the elevator doors. As they opened, he tensed, but it was empty.

Climbing aboard, we shuttled toward my family home, and I let him step out first before I finally made my way to my old front door.

She was standing there, waiting on me, looking frail and a lot older than I'd expected. We hadn't kept in touch much, mostly because she was out of it and had an odd perception of the passage of time. I understood that though—when I was in one of my moods, I shared that trait.

Mom opened her arms to me though, and biting my lip, I walked straight into her embrace.

She hugged me tight, far tighter than I'd ever imagined, which made me realize she'd missed me, and I burrowed into her right back.

"Been too long, Aela," she chided, squeezing me with each word.

"Yeah, it has, Mom. I'm back now though."

She grew tense at that, then edged away from me to look at me. I was taller than her now—when had that happened? We shared the same features, delicate but somehow bold with our strong eyebrows and high cheekbones, our eyes were faintly inset, but they were richly hued, as was our hair, although hers was more streaked than when I'd been a kid which told me it was salon dyed. I could easily remember her doing her own hair and always messing up.

My lips twitched at the memory.

"Your son's here?" She peered around me into the hall, then jerked in surprise to see George. While he was young, he wasn't *that* young.

"That's my new guard," I explained. "Seamus isn't here. I didn't bring him this time. I didn't expect to visit, to be honest. We were driving past and I just thought I'd come see you."

She squeezed my hands, but her gaze remained on George. "You have a guard."

"I do."

Mary glanced up at me. "He's claimed you?"

I dipped my chin. "He's in the process of it."

Her eyes cleared for a second. "The shooting. Of course. Bad business. Bad business. Your father almost got his last week. The Italians are crazy, running around like something from an action movie. Uncaring if innocent people get hit." She grunted. "Animals."

We weren't exactly well behaved, well-modulated examples of humanity.

"I can't stay, Mom," I told her. "I just wanted to come see you."

"You can't stay for coffee?" she asked, and her disappointment was actually a salve.

"No. Not today. But another time, I'd really like that."

She smiled at me, the smile reflected in her eyes as she reached up and touched my chin, letting her fingers slip over my cheek as if she was 'seeing' me with her hands. "Come whenever, and bring Seamus. I want to get to know him."

It was on the tip of my tongue to tell her she could have known him for years, but there was no point in being bitter about this. No point at all.

I nodded. "Will do. Dad still spending his nights at the Tavern?"

"Yes." There was no disapproval in either of our voices. "If you come before eight in the evening, and after ten in the morning, you'll be able to avoid him."

"Good to know." I leaned down and pressed a kiss to her cheek. "I missed you."

"I missed you too," she replied, and I realized she sounded surprised, but I got it. Not that she missed me, but that she felt anything at all.

She'd been in a doped-up haze for decades, and my father didn't really give enough of a damn about her to try to help her. I'd always felt bad for leaving her with him, but when it had come time for me to admit I was pregnant and that I needed help, she'd just aided me in getting out of the country. Had never offered to come visit, had never helped with her parents who'd always disapproved, but believed too much in family bonds to ever throw me out onto the streets.

Bitterness welled in me, but I tossed it out like I was throwing out so much at the moment. I could hold onto it, keep it close to my chest, or I could move on.

I was deciding to be an adult.

If Declan didn't hold a grudge against me, then I decided that I could woman up too and be a bigger person.

"I'll see you soon," I told her, reaching for her hand and squeezing again, before I pulled back and retreated to the elevator.

I hadn't expected to see her today, hadn't thought to visit since I'd made it back to the city which I knew was pretty horrible of me, but as I stared out of the elevator, her gaze was glued to mine until the doors closed.

There was regret in hers, a regret that I knew came from everything she'd missed out on, and the sight of it made me feel better. Made me feel like there was something to work with rather than just batting my head against a brick wall.

My life was coming together in pieces I'd never have expected because, even though I'd spent every day wondering if that day would be when Declan learned of Seamus, I'd never really thought about the aftermath. Had just thought about the main event.

Nothing was going down as I'd anticipated.

I'd thought he'd hate me, had thought he'd make my life miserable, and I had a feeling that, in different circumstances, he would have.

He'd have detested me for denying him Seamus, would have taken pleasure in making me miserable, in sucking all the joy out of my life and making me live as a shadow of my former self.

But he'd been shot and as horrible as it was, I thought the next time we went to church—because that was in the cards, and that was another culture shock for Seamus that was heading our way—I'd give my thanks to the Almighty for the gift of those bullets because Declan had almost died, and that changed a man's perspective.

Which, in my predicament, couldn't have happened at a better time.

DECLAN

THE RIDE TO OUR PARENTS' compound took place in relative silence, especially since I was thinking about everything there was to discuss, but sometimes, with Da, there was no point in discussing beforehand and getting your story straight. He always knew.

Like a shark scenting blood, he knew how to drag out the information he wanted.

A part of me was still bewildered that, all these years later, he hadn't figured it out sooner. Pulling the wool over his eyes was close to impossible but, somehow, I'd done it when I was a dumb kid, dicking around with a bunch of other dumb kids.

As it stood, he wasn't aware I was being blackmailed, or that we were looking for a blackmailer, and because Conor made it a habit of keeping Da in the dark with his IT exploits, I wasn't worried, not really, about him having given me away.

Conor had been right though. If ever there was a time for Da to find out that I'd lied, it was now. But that didn't mean I was eager for the truth to be revealed.

I'd made a lot of mistakes along the way and had paid dearly for them. My son was a stranger to me, one I was slowly coming to know, but still a stranger. And Aela, while anything but foreign to me, was a delight I couldn't believe I'd had to live without for so many fucking years.

Regret hung heavy on my heart, and I knew it changed me. Whether it was for the better or for the worse, I couldn't say. Maybe I wouldn't be able to. Maybe it was my family who'd see the difference.

"You're quiet."

I cast a look at my elder brother. "Got a lot to think about."

"I'll bet. Wish you'd told me before," he said gruffly. "Always did hate it when you kept things from me."

A short laugh escaped me. "If I'd gotten you involved back then, you'd be as fucked as I am now."

"Da'll punish us, but he ain't gonna kill us," Brennan groused. "Ma would never let him."

I loved that he qualified that, loved that he knew he had to.

Da wasn't the most rational of men, and he had episodes where he went a little batshit crazy. The only constant that kept him sane was Ma.

Of course, that sounded insane. A person wasn't lithium. They couldn't take a goddamn personality disorder and even them out, but Magdalena O'Donnelly was Aidan O'Donnelly's miracle.

We all knew it.

All knew to dread a day where she died and he stayed around without her.

If God really did exist, and my father believed more than most, then He'd take Da out first, then her.

Not that I liked to think about them dying, but sometimes, in our world, death was a conversation that was forever on the tip of the tongue when compared with most folk.

Not a year went by where some shit stunt like what had happened to me didn't befall one of us. Then there were the guys around us. Rogan, the man Brennan and Eoghan had set onto Aela at first, was Ma's favorite guard. He was dead now, and there was no coming back. Not unless he was the next coming of Jesus, and I highly doubted God was capable of that level of mischief. Sending back His son as a hired gun? Highly unlikely.

"Do you think it's Cillian?" Brennan asked when I didn't reply to his earlier comment about Ma.

"No. I don't. I think someone stole his identity, I'm just not sure why they would."

"I think you like to make shit complicated."

My lips quirked. "Maybe. I'd prefer things to be simpler though."

"Declan, you and simple ain't never been friends."

I heaved a sigh. "I hate to agree with you, but you're not entirely wrong."

"Was he mad about Deirdre?"

"What do you think?" I rumbled. "He'd told her everything so she could trap me, and I don't think he did it because he thought we were Romeo and Juliet. He wanted her to surge through the ranks and so did she."

Brennan whistled. "I knew you hated her, could never figure out why you were with her, but I have to give you credit, bro. There's a reason why Da never realized what went down that day. You're a fucking good actor."

"Is that your idea of a compliment?"

"Better than calling you a good liar, no? Thought I was pulling my punches."

"I'd stab another man for calling me a liar," I grumbled.

"You can't stab shit at the minute. I saw you in the parking garage. You looked like I could push you over with my pinkie."

I flipped him the bird as we rolled to a halt outside my parents' compound.

The house was completely unlike the old mansion where my folks had lived which, to be honest, had been a damn sight handier. Closer to the city, not so far away from my place, and bigger too, but they liked it here, and it was safer for them.

No matter what we did, the enemies came at us like rats out of a sinking ship. Da blamed Conor sometimes for his coding letting us down, but we were the ones at fault. If we didn't make another enemy every time we took a dump, it wouldn't be so hard to keep us goddamn safe.

They'd be better off at the top of a high rise. Sure, a sniper could get to them, but it was a lot fucking harder. Here, there were endless yards of perimeter walls to secure, two gardens, a pool area, never mind the driveway which was barricaded like my folks were living in Fort Knox. But Ma refused. She said she liked living in a house.

For Aela, I was contemplating moving into a brownstone I'd bought last year when Finn had brought it to my attention. He knew I liked the Upper East Side, had seen the rundown dump and had figured I might like a change of pace.

That he thought that said I'd been changing for a lot longer than I recognized. For a lot longer than Aela and Seamus had been in my life.

A man had to settle down at some point, I guessed. I was ready for that, but my brain, my *body* wouldn't allow me to do anything of the sort with a woman who wasn't her.

It was why I forgave her so easily.

Why I was willing to move past things, to forget ancient history. I wanted her anyway I could get her, and I knew I wasn't the best deal on the shelves. Not when she was as good a mom as she was.

"I'm going to need your help, Bren," I rasped, as he pulled to a halt beside a massive fountain of a kid pissing into a pool.

"With what?"

"Seamus." I blew out a breath. "He ain't like us."

"Didn't need you to tell me that. I met the kid, you know?"

"Yeah. You did." I cut him a look. "Surprised you guys have been giving me so much slack."

"Not like we had a choice."

"No?" Curiosity had me turning to him.

"Ma told us to back off. Sounds like she and Aela had a little confrontation. Apparently it resonated."

Because I could easily see Aela giving Ma shit, and because I didn't doubt Ma had deserved it if she was laying down the law, I decided not to get in her face over it. Quite clearly, they'd gone against my wishes, but Aela had held her own. If she hadn't, we'd never have had as much peace and quiet as we'd had these last couple of weeks.

Oddly proud of her, and the fact she wasn't scared of my tyrant mother who was wed to a man who made tyranny look friendly, I climbed out of the car with barely a wince as Brennan said, "Don't worry. If he won't let go of the topic, of bringing Seamus into things, then I'll let him in on some news."

I arched a brow. "What news?"

"I'm getting married."

My eyes flared wide. "Who the hell to?"

His lips twitched. "Think I should key the woman in first before I tell you."

"What the fuck, bro? You can't just drop that on me and not expect me to ask questions."

"Got no answers. Not yet. But it'll stall Da for a while."

"Wait, so it's a joke?"

"No. It's not." His smile was grim. "You aren't the only one who has a past, Declan. We all made mistakes. Some are impossible to rectify, but some can be if you just try."

With that cryptic statement, he stormed off, leaving me to stagger toward him down the stone path.

I headed inside, instantly wincing when Ma barreled out of nowhere to hug me. It always astonished me just how strong she was, but I appreciated it. I couldn't deny it. I squeezed her back even though it hurt, and when she peered up at me, concern on her face and relieved tears in her eyes, I couldn't fault her.

Just like Brennan had said, we all made mistakes. Ma's mistake had been to let Da get away with murder. I couldn't hold it against her, not after Da had gone full throttle crazy when she'd been abducted by the fucking Aryans nearly twenty-five years back—the repercussions of which we were still dealing with to this day.

I kissed her temple and murmured, "Good to see you, Ma."

"Even better to see you, son." Anxiety danced in her eyes, and I wondered if she was concerned that I knew about her visit to Aela and apparently stirring shit when I'd asked her to do the opposite, but when I said nothing, she licked her lips and asked, "How's Seamus? Are you ready to bring him to Sunday lunch yet?"

That was four days away. I guessed I had time to prepare my kid, my *atheist* kid who didn't believe in God—a discussion we'd had after watching a show called *Naruto* of all things—to church and then to the family home.

"I'll see what I can do."

Whether I liked it or not, life was starting to butt its head against our doors. Aela and I had lived in a little cocoon. A small bubble that kept the past, present, and future from colliding with us.

Our time had come, however, and while we'd navigated this small storm, I had to wonder if the hurricanes that were a part of this world were something we could survive.

SEVENTEEN

AELA

IT WAS Seamus's first day of school.

The first day where Declan could officially return to work, and that was because he'd had the all clear.

I was nervous for both of them, but nervous mostly for myself.

The all clear, an empty nest, I knew what that meant.

No way was Declan returning to work today. No way. No how.

This was it.

The start of something that had been brewing for decades.

I licked my lips as I dropped a couple of pancakes on Shay's plate. He was wearing a uniform that he'd been bitching about since I'd bought it, which looked like something from a private school in the UK. That place Prince William had attended, with a blazer that came complete with a hat of all things.

I'd admit, not to him of course, that he looked like he belonged in a Charles Dickens' book.

Biting my lip to hold back my smile as I dished out some for Declan too, I caught his eye, saw the gleam of amusement in his gaze and both of us forced our features to freeze because Seamus had more of an ego than he'd like to think he did. He'd get snappy and snippy if we laughed at him, and sure, sometimes he might need that, but on his first day of school? Nope.

That Declan was in agreement boded well for how we meshed together.

I was a 'don't sweat the small stuff' kind of person. Even though I'd been close to him once upon a time, I'd never have thought he was like that too.

It was Friday. Because money talked, we'd managed to get his uniform sorted out by yesterday, and that was why, four days after the tour, he was about to become a Midlands' boy.

Anyone who was anyone knew about the Midlands' reputation. It was going to make his name, cement his ties. It would be better if he'd attended from a younger age, but four years was enough to make a good impression, and he was used to being around new people, used to having to make friends.

He'd do his damnedest to fit in because he had a pet project—world domination—but until that happened, he had to adapt to an antiquated uniform.

I cleared my throat as I served myself too, then drizzled maple syrup over my small stack.

Fiddling with my earrings, I asked, "You sure you're going to be okay driving with Liam?"

Seamus scowled at me. "I'm not four, Mom."

I hated that he was growing up, even if it was just how the world worked. The first day of his Rhode Island school had involved me driving him there, picking him up, and then heading for a snack afterward.

Over the local coffee milkshake, something called a 'coffee cabinet' that I was actually starting to miss, he'd told me about his day, and we'd talked strategy—the kids to avoid, who to befriend.

Maybe it was the Five Pointer in me, but that was how I approached every scenario. Anyone who wasn't in the life had to be viewed clinically until their stance could be judged. Their weaknesses dissected and their strengths calculated.

I'd passed that onto my kid. For his own safety.

We had traitors in the Five Points, not many, but a few—and they never lived long to tell the tale afterward. That was what I'd taught my son. You didn't rat, you didn't let yourself get backed into a corner. You stood strong, stayed close to your friends once you made them, and didn't trust them at first until they proved themselves.

Of course, I'd befriended Caro... so maybe my judgment wasn't up to much?

"I know you're not four," I murmured, as I worried over how well he'd do today... like he was four. "Doesn't mean I don't want to make sure you're okay."

"You'd feel pretty crappy if she didn't give a shit though, wouldn't you?" Declan inserted smoothly, his eyes lifting from his breakfast to glance at Seamus who scowled at him.

"Mom always gives a—"

"Careful," I teased. "Can't be swearing at that fancy ass school."

He heaved a sigh. "Mom always cares."

"Yeah, and aren't you lucky she does?" Declan pointed out, making me smile inwardly.

He was a clever one. I liked that. I liked that he made Seamus see how fortunate he was without me having to do a damn thing. It wasn't that I wanted my kid to be grateful, because ever since he'd hit his teenage years, that was as hard as asking him to find world peace amid the laundry that collected on his bedroom floor.

But it brought perspective, and I was all for that.

I had high hopes for my son. Not because I needed him to be a politician or a lawyer or someone that mattered in the world. But because he wanted that. He was too bright a spark to just waste, and sometimes, when I looked at him, he gave me hope.

The future was dark. When I looked at him? He was a lightbulb that fizzled in and out, giving me a promise that things would get better if there were enough kids out there like him who cared.

"Yeah," Seamus admitted sheepishly. "I'm lucky."

Declan hummed. "My ma didn't ask if I was okay to go to school with my guard."

Shay frowned. "Why didn't she? Didn't she care?"

Lena and Aidan were the strangest parents in the world. Everyone knew how they felt about their sons. They'd kill for them. They'd break bones to make sure they were safe. But that wasn't my idea of love.

"She cared," Declan murmured, "but they wanted me to be strong. They wanted me to be independent."

"Can't exactly be independent at twelve," I interjected softly, knowing that was the age he'd been tossed into the shark pool.

He shrugged. "Nope." His smile was rueful.

Seamus didn't understand the time reference—why would he?

Peering between us, he heaved another sigh. "Okay, Mom, you can take me to school."

I snorted because he sounded so long-suffering that I joked, "Oh, you'll let me grace you with my presence, huh?"

Sure, I wanted to bone his dad like I'd just taken some Viagra, but these days were impossible to replace.

When he grinned at me, the cheeky little monkey, it was like he was five again. "Yep, I'll let you."

But his shoulders weren't hunched, and he wasn't scowling at his breakfast.

I had to sigh.

He'd wanted me to be there. But he thought he was too old for it.

I gulped.

This was down to Declan.

I shot him a grateful look, and his lips quirked at the corner, even as warmth filled his eyes.

Goddamn, he was so getting lucky today. Something he registered, because he gritted his teeth and focused on his breakfast, but not before I saw the banked inferno that flickered between us like someone had just set fire to all the goddamn paper walls in the penthouse.

Of course, two hours later, one kid dropped off at school, and a pussy just *dying* for Dec's dick, I wanted to scream when I walked inside and found the place empty.

What the hell?

Where was he?

I looked in all the rooms, trying to see if I could find him before I gave up, registering that he'd been called into work.

I'd saved the kitchen until last because he wasn't the kind of guy to sit there without someone else in it. The kitchen was his mother's place, so it figured he'd associate that with her, with women, and not necessarily with comfort. Especially if it was empty.

But when I found the box on the table, I frowned at it and wariness hit me. It was regular cardboard.

Faintly beige, faintly brown. The corrugated kind.

I licked my lips, recognizing how messed up it was that I found myself checking the base for fluids...

When I registered it was dry, *bone* dry, I headed toward the table where it was located. Sucking in a breath, I jerked the lid off, almost dreading what I'd find, then I sagged, hands flopping onto the table when I recognized what it was.

A Kevlar vest.

There was a note pinned to it too.

Wear it if you go out. I have one for Seamus as well. They only just arrived.

Da called. I have to go out, but I'll be back before Shay gets home from school.

There's a present for you in my bedroom. I'll give it to you later.

Dec

It was short and sweet, everything he wasn't.

I plucked my bottom lip, wondering what the gift was and why he hadn't left it here now. Better that than thinking of the fact I had an addition to my wardrobe—a bulletproof vest.

Shit like this was a reminder of the anonymity I'd left behind.

The threat was high if they were making the women and kids wear Kevlar, and I was surprised we weren't being shoved into lockdown if that was the case.

I rubbed a hand over my face as I slumped in the chair that I'd taken to sitting in. Funny how routines grew. I sat facing the view, Declan sat to the side, and Seamus faced us both. We took those seats every day, and not one of us had mentioned it before. We just did it.

That was what family did, didn't it?

Like, with couples, one of you just always took the left side of the bed in a motel/hotel. One of you tended to have the remote, and one of you always knew where everything was in the house...

I'd never had that. It just wasn't in me to want much from a guy, not when I knew what the real thing was. So to suddenly be experiencing all this was very strange.

And to be doing so with Declan... well, I couldn't say it made the Kevlar worth it, but neither did it make me want to run for the hills.

I'd missed him.

More than I'd even realized.

Which was dumb, I knew, but I'd been too busy to really think about it. Raising a kid, forming a career, making a name for myself, it took time and energy. That didn't take into account the rather nomadic lifestyle I'd forced on us since Seamus was a toddler.

I didn't like to think back to that point, when my grandfather had tried to shotgun me into marrying a local boy whose boots he'd thought I should lick in gratitude because he was willing to 'take Seamus on'.

I'd had needs. I'd enjoyed the men I'd screwed. But marriage? If that ever happened, it was for Declan.

Beyond stupid, I knew, and even more than that, irrational.

But who said a woman always had to make sense, huh?

I dragged the Kevlar out of the box, stared at the paradox that was the slimline bulkiness, and winced at the weight of it in my arms.

Because this was the first morning I had to myself, where the penthouse was empty, where I had time on my hands, I knew what I was going to do.

Shopping.

I hated it, but when it involved getting art supplies, it gave me a lady boner.

Though I hadn't dressed up for dropping Shay off at school, I'd worn a nice skirt and shirt with no rips and no skin showing. I'd felt like Mrs. Goddamn Brady, but I didn't want him to be ashamed of me, and I knew the blue in my hair would be gone soon because Midland moms wore pearls, and didn't have jewel-colored hair and tattoos.

The tat I couldn't do shit about. The hair was manageable.

Grunting at the thought, I unbuttoned my shirt, dumped it on the table, then reached for the vest.

It was deceptive. Looking at it, I knew Dec had just dropped a fortune on us, which made me feel oddly warm inside. The Kevlar represented so much; his affection, his caring. As much as I hated it after I slipped it on and tied myself in, it made me feel good for that reason alone.

It was custom, I realized, as lightweight as these things could be, and had thin straps, and knowing that I mattered to him enough to go to the time and effort of buying something like that made it more than worth having to wear it.

Redressing in my shirt, I winced as it pulled a little tighter now, and because the bulletproof 'cami' ran so high up the chest, it looked like a bulky undershirt.

Still, there wasn't much I could do.

Dressed appropriately for my current situation, wondering how Dec had managed to get a custom Kevlar vest for me in such a short space of time, I headed on out.

I was about to go shopping *Pretty Woman* style, except I'd be buying things that fed my soul and not the capitalist machine.

And I couldn't fucking wait.

DECLAN

"WHAT DID he want to talk to you about?"

I gave Brennan the side-eye. "Caroline Dunbar."

Bren grunted. "Fucking bitch."

She was that. One hundred percent.

Always in our business, always sniffing around. Didn't stop me from feeling guilty when I thought about why she was on this goddamn crusade of hers.

Bren, like always, was a mind reader. "Not your fault her father was a fucking snitch."

I winced, hating to think back to that night.

I might have been inducted into the life at twelve, but Da had let me wait until I was seventeen to make my first kill. That he'd waited so long and had made me do that when I could be tried as an adult had always been proof of what Jimmy D had snitched over.

I'd never known how bad the dumbfuck's betrayal had been, but that Da got me involved was clue enough.

"Never liked killing," was all I said.

"Think I do?" Brennan arched a brow as he pulled up at a red light.

We were driving back from Da's compound after another impromptu meeting. Last time it had been about Shay, about what role he could play in the Five Points, about Ma wanting to meet him, and Da wanting me to make that happen. As a result of that conversation, we hadn't spoken since, because he wanted me to essentially Shanghai Aela, not take her wishes into consideration at all. What he didn't seem to understand was that they weren't just her wishes.

I loved my parents but they had a way of doing things that was decidedly not of this Millennium, but the last.

Still, when the old man summoned, we drifted to his door, and like he'd thought I might not comply, Brennan had shown up at my penthouse to give me a ride.

Like I couldn't drive my fucking self.

"Why do we put up with this crap?" I muttered. "Dealing with Da, letting him treat us like we're soldiers first, sons second?"

"It's all we know." He twisted his wrist, the one that was weak, that popped with the move. The one he kept on breaking because Da had used that as his 'punishment wrist'.

I'd seen the way Da did that and had learned my lesson. Eoghan had as well.

Brennan had been a lot more of a rebel than he'd ever let on.

He toed the line to a certain extent, that was why news of him getting engaged soon came as a surprise. He tended to do what Da wanted. Not in a way that made me think he was a brown-noser, because if he was that, I wouldn't like him so fucking much.

Brennan had changed for real after Ma had been targeted by our enemies, and ever since, he'd toned things down. Turned a lot more serious.

Couldn't blame him.

"That's no reason to stick with it," I grumbled.

"No. It isn't. But we love the family. We just don't like the life. Even if the life is all we know..." He broke off, his gaze focused on the rearview mirror before he mused, "Anyway, what else would you do with your days?"

"If I wasn't running drugs, stolen cars, and guns, you mean?" I rolled my eyes.

"Yeah," he replied, his tone serious. "What would you do?"

My scowl returned.

I didn't fucking know.

"You're only questioning things because of Seamus, and I get it. I am too. I'm hoping you're going to break the mold with him. Not gonna let Da do his usual shit. He takes over because we let him have too much sway. It's about time we started getting in his face about the stunts he pulls."

"He's only gotten away with it for so long because he's unhinged and we're all half-terrified he's going to kill us. But he's getting older."

"Older doesn't mean weaker," I retorted. "You and I both know he'd shoot us in the head if we didn't, as you said, toe the line."

He shook his head. "No. Haven't you noticed? He's changing."

"He is?" My brow puckered. "Since when?"

"Few years back. They never talk about it, but he's calmed down a lot. Wouldn't be surprised if Ma got him on meds or something. He doesn't have those blackouts like he used to have."

I blew out a breath because he wasn't fucking wrong.

"Jesus," I whispered, "how the fuck did I forget about that?"

"Not like we have time to smell the daisies, bro, is it?" His gaze flickered to the rearview mirror again.

"We got a tail?"

"Yeah." He grunted. "Least it's only the Feds."

"Fucking Dunbar," I groused.

"What did Da have to say about her?"

"He wants Eoghan to take her out."

"She's a nuisance, but she isn't *that* much of a nuisance. Not worth us raising hell with the Feds."

"Why do you think we were arguing?" I countered with a short laugh, watching as he maneuvered onto the highway that would take us to my side of the city without getting stuck in traffic.

Of course, traffic was a way of fucking life for us, but we avoided it where we could.

"Surprised he consulted you," Bren commented, his brows high.

"Yeah, I was too. Think he only did it because he wanted to talk about Shay again."

Brennan cleared his throat. "Don't like to talk about the kid this way, because he's cool, but you know how much leverage he gives you with them, don't you?"

"Yeah." I gritted my teeth. "I do."

"Gonna play that card?"

"If it means keeping him safe, hell fucking yeah."

Brennan flashed a grin. "Good."

His cell went off, making the console flash with Aidan's name.

"Answer call," Brennan rumbled. As it connected, he said, "I'm on speaker with Declan, Aid."

"Nice timing," was Aid's reply.

"Hey, bro."

"Hey, Dec. You doing better?"

"Still aching, but on the mend."

"Good, good. Gonna see you on Sunday?"

I pulled a face. "Yeah. Don't think I can get away with it for another week."

Brennan and Aid snickered, but Bren quickly told him, "We've got friends."

Silence fell at his words, and I knew Aidan was registering what that meant.

"Everything okay?" Brennan continued.

"Yeah. Got great news actually." He cleared his throat. "Managed to get the property in the Bronx secured. The offer was accepted."

My brows rose. "What property?"

"Aid had one of the kids on his crew enlist," Brennan whispered, "with the Italians." Then, to Aidan, he said, "They didn't do much research, did they? You offered under the asking price."

"Because the dumbfucks are desperate for the cash," Aidan retorted. "They're acting like lunatics and need to pad their accounts."

"Well, Don Fieri doesn't have much to live for anymore, does he? Ain't got anyone to pass all the family jewels onto with both his kids dead."

I cut Brennan a look. "Are we getting our friends from school involved in the project? It's a fixer upper, right?" *Did you ask the bikers to get involved?* I asked, referring to the Satan's Sinners' MC we had familial ties as well as business links with. This conversation was going to wear on my last nerve because we'd have to speak in code. If we had a fucking tail, then the car might be bugged too.

"Nah. No need." Brennan shot me a dry smile which told me that was a lie.

If the Sinners dirtied their hands, then I realized the Italians must have hurt one of their women. Shit, I'd missed out on a lot more than I'd thought if that was the case.

"Dec, you need to figure out why. Maybe there's something we can use."

For leverage. "I'll try."

"They're your friends, not mine. I'm glad you'll be catching up with them soon," Brennan groused. *And not me.*

I smirked because Brennan didn't like talking more than ten words to anyone unless they were one of his brothers. "I quite like Nigel. He's like a shark." 'Nigel' was code for Nyx.

Aidan snorted. "Like Da."

"Nah, more rational. Plus, who doesn't like a man who does what he does for fun?"

Aid and Bren grunted their agreement, knowing Nyx's idea of 'fun' was killing kid fuckers before breakfast.

"You won't be hearing much from Nigel anymore. Remember? He's busy now he got that promotion."

"Shit. I forgot. Who is it again?"

"Padraig."

I arched a brow. "Christ. My memory. You tell him we're linked?"

"We had an interesting conversation about family. He seemed to think his mother was some kind of..." He shrugged. "I don't even know. I mean, we all know his ma was a slut, but he was pretty sure his stepfather was gonna throw her out and replace her with a new model."

"He wishes he could," Aidan muttered dryly.

I grimaced, because if I was married to Leanne, I'd want to divorce her as well. Shame we were Catholics...

"Anyway, that's great news about the new house. What's the end goal?"

"Brilliant location to set up shop. Not going to get much out of it at first, not with—"

Brennan slammed on the brakes. But it was too little too late even if his responsiveness probably saved our asses.

We collided with the vehicle in front, their back end buckling like it was made out of glass.

I jerked forward, the seatbelt pulling tight against my belly and chest where the wounds were still sore. But Brennan didn't fare much better. His head bounced off the steering wheel with an audible crack, and he was out like a light.

I hissed out a breath as Aidan snapped, "What the hell was that?"

"Car in front," I rasped, "stepped on the brakes."

"You okay?" he demanded.

I let out another hiss as the vehicle ahead didn't limp along to the side of the road to exchange goddamn insurance providers.

No.

The driver and passenger leaped out with bandannas covering half their fucking faces, Kevlar vests on their torsos, and semi-automatics in their hands.

At that moment, my life flashed before my eyes.

It hadn't done that when I'd been on the *Famiglia* compound, hadn't even when I'd been bleeding out and felt sure that I was looking at a blue-haired angel back in the 'hospital' when I'd seen Aela before I passed out for real.

Now it did.

Now, I was loaded with regrets for what I was going to miss out on.

They wouldn't miss at point-blank range.

It took two seconds for those thoughts to cross my mind, and another second for me to pull out my gun.

I had to act.

Fast.

And three seconds weren't fast enough.

EIGHTEEN

DECLAN

I WASN'T great with a gun. My aim wasn't perfect, even though I visited the shooting range more often than any of my brothers, which they gave me shit for.

I dealt in weapons, but I couldn't shoot half the fuckers.

Now, shit was different.

I had to get this right or Seamus wouldn't have a dad, and Aela?

Christ.

What would happen to her?

Da would pull something. I just knew it. He'd take Seamus away from her, and she'd—

No.

I couldn't fail.

Quickly shooting out the windshield, I managed to get another round off. The shooter on the passenger side went down with a speed that left me wide-eyed, but the other guy, the driver, managed to hit the fender and, worse luck, fucking Brennan. Only in the shoulder, thank God, but that was too much.

The kickback from my gun shouldn't have me shaking like a goddamn kitten, but I was fucking exhausted all of a sudden. Adrenaline was still riding high in my veins, but instead of making me feel like I'd ingested ten million Red Bulls, it just left me feeling woozy.

I got off another shot, watched as it went too low, and cursed because that gave him the opportunity to shoot us. Only, his leg buckled from my bullet and he went down, screaming like a bitch as he collided with the asphalt. Before I could feel even a whisper of relief, flashing lights appeared in the rearview mirror, and two guys in FBI jackets jumped out with weapons in their hands as they scanned the scene.

Aidan hissed, "Dec, what the fuck's going on?"

"They're down," I rasped, my gaze on the agents who were casing the area.

"Thank fuck!"

One of the Feds flashed their weapon at me, but I scowled at him even as I made sure I dropped my gun on my lap and raised my hands high. They moved out to the shooters, one going to check the pulse of the guy I'd taken out, and another going to the fucker rolling around, screaming like I'd shot off his cock.

Goddammit.

Today was not going to end as planned—with me getting my dick wet in the pussy I'd been craving for over fourteen fucking years.

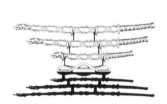

AELA

"*MO GHRÁ.*"

His voice shouldn't make me melt, but it totally did. Combine it with the endearment he'd only ever used with me? Say goodbye to my panties.

"Hey," I greeted, as I stared at New York's answer to my wet dream.

The art supplies store was twice as large as the one I'd used back in Providence, and before he called, I'd been drooling over the array of Winsor & Newton oils. But Declan beat oil paints, acrylics, and even charcoal.

Yeah, that was how hot he was.

"I need to ask a favor."

As I picked up a tube of Winsor Orange, peering at the label before ducking down to see if there was a bigger version since I'd need a lot of it for the painting I had in mind, I asked, "What's that?"

"I could ask anyone to come get me, but I want to see you."

Unease filled me, and I replaced the tube on the shelf, twisting around to look at my paradise to give me a semblance of calm.

It didn't work.

Even surrounded by narrow aisles with tall shelving units loaded down with any and all mediums that my heart desired, concern had me stuttering, "W-Where are you?"

"I'm at Belvedere Central."

My eyes flared wide, but that he was in an actual hospital, as crazy as it seemed, filled me with relief.

I knew the Points only used setups like the one he'd been operated in when the injuries were from illegal activities.

Gulping, I asked, "Why are you there?"

"Because Brennan got shot."

My heart stuttered a little. "Is he okay?"

"Flesh wound, in and out. I promise, he's fine. Wouldn't be asking for you to come collect me if he were badly hit."

The logic had me releasing a shaky breath. "What the hell happened?" I questioned as, with no guilt, I dumped my loaded basket on the ground and hurried out of the store.

When George saw me—he'd stayed outside, guarding the door—his blank expression morphed when our gazes clashed.

His shoulders straightened, and tension filled him as he scanned the area, looking for a threat.

I grabbed his sleeve. "I need to get to Belvedere Central," I told him.

A second later, he had his cell in his hand. "Bring the car around, Jerry. Now. Emergency."

"I'll explain when you get here," Declan murmured in my ear.

"Won't be long. I'm only on 7th Avenue. Just around the corner from Carnegie Hall."

"Ask for the West Magdalena Suite."

"Will do."

Because I kind of wanted to cry, I cut the call instead. The panic inside me was ridiculous, considering he was fine and that Brennan, while injured, had been hit with a clean shot.

Even though George had said the magic word, 'Emergency,' it still surprised me when, barely two minutes later, the SUV was swinging around the corner and the brakes were squealing as Jerry roared toward us.

I didn't need hustling in, but George hustled me anyway, and the second our asses were on our seats, the engine groaned as Jerry made the ten-minute drive in five.

George was out before me, a miracle considering I nearly face-planted in my haste to get out of the vehicle, but he had his hand on the bulge at his shoulder as his head whipped from left to right, making sure there was no active threat against me.

The trouble was, if someone was stupid enough to have tried to take out an O'Donnelly then the trivial turbulence between factions had just morphed into an all-out war.

Aidan Sr. was going to lose his shit over this.

I just knew it.

Terror for Seamus was a solid weight in my stomach, for what this might mean, for what it represented, and I was inordinately glad that he had a guard on him at school. It was a wonder I could get air in and out of my lungs as I ran to the reception and asked for the suite Declan had named.

The instant I uttered 'West Magdalena Suite,' the receptionist's air of boredom disappeared. Her eyes flashed wide and she jolted to a standing position. Immediately keyed into the fact that was the VIP ward, I wasn't surprised when she muttered something to her coworker and beamed a sympathetic smile at me.

"If you'd like to follow me, ma'am?"

I dipped my chin, and with George at my back, strode down the busy corridors to the elevator.

A few minutes later, spat out onto the right floor, I burst into tears when I saw Declan standing there.

I had no idea how he'd known we were coming, unless Jerry had texted him because George was still on edge—had even patted his gun and stepped in front of me when the elevator doors opened so he hadn't been the one who'd messaged Dec. How was unclear, but I didn't give a damn. I was just glad he was waiting for me because I could hurl myself at him and hug him tight.

As scared as I was for my kid, it was way too easy for my 'programming' to kick into high gear. This was what I'd been raised with. This was all I knew.

Men got taken down, men got jailed.

Women sat at their bedside, women watched as their men were locked away.

I didn't like the programming, but it kept me in good stead and would continue to do so, because as much as I hated this, hated what my world was becoming, the second Declan's arms moved around me, I knew where I was supposed to be.

It was the only thing that made sense, even if he was the source of all my confusion and concern. It didn't matter.

My body, heart, soul, and mind were all in agreement.

There was no backing out of this.

No moving away.

No hiding behind walls or ignoring my feelings.

I loved this man.

Enough to endure whatever shitstorm was coming our way. Enough to deal with it and take it on the chin, because life was so fucking short.

Brennan was the one being sewn up today, but Dec had only just gotten out of an IC-goddamn-U. There were no guarantees. No promises.

You had to take what you wanted.

What you needed.

And Aela O'Neill?

She wanted Declan O'Donnelly.

Until death did them part.

NINETEEN

DECLAN

RUBBING the back of my neck with a towel, I headed out into my bedroom and saw Aela lying on the bed. Her feet were crossed at the ankle, her arms were behind her head, and the distinctly masculine pose had me coming to a halt and smirking at her.

"I feel like I'm being sexualized," I teased.

Her nose crinkled. "Objectification is no laughing matter."

"I think I can deal with it, this once at least." I arched a brow. "You okay?"

"I'm worried about the Feds."

"Don't be. They always sniff around us, and if anyone has to worry, it's not us but the *Famiglia*. They were the ones who had Feds as witnesses to their shootout." I had to laugh. "If there could have been a better time for us to be tailed, it was then."

"Is there ever a good time to be tailed?"

"No. Never a good time to be shot at either." I jerked my chin up. "Know what I was thinking when it went down?"

"No. What?" she asked softly, quietly. Her gaze was wary. Uncertain. Totally unlike my Aela.

"You. Seamus. I was thinking about how, when it happened before, my life didn't flash before my eyes, and this time it wasn't my past but a potential future I was missing out on." I sighed. "Messed with me. Made me a better shot, though, so I can't complain."

"A better shot?"

I nodded. "I'm a shit shot," I told her drolly.

"Should get Seamus to help you. He's damn good. Can hit bullseyes from forty yards."

Rolling my eyes, I grumbled, "Of course, he can."

"Hey," she murmured, "I'm not teasing. It would be a good way for you two to get to know each other. To have a thing. You know? If he's teaching you, then he has a position of power over you. Kids like that shit. Makes them feel important."

"He is important."

"I know. He's everything."

I swallowed, because before, I'd have scoffed. Now? She was right.

He *was* everything.

What was the point to anything without thinking of a future with him in it? Without wondering how to make the future brighter *for* him?

It was like my investment before had been solely in the present. Now that I had to think of him, it changed my perspective for the better.

"Okay, I'll take him this week. I'd have him carrying if I could."

She laughed a little. "I'm not sure that fancy pants school would like him armed."

"Probably not."

My grousing had her laughter deepening, then it softened, and she inquired, "You pulled strings to get him in there so late in the term, didn't you?"

I shrugged. "He wanted to go there so go there he will." I tossed my towel back into the bathroom, twisting around to do so. The move pulled muscles I really wished I hadn't pulled and, making sure my grimace was hidden when I faced her, I sighed when I realized she'd seen everything anyway.

She was an artist, for God's sake. A student of the human form and expression. Pulling the wool over her eyes was never going to happen.

"Thank you for doing that," she rasped. "It will make it easier for him to settle down."

I nodded. "I want him to be happy. I know that if he's happy, you will be too, and I want that just as much."

She stared at me for an inordinately long time, like she was trying to judge how truthful I was being. I wasn't sure if her X-Ray vision picked up on anything, but after a little while, she murmured, "I really don't want you to get shot."

I had to laugh. "Well, that's not on my to-do list either."

"Good to know," she sniped, but her eyes narrowed. "In fact, I want it so little that I didn't know—"

When she broke off, I tipped my head to the side. "You didn't know what?"

"It made me realize that nothing has changed for me. Nothing, Declan. It makes me feel like I'm seventeen again, and I'm most definitely not that.

"I always knew the day would come where you'd find me and discover the truth about Seamus. Every day you didn't, every month that passed and year that dwindled away to nothing, I breathed a sigh of relief. Each year with me, away from you and the family, was important. It imprinted *my* values on him. I didn't want to be like Mom, and I would have been if I'd stayed with you.

"I'm not saying you wouldn't have treated me better than Dad, because I think you would have, even if I'd been a lot less independent back then, but I didn't want to be that. And I wanted him to be raised outside of the life.

"Everything I did as a kid was about not showing Dad up, about making sure I hung around only with Points' families. I didn't want that for him."

"You want him to be normal," I murmured softly, and for the life of me, even as she pissed me off, I got it.

How couldn't I?

When I was a kid, growing up, I'd felt like a changeling. Plopped into a macho household where things like the arts were disdained. Da had thought I was gay for half of my childhood, for Christ's sake. That was before I'd even discovered things like the opera and ballet!

My friends all had to be from Points' families too, and within those friends, I was well aware that a lot of the guys wanted to hang around me for who I was. It was well known that the kids you grew up with, who you were close to, would be a part of your crew. They'd grow with you, get promoted to run with you, and that meant knowing if someone liked me for me was impossible.

I'd been held back a year in school simply because I'd been so behind with all the shit Da had shoved on my plate when I was a fucking teenager in an attempt to toughen me up.

Eventually, I'd learned to keep my trap shut. Never to talk about things that mattered to me, because if I did, then he'd think I needed another dose of goddamn tough love.

"You're not mad at me for wanting that, are you?" she whispered softly.

"How can I be when I was raised the way I was?" I scratched my chin. "I'm not saying I like it, and I'm not saying I appreciate you lying to me the way you did, but for his benefit, I understand, and in some ways, I'm grateful. He's a well-rounded kid, Aela. I don't know if he'd have been like that if he'd been raised like us."

"Thank you."

I ducked my head, and muttered, "What were you going to say? Before I interrupted you, I mean."

She blew out a breath. "For as long as I knew you'd find us eventually, I had plans in motion. I knew that if you'd turned into a prick, or, I don't know, if you were going to abuse me for what I did—"

"I'd never do that!"

"I didn't know that. And I'm not sure your da doesn't want to slap me around, Dec."

"Just let him fucking try," I ground out, my fists bunching at the thought. "I'll fucking kill him before I let him take a step toward you in violence."

Her lips curved into a tiny smile. "My hero."

Surprisingly, there was no mockery in her tone.

And it warmed me.

She meant it.

Fuck, it had been a long time since I'd been anyone's hero, and even then, it had been her. Before I'd turned into the villain, before she'd run off and I'd had no choice but to let her flitter away.

She cleared her throat as our eyes caught and held. "I had plans in motion," she repeated. "I knew I might have to get out. And today, everything inside me was screaming danger, danger, that I needed to take Seamus away from this insane life, but the thought of not being with you, Dec, it hurts just as bad as it did when I was a kid."

"I don't want that. I want you. I want this. Us."

My throat felt too thick when I swallowed. "I want that too. You and me. I want that."

She leaned up on her elbow. "I've only ever wanted you, Declan. Even when I ran, I never stopped wanting you."

"Then why did you go?"

"Because you looked at me like you hated me, and—" She blew out a breath. "You looked at me like Dad looks at Mom."

My brows shot up. Whatever I'd expected her to say, it wasn't that. "Your dad hates your mom?"

She shrugged. "He's never there. She's always alone, high on fucking antidepressants or whatever the crap it is she's taking now. He never kisses her, always treats her like crap. She's like his slave. I don't like it, but what can I do? She won't leave him. I asked her to come with me to Ireland," she explained softly, "but she wouldn't."

"It sounds like he's just old-fashioned," I replied sympathetically. "You know what the old guard are like."

"Dicks?" she grumbled, making me laugh.

"Yeah, dicks."

But she shook her head. "I know why he hates her."

"Why?" I asked softly, moving over to her.

It was still fucking hard getting onto the bed, and I felt like I was about ninety, but I managed to do it without plopping down and looking like a fool.

This was the first time she was talking to me about the shit that mattered without me raising the subject. The first time we were in bed together where my dick could get hard without my balls turning blue.

This was relationship stuff.

Not just sex.

More.

Just... *more.*

She watched me, and I loved that she didn't offer to help, just wished she'd look away in case I had to bellyflop onto the sheets... thank fuck I didn't have to.

"My birthday is six months after their wedding anniversary."

I tensed. "Oh."

She bit her lip. "Yeah. So, you know what that means, don't you?"

"She either trapped him, or it was accidental, and he still feels trapped."

"Yeah."

"But you didn't trap me. I remember the day the condom broke like it was yesterday, babe. I would have never blamed you—"

"All I thought was that you hated me, Dec. I thought things had changed because of Deirdre. You'd always been weird with her, and when she died, and it all went south, I just thought you felt guilty and blamed me.

"If I'd told you the truth, what would have happened? I'd have been stuck in a marriage like Mom's. I'd have been tied to you even though you loathed and hated me. Resented me for trapping you, resented me for being the one who was alive when Deirdre was dead."

"You had to know I fucking hated her," I rasped. "She never managed to figure it the fuck out, the dumb bitch, but you weren't her. I felt your eyes on us whenever she touched me."

Pain flashed over her features, pain I regretted causing. Not just then but now. "It seemed that way, but you never left her, did you?" she whispered. "You never made a move to dump her, and you kept me on as your side piece. I know why now, but you never told me back then, and I never expected you to. You're an O'Donnelly. I'm an O'Neill. Never the two shall meet and all that crap. What I was getting from you was more than I'd ever thought I *could* get. At least this way, I had your baby too."

The words weren't ones I'd expected to ever hear from Aela's lips.

"You wanted my kid?" I rumbled, the words low, husky.

She tilted her head and met my eyes. "I did." She licked her lips. "I do."

For whatever fucking reason, my body loved the idea of that more than I could say. My dick pinged to life, and I knew she had to see it through the towel. I felt like I had the leaning tower of goddamn Pisa down there.

Her eyes drifted down my body, and when they stopped at my dick, and her breath hitched, I groaned.

She cut me a look, and whispered, "That for me?"

"Always been for you," I murmured. "Always."

A groan escaped her and her hand went to my waist even as she was moving forward, rolling onto me so she was straddling my calves—the position had my heart speeding up, especially when her hands went to work on the knot, and when she parted the towel and lowered it down, I nearly fucking cried.

Jesus fuck.

It had been too goddamn long since I'd felt her mouth on me, and the sweet perfection of it had my hips bucking. She tongued the tip, smoothing it around the glans before shaping me with her open mouth, rimming her soft lips up and down the column of my shaft. Her tongue fluttered along the vein down the back, and when she reached the base and hummed, I groaned again when she moved up and began to suck me down.

There was no artifice here. No intent to do anything other than taste me. For *her* enjoyment.

She hummed and mumbled as I bucked my hips, but she did it for herself, and somehow that made it even sexier.

When she pulled back, her lips were glossy with saliva, and I groaned at the sight before I watched her purse them and spit dribbled down to coat the tip. I gritted my teeth as she followed the trail, sucking on me like I was a lollipop and she was intent on getting to the bubblegum beneath.

I watched her work, getting off on seeing her intensity, and then she spiced things up a notch by pulling her skirt up and slipping her hand beneath it.

Fuck.

I loved that she got off on this shit. I remembered from before that whenever she went down on me, she'd usually end up fingering herself, which though vanilla as fuck, had to be the hottest shit I'd ever seen, and trust me, when you were an O'Donnelly, most women went above and beyond to stay in our beds.

I'd had all kinds of shit pulled, from kinky to weird, all in an effort to be memorable, and while it had worked, to a certain extent, nothing stuck with me like this.

It was... natural. Because it was *Aela*.

She didn't have to pull out a black rubber dildo that had to be bigger than the Hulk's cock, slide it in her asshole, and then fuck me with it in for it to stick out in my mind.

Nope, she just had to finger herself while she was sucking me because *she* wanted to suck me.

Not to impress me. Not to get me hot.

For herself.

I fucking loved that.

Fuck.

I clenched my eyes closed, grunting as she moaned around my dick as her fingers worked their magic on her, and even though I'd been content to let her suck me, to own it, I couldn't just lie there anymore.

I had to get involved.

Grabbing her hair, I rolled it around my wrist and used it to tilt her head back. She pouted but obeyed, then rasped, "You got a problem?"

"Yeah. Show me your fingers." She bit her lip but obeyed, pulling out her slick digits from under her skirt. "Coat my cock in it," I ordered, watching her with narrowed eyes until she followed my order. As she twirled the tips around my cock, I raised my chin. "Taste it. Just where you touched."

She stuck her tongue out and moved it around in the same pattern as she'd stroked her fingers, and I groaned before I tilted her head back again, and muttered, "Show me your cunt."

A mumble escaped her a scant breath before she ignored my command and sucked me down. From tip to goddamn root.

Well, fuck.

How was I supposed to grumble at that when it felt like fucking heaven?

Arching my hips, I shoved my dick as far into her as I could, loving when she groaned. I just knew her pussy would be even wetter, and as much as I wanted her to carry on sucking me, I wanted inside that little cunt more than I knew how to handle.

Hissing when she swallowed me down, sucking and choking me with the tight clasp, I grabbed her hair and whispered, "You asking for that ass of yours to be spanked?"

Her head bobbed down, and my eyes felt like they were rolling back in my head.

My threat of punishments was only getting her wetter, and that wetness was nowhere near where I needed it.

Fuck. Talk about a Catch-22.

Deciding that she was going to do what she was going to do, and apparently I didn't have a goddamn say in it, *this time,* I sank back against the sheets and watched her. But it didn't sit well with me.

I'd watched a lap dancer.

I'd observed an old mistress doing this shit, uncaring if she got hers, not even really touching her after she got me off.

Aela was not those women.

She was mine.

Had been since I'd claimed that cunt as my own.

Because I needed her to know that, I growled, "That little cunt sopping wet for me?"

She swallowed.

"I bet it is. Bet it's so fucking wet, it's drenching your skirt."

She moaned.

"Bet it's so goddamn empty, just waiting for this cock to fill it."

She sighed.

"Why don't you show me it, baby? Huh?" I thrust my hips up. "Why don't you show me that glorious little pussy that's always been mine?"

That had her slowing down, and when she peered at me under her lashes, I knew she liked that.

Fuck, I knew she liked everything I had to say, but that one in particular...

"Show me what belongs to me," I ordered, and like I'd told a genie my wish, she obeyed.

She sat up on her knees and slowly lifted her skirt, raising it higher and higher, revealing her thick thighs and a pussy with that landing strip my dick was just ready to come on.

"Spread your thighs so I can see."

Once more, she did as she was told. But she was watchful, taking me in, observing and listening as her tits strained against the confines of the vest with every shaky breath she sucked in and out.

I looked at that juicy pussy, the glorious slickness that made my mouth water, that I'd tasted several times since she'd come back to me, but I'd never get sick of looking at it, fucking it, sucking on it.

I growled under my breath at the thought and, grabbing my dick, demanded, "Come over here, princess. I need to fill you all the way up."

Though she gulped, she drifted forward on her knees, not making a move to strip. I wanted her like this for our first time. Not skin to skin, but with me naked, bare, and her covered. I wanted her to feel the power exchange here.

She could be fully dressed or bare-assed naked, and I'd still have command over her body.

Because it was mine.

Just like my scarred and fucked up one was hers.

I twisted slightly to stack up some pillows behind me and, once again, my torso protested the move thanks to my recent injuries even though our doc had cleared me for regular activities, but there was no way in hell my mind was focused on anything other than my dick and getting it inside her.

When I sank back, her gaze was glued to my cock, and when she grabbed it, held it firmly in her fist and cocked her leg over me at the same time as she sank down onto it, I hissed as finally, fucking finally, I found my way back home.

Blowing out a breath as she slipped down on me, her features tightening and releasing in a way that told me she hadn't fucked someone in a long while—a thought that pleased me even if she should never have known any other cock but mine—I waited with bated breath for her to settle on top of my lap.

Each cosseting inch of that delicious cunt surrounded me like wet silk, and the pressure of that vise-like grip was beyond paradise.

I reached out, one hand coming to her hip, the other slipping between her thighs so I could rub her clit. She moaned and I felt the slight give in her cunt as she relaxed some, and when she kind of slumped on me, I figured I'd hit the right spot because her pussy was tighter than ever, but she was a shivering mass of sexy goo on top of me.

Groaning when she bit her lip, her eyes colliding with mine in a way that made me wonder if she could see into my fucking soul, she murmured, "This dick is mine."

My top lip quirked up in a smirk. "This cunt is mine."

She dipped her chin. "Just so we know how this shit works."

I narrowed my eyes on her. "The second I saw you again, it was like time had rewound itself." I tapped her clit. "Should never have belonged to anyone else."

That had her gulping, and I knew the words resonated with her because she grunted then rewarded me by sitting up and slowly taking me again. A shuddery breath escaped her before she moaned and started up once more. Her hips began to writhe and wriggle from side to side in looping circles like she was belly dancing, and fuck if it didn't feel like magic.

As she moved over me like a pro, I rubbed her clit, and her mewls and moans, and the squeezing of those tiny muscles had me barely holding back from busting my nut.

I needed her to get hers first before I blew my wad, and I said that fully aware of what I was doing.

I figured she did too.

No condom.

A part of me hoped she didn't have an IUD in, but I figured she was too smart not to have one... more's the pity.

As I slipped my fingers through her juicy folds, I watched as she started to pant. Her cheeks flushed, color blooming over them and along her chest, and suddenly, I realized something.

She was still wearing her Kevlar vest.

The notion blew my brains out.

Unable to stop myself, I let go of her, and though she complained, I grabbed the hem of her shirt and tugged it open, uncaring that the buttons pinged to the ground in discontent.

When I shaped my slick fingers over the vest, I eyed it and her tits. They were firmly held in place by the sheath, but they were generous enough that the jiggle was real.

I started working on the straps, wanting to see her tits, but I barely had a minute to enjoy the view or to feel it, because when I flung the vest onto the ground, reached up and cupped the bounty of flesh before squeezing the nipples with my fingertips, she exploded around me.

And she was loud.

Beautifully, gloriously loud.

Her head tipped back as she screamed out her joy, and I was almost disappointed that I owned the whole floor because I'd have liked my neighbors to have heard that.

The sound was enough to take me to the brink.

The way her pussy did the fucking tango around my shaft?

There was no way I was going to be able to hold back.

When I came, I filled her to bursting as I grabbed her hips and ground her down onto me as I used brute strength to urge her into maintaining that pace. She clutched at me and clung, her body taking everything I had to give and more, until there was no delineating line between her and me.

We were just *us*.

Which made me hiss out her name before I hauled her down against me and hugged her tight to my chest.

This woman was mine.

She belonged to me.

I owned her.

But fuck if she didn't own me too.

TWENTY

AELA

THOUGH I'D BITCHED about our first fuck not having an audience of three glorious, stolen paintings, I was in a much better mood after I came.

Which was only natural.

And today was the kind of day where you needed the extra help of a bunch of endorphins and hormones, because my kid's uncle had been shot, my childhood sweetheart had to kill a man and lame another, the Feds had been at the hospital and were sniffing around Declan and Brennan for interviews, which could easily turn into something more if they decided Declan's offense wasn't self-defense, and...

Well, yeah.

It had been a long day.

Still, Declan had given me two gifts today—I was coming to see that was his style. Never just one present, but always two. An orgasm because I refused to accept the Kevlar vest as a gift, and a pair of tiny jade earrings, which were so pretty I'd removed a set of my faves and slipped in the small cabochons. Which, knowing Dec and his fetish, had probably belonged to some ancient empress or something.

Fuck, if that didn't just get me wet again...

After a day like today, however, the last thing I'd anticipated was having Conor show up at six and declare, "I'm hungry."

I blinked at the sight of his face in the intercom and arched a brow. "So? Go to a restaurant."

"But I'm here." He beamed at me. "I brought cannoli."

"Where the hell did you get cannoli?" Declan demanded, appearing behind me. One hand moved to my shoulder, the other to my waist in a move that was distinctly proprietary, and that had me feeling the heat of him along my back.

It reminded me of earlier, reminded me of how perfect that had been.

Sure, three glorious works of art hadn't watched me get off, but there was always tonight. And tomorrow.

I sighed at the thought before I tuned in as Conor muttered, "Well, I wanted 'em."

"You mean you went onto *Famiglia* turf for *dessert*?" Declan queried, his tone suggesting Conor had gone around the bend.

I couldn't blame him.

"No, there are other places that make cannoli that aren't on their territory," he said with a huff.

"Not many, and not between my building and yours," he hissed. "Goddammit, Kid. Get your ass up here. We need to have words."

Conor rolled his eyes. "I can hardly wait." Then, he shot me a cheeky smile. "I'm excited about dinner though, Aela. Thank you for inviting me."

Before I could tell him I hadn't invited him to anything, he was already in the elevator and heading up to the penthouse.

I twisted around to glower up at Dec, who pulled a face. "I can order in."

Grunting under my breath, I trudged away from him. It wasn't that I didn't like Conor, I just wasn't in the mood for being around Declan's family. When they were involved, shit hit the fan, and we'd already been splattered in enough of the brown stuff for one day.

When I made my way into the kitchen, I saw Seamus was still sitting there.

At the same time as we'd bought his uniform, we'd grabbed him a desk and a chair for studying. While he had a perfectly fine computer, Dec had also bought him an iMac, which had arrived yesterday along with his uniform.

How they pulled the moves they did, I'd never know.

So, with his room furnished for the most part, and until we really settled in and started changing things up which we'd have to do because I couldn't live with paper screens for walls forever, *or* alternatively, move, I'd anticipated him to be glued to his bedroom.

But he wasn't.

He was here. At the kitchen table, studying.

It made me happy to see though, so I didn't comment on it. If I did, he'd probably stop doing it.

Damn teenagers.

Without saying a word because he was typing away on his laptop, and I didn't want to disturb him, I headed for the fridge, peered inside, and decided there wasn't enough to feed an extra mouth. Nor could I be bothered with dealing with the dishes, so I grabbed my phone and started scrolling through the options.

"Want Korean tonight, Shay?" I asked when he'd stopped typing.

He hummed. "No. Pho?"

I hummed back as I sank into my seat and made my selection. When I heard mumbling in the hall, I decided Conor had arrived and Declan was telling him why entering another territory for dessert when the Five Points was at war was a bad idea.

Cue eye roll.

Like he needed to be told.

Conor was one of the smartest bastards I knew. Whatever he did, he did it for a reason, which told me if he'd been on Italian turf, then it was for a purpose.

Though I was curious, curiosity wasn't something that could be nurtured in the life. I'd never get any answers to the ins and outs of their business, and to be frank, I didn't want to know either.

Mostly, I just wanted to make sure that we were all safe.

That was the extent of the shit I needed to know.

As the guys walked in, Declan heading over to the fridge to grab some drinks, I presumed, I asked, "I'm ordering pho for Shay and me. Want some? Or do you want something else?"

"Pho?" Conor echoed, nose crinkled.

My lips twitched. "Yeah. Pho. You still only eating Irish, boys? There's far more to this world than just stew and potatoes."

Declan caught my eye over Seamus's head, and though he didn't have to say a word, I felt his heat, his intensity in that narrow-eyed stare as he silently told me *eating Irish* was the best and *only* dish on his personal menu.

Sigh.

I couldn't wait for him to go down on me again.

"Be still my heart," Conor was teasing, drawing me from thoughts of oral sex and my man. For shame. "You mean there are more staples out there?"

His gasp had me laughing even though Dec had just reduced me to a melting hot pot of hormones. "Shock shock, horror horror, no?"

His eyes were twinkling, but he grumbled, "I wanted a home-cooked meal."

"If you wanted that, then you should have probably stayed at home," Shay retorted, making me laugh. "That's where you tend to find that kind of thing."

Conor groused, "Hey, I thought we had an understanding. I'm the cool uncle. That means you have to be nice to me."

Shay snorted. "Yeah, that might have worked when I was five."

"How old are you now?"

"Not five."

I laughed at my kid's dry rejoinder, and with a patience that was earned by Shay giving his uncle crap, I queried, "What do you want to eat, Conor?"

"Why are you even here?" Declan groused. "You have plenty of food at home."

Before he could grumble much further, the buzzer rang. He looked at me, and I looked at him and shrugged. "I don't know who it is. Not like I know anyone here anymore."

Well, I did, but I highly doubted Mom would feel comfortable coming to an O'Donnelly's penthouse. Even if her daughter and grandson were living in it.

He heaved an impatient sigh, which amused me as my patience was increasing as his decreased, and he stormed off.

"Fuck's sake," I heard a couple of minutes later, before he returned and said, "Brennan's here."

I shrugged. "He should be actually. It should be a rule. You can't eat dinner alone if you've been shot."

Shay bit his lip at that, and while I knew I shouldn't be joking about it, I had to.

People did things like that in this world. They got shot, had the shit kicked out of them, and came back with black eyes and stab wounds.

It was violent.

It was dark.

It was grimy.

He needed to get used to that. Even if I wished I could keep him squeaky clean for an eternity, it just wasn't possible.

Conor arched a brow at my levity, but commented, "I didn't think you'd have told him."

"Like he said, he isn't five," I said softly, sharing a gentle smile with my son.

Clapping him on the back, Conor remarked, "Don't worry. Dec was telling me in the car the other day that you want to be a lawyer. If you work behind a desk like me, you don't get shot."

Declan called out, "Bull."

Conor's nose wrinkled. "That was a mistake."

"Almost shot himself in the foot," Declan shared dryly, as he grabbed his beer and tossed it back, taking a deep gulp.

Shay's eyes flared, but he twisted to face Conor, his curiosity clear. "You shot yourself in the foot?"

"Now, Seamus, the key to being a lawyer is getting the facts straight then twisting them," Conor chided. "The key word there is *almost*. I missed by a whole eight inches."

Declan smirked, then peered out into the hall which clued me in to the fact that the elevator doors had whirred open.

When he dangled a beer in the doorway, a hand grabbed it, and Brennan took a deep pull before sighing. "Damn, I needed that."

Seamus frowned. "Are you supposed to drink when you've just been shot?"

"Or cracked your head on the steering wheel?" Conor grumbled, his tone disapproving.

"No better time *to* drink," Brennan replied with a wince as he moved deeper into the room and slumped at the table. "Christ, what a day."

That about summed it up.

"Shouldn't you be in the hospital?"

Brennan shook his head, but his lips twitched at the unease in Seamus's voice. "No, it was only a flesh wound."

That had me arching a brow because I knew the bullet had gone through his arm. He had a flesh tunnel—bicep style.

Still, who was I to argue? They were probably used to being human sieves.

"I'm ordering in because I refuse to cook for you all," I interjected, before Seamus could get into a discussion about only God knew what. There were hospitals, guns, shootouts, and mafia wars on the table, and I'd prefer for there to be actual dishes of food.

Suddenly, I was ravenous.

And after the way I'd spent most of my afternoon, it was an honest hunger, that was for certain.

Brennan's eyes lit up. "What are you ordering?"

"Pho."

He snorted. "You'll never get Conor to eat that."

"It's good," Seamus protested.

"Hates anything with much flavor," Brennan said wryly. "I'll have it though."

I dipped my chin when he gave me his preferences, and I looked at Declan who shrugged. "I'd prefer a steak."

"Oh, I can deal with that," Conor chirped.

Rolling my eyes, I ordered the pho for the three of us, then set up another order with another restaurant that I remembered was popular with the Five Points' members for the steaks.

The fifty minutes passed swiftly, but the rest of the evening blurred too.

I had to admit, I'd never thought I'd ever be close to Declan's family, because why would I? I was a gofer's kid. I never should have mixed with the lofty upper ranks of the Five Points, but they were around my table, eating and drinking, laughing and joking, making my kid one of them.

Seamus lit up around his uncles, and I knew, then and there, that he'd been missing this. Even without knowing what he'd been missing, it was this.

Male company. Family.

It had always been just the two of us against the world. That was changing, morphing, and even though not all of those changes were good, even though there was danger here, even though... even though... even though...

It was all a 'what-if?', wasn't it?

But seeing him laugh, knowing he was with people who instinctively accepted him because he was blood, it filled me with warmth. There was a promise of family here. Sure, his grandparents, on both sides, were a disappointment, but his uncles would more than make up for that.

I'd seen it before, but tonight just reaffirmed it.

Seamus was safe with his uncles, he had a family, he had a wider reaching support system, and I couldn't be anything other than joyful about that.

TWENTY-ONE

AELA

I GRIMACED THROUGH ANOTHER HYMN, trying to remember how long this would go on for.

The last time I'd been in St. Patrick's Catholic Church was Deirdre's funeral, so the memories weren't great. That wasn't my last time in church, more's the pity. My grandparents had insisted on it when I lived with them. So it had been at least a decade since I'd attended a Sunday service, and in my opinion, a decade wasn't long enough.

Seamus was in total agreement.

I'd managed to get him here on two conditions.

One, he could mess around on his phone throughout the sermon. Thank God Conor sat beside us. He looked as bored as Seamus and me, and together, the two were splitting a pair of AirPods and watching what looked to be some guy making mozzarella from scratch. Go figure.

Two, he was 'owed' a day. That meant we'd go wherever he wanted, eat whatever he wanted, and do whatever he wanted.

I was actually looking forward to that part because he wanted to go to Coney Island, and it had been a lifetime since I'd been there. I knew it would be a blast.

Mostly, I was touched he wanted to go with me at all. I figured that would be something he'd do with friends from school when he stopped psychoanalyzing them long enough for them to become friends, of course.

Barely refraining from yawning, and contemplating buying myself a set of AirPods to get through the sermon from the ever difficult Father Doyle—

a man who astonished me by still breathing, because he'd been ancient when I was a kid—I put some of my weight onto Declan and tried not to tip my head onto his shoulder.

If I could have napped, I would have.

Man, if this wasn't an order from up high—and no, I wasn't talking from God—I'd have cut and run from today, but we were heading straight from here to the O'Donnelly's house, and the kid inside me who'd been blushing and enamored of their power still found it hard to wrap her head around the fact she would be breaking bread with the rulers of our little kingdom.

I wished we could have gone straight there. I'd actually murder a Sunday roast, because I hadn't had one in years, and from how Conor had waxed poetical about his mother's cooking, I knew I was in for a treat.

Deciding to rest my eyes for a while, I thought about last night and the night before.

I was still sneaking out of his bed to get back into my room for Seamus's sake, but damn, the man had learned some moves since I'd been gone.

I couldn't even find it in me to be jealous, not when I thought about what he could do with his dick now.

Sheesh.

Just the thought started to get me a little horny, which was gross in church. Hell, even I had standards.

Before I could think about how perfectly his cock filled me, all around us, people started to move. I opened my eyes, widened them a few times to wake them up and make sure I didn't look like I'd been sleeping, and watched as the rows in front filed out.

I knew, point blank, this had to be one of the busiest parishes in the city. Simply because of Aidan Sr. It was a part of the life to come here every Sunday, whether you were a believer or not. He didn't care. His men had to go to confession too, because that was as integral as having loose morals where crime was concerned.

The hypocrisy never failed to amuse me.

But, as a result, the pews were full. Every single one of them. From left to right. Jam-packed like sardines in a can. Even the two naves were. I was pretty sure it was a damn fire hazard!

It helped that Aidan Sr. had his guys on a short leash. The first row filed out, followed by the second and so on. It was anal enough that the pews themselves walked out from left to right like it was some kind of simple dance.

Because we were in the second row, I nudged Seamus with my elbow, and taking the hint, he quickly turned off his video and muttered, "I'll send you the link later, Uncle Conor."

I smiled at that, not just at the fact he'd called him 'Uncle,' but that Uncle Conor wanted to finish watching the mozzarella video.

It fit that the two of them got on well considering Conor was an over-sized kid and Seamus was an undersized adult.

Shay managed to tuck his phone into his pocket just in time for us to leave the pew. My ass was numb, and it was fucking freezing in St. Patrick's as we moved down the aisle.

I kept my gaze locked and loaded on the back of Declan's head, well aware that the masses would be watching Shay and me as we exited the church. With no desire to catch my parents' eye either, I had no doubt that the women of the Five Points, and the Old Wives' Club—the wives of fallen Pointers—would be chatting up a storm about me. It was a wonder my ears weren't burning already, because I had to reason that they'd be calling me all kinds of crap behind my back.

It took a while, because Father Doyle stood and said farewell to every parishioner. At least, he did to the ones in the front pews which seated the most powerful members of the mob.

When it was our turn, he turned his focus on me and reached for my hands, sighing. "Aela O'Neill, how long it's been since last we met."

There was no point in pulling my hands away, even though I didn't like the old bastard. There'd never been any funny business with him, but he was quick with a ruler to the palm if you didn't obey fast enough in Sunday School.

Bastard.

In my mind, I told him it hadn't been long enough 'since last we met,' but I just shot him a pained smile. "No, quite a long time, Father."

He cut a glance at Seamus. "An unwed mother—Declan..." He tutted. "It's a sin, child. I hope you'll be rectifying that soon enough. We don't want the wee lad to be feeling his illegitimacy now, do we?"

I narrowed my eyes on him. "It's 2020, Father. I don't think anyone even notices—"

Doyle raised a hand, which immediately pissed me off because he expected me to obey, and with Aidan Sr. hovering about, I knew I had to. Goddammit. "The Father sees all. Knows all, Aela. He's well aware that you acted in a slatternly manner, and when I see you next in confession, we'll be sure to discuss how you can atone for your sins."

My jaw clenched, especially because this was not a conversation I wanted to be having in front of my kid. Not only that, I knew the people behind me could hear. Sure, that was mostly Declan's brothers and his family, but the family would be the ones who agreed with Doyle!

"I won't be attending communion, Father."

He blinked at me, and the man's arrogance, as well as a position that was reaffirmed by Aidan Sr., not the Father himself, had him braying with laughter. "I shouldn't laugh, child, I shouldn't, but that was mighty amusing. I didn't realize you were such a funny lass."

"I'm not joking," I murmured, and I felt Declan tense up at my side.

I didn't shoot him a look because I didn't need his backup to stand tall and proud.

I'd deal with this farce of a service once a week, but I wouldn't be laying myself prostate in front of Doyle or anyone, and I had a voice in my head that would let me tell the dick that.

"You have to be joking," Doyle sputtered. "Once a week. That's the rule."

"Maybe in your world, but not mine."

Declan cleared his throat, but he surprised me by not saying a word.

I'd almost expected him to pacify Doyle, and the way he kept looking at my man told me Doyle expected it too. But he didn't. He stood tall, shuffled every now and then from foot to foot, but otherwise, he let me have my voice.

I wasn't sure there was anything else he could have done that would have made me so damn happy.

He wasn't cowed, wasn't scared of the consequences. No, he just knew I could handle it. He was there with Kevlar vests and guards when danger came, but Doyle was just a snippy old bastard who needed to meet his Maker to get a life.

"We must discuss this some other time," Doyle rumbled, his gaze dancing between the three of us. "This is most concerning, Aela. I'm truly worried for your immortal soul."

"I wouldn't bother, Father, it's been a lost cause for nearly a decade and a half."

"It's never too late to beg for forgiveness. To seek redemption."

I shrugged, but before I could gripe at him, Aidan Sr. called out, "What's the holdup?"

Doyle's eyes flashed with concern before he nodded at us all, his features one big pucker of discombobulation, and we strolled away.

Seamus, the second Conor was dealing with Doyle, muttered, "What a jerk."

My lips twitched. "Yeah. He hasn't changed much. How does he sound more Irish now than he did when I was a kid?"

"A miracle," Declan said glumly. "It's the only thing about him that *has* changed."

I knew why he was glum too.

"He'll tell your father."

"Of course he will."

Seamus peered over at us. "He can't make us go, can he, Mom?"

I shrugged. "Your grandfather likes to get his own way," was all I said.

"Then he needs to learn he can't always." His brow furrowed. "Isn't that something you learn as a kid?"

"It is, but I think your great-grandmother skipped that lesson."

"Or four," Declan muttered, scrubbing a hand over his face.

And again, he endeared me to him more than he could ever know by not trying to sway me into agreeing with him.

He didn't say a goddamn word, just looked miserable at the prospect of the conversation that was in all our futures. I couldn't say I blamed him.

The last couple times I'd met Aidan Sr. were a couple too many.

As we headed over to Dec's SUV, a shiny Porsche that gleamed in the sunlight, George straightened up. He'd stayed outside to watch over the vehicles. Either this was new, something the upper ranks necessitated, or it was because of the war.

It pissed me off that I knew why too.

Not because they thought some punk kids were going to take off with one of the classic sports cars here, but because they were making sure that no other faction could plant a car bomb while they were otherwise engaged.

That was the lofty world I lived in now.

When I climbed into the SUV after Dec opened the door for me, I watched as he rounded the fender at the same time as Seamus leaped in behind me.

He was relatively quiet as Declan got behind the wheel and started the ignition, but he'd been quiet since Conor and Brennan had come around for dinner.

Used to his moods, I left him in peace, and Declan was relatively quiet, too, on the drive out of the center of Hell's Kitchen and toward the highway that would take us off Manhattan and lead us into the city itself.

Was I surprised the leaders no longer lived in the epicenter of their territory?

Sure, but I got it. They weren't exactly figureheads. Anyone who was anyone knew to fear where angels wouldn't tread where Aidan Sr. was concerned, and he was probably as much of a prime target now as he'd ever been.

I turned to watch the scenery go by. Expensive stores, landmarks that I'd visited a time or ten in my years here, the busy roads that were crammed with cars even on a Sunday. We passed fancy restaurants and skyscrapers that were engineering feats.

The energy here, the vibe, was something that couldn't be replicated, and I had to admit it was inspiring as hell. I hadn't anticipated that, but I considered it a boon, especially with all the external crap I was having to deal with. My muse should have left the building, but instead she was here, alive and kicking, and loving the chaos into which we'd fallen.

I was having a hard time settling down on my next project, that was how heavy the barricade of inspiration was, but I'd know, when the time came, what I needed to do.

"You doing okay, Mom?"

My brows rose at the question, but I turned around to look at Shay. "Takes more than a crotchety old priest to get under my skin, butt face." When I let my gaze drift over him, his sheepish grin revealed a multitude of things. Most of them being that he was nervous.

Not that I could blame him.

I'd tried to keep this Sunday ritual low angst, teasing him as I bribed him to come to church, stuff like that. But it had to be intense. He was about to meet a set of grandparents for the first time ever. They might love him, they might loathe him—he didn't know, did he?

I mean, *I did.* I knew. He could be a little bastard and the O'Donnellys would still bring him into the fold. That was how they worked.

I actually kind of liked that about them.

Family went deeper than personality.

It was bone deep, *blood* deep. You could be a prick as a person, could be going through a rough patch that made you a pain in the ass, and you'd never stop being blood.

Every time I met them, that was rammed home to me.

"I didn't like what he was calling you," Shay admitted, and he shot his father a glare under his lashes. "I should have said something."

I knew what he was getting at, but I twisted it around and asked, "Why should you? I said it all, didn't I?"

"You should have had backup," he argued stubbornly. Another glower aimed at his father making an appearance.

"I have a mouth in my head, don't I?" I winked at him. "If I'd needed your father's or your help, kiddo, I'd have asked for it. I knew exactly how

Doyle was going to be. He's old school. He's Old Testament. How you were born might not be the way his church likes it, but I stopped giving a damn about those ways when I was seventeen."

Shay's brows rose. "Then why are we going to church if you don't care about it anymore?"

"Because it's important to your grandfather."

Shay's frown lightened some, and he tipped up his chin. "Oh."

I reached between the seat, loving that he held out his hand to grab mine. "I love that you wanted to defend me, but don't forget I kick butt too. Who's the one who put that bitch at the PTA meeting in her place last year, huh?"

His eyes lit up before he burst out laughing. "That was hilarious! Oh man, you really shut her up."

When Declan started chuckling, I wasn't surprised. Shay had an infectious laugh. "What happened?" he inquired, snickering all the while.

I wafted a hand. "We were arguing about the homecoming dance, of all things—"

"Wait, you were on the actual PTA?"

His surprise had me grumbling, "I like to pay it forward, and I wanna know what's going on wherever Shay is. I don't think Midlands will let me in unless I let my blue hair fade out, though."

At that, Shay groused, "I like it blue, Mom."

"Thanks, baby," I replied with a grin. "But future presidential candidates' moms can't have blue hair and more than one piercing in their ears."

Eyes twinkling, he said, "Well, I'm not that yet. Enjoy yourself while you can before you have to behave."

That had me snickering too. "You're all heart, kid." I loved the sparkle in his gaze, it filled me with warmth to know that he was less anxious and that was something I'd helped ease. "Anyway, the homecoming dance. Yeah. So she wanted to bring in like a pony and a magician act, and all this stuff, and I was like, 'It isn't a five-year-old's birthday party.' She got in my face, threw some water at me, screamed at me a little, and I just said, 'No wonder you wanted it for that age group, seeing as you're acting like a five-year-old right now.' She was wicked pissed."

"It was hilarious. I wasn't supposed to be there, but Caro couldn't babysit. Mrs. Jayden turned bright pink and stormed out."

"Queen of the one liners. That's me," I joked. "And in that old school, they were all swanky and snippy. Being likened to a kindergartener hit her straight in the ego."

"They'll probably be even worse at Midlands," Declan pointed out, but he was smiling.

"Yeah. Probably. You're going to be rubbing shoulders with senators' grandkids, Shay, seeing as the country's run by a bunch of old, white dudes."

Dec rolled his eyes. "Still fighting the establishment, I take it."

I rolled my eyes right damn back. "It's what I do."

"Your mother was a lot more idealistic back when I knew her, Shay," Declan told him, and when I cast my kid a glance, any unease had faded away. It was almost charming to see him eat up the words, like he wanted to know what I'd been like. It hit me then that he'd only ever gotten a pretty one-sided view of me. "She wanted to change the world."

"I wanted to go into the Peace Corps," I agreed, and I smiled at Shay. "But you changed all that, so I decided to make money instead." Tongue-in-cheek, I winked at him. "And because we live in a capitalist sinkhole, the more money I made, the more of a platform I had, and the more I could shine a light on the shit that goes down everywhere."

"Rebel, rebel," Declan teased under his breath.

"Still my favorite Bowie song," I teased back, loving his grin.

"Did you know that every piece of Mom's art has a message?"

Declan shrugged. "I didn't, but I can see why. My favorite is *Rats at Dawn*. Charming name there, by the way, honey."

Butterflies spilled through me. "You have a favorite?"

He gave me the side-eye. "You know I appreciate art."

"The classics. Not modern art."

"Everything in its proper place." He cleared his throat. "A few years ago, I found out about you. Did some research. You have good techniques."

He'd known about me for a couple of years but hadn't stormed into my life?

I wasn't sure how I felt about that, wasn't sure if my perceptions were skewed because he liked *Rats at Dawn*. Despite the less than charming name, it was an oil painting I was particularly proud of.

I'd been in London at the time, and we'd been staying in Canary Wharf, one of the financial hubs in the capital. I'd taken to waking up at dawn and drinking coffee on the banks of the Thames while watching the city wake up as I froze my ass off.

I'd watched joggers return from their morning run head inside, get changed into slick suits, and return with expensive cases in their hands. They were the banker wankers that were so often vilified, so I'd done a little more vilifying.

A rat morphed into a jogger morphed into a city fat cat.

That collection had all been around an animal. And not always the pretty ones either. There was a kraken amid that set too.

My muse was weird. The public? Weirder still. *Rats at Dawn* had sold for a million at auction last year.

Realizing that I'd fallen silent when I wanted to keep Shay's mind off things, I muttered, "I'm glad you liked it."

"*Rats* was my favorite. Remember that time in London where we—"

As Shay reminisced, I let him, chiming in here and there with things to make him laugh. But my brain was whirring. Not only had he seen my art, known who I was for a couple of years, Dec had a favorite. Thought I had 'good techniques'.

I hated that I was nervous. Hated that he'd turned me into a goddamn fifteen-year-old again when I was about to go to his house, meet his family for the first time in a proper setting.

Never in a million lightyears would I have expected to ever be rolling up to the O'Donnelly home for Sunday lunch, but that was how surreal my life was now—as surreal as my art.

It took a while because they lived off the beaten path, closer to upstate than the city, and it made me empathize with Declan because I knew he had to visit often and it was a bitch of a drive, but the house itself was beautiful.

A one-story building that was too short for two floors, but too tall for just the one, which I figured meant the sprawling home had super high ceilings. From the road, it was like the place was a high-security prison. The walls were tall, glass glinted on the ramparts, barbed wire glittered in the sun, and cameras twisted here and there as the car drove to the driveway.

There was a guard station, signage for several alarm companies, and to get through the gate, Declan had to roll to a halt, open his window, and salute the guy sitting in the booth.

As we drove inside, the prison vibe disappeared to be replaced with a beautifully landscaped garden that paved the way to a house that belonged in Hollywood.

It was light and breezy, lots of windows, lots of French doors that led to a terrace that ran along the side of the property. In the distance, I could see the gleam of a pool and a lot of seating areas.

"You grew up here?" Shay asked Declan, and I could sense his eagerness to know more. To learn about his dad.

"No," Declan replied. "They moved here a few years ago."

Didn't take a genius to figure out why.

Security threat.

Christ, I'd barely been back a month and I'd heard that so many fucking times.

"Where did you live when you were a kid?"

"In Hell's Kitchen. When I was really young, we lived in an apartment."

That had my brows surging high because I hadn't known that.

His hand drifted over to me, and for the first time, I wondered at *his* state of mind because he never touched me in front of Seamus, something I really appreciated, but his hand settled on my leg. His palm wasn't dry. Not exactly sweaty, but I just got the feeling he was nervous.

The notion soothed me because it made my own agitation feel normal. I wasn't scared of the O'Donnellys, not anymore, but the kid in me, the kid who had taken one of their own from them, who had sneaked around with Declan, well, that kid was bricking it.

As we pulled up to a halt, the door opened. Lena and Aidan Sr. could only have recently arrived themselves, but when Lena surged out, I sensed her excitement.

Truthfully, I was surprised she didn't have more grandkids roaming around. I'd have thought they'd have tried to marry their sons off earlier, but apparently they hadn't.

The older woman stood on her front stoop, wringing her hands. I twisted around to look at Shay, saw he was watching her, and murmured, "That's Lena. Remember, be polite and respectful. They have a different way of life. Watch and take note."

I'd told him the same when we'd traveled with some Roma back in Ireland and when we'd traversed the desert with a nomadic tribe of Bedouins.

I figured it was fitting that I told him the same with a bunch of people who were Irish Mob. A culture all on their own. A society that lived with its own rules.

Declan had killed someone this week, shot another's foot, but he hadn't spent a lick of time inside a police station... that was how it worked when you were an O'Donnelly.

"I will," Shay promised, but he was a kid. His assurances didn't always mean that much.

Like that time with the Bedouins, when he'd asked why the leader was called a Sheikh, when he'd learned that Sheikh meant 'old man,' and the leader of the tribe had been in his late thirties...

I'd thanked God for the fact we'd had someone translating for us and, kindly, the translator hadn't communicated that part.

Sometimes, questions just came out, and with Seamus, more than most. He was inquisitive by nature. Protective too.

I wasn't surprised he'd raised Doyle's conversation, because he'd stayed quiet and hadn't said anything, he'd be feeling guilty.

Somehow, and I had no idea how, but I'd instilled an honor code in him. Sometimes, I wondered how I'd done such a good job, but then I'd come back down to Earth when he took a twenty-five-minute shower.

I climbed out of the SUV, and as Shay closed his door, I hooked an arm over his shoulders. When he hugged his around my waist, we walked as a united front toward the grandmother who, quite clearly, longed to meet him.

Aside from the one-armed hug, he was stiff and tense, and I didn't bother trying to ease that. He'd be that way until he was home tonight, and that was okay. I didn't blame him, either. I'd be happy when I was climbing into my bed tonight too.

Well, happier when I climbed out of it to head into Declan's...

"Seamus," Lena whispered, her eyes lighting up as they drifted over him.

He looked cute in his suit, and even though I figured he could have come in pants and a shirt, I thought it best to start off properly... the suit and the Kevlar vest? More reasons why I owed him big time. Hence the full-on day trip to Coney Island.

"Hi," he said awkwardly, lifting a hand and waving it.

She smiled at him, then stepped forward at the same time Aidan Sr. loomed in the doorway.

His eyes were on me, and not even for a scant second did they flicker over to Shay or to Lena. It was the strangest feeling, being at the center of someone's focus who was capable of killing you, who'd feel no remorse over it because he had a different honor code.

It was like when you went to a zoo or an aquarium and a lion or a shark stared at you through the cage/glass. You were well aware that, without the pen, you'd be chomped up and spat out within seconds.

I was face to face with a predator, and even though my heart sped up, I wasn't scared.

It boggled my mind, but I wasn't.

I tipped my chin up and stared him down just as hard as he stared at me, until Declan barked, "Da, stop it."

His gaze cut to his son, and they glowered at one another for a minute before Lena turned to her husband and grumbled, "Stop looming, Aidan. Get over here and meet Seamus."

Aidan licked his lips and took a few cautious steps forward. In fact, everything about him spoke of his nerves.

The distinct difference between before, when he'd been looking at me with the cold, glass-eyed stare of a predator, to now was difficult to acclimate to.

Every frickin' mommy instinct inside me was screaming to get my kid away, demanding I head for the hills with my boy, but hadn't I just been saying what was the complete truth?

These guys wouldn't kill family. They'd kill *for* family.

Maybe he knew what was going through my head, maybe he got it, because Declan was behind me all of a sudden. He was there, and I felt his heat, and he didn't move as Aidan held out a hand for Seamus to shake.

The next few minutes were surreal. Lena fussed, Aidan stayed silent, and Seamus didn't really soften that much. He smiled and awkwardly answered the questions Lena asked, and in the end, I knew that with Lena trying to force fourteen years of grandmotherly instinct onto him, she wasn't going to get anywhere.

However, before I could utter a peep, Declan murmured, "Ma, I think Seamus would really like a drink."

Lena tensed, then her eyes flashed wide. Her red hair wasn't as bright as I remembered from childhood, streaked liberally with silver and gold now, but it glinted in the sun as her hands came to cup her cheeks. "How could I forget my manners?"

She dragged Seamus off inside the house with him looking back at me with wide eyes that asked me to intervene, but when Aidan spun around to follow, Declan barked, "Da," and my attention was averted.

Aidan, scowling, peered over his shoulder and groused, "What?"

"I told you about this before. You want Seamus in your life, you don't treat Aela like she's public enemy number one." Everything inside me heated up at that. Fuck. I didn't need him to defend me against goddamn Doyle, but his dad was different. I needed all the help I could get. "You treat her with respect."

"You ain't taking that boy anywhere."

"I'll take them both anywhere I damn well want. I'm not having you disrespect Aela. You got me?"

Aidan squinted at me and raked me with a disapproving glance before he shrugged and strode into the house.

"That didn't go too badly," I muttered, but before he could reply, the sounds of vehicles coming down the driveway made themselves known to me.

In a matter of moments, I'd been formally introduced to Aidan Jr., who I'd only seen glimpses of at Declan's hospital room, and Finn O'Grady, his wife Aoife, and their baby boy Jacob. I glanced between them all, surprised because though I knew the names, and everyone in the Points was well aware that Finn was high up in the ranks but also like family, there was a disconcerting similarity between the two friends. I knew they'd met in school, so I wasn't sure how that was possible, but the thought was rammed home when Eoghan showed up with his wife, Inessa.

There was a distinct similarity between them all.

I'd met Finn, Aoife, and Inessa back that night when everything had changed, when Amaryllis, my ex-student, had come to me for help. But I hadn't exactly gone out of my way to get to know them. If anything, I'd been more worried about getting childcare for Seamus, and then, when I'd heard about Declan's injuries, my focus had been solely on him.

Inessa had been kind though, Aoife too. Both women were at ease with the brothers in a way that shouldn't have come as a shock, but still did because I was used to thinking of them as O'Donnellys and not regular men.

Still, these were the ones I knew the least, so when Brennan and Conor showed up, Conor driving, relief hit me. Declan, with his arm around my shoulders in a position similar to how I'd held Seamus close earlier, turned to face his other brothers.

"You drive like a fucking lunatic," were the first words that managed to cross the distance.

Conor scoffed. "I drive like a regular person."

"A regular person who needs goddamn glasses. You didn't see that SUV in front of you, did you? How the fuck you didn't rear end them, I'll never know."

"Because rear-ending is your fucking specialty?" Conor mocked, earning himself a bird flipped his way from Brennan.

"No swearing. Jacob's a prodigy in the making," Finn rumbled, "I don't need him spitting out curse words."

Brennan scowled at us en masse, before he groused, "Whose idea was it for boy wonder to drive me home?"

"I won't be kind next time," Conor grumbled.

"You can drive back with us," I offered, knowing Seamus would appreciate that. He liked Conor and Brennan, and even though he'd seen more of them, I knew it wasn't just having been around them that made him like their oddball humor. There was a real 'odd couple' vibe between the two brothers that, I couldn't deny, was amusing as hell.

"Thank you," Brennan muttered, crossing himself in relief. "I didn't survive a shootout once this week to die in this dick's passenger seat."

I was grateful to both of them for breaking the ice, because ice had never been broken more perfectly than it was right then. It was easy to slip between Conor and Brennan, for Declan to be at my back. I knew them. I got them. They were, I realized with no small amount of astonishment, my kind of people.

Maybe I should want to hang around Aoife and Inessa, but they were, well, girly girls. They wore dresses and skirts, Inessa even had a patterned silk scarf around her neck that screamed Hermès, which I'd seen her use to cover her hair in church, whereas I wore black pants, a camisole on top of my Kevlar vest, and a structured, slim-fitting leather jacket.

As we all trudged inside, heading for a large living room that was dominated with a massive TV screen, and an equally massive sofa, what took me aback the most was how, wherever I looked, there were frames on the walls.

Picture on top of picture on top of picture.

It was incredible.

A still life movie of the O'Donnellys from birth to adulthood.

Entranced, I drifted around, taking stock of the different images, easily picking out the ones which were Declan. They all had the same bone structure, that mouth that was quick to smile, grimace, and snarl. They each were dark, some a little lighter here and there, but all of them—Finn included, were Black Irish.

As much as I loved seeing Declan, I had to admit—Finn fascinated me.

Not because he was beautiful, which he was. As an artist, I had to appreciate that there was something about him that took him up a level. Aoife was definitely a lucky lady. But there was something undeniable. Indefatigable.

Something that I'd never heard rumors about, which meant either Aidan Sr. had squashed them into dust a long time ago, or... well, nobody had ever figured it out.

It didn't seem likely.

In fact, it seemed impossible. I couldn't be the only one who saw the similarities, could I?

As I studied a picture that had my lips twitching when I took note of Conor shoving an ice cream cone in Declan's hair, I wasn't surprised when someone came to stand behind me.

I thought it'd be Declan or Seamus. Hadn't expected it would be Aidan Sr.

Never turn your back on an enemy...

"Lena always had her camera stuck to her when they were boys," he said softly, reminiscently. "And that was before the day of the iPhone, where every single picture had to be processed. Some would be ruined, some would be exposed, the film might be damaged... it mattered to her."

"I can see that." I cut him a look. "I'll get some pictures of Seamus to you for the wall."

He arched a brow, but he registered that I was on the same page as him. "It would be a kindness. She likes to document everything."

"That much is clear," I mused. "There a reason?"

"Her mother had Alzheimer's. She's terrified she'll get it too and forget them."

I'd never deny that the O'Donnellys were held up as monarchs of an unofficial kingdom, but hearing that humanized Lena in a way I couldn't have expected.

She was the ice queen.

She ruled over the Five Points, just a step behind Aidan, making sure he kept his head. The cold to his intense heat that burned and burned, never seeming to drain, impossible to extinguish.

Everyone knew of his mercurial tempers, the moods that could see him fell a dozen enemies in a knife fight. He was lethal.

Deadly.

But I was looking at a picture of him in a drenched suit with a bunch of boys giggling around him after they'd, quite clearly, pushed him in a pool that gleamed behind them.

It was an insight into people who were revered—and feared—as gods.

Unnerving.

"If you're going to give me crap about Seamus, don't bother," I warned softly, my focus still on the photos.

"Leave the girl alone, Aidan," Lena chided, slipping up behind me with a silence that jolted me.

"I was merely conversing with her. She's interested in the pictures. Said she'll give you some."

"Oh!" Her voice changed. Morphing from concerned and a little chastising, to surprised and excited. "That would be lovely."

"I have many," I told her with a genuine smile. "I wasn't as prolific with a camera as you, but I certainly took enough to drive him crazy."

"The boys were used to it. I took pictures all the time." She reached up and ran her fingers over a shot of a grumpy Declan in what looked like his communion suit. "Such a quiet boy," she said softly. "We never understood him."

"He's not quiet," I countered, twisting to look at her better. I felt a lot less ill at ease knowing Aidan Sr. had wandered off, because while I didn't doubt Lena could cut me down effortlessly, I also knew she wouldn't because of Seamus.

Only a woman with five boys could sense how close a mother and son would be. Hers were all incredibly protective of her, after all. Seamus was of me too. For so long, it had been us against the world...

"No?" She shrugged. "He was very different than the others. Never interested in sports, though he played to keep his brothers happy, never interested in books, never interested in anything at all."

I found that hard to believe, especially as I knew he was fascinated by the arts. Enough that his home was a rogue's gallery—literally—of stolen artwork. Nobody who was that obsessed, who spent a couple of million on a safe to protect lost paintings, could be classed as 'uninterested.'

She just didn't know him.

And that saddened the hell out of me.

"I see you disagree," she observed softly. "There's plenty a woman never learns about her son. That's how it should be. He's lived in his father's shadow since he was a boy... it's time that changed, I think."

She drifted away without another word, no sign of distaste or disapproval in her statement, but neither was there any appreciation. But that was okay. Very likely, I wasn't good enough for her son, but he disagreed and I was more than happy with that.

A few minutes later, Brennan disrupted me by asking, "What's caught your attention?"

If it had been Declan, I'd have talked about Finn. Maybe mentioned his parents' strange way of breaking the ice. Instead, because it was him, I murmured, "I like seeing you all this way. It reminds me that just because everyone in Manhattan is terrified of you, I don't have to be."

He snickered. "Not just everyone in Manhattan."

Chuckling, I teased, "Most of the East Coast, huh?"

"Well, I hate to be modest."

"He does. Hate to be modest," Declan inserted, his hand slipping around my waist as smoothly as he slipped into the conversation. "Did the folks give you shit?" he grumbled. "I'm sorry, I was helping Shay out."

I arched a brow. "With what?"

"Man stuff."

What went up, had to go down—my brows furrowed. "What kind of man stuff?"

"Things women don't understand."

He and Brennan shared a look, but while they both seemed to understand, I really didn't. "Huh?"

"Never mind. Just know I'd have come and saved you if I'd been able to."

Despite the mystery, I patted his hand. "I know. They were semi-decent."

"I, on the other hand, could have saved you, but I decided it was time to rip off the Band-Aid," Brennan remarked, lifting his glass and taking a sip of what looked like a Bellini.

The big, tough Irish mobster rocking a sling on one shoulder and a holster on the other while holding a slender flute of champagne with peach juice was more than discordant.

In fact, it was jarring enough to make me want to paint it.

I didn't particularly want Aidan Sr. or Lena's approval. It wasn't something that would keep me up at night. If they hated me, they hated me.

So be it.

I wasn't, and never had been, an ass-kisser. With Aidan Sr. in particular, I wasn't sure if getting rimmed was a surefire way to make him hate me more. All I could do was be strong, stand firm, and believe that I made the right decisions along the way.

Better communication might have kept Declan and me together, but back then, I didn't think so. He was young, and like Lena had said—under his father's thumb. I'd known that way back then. He'd come to me so many times after doing a job, and though he hadn't said anything, I'd felt how lost he was. Sometimes, when he was inside me, that was the only time he'd felt *found.*

He'd even told me that once.

And it had resonated with me in a way that was beyond comprehension.

That had been better than an 'I love you' in my mind. To this day, it still probably meant more to me than any of the random crap men had a tendency of saying when they thought themselves tied to a woman.

But I knew, then and there, that I'd paint all of Lena's boys and gift her the portraits.

And just like I knew she'd adore them, I knew they'd be my best work. Ever.

My muse had come to a decision—the O'Donnelly sons were going to be my next magnum opus.

DECLAN

SEAMUS'S CHEEKS were still red an hour later as we sat down for dinner. Because Inessa was more his age than ours, I understood his fascination with her, and I especially understood the impromptu boner that had him scurrying out of the room like he'd shit his pants.

At first, I'd thought Ma had said something to him, so I'd rushed after him and grabbed him to make sure he was okay. His glittery eyes, the red cheeks, the way he held his jacket close to him?

It was amazing how much I'd forgotten about being young. And it was amazing how fucking ancient that made me feel.

His voice still squeaked every now and then, and since he'd come to New York, he'd had a few zits, a couple of pimples. Nothing terrible. His top lip was getting some fuzz, and I was inordinately pleased that, when his beard came through, I'd be around to show him how to shave it.

I didn't think there'd be much I'd be able to teach him, because Aela had done a bang-up job, but the man stuff? That was the crap *she* didn't know.

And apparently I needed a reminder too, because until Shay went through the stuff, I couldn't remember half of the crap that happened when you were a teenage boy.

Still, with his secret crush for his aunt under control—a thought that still made me want to laugh—I made sure that I grabbed a dish, held it for

Aela as she served herself, then took what I needed too. I wanted the family to know she meant something to me.

She wasn't a bitch.

She wasn't here simply because she'd been the womb who dropped Seamus.

She was mine.

As I maneuvered my overwhelmed plate, chatter started around the table. As usual, I listened. Among so many voices, it was easier just to tune in, figure out what was what. There were so many big personalities around here that I preferred just to sit back and let them talk.

"You'll never guess where Eoghan took me last night, Lena."

Ma arched a brow. "Where?"

"The Bolshoi Ballet is in town," she enthused, which had my ears pricking up with interest.

Fuck, I was really out of it if I didn't know they were in the city.

"What did you see?" Aoife asked. "I've never seen a ballet, but I'd really love to go."

"*Swan Lake*. It was incredible. I've been to a few but—"

Da, with his elbow on the table and his fork hanging from his hand, scowled at her then glowered at me like it was my fault I'd infected her with an appreciation for the ballet. "Looks like you're not the only one who gets a kick out of watching a bunch of faggots, Declan. Why you'd want to watch them run around in fucking skirts—"

"Language," Ma grumbled.

My mouth tightened because I knew what was coming, only, it didn't.

"Is that a homosexual slur?"

I could feel the entire table grind to a halt at Seamus's question. Nearly everyone stared at him, but I cast Aela a glance and saw she was smirking into her roast beef.

"Yeah, it's a homosexual slur, kid," she confirmed.

"You can't say things like that," Seamus piped up.

"Sure I can. A man can say whatever he wants when he's at his own table," Da rumbled, but I could sense he was only being patient because Seamus was who he was.

"You can't. It's insulting. Not only to anyone who's gay, but also to Dad. I mean, he quite clearly *isn't* gay. And just because he likes art and things doesn't mean you can talk about him like that."

Well, if that didn't break my fucking heart.

I swear to fuck. My eyes prickled with goddamn tears at not only the first time he ever called me Dad—and I was no fool, I knew the second we were outside he'd go back to calling me Declan or not calling me anything at all—but that he chose to do so now? While he was defending me? Just... fuck.

Conor cleared his throat. "How messed up is it that the only person who's ever defended Declan at this fucking table is his fourteen-year-old kid?" He dipped his chin. "Kudos to you, Shay."

Unease drifted over the diners. I felt it gathering like storm clouds over us, shadows forging and dispersing as people's attention drifted toward me. I kept my head down, like I usually did while I was under this roof, and carried on scraping up my food.

The second I could get out of here wasn't a second too soon.

"A man shouldn't be prancing around in tights," Da ground out, and I knew he wasn't happy about Seamus giving him lip. "And a man sure as fuck shouldn't be wanting to watch a *nancy boy* prancing around like a fucking fairy."

I could feel Seamus bristling from two seats down, but Ma sniped, "Aidan, shut your fool mouth."

"No, if you don't address issues then they're impossible to resolve, Lena," Seamus interjected, his tone calmer than his expression belied, like he was fourteen going on forty. "It's a very antiquated way of thinking, Aidan. I'm sure you know that, and clinging onto your old-fashioned thought processes might seem more comfortable to you, but all you're doing is being prejudiced against a lot of innocent people who only want the right to live their lives as they want, with who they want. They're not hurting you, so why should it bother you who they're with?"

"Because it's not right. It's Adam and Eve, kid. Not Adam and Steve," Da remarked, but something had shifted.

He'd gone from being pissed to being amused.

Though I'd heard his bullshit more times than I could count, it didn't stop me from gritting my teeth over the conversation.

For a helluva long time, he'd thought *I* was gay, so I'd heard it all as he attempted to scare me straight. Which wasn't easy when I was already straight to begin with.

"That makes no sense. A lot of animals engage in homosexual activity. It's perfectly natural. Anyway, you're talking about ballet. Most ballets are about tragic romances, aren't they, Mom? Remember that one we went to see in Paris? It was about that girl who fell in love with a guy—"

"You've been to Paris?" Aoife asked, her eyes lighting up. The abrupt question, however, told me she was trying to change the subject.

"Yeah. We lived there for a year," Seamus confirmed. "It was brilliant.

Lots of museums and lots of cultural things. Just because I enjoyed going to the opera and the ballet doesn't mean I'm gay," he pointed out, but his voice broke, and I didn't have to look at him to know he was doing his level best to avoid drooling over Inessa. "And anyway, going there is a great way to socialize with the right people. It's like golf. Does anyone even like it? But most businessmen play because you can talk business on the green."

"Is this kid for real?" I heard Aidan Jr. mutter.

For the first time, my gaze snapped off my meal and onto him. "Yeah, he's for real, and I think he's fucking brilliant. Hasn't Aela done a great job raising him?"

"Yeah, I agree," Conor added, backing me up, and I'd give him a steak later on in the week as a thank you. "She has. He's got world domination on his list of things to do. You only aimed for the city, Da, Seamus wants the country, at least."

Da, being the nutcase he was, found that hilarious, and as he chuckled like a loon, slapping his leg like he hadn't heard anything so funny in all his life, somehow, it shifted the conversation onto Seamus. He talked about his new school, about his classmates and how many bodyguards they had for some reason, and he talked about the places he'd been and had seen.

By the end of it, if his staunch defense of me hadn't cleared it up, I knew my family was impressed.

Not only was Seamus mature, independent, and kind, he had brass balls.

And with the O'Donnellys? That was exactly what you needed to survive.

TWENTY-TWO

AELA

AS I RUBBED my hair dry, I watched Declan as he started to stride from one side of the bedroom to the other. I knew he was on the phone with Conor, and the reason I was listening in was because I'd heard him mention Caro's name a few times. As well as a couple of curse words in reference to her.

My childhood was too deeply ingrained in me to think of her as anything other than a pig, but I was infinitely curious about why Declan was so pissed. Caro had been investigating me and my clients, a case that had disappeared thanks to the four-grand-an-hour attorney the family had procured for me, so I wasn't sure why she should be causing the O'Donnellys much of an issue.

Trouble was, in my position, I didn't expect to learn all that much. Women never did.

Heaving an impatient sigh at the outdated thought process, I alternated between wanting to know and sulking over the status of women in the Five Points. I mean, it wasn't like I *wanted* to get involved, but being out of the loop sucked.

When Declan turned around and saw me, I could tell he hadn't realized I was in the room.

Because that meant I was slipping under his defenses which, in my opinion, boded well for our future together, I watched him end the call with his brother before I asked, "What's Caro doing now?"

"You heard that much, huh?" he questioned sheepishly, rubbing a hand over his chin as he eyed me up like I was his ma's apple crumble.

I'd eaten that today, so I knew it was the bomb.

"I did."

"We have to pay her a visit in the morning. Conor was just setting it up."

"How come?" I arched a brow. "Didn't realize FBI agents were on speed dial for mobsters nowadays."

"Now, now," he chided, lips twitching. "You know we prefer to be called businessmen."

That had me snorting, even as I tossed the towel I'd been using to dry my hair behind me into the bathroom. All the while, he watched me, his gaze trickling over me like liquid silk that he poured over every inch of my body.

While the day had been long, hella long in fact, I was beyond grateful to be home and for the ordeal to be over, but the heat in his eyes made my fatigue vanish in an instant.

I'd never thought to experience the likes of it again, and I was enamored by the way he made me feel as if I was fifteen once more.

"I didn't expect that today."

Because my mind was on sex, and his wasn't, it took a few seconds to register what he was talking about. "Seamus? You mean him defending you?"

"You mean him doing what no one in my family has ever done?" His scowl took me aback before he muttered, "No one has ever understood my love of the arts." He strolled over to the wall safe, and started the process of opening it.

When the beauties within were revealed, I swallowed at the sight of them, and murmured, "I like the fact that you and these three come as part of a package."

"She wants me for my art," he grumbled under his breath, but his smile shone through his eyes, taking away the bleakness buried there after talking about his family. "Funny how they don't get it, but you do. So perfectly. And Seamus too."

"He's my kid. How couldn't he understand art? It's fate that you like it as well."

"Can I ask you a question?"

"Of course." I didn't bother to be wary over what he might ask. There was no point in lying.

The distinct difference between being the aforementioned fifteen-year-old and the sensible woman standing here today was that I didn't have it in me to play coy.

I was all in at this point, and I wasn't going to hide it.

"Did you ever expect us to start up again? You said you knew the day would come where I'd find you... did you expect us to get together?"

I blinked, but replied honestly, "No. I didn't. I thought you'd be married by now."

"So you just thought I'd set you up in an apartment?"

Warily, I fingered the hem of the towel that covered me, keeping my head bowed.

"Shit."

His curse had my shoulders hunching, because I knew he got where I was coming from. "You couldn't seriously think I'd top you?"

"It was one of the major reasons I worked so hard to be successful. I needed to keep myself safe."

"You seriously thought so badly of me?"

"You were like a different man after Deirdre died, Declan," I rasped. "Nothing like the boy I loved, and all I could think was that I was a side piece and she was supposed to be your bride. I thought you'd be wishing I was dead and not her."

He scrubbed a hand over his jaw, contemplating my words even as he was shaking his head. "I wish I'd known how badly I'd treated you. Maybe I'd have expected for you to run off. I just thought you'd stop calling, stop trying to see me. I never imagined you'd go all the way to fucking Ireland to avoid me."

"Did you look for me?"

Pursing his lips, he grumbled, "Of course I did. But it was too late when you were out of the country, and I had to keep it on the down low."

"You could have followed me," I said softly.

"I could have." He sighed. "I should have."

"Why didn't you?"

"If I tell you that I have no idea why, would you believe me?"

My lips twisted. "You have no reason to lie to me."

"I don't," he agreed. "Did you keep tabs on me?"

"Some. Enough to know you were alive."

He shot me a rueful smile. "These past couple of years, I kept tabs on you. Nothing too heavy or I'd have found out about Shay sooner, but about your art."

"I know you did—you said you liked my work today."

"I can't stop thinking about how different shit would be if I'd come after you." He blew out a breath. "It makes me feel so fucking guilty."

My life and his would have been a hell of a lot different if that was what had happened.

Was it crazy that I was glad we'd been separated? I wished Declan and Seamus were closer, and that was my sole regret, but I was a stronger woman for all my experiences. The kind of strong woman that a man like Declan needed.

It was crazy, wasn't it? How I could contemplate marrying a man who gunned down attackers one day, then could be sitting around the family dinner table, his shoulders hunched as his father insulted him the next?

"Don't, maybe we're the people we need to be now because of what we've gone through separately."

His smile was rueful. "Don't think you'd have been as ballsy today with Da if we'd married when we were young."

"No," I agreed, and because that was the segue I needed, I stated, "My turn. For a question, I mean."

"Shoot."

"Finn's related to you, isn't he?"

He reared back at that. "Huh?"

I shrugged. "Your bone structure is the same. The coloring too. It's uncanny. And I swear, when Seamus was a boy, he looked like Jacob. Sure, his baby features are still developing, but it's like looking at a mini Aidan."

He was shaking his head in disagreement. "No." His voice was the sternest I'd ever heard it. "No. Finn's like a brother to us, but he's a friend of the family."

"I know he is," I replied softly. "I've been away a long time, but not *that* long." Because he didn't want to hear it, because he didn't even want to register it, I decided the only thing to do was to move closer to him and to take his mind off things with a kiss that would lead to action and not more thoughts.

The past was bleak, loaded with what-ifs and what might have beens, and it was murky enough to make me want to avoid thinking of it. The present was bright, and the future loaded with hope that I longed to come true.

Dec and I were rattling along well together, merging into a cohesive unit that I knew Seamus was the direct reason for, but there were signs that he needed me as much as I needed him.

The way, today, he'd placed his hand on my thigh. How he'd let me have my voice. How he'd tried to protect me, shield me from his family.

I'd expected to be killed, to be mistreated, to be yelled at. Instead, I was being treated like an equal. Like someone who'd made as many mistakes as Declan had. It hit me then that the reason he was cutting me so much slack was that he wanted a second chance too.

That, maybe, for as long as I'd been pining for him, he'd been pining for me.

I hoped that was the case.

Really, truly, I did.

And then, I didn't think because as I moved over to him, he tugged me into his arms, and after placing his hands on my hips, jerked me upward so that I could hook my legs around his thighs.

His touch was harder than usual, a little rougher, but I didn't, *wouldn't* complain, because I knew why.

I'd stirred up something in his mind, something to do with Finn and his father. He was denying it, trying not to think about whatever had cropped up, but that was the trouble with Pandora's box. Once it was opened, it could never be closed.

So I let him take solace in me. I let him enjoy my body and use me as a respite because I wanted to be that for him.

I wanted to be his everything.

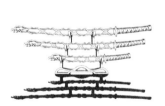

DECLAN

MY MIND BUZZED with thoughts I didn't need to hear, didn't *want* to hear. I wasn't sure where she'd gotten that crap about Finn, but it drove me crazy, to the point where I was a little rougher with her than I intended.

I never treated her with kid gloves, something I knew she enjoyed. I treated her like a woman I needed, *craved,* and that seemed to get her as hot as she did me.

So because she didn't complain, I pushed her against the wall. I knew she loved that the paintings were 'watching' us, and that drove things up to another level for me too. Fuck, we gelled so well that it blew my mind how we could be so different yet so perfect for each other.

So perfect *now* for each other.

She wouldn't be this Aela if I'd wifed her when I was a kid myself.

She wouldn't be this strong, this fiery, this ballsy if she hadn't led the life she had.

With my dick grinding into her, I held her up with force alone so I could reach up and cup her face. She stared at me with eyes that were hazed with lust, and it stirred me like no other woman could. Just to see that she was aroused was enough to make me want to pinch myself.

Framing her cheeks, I murmured, "You know what blows my mind?"

She blinked. "What?"

"That we had to go through all the shit to be here right now. To be the people we are."

"We did," she confirmed softly.

"It fucks with me to think that I like this you better than the old you."

Her brows rose, but her lips twitched. "I think there's a compliment in there."

"There is. A massive one. The old you got my dick hard." I ground my cock into her. "This you makes me feel like I'd kill to get inside you. I never thought I could feel this way for a woman. Never thought I'd love someone so fucking much just for how they go through life, butting heads here and shouting people down there."

Her eyes flared wide. "You love me?"

I dipped my chin. "Think it's time you knew that. I loved you before, but I'd have married Deirdre, I'd have been her husband in name only, but you'd have been on the side, and if there's one thing I'm glad about, it's that you never had to be there.

"You deserved so much fucking more than to be a mistress, but I'd have done that to you because I'm a selfish fuck. I'm a jackass who loved you but would have put you in that position anyway.

"I didn't deserve you then and I don't now, but I love you. For what it's worth, Aela, I do." I sighed. "I just... I dunno. I had to get that out. Had to tell you."

She licked her lips. "I loved you even if you were a prick. But I like you now. I didn't realize how important that was when I was a kid. I was in awe of you. Overwhelmed that Declan O'Donnelly wanted me, and that he trusted me, and I loved you, but I didn't know you.

"Even though we've been together barely any time at all, I feel like I know you so much better now. I love that you let me have a voice, I love that you'll have my back, and I love that you love Seamus." She reached up and cupped my chin, those sapphire blue orbs piercing mine as she rasped, "What I'm trying to say, Declan, is that I love you, but I *like* you too."

As always, she cut straight to the heart of the matter. Making sense out of the shit I'd spewed. "Yeah," I breathed. "I like you too."

"I love that you're a fanatic for art, and that half the stuff in this place is stolen. I love that you have layers. You're like an onion. Before, I guess I just thought you were one-dimensional. An O'Donnelly. That defined you *and* described you. But now? You're so much more than that, and I see it and want it all for myself."

Bowing my head, I licked her lips, tasting her and whispering, "You can have all of me, Aela. All I have to give." When she surged forward, I was surprised when her hands gripped my hair tightly, with a force that stung. She held me to her, clung to me, her knees pinning me in a hard grip around the waist as she rocked against me like the words were all she needed to let loose.

And if I'd learned anything about her, it was that she didn't need much of anything to let loose.

Thank fuck.

I levered a hand between us so I could unfasten the knot of her towel. It didn't go anywhere, not squished between us the way it was, but as she thrust her tongue into my mouth, my other hand went to my fly. Her pussy was there, bared by the split in the towel, and I groaned at the hot silk that rubbed my knuckles as I tried to work down my fly.

When I managed to get my dick loose, I held it before I traced it through the juices that slipped from her slit. Al-fucking-ready. Goddammit, what she did to me.

I kissed her like I was dying, kissed her like today was the last day of my life. Fucking her there as I teased her slit with the tip of my dick, her nails dug into my scalp. She scraped down, dragging nerve endings to life, and I grunted into her mouth, the grunt morphing into a groan as she dipped her teeth into my bottom lip.

The prick of her teeth, the drag of her nails, it felt phenomenal. Made me feel fucking alive.

She whimpered as I angled her, no longer teasing her, and urged her down onto my dick.

She took me like she always did—like her pussy was mine. Forged for me. Made to hold my cock.

As I filled her, she groaned, her mouth tearing free from mine as she panted out a breath, her head flopping into the wall as I let my lips drift across to her ear where those earrings of hers as well as the jade ones I'd gifted her glinted between strands of bright blue hair. I sucked on the earlobe, then dropped down so I could give her a hickey.

Biting down, I felt her pussy quake around me, cosseting me and drawing every ounce of cum from my dick.

Gravity impaled her on me, and the feeling was beyond anything I could have dreamed. Unable to stop myself, I grabbed her arms and pinned them overhead. The movement had her towel flopping to the ground, and I groaned as, dropping my head, I managed to grasp one of her nipples. Fluttering my tongue around it, I sucked hard, nibbling the tip before I started to rock even harder into her.

Her back arched, giving me more access, and as I bit the tip, she released a shaky gasp, her breath stalling in her chest for a handful of seconds before she released a keening moan. It powered through my senses, even more delicious because I knew she was trying to keep quiet but was finding it hard.

Thanking God Seamus's room was on the other side of the apartment, I watched her come, felt it, reveled in it, as I let her fly free. With each pulsation of her pussy around my shaft, I was a goner, and I only held on because every thrust I made had her drawing in air like she was a drowning woman searching for oxygen.

When I moved to her other nipple, biting down a little harder, no teasing, nothing but need and want merging together as my balls drew up tight, she came again but she struggled in my hold, her arms bucking against me, wriggling and writhing against the wall in a way that had me exploding into her.

As my cum drenched her, I groaned, letting go of her nipple and burrowing my face into her throat, biting her there as I moaned out the fucking relief that came when I was inside her, when I was allowed to let go, to merge with her.

Nothing beat this feeling.

Nothing.

No one beat her.

She was mine.

No longer my filthy little secret, but my woman. At my side. Where she should have always been.

TWENTY-THREE

DECLAN

I PEERED AT CONOR, then down at the files he'd handed me.

"You shitting me?"

He sniffed. "When have you known me to shit you when it comes down to business?"

I rolled my eyes. "All the fucking time?"

His lips twitched. "Well, this is different. You've paid nearly one and a half million to this fucker. I ain't about to play you around anymore. You were a kid. We all make mistakes." He pulled a face. "I know I sure as hell did."

"What? Breaking into NASA wasn't a highlight of your misspent youth?"

"Oh no, that was the best fucking day of my life. I'm talking about not fucking Janie Petersen." He whistled. "She'd have had my balls in a vise, and I'd have loved every minute of it."

"Do we really need to hear about how you seriously need a dominatrix to keep you in line?" Brennan groused.

I smirked at him. "I can just see Conor in a gimp suit, can't you?"

"I'd rock it, just like I rock everything." He blew on his nails, making me wonder how the nerdy fuck always managed to look cool no matter what he did.

I'd hate him if I didn't love the shit out of him.

"You seen this?" I asked, waving the file at Brennan.

"Course. Wouldn't be here if I hadn't."

"True." I tipped my head to the side as I stared in the rearview mirror. "Tail free."

"Not just a pretty face," Conor commented, making me shake my head as I laughed. "Better than Brennan, at any rate."

"You drive like you belong in an insane asylum," Brennan grumbled.

Because I'd already heard this three fucking times today, I grumbled back, "Look, as much as I love the matinee, I have places to be. People to see."

"Yeah? Like who?" Conor sniped, giving me the side-eye.

"My woman?" I retorted.

"Yours, huh?" He hummed under his breath. "Proposed to her yet?"

"Nah. I don't need to, do I? She has to know it's in the cards. What with a man who makes you look sane behind the wheel for a father."

"Every woman needs the romance, bro," Conor retorted, shaking his head at me like I was a lost cause.

Goddamn nerve.

Dude's longest relationship was with his right fucking fist, and here he was, giving me shit?

"He's right," Brennan confirmed. "You should propose. She'd dig it. Just because she's not all girly girl doesn't mean she wouldn't love all the cutesy shit. In fact, I bet she'd really love it."

My brow furrowed. "You think?"

"Yeah. I do." Brennan nodded. "You got a ring picked out?"

"Well, yeah, but I was just going to give it to her when we were ready to get hitched."

"On the day itself?" Conor shook his head again. "Declan, I swear to fuck, for a guy who loves all that tragic romance, all the arts and stuff, you're clueless, aren't you? Let me guess. You want to get married in front of a justice of the peace?"

"Don't see why not." I shrugged. "We're both private people."

Conor scowled at me. "We're a private family, doesn't mean things don't have a time and a place."

"I refuse to go through what Eoghan did," I argued. "Hell, I went through all that shit so he didn't have to! I'm the one who had to prop Inessa up because he was chickenshit. If anything, he should go through it for me."

"Nah, Inessa meant jack to him back then. Aela matters to you." Conor pursed his lips, eyes narrowed like he was deep in thought. "In fact, I tell you what. I'm going to plan your service. You don't have to do shit, just turn up on the day at the place and time when I tell you. I bet she loves it."

I glared at him. "What the fuck do you know about this shit?"

"Doesn't take a goddamn degree," he retorted, holding out his hand. "We got an agreement?"

"So long as it's not that whole dog and pony show like Eoghan had to deal with."

Conor snorted. "Bro, their ceremony was all for show. This isn't."

"Isn't it? Gotta make Seamus legit before you get me shot again," I groused, waggling the file he'd handed me in his face.

"Well, okay, if you want to think of it that way, then do." He hitched a shoulder. "Not gonna affect me."

A breath gusted from between my lips as I conceded, "Okay. Go for it. But I get to take full credit with Aela."

"That's it," Conor joked. "Start married life off the right way—with a lie."

My nose crinkled, so I reached up after I shook his hand, scratched it, and flipped him the bird. "But I'll tell you when and where—when I've made a decision."

He just grinned at me, then pointed to the file. "Now. As you so rightly said, I gotta get you shot."

"This just seems insane to me," I replied, my attention averted. "Caroline Dunbar can't be behind the blackmail. She's too much of a stickler for the rules."

"She's always had a boner for you," Conor argued. "Ever since Jimmy D."

"How the fuck she knew you were behind it, I don't know," Brennan rumbled, his body angled toward the front of the building we were watching for signs of life.

If that bitch had a tail on us, we had one on her. We knew every move she made, and if she took a piss or went for a shit, then we knew about it.

That was why we were waiting for her to come home.

This afternoon, when my brothers had burst into my office at the warehouse I managed, both of them looking like they'd found a treasure map with an 'X' marking the spot, then had reeled off the tale of how Conor had discovered exactly who the blackmailer was, the day had long since spiraled out of control.

I wasn't even sure what we were doing here.

So I said as much. "What are we supposed to do? Confront her?"

"Yeah. Of course," Conor grumbled. "You think I tracked that account through a gazillion goddamn VPNs and IPs and spent a week solid tracing it just for you to carry on paying? You owe me the ten grand you were going to give her."

I griped, "That's it. Remind me why I didn't get you involved before."

He sniffed. "You're a dumbass, that's why." Then he heaved in a breath. "Of course, I know it's because we never stuck up for you as a kid, so you didn't trust us. But I think you trust us now, so that's something."

I tensed up. "Course I trusted you. We're kin, ain't we?"

"We are, but when Seamus stuck up for you on Sunday? Well, man, it just rammed it home how we never did that when Da used to give you crap about liking museums and shit, you know?" His shoulders wriggled. "Then I thought about all the time you were paying that bitch hush money, and it fit that you didn't think you could trust us with the truth. But you trusted us with Seamus and Aela, so I knew shit had changed."

My own shoulders weren't just wriggling, they were up by my ears.

"That true, Dec?" Brennan asked softly.

"Maybe," was all I said a few minutes later after the silence grew too thick for me to deal with.

Fuckers knew how to get me to talk.

I cleared my throat. "It's old news."

"Nah. The history is always part of the present," Conor stated too sagely for my liking. "We're here for you now, and we're going to make the bitch pay."

"You swept the car for bugs, didn't you?" I inquired drolly.

"Duh," he rumbled. "I think we need to get in there, tell her we know what her game is, and if she's going to threaten you then we can threaten her back. I can easily show the Feds how I traced the bank account."

"Stalemate," Brennan chimed in.

"Exactly. I love it when a plan comes together." Conor rubbed his hands together.

"Until she calls our bluff. I don't want to go to jail—"

Brennan snickered. "Like you would. The director's in Da's pocket, Dec. Fuck, you know that. You ain't going nowhere."

Unease whispered through me. "You don't know that."

"What? You want to kill her?" Conor queried, like he was asking if I wanted ketchup with my burger.

"Might have to," I answered with a sigh, reaching up to pinch the bridge of my nose. "I don't want to, not with the shit it will stir, but you never know with her. She's a fucking slimy bitch."

"That she is," Brennan agreed. "She picked the perfect job for someone like her. A pig can never be trusted."

I nodded, totally on board with that. "Just like her father," I added.

"Yeah. Just like Jimmy. Fat fucker," Brennan agreed.

"Seamus would say you're being fattist," Conor pointed out. "Hey, Dec, did I tell you how much I love your kid? He's fucking awesome."

I grinned. "You think so, huh?"

"I do." He cut me a look. "Did you talk about what he wanted me to show him the other night?"

Brows lifting, I replied, "No. I don't think so. He's been quiet since school started for real. What did you show him?"

"Sweet fuck, tell me you didn't explain the birds and the bees to him. He'll never get his leg over if you did," Brennan mocked.

Hiding a laugh when Conor scowled at him, I questioned, "What was it, C?"

"He wanted to learn about the family."

"What about it?" I asked warily.

"Whenever he searched the O'Donnellys, he kept getting the wrong information—mostly because it's part of my job to make sure that people get the wrong information. So I pointed him in the right direction."

Brennan heaved a sigh. "I swear, Conor, you're a brilliant idiot. Why would you show him that shit?"

"He needs to know."

Dread filled me, but then, there was no point in dreading it. What had he just said? *History affects the present...* I didn't want Shay to know about the family's roots, but he had a right to. But it sure as hell put a slant on why he'd been quiet recently.

"Wait, you mean he challenged Da knowing what he does about him?" And he'd called me 'dad' afterward too.

"Yeah. Swear, that kid's got brass balls," Conor remarked with a grin, and because I'd thought that about Shay too, I couldn't disagree.

"Fuck, he sure does," Brennan agreed. "Thought Da was going to lose his shit when Seamus put him in his place."

My lip quirked to the side. "Was definitely the best entertainment I've had in a long while at the Sunday roast."

"You really hate it, don't you?" Conor asked. "Being at home? Being around the folks?"

I shrugged. "I love them, but they don't get me. They don't have to either. I'm a grown man."

"Yeah, but—"

Before he could say another word, the deep throb of some straight pipes rattled down the street.

"Fuck, I hate Harleys," Brennan groused. "Why do they have to be so loud?"

"It's a fallacy, actually," Conor intoned, in know-it-all mode. "They say that if the pipes are loud, ongoing traffic will hear them, but the sound from the exhaust goes straight out of the back end. All it does is make them go deaf prematurely—"

"And piss pedestrians off," Brennan grumbled.

As the bike approached, I tilted my head to the side, recognizing that it wasn't a Sunday rider on the back of it.

"Biker," Conor confirmed.

"No tags," I murmured.

"Does there need to be? Nearest MC to us is the Sinners," Brennan pointed out.

"He's not wearing a cut." I lifted my cellphone and as the biker drove by, I snapped a photo, full frontal and a real beauty, then immediately sent it to Conor, whose own cell buzzed as he received it.

When the guy got off the bike and swaggered over to the thin house where Caroline Dunbar lived, a house that in no way looked as though she was spending the ten grand I'd been sending her every month for a decade, my brows rose high. When I cast a glance at Brennan and Conor, saw they were equally as surprised, the three of us settled in for the long haul.

We were curious now as to what the fuck was going on and what exactly Dunbar had gotten herself into.

AELA

WHEN I TOOK a seat at the Plaza, I peered around the fancy hotel, impressed despite myself.

I'd been able to afford to eat here for a long time, but I just never had. Now, I was here for a different reason.

Afternoon tea.

And I'd prefer to stick pins under my nails.

Still, the place was nice. A massive chandelier hung suspended over a gleaming antique central table that was loaded down with seasonal flowers. It sat atop a rich Turkish rug, which lined the perimeter of the room. The walls were like something from an Austen movie—that strange kind of gilded paneling—but what I loved the most was the overhead dome that let in the meager light from a crappy New York day.

It made the place like a greenhouse, which was fitting considering the name—The Palm Court. There was a stand with flowers on it above the shelving units of the bar, but more impressively, there were a huge pair of palms that dwarfed the servers flitting about.

Mostly I loved how the table I was seated at was mirrored, and it reflected the intricate metal lacework of the dome without me having to tip my head back to gape at it.

A little too rich for my blood, I'd never have selected this as the place where I'd like to meet Aoife and Inessa, but hey, this was their suggestion.

I'd never been a 'brunch with the girls' kind of woman, mostly because I'd always been on the move. It made it hard to make friends, especially ones you had a standing date with. Of course, there was the debacle with Caro, but seeing as she liked me for who I knew, and not what, I dismissed her entirely from my memory banks.

Still, when I'd received the text from Inessa this morning, I'd been grateful to be included. Surprised, but grateful nonetheless.

With Declan back at work, and the apartment all to myself, I was left in my makeshift studio, working. Not that I was complaining, because I was busy making the preliminary sketches for Seamus's portrait.

I'd decided I'd give Lena his and Declan's portraits together, and then gradually work my way through the brothers.

I knew it was a way of softening her up, and I also knew that if she did soften toward me, Aidan Sr. would stop giving me so much shit whenever we met up.

Sunday lunch could have gone better, what with Seamus calling his grandfather out for being a homophobic prick—

"Aela!"

I smiled at Aoife when I saw her wading through the crowd with one of those baby car seats in hand. She plunked him on a chair, made sure he was stable, then bent down to kiss my cheek. I hadn't expected that, so I jerked back in surprise, but then stilled when I felt the soft brush of her lips against my cheek.

"Sorry, I didn't expect that," I said dryly, leaning over to give her the same treatment.

She beamed at me. "It's okay. I just—" Her smile was infectious. "Well, I wanted to give you a proper greeting."

I knew my eyebrows had to be kissing my hairline at that. "Any reason in particular?"

Her smile morphed into a grin. "For daring not to go to confession."

Ah.

I rolled my eyes. "Aidan Sr. nearly had a conniption, didn't he?" Things had derailed after the homophobic prick thing, that was for sure.

"You know he's mad when Lena tells him to walk it off in the garden." She raised her fist, lifted it over the table, and laughing, I bumped it with mine.

"What's the fist bump over?" Inessa asked, approaching the table, looking more put together than any eighteen-year-old I knew.

Hell, I'd been a mess at her age. A single mom who'd upended my entire world to protect my kid, but she was so seamlessly elegant I was envious.

She wore a simple black sheath dress, a shearling coat, heavy leather boots, and carried a Gucci bag. She tied it together with a pair of sunglasses in her hair, which she had to be using to keep her blonde locks out of her eyes because it was grim as anything outside.

Aoife, on the other hand, looked a lot more normal. She wore a pair of skinny jeans, a flowing t-shirt with a flamingo on it, a simple brown leather jacket, and some loafers.

Just like me, they wore Kevlar like it was an accessory, but I was definitely underdressed in my gypsy skirt, shitkickers, and tee, but that was purposeful. I was an anarchist, for Christ's sake. Eating at a place like this was bad for the rep.

And it was totally worth the looks I kept getting from the staff.

I mean, it wasn't like I was the only person who'd walked through these doors who had blue hair.

Surely rock stars had come and visited?

"I was just saying how she's brave for telling Aidan Sr. where to stuff it."

"Confession," Inessa said sagely, waving at me in greeting before bending down to kiss Jacob's forehead. As she did, I saw their guards bump knuckles at the back of the bar—Billy and Limerick. Christ, it had been a *long* time since I'd last seen them.

"Yeah, confession." Aoife grimaced. "I swear, it's like living in a monastery, except with killer monks."

I laughed at that. "You're not far off."

"I don't know," Inessa countered. "I can't see any of the brothers being celibate for long, can you?"

The three of us shared a glance and started snickering.

"Definitely not," Aoife replied with a cheeky grin.

"Yeah, *no*," I added.

"Thank God for manwhores too! Especially when they're reformed," Inessa commented.

"Can they ever be reformed?" I mused a little wistfully.

"Depends. According to Lena, she kept Aidan tied to her by always putting out," Aoife said dryly.

Crap, if that wasn't the most perfect segue ever into what I'd been talking to Declan about the other night.

But was it wise?

"There was never any talk of Aidan cheating," I started weaving.

"When Finn and I first got engaged, she told me to expect men to cheat, but when Inessa came to Sunday lunch, she said that to tie a man to us, we had to get them drunk on us."

"That's a contradiction, isn't it?" I asked.

"I thought so too," Inessa grumbled, as she played with a little soft toy Jacob had in his carrier.

A server came and handed us a menu, and after we'd made our selections and had tea dropped off for the three of us, I had to admit, I was chomping at the bit to ask what I probably shouldn't.

Some things were family secrets for a reason, after all.

But I never had been able to leave things well alone.

"It's funny how close Finn is to the family," I started, curious if they'd get my drift. I couldn't be the only one who'd seen the similarities between him and the rest of the brothers, could I? And after Dec's response, I knew it was going to be swept under the rug. Which I was okay with. I just wanted to know the truth.

My reason wasn't very palatable either.

I knew, for the rest of my life, that Aidan Sr., no matter what I did, no matter how many portraits I gave to Lena, was going to throw my past in my face.

If he'd cheated, I wanted ammunition too.

I never said I was a nice person...

"The boys grew up together," Aoife replied, but her tone was a little more wooden than before.

I shrugged. "I mean, I know. I was there." I shot her a smile. "I just never noticed the likeness before."

Inessa gave me a look before immediately taking a sip of tea. "I don't know what you mean. Likeness?"

"You know... how he looks like Aidan Sr.?"

"It's because they're all Black Irish," Inessa murmured. Then, she sighed. "Thank God for the Black Irish." She replaced her cup onto the saucer, then gently squished Jacob's cheek. "This one is going to be a heart-breaker, just like his daddy."

"And his uncles," I interjected dryly, not willing to let this drop.

I wasn't sure why they'd invited me here, but I'd figured it was to pump me for information. I highly doubted they wanted to be friends with me. I'd long since learned that I wasn't a likable person because the day Deirdre had died, and I'd headed off into the great unknown, I'd made a decision.

I wouldn't kiss ass ever again.

And being friends with Deirdre had made me stink of shit because I was that far up her butt.

As far as I'd ever been able to see, that was how friendship worked.

Aoife squirmed on her seat at my statement, but she tilted her head to the side and noted, "You're grumpier than I'd imagined an artist would be."

I had to laugh at that. "I'm not grumpy."

"No?" Aoife arched a brow. "Just rude then?"

I grinned at her. "Touché."

Her eyes twinkled a little. "What do you want me to say, Aela?"

"That Finn is Aidan Sr.'s by-blow?"

"By-blow?" Inessa repeated, her brow puckering.

"His illegitimate child," Aoife answered. "I need to get you hooked on historical romance next."

Despite myself, interest hit me. "You like romance books?"

"Yes. We do," was Inessa's retort, but I sensed her bristling ahead of schedule.

I raised my hands in surrender, because even though I wanted answers, I wasn't a total bitch. Even if romance books *hadn't* been my jam, I'd never give them crap about that. Someone's taste was their taste, and I celebrated that.

The world would be a boring place if we all weren't individuals and unique with it.

"I love romance books too." When they gaped at me, evidently disbelieving my claim, I reached for my cellphone in my purse, scrolled onto my kindle app, and shoved it at Aoife. She peered at the covers and laughed.

"You like mafia romance?"

I didn't have to look in a mirror to know my eyes were twinkling. "Very fitting, no?"

"Very." She pursed her lips. "Why do you want to know if Finn is what you think he is?"

Because I wasn't going to bullshit, I murmured, "So if Aidan Sr. tries to have me killed or something, I can hurl that at him."

Inessa scowled. "Why would you do that? If he has you killed, then he wouldn't be there to hurl anything at. Not even your shoe. Plus, they send" —she muttered under her breath— "Eoghan... out on those jobs. He wouldn't hurt his brother like that."

I loved that logic, especially because it was clear she'd been raised in the life. I mean, I knew that already, she screamed Bratva with her stiff manner and her stern disposition, but Aoife most certainly wasn't like us.

While I knew she must know *something* about how the Five Points' world worked, it was obvious that she hadn't anticipated my answer.

Ironically enough, it was clear to see that she liked it too. Taken aback, sure. Liked? That was something *I* hadn't anticipated.

She reached for her cup of tea and stared at me over the rim. "I don't think he'd kill you. Lena's wanted a grandchild for a long time."

"She has Jacob."

"She'd have had Seamus, too, if Declan hadn't done whatever he did that made you hide him."

"It wasn't his fault," I defended. "Not totally. I thought he'd think I was trying to trap him, and when Deirdre, his girlfriend, died the way she did..." I shrugged. "I hate to say it when you've just brought a baby into the world, but what kind of life is it for a kid?"

She grimaced. "Did you think that thought didn't cross my mind when I got pregnant?"

"I can imagine it did. All I could think was that I wanted to protect him. Keep him safe. And there I was, pregnant, standing over my friend's grave. A friend who'd died because she was following her boyfriend who she thought was cheating... because he was. With me."

"It wasn't your fault she was following him." Inessa shrugged. "I never expected Eoghan to remain faithful to me. Lena is right that we can't expect it of them."

I scowled at her. "You bet your ass we can expect it. If they say they love us, then we can expect it."

"I agree."

Inessa shrugged. "I don't disagree, but I just... I was raised a different way."

I sighed. "I was raised the same way. I know how often the men cheat. I'm sure my dad did too, and that I've probably got younger brothers and sisters roaming around the city, but... when they tell you they love you, they shouldn't cheat. It should be like a law or something."

"That is my kind of law," she concurred with a soft smile.

I didn't need to hear her say it to know that Eoghan loved her, and that she loved him in turn. I'd seen them together, and a blind man would know about their feelings for one another.

I didn't think it was puppy love either. Eoghan wasn't, and never had been, a puppy.

Having met him as a kid, having seen him in school, he'd been born and raised a pitbull. A nasty one.

Aoife studied me until her attention was broken when the server arrived with a tiered dish that had scones and petit fours and small, crustless sandwiches on it.

Tiny knives and forks were propped on gleaming linen napkins alongside bone china plates.

Because I was a dessert first kind of girl, I served myself a petit four and a scone, and as I smothered the scone with jam and cream, the silence grew tenser with every passing moment.

Until, eventually, Aoife blew out a breath, and muttered, "You didn't hear this from me..."

TWENTY-FOUR

DECLAN

WHEN SEAMUS HIT the target three times in the chest, I glowered at him. "How did you do that?"

At his age, I'd been hitting paper dicks with how low my shots were running, and while I was a lot better now, I was no Eoghan.

I'd exaggerated when I'd told Aela I was a crap shot, because in my world, a crap shot meant being put in a body bag ahead of schedule. But the idea was a good one. It was a way of giving my kid the power, and I was all for that.

Life always had a way of working out how you least expected it, so I wanted to make up for time lost as well as getting to know the real him.

The Seamus that Aela never really saw because she knew him inside out.

I could do a Da, be a prick, and shove my way into his life and make him listen, or I could be his friend.

I'd never been like Da. Never wanted to be. So being a friend was more than enough for me to be happy.

He grinned at me, a little cockily, but he deserved it. Neither was he embarrassed to admit the truth, "Practice."

"Not skill, huh?"

He snickered. "Maybe a little."

I shoved down the plastic glasses I wore and leaned my elbow against the stand on the gun range where we were firing shots.

The paper target was flying toward us, confirming what I already knew

—Aela had made sure he was comfortable with a weapon. That had to have gone down like a lead balloon in Europe. They weren't as gun happy as we were over here in the States, but I was glad. At least I knew he was safe.

Now I just needed him to turn twenty-one so he could get a license and carry.

When he eyed the small holes in the paper, he murmured to himself, "Not bad."

I arched a brow. "Couldn't have done much better. Three in the center of the chest? Not even the nine circle, but right in the middle?" I whistled. "You did good, kid."

His nose crinkled, but I knew he liked hearing that.

My practice went down on the streets, but I'd keep this up if it meant getting some quality time with my boy. Especially since he seemed to enjoy it.

"Thanks."

As he unclipped the target, I asked, "You want to grab a burger?"

He twisted to look at me. "Can we?"

"Sure thing." I rubbed my hands together. "You got something in mind or can I pick?"

"You know the city better."

"That I do." I eyed him. "You like milkshakes?"

"Duh."

I grinned. "Then I know the perfect place."

As we finished up on the range, leaving with a tip of my head to the owner, the wife of an ex-Pointer who'd died back in the eighties and was an integral member of the Old Wives' Club—a bunch of savages who were the wives of dead brothers—we headed for my car.

The alarm beeped as I unlocked the door, and when we climbed in, he carefully placed the folded paper target in the glove compartment.

"You going to show your mom?"

"Yeah, it'll make her feel better."

"It will?"

"She likes to know I can protect myself."

I pursed my lips at his words. "Question, did you ever, before I came into your life, I mean, need to shoot a gun?"

"Once or twice."

That had my eyes widening, and I stopped, taking a moment before I started the ignition to twist toward him. "Once or twice?"

He shrugged. "Once when we were in Mexico. Someone tried to kidnap us. It was nuts."

"They tried to kidnap you?" I intoned, and I knew he sensed my anger because his shoulders hunched.

"Yeah. Like I said, insane. Mom got shot in the belly. After she healed up, the guy Mom was working for brought us into his compound even though, before then, she used to insist on having her own place. She wasn't happy, but it was a big job and she was totally mental over it."

"What do you mean?"

He hummed under his breath. "You know, when she goes gaga over a piece?"

"I've never seen her like that."

"Give her time," was his wry retort. "This is probably the longest she's gone without something driving her. She gets really involved in stuff. Forgets to eat, never knows what day it is or time it is, things like that. "

I knew how that went... *once upon a time,* I'd been at the center of that focus. And now that I thought about it... I'd seen her scar there. It was small, and when I'd seen it, I'd been going down on her so my focus had been elsewhere.

Shit. She'd almost fucking died.

Anger and distress made my voice husky as I demanded, "What was the other time?"

"It was a mugging that went wrong. Mom isn't very good at just handing over her purse. She almost got pistol-whipped, and would have done if I hadn't grabbed her gun and shot the guy in the foot."

"Good job, kiddo."

He pulled a face. "I was aiming higher."

Despite myself, I had to laugh. "Ouch."

"Yeah. I was meaner back then."

"Probably because you thought it was only for pissing out of."

He bit his lip, but I knew he wanted to laugh. "You swear a lot, don't you?"

Unoffended by the question, I told him, "Yeah. But..." I paused as I tried to figure out how to say what I wanted to say. "They're just words. Only as powerful as you make them. For me, it's part of the role I play. I'm so used to playing the role, I use them more than I like."

"Why play a role at all?"

"I don't have a choice. I never did." I tipped my head to the side. "You, on the other hand, will always have choices."

"Why?"

"Because you met my father. I'm not him. Plus," I said with a shrug, "Aela raised you well. She raised you to be different, and I like what I see. If we'd been together when you were born, I don't know if things would be the same. As much as I hate that I'm a stranger to you now, I'm almost glad if it means your path is different than mine."

He blinked at that, and I knew I'd surprised him with my answer. "I-I think that's probably the nicest thing you could have told me."

"It's the truth. I want what's best for you," I said, and I meant it.

"Unlike your father."

"Unlike him," I confirmed.

"Why's he like that?" he asked warily.

"He's a product of his environment. Just like I am. Just like you are."

"Do you hate him?"

I stared at him, not totally surprised by the question. "When I was your age, sure. He wanted me to do things..." My voice waned because he didn't need to know *what* things. "He wanted me to be something I wasn't."

"Why did you conform?"

"I didn't have a choice."

"We always have choices."

"Not in my world."

"It's my world now," he rasped.

"No. I'll make sure it isn't."

"You sound so sure."

"Because I am."

He bit his lip. "I asked Uncle Conor for—"

"I know. He told me. Didn't like what you read?"

"I mean, I've seen *The Sopranos*." He hesitated. "Don't tell Mom though."

I had to grin. "I won't."

"I know what a crime family does and things, but..."

"But what?"

"It's not like *The Sopranos*," he said miserably. "It's real life."

"It is."

He licked his lips. "If I saw—"

I tipped my head to the side when he broke off. "Saw what?"

"Nothing."

My brow puckered, but I reached over and cupped his shoulder. "What is it? You can tell me."

"Nothing. I promise." He cleared his throat to suddenly hide the squeak, and while I knew he was hiding something, what could I do? Get out a knife and threaten him?

I could see that going down well with Aela.

So, even though I knew he was lying, even though I could see from the sudden storm clouds in his eyes that he badly needed to share something with me, I just murmured, "You won't be getting involved in my world."

He peered up at me with relief in his gaze, but he inquired, "Why is Aidan so mean to you?"

"Because he wants me to be something I'm not, and even though I do as he asks, do what he wants, and have never said no, it's not enough."

"Why?"

I blew out a breath. "That's a tough question, kid."

He shrugged. "Someone has to ask them."

"True." My lips twisted. "If you asked me before I found out about you, I'd have said because he wanted me to be better."

"But now?"

"I'd say because he sees me as his failure."

Seamus's eyes widened. "That's mean. You're not a failure!"

Though his defense was appreciated, I shook my head. "*His* failure, kid. He made me into what I am. Even though he had to work hard to shove me into that mold. So, when he looks at me, he knows I'm this because of his choices.

"When your mom looks at you, she sees a kid who took the bull by the horns and made things happen. She gave you your head, let you do what you wanted, and when you're older, and you're a fancy lawyer or the president, she'll know that you had the brains and the smarts to get there on your own."

He frowned. "I think I know what you mean."

"Good."

"When he looks at you, he sees what he made you, not what your potential should have allowed you to be."

"Exactly." I cleared my throat. "That's hard for anyone to deal with."

"I'll bet." He stared at me, then slowly asked, "What did you want to be?"

"That's the irony."

"Why?"

"Because I have no idea."

"You must have had goals. Dreams."

"I never allowed myself to have any. It would have been too painful."

"Mom said you loved art. She said that she doesn't know how I'm about as useless with a pencil as she is with a wrench when you and her are so artistic."

"I'm not artistic," I countered. "I just like looking at it."

"Did you never try?"

"I used to doodle, but nothing more than that."

"Wow." When I arched a brow at him, he wriggled his shoulders. "That's sad. You could have been like Mom."

"Maybe. But I never bothered worrying about it. This is my life. I am who I am."

"Won't Aidan try to do to me what he did to you?"

"Without a doubt," I told him, which had dismay flashing in his eyes. "But, Shay, you're my son. Not his. I already warned him to leave you alone.

"Now, despite that, I hope you'll have a relationship with my parents, especially Ma, because she's good people."

"How is she good people when she let him do that to you?"

"Because she loved me. Because she tried to defend me. But Da isn't someone you can battle that often without getting worn down."

"What if he wears you down?"

"He won't," I told him, aware my tone had hardened. "I never bothered fighting for myself, Seamus. I saw no point. I am who I am. I was born for this life. But you weren't. I'll fight for you like I never fought for myself, and I don't give a damn if he and I lock horns every day for the rest of my life— I'll never let him control you. You'll do what you want to do. You'll make mistakes and succeed and you'll be as normal as you want." I shrugged. "If you want in the life, then that's your choice, but somehow, I don't see that for you."

He blinked at me. "I want to be president."

"Why?" I asked, but my lips were twitching because I knew he meant it.

"Why not?"

I laughed. "True. Why not an astronaut?"

"Not interested. The president sees all, hears all, knows all." Interest gleamed in his eyes. "That's my kind of game."

"Hardly a game when you make all the rules."

"Best way to win."

I tipped my head at that. "You want to be president, then I'll help make that happen."

He pursed his lips. "I'd say that I want to do it fair and square, but everyone knows that you make it to the top by lying and cheating."

"You're too cynical for your age," I said dryly.

"I'm a realist."

"Your ma'd say you were an idealist." I smirked a little. "You're fourteen. You should be thinking about boning the hottest girl in your class."

"She isn't as hot as Inessa."

Even though I knew I had to caution him, I'd admit to loving that answer simply because it meant he was opening up to me.

Fuck, maybe being his friend wasn't impossible.

"You read up on us..." I cocked a brow at him. "You know what Eoghan does for a living."

He grinned at that. "Doesn't that make it more fun?"

I snorted. "Stick to kids your own age, bud. They won't get you shot, and I'd hate to have to kill my own brother. Da might be a jackass, but I love my brothers."

"You love your mom too."

"I do."

"I'm not sure she deserves it."

"Maybe not, but I love her all the same. And, like I was saying, I hope you'll get friendly with her because she'd love to be a part of your life, but if you don't want to, then you don't want to."

"You're more accommodating than Mom is."

"What makes you say that?"

He shrugged. "She usually makes me do stuff I don't want to."

"That's what moms do," I replied wryly.

"I guess." He heaved a sigh. "Are you and Mom going to get back together?"

"Would it upset you if we did?" I'd expected this question earlier, if I was being honest.

"No. She never really stopped loving you anyway. It'll be nice to see her happy." He narrowed his eyes on me. "You will make her happy, won't you?"

"I'll try. That's all I can offer."

"You've seen how good of a shot I am."

Snickering, I said, "I did. And I meant it. I'll try. Nothing is ever simple. Not where love is concerned."

"You love her?"

"Always did. Never stopped."

"You didn't look for her."

I heard the accusation. "I didn't."

"Why not?"

"Because I got mixed up in things I shouldn't have, and... she lied to me."

"What about?"

Uneasy with the direction this conversation had taken, I looked away and stared at the Merc beside him.

"Ah."

My gaze darted back to him. "What?"

"She lied about me."

"That's one way to phrase it." I grunted. "If I'd known the truth about you, I'd have left no stone unturned, Seamus."

His eyes gleamed at that, but all he said was, "She's very protective."

"She is. She has every right to be. It's a mean world out there. Every kid should have a mom who protects them."

Shay studied me with the zeal of a scientist, and the cold, hard reasoning of a calculator. It was weird to feel flayed open, but this was my kid. Looking out for my woman. I wasn't going to fault him for it.

Expecting another question, he surprised me by declaring, "I'm ready for that burger now."

Assuming I'd passed whatever test he'd set me, I muttered, "I was ready five minutes ago." And with that, I set off, somehow feeling like we'd cleared the air and had set the stage for the next few acts of our life.

I wanted him to know I was here for him, that I'd fight for him, *and* for Aela. It would take more than one session at a gun range and a chat before a burger to make him realize I meant exactly what I said, but we had time.

And I was more than grateful for that.

But, as we pulled into a drive-thru, after we checked the menu, and just before I could order, he told me, "You can tell Mom to stop sneaking in and out of her bedroom every night."

My lips curved into a sheepish grin, and when the intercom squeaked, I gave our order, and we never spoke about Aela's nightly escapades again.

Just like a real father and son wouldn't.

TWENTY-FIVE

CONOR

THE SECOND MY computer screen went blank, I knew what had happened.

"Goddammit," I groused under my breath, unsurprised when bright green text flashed onto it.

I swore, this bitch had a Matrix obsession—only ever did things in black and green.

Lodestar: **I know what you did last summer.**

aCooooig: **I'm not Freddie Prinze Jr.**

Lodestar: **Shame. Always had a crush on him.**

aCooooig: **There a reason you hijacked my hardware?**

Lodestar: **Fun?**

aCooooig: **Fuck. U.**

Lodestar: **Ouch. You trying to hurt my feelings?**

aCooooig: **If you infect my hardware again, you'll wish that was all that hurt when I'm through with you.**

Lodestar: **I thought you liked playing?**

aCooooig: **I do. Just without the ten grand price tag every time.**

Lodestar: **It's true what they say then.**

aCooooig: **About what?**

Lodestar: **The Irish. Tight.**

aCooooig: **My ass is tight. And it's the Scots. The Irish are flush with cash when they're happy.**

Lodestar: **Good to know.**

aCooooig: **There a reason you're here? Hijacking my computer?**

Lodestar: **Yep**

aCooooig: **Care to share?**

Lodestar: **Seen the traces you've been running**

aCooooig: **Which ones?**

Lodestar: **All of them, little bird. Flying all over the web like you have. You're lucky I'm the first one to spot it.**

aCooooig: **Specifics.**

Lodestar: **The Fieris?**

aCooooig: **There a reason you got in touch?**

Lodestar: **I just learned we're working for the same side.**

aCooooig: **Excuse me?**

Lodestar: **Your code tells me you can read, so...?**

aCooooig: **What the fuck are you talking about? Same side?**

Lodestar: **I'm friends of your friends.**

aCooooig: **Since when?**

Lodestar: **Since a long time. Any enemy of the Fieris is a friend of mine.**

aCooooig: **Why?**

Lodestar: **You'd have to know what *I* did last summer before I'd tell you that.**

aCooooig: **I always had a crush on Buffy.**

Lodestar: **Pity for you I look nothing like her.**

aCooooig: **Shame.**

Lodestar: **Now you know how I felt.**

aCooooig: **Come on then, enemy of my enemy. What do you want to tell me?**

Lodestar: **Who says I want to tell you something?**

aCooooig: **The fact you got in touch with me?**

Lodestar: **Maybe I just felt like talking to someone on my level.**

aCooooig: **Oh.**

Lodestar: **Oh. Anyway, the Fieri Jrs.? They're dead now.**

aCooooig: **I know.**

Lodestar: **That why you looking into the other families inside the Italian mafia?**

aCooooig: **Yeah. Trying to figure out who's going to take charge once Benito dies.**

Lodestar: **There are three families in total.**

aCooooig: **One to the left and the other to the right of Benito Fieri.**

Lodestar: **Yeah. The Rossis are second in line. But Benito's power is still in full force. When he dies, that's when shit will change. And unless the Bratva hire a sniper, I just perused the transcription of his recent visit to the doctor—clean bill of health. Only the good die young, I guess.**

aCooooig: **How do you know this? I've been scouring and I didn't know.**

Lodestar: **I've made it my business to learn everything about the *Famiglia*.**

aCooooig: **Thank you.**

Lodestar: **No worries.**

aCooooig: **You helped me. I can help you.**

Lodestar: **How? I don't need any help.**

aCooooig: **Everyone always needs a helping hand at some point.**

Lodestar: **Not me.**

aCooooig: **Yeah? Well, how about this?**

aCooooig sent a link

Lodestar: **You trying to malware me?**

aCooooig: **No need. Had malware on your system for as long as you had it on mine. Check it out.**

Lodestar: **What is it?**

aCooooig: **You'll find out soon enough. We've only got a few 'friends.' Maybe you'll get this fucker's face out there.**

Lodestar: **I know him. What did he do?**

aCooooig: **Seen fraternizing with a corrupt Fed.**

Lodestar: **Jesus.**

aCooooig: **About sums it up.**

Lodestar: **Thanks for the heads-up.**

aCooooig: **Happy to help.**

Lodestar: **I'm sure.**

aCooooig: **There's no need to keep on fighting.**

Lodestar: **Who said we're at war?**

aCooooig: **My bank account.**

Lodestar: **Mine suffered just as bad.**

aCooooig: **You got eyes and ears in all the families in New York?**

Lodestar: **Now...why would you ask me that?**

aCooooig: **Interest.**

Lodestar: **Huh?**

aCooooig: **Well? Do you?**

Lodestar: **Maybe. What are you looking for?**

aCooooig: **Bunch of rats.**

Lodestar: **I like rats.**

aCooooig: **You like snitches.**

Lodestar: **Rats make good pets.**

aCooooig: **I'm sure, but this kind doesn't.**

Lodestar: **Agreed. I heard the Westies are having a little problem with vermin.**

aCooooig: **You did, huh?**

Lodestar: **I did.**

aCooooig: **Know who and why?**

Lodestar: **I can find out.**

aCooooig: **You sure you don't already know?**

Lodestar: **>.>**

aCooooig: **I'll pay for information.**

Lodestar: **Who are you?**

aCooooig: **Someone whose family suffers when a rat takes a bite.**

Lodestar: **Hmm. Maybe there's nothing I want.**

aCooooig: **You don't like justice?**

Lodestar: **Sure I do.**

aCooooig: **Lots of chatter about the Fieris.**

Lodestar: **Always is. That's what people do. Chatter.**

aCooooig: **True. People always talk.**

Lodestar: **Always.**

aCooooig: **What do they say though?**

Lodestar: **If I were you I'd be looking for someone.**

aCooooig: **Who?**

Lodestar: **Fed.**

aCooooig: **Bastards.**

Lodestar: **Yeah. This one is a real fucker.**

aCooooig: **What did they do?**

Lodestar: **Fingers in a ton of pies. Some say this one has a grudge against the Five Points.**

aCooooig: **Plenty of them out there.**

Lodestar: **Naturally. You make a lot of enemies on your way to the top.**

aCooooig: **Truer words.**

Lodestar: **You know of a corrupt federal agent with beef against the Irish?**

aCooooig: **Maybe.**

Lodestar: **Well, a little birdie twittered and told me that the Fed is a go-between.**

aCooooig: **Between who?**

Lodestar: **A bridge between anyone who hates the Irish and wants to find their way into the *Famiglia's* inner circle.**

aCooooig: **Motherfucker.**

Lodestar: **Exactly.**

aCooooig: **I know who it is.**

Lodestar: **I'm sure you do.**

aCooooig: **I owe you.**

Lodestar: **Yes, and I always come calling for my debts.**

aCooooig: **Honey, ever heard of '*laissez les bon temps rouler*'?**

Lodestar: **I don't speak French.**

aCooooig: **That one's worth finding on Google Translate.**

Lodestar: **Maybe.**

WHEN MY COMPUTER screen returned to normal, I sent crawlers through my system to kick her out of there, but after that was in place, I started a group call and, when all my brothers were scowling at me, I told them, "Houston, we don't have a problem."

TWENTY-SIX

DECLAN

"WE *DON'T* HAVE A PROBLEM?"

Conor beamed at me. "No. We have a solution."

"To which problem?" Finn asked. "And did you really have to wake me up at three AM? Some of us have to be up like regular people."

Conor blinked. "It's three AM?"

"Never mind," Finn said with a yawn. "What solution and which problem?"

"I found out who Benito Fieri's heir will be."

"Didn't we already know that?" I asked with a frown. "Only the Rossis and the Genovicos hold any power in the ranks. You know they have a different power system than us."

"Yeah, their way makes no sense," Aidan grumbled, rubbing his hand over his face. "Who has three families in charge? Why three as well? Why not a council?"

"We only have one family in charge," I pointed out. "And when Da dies, you'll take over, and when your kids are old enough, they'll be more important than my kids."

"It's royalty, is what it is. Considering Da hates the British, I wonder if he realizes he runs his world in the same vein as the Windsors," Brennan commented with a small laugh.

My lips twitched. "Think we're getting off topic."

"We are, and some of us have people waiting for us back in bed," Eoghan groused.

"Marriage has made you a real killjoy," Conor remarked. "You'd think a regular lay would have perked you up."

"I was plenty perky before you dragged me in on this group call."

I had to laugh, and so did the others. We all knew that when the *Mission Impossible* theme song rang on our cells, because Conor was still in Fourth Grade, that we had to answer.

"Well, you can get back to boning your wife after we've discussed this. Lodestar got in touch."

"She did?" I scowled. "Why? I thought you and she were enemies."

"She went out of her way to tell me we had mutual enemies so that made her a friend."

"Sounds like your kind of psycho," Aidan rumbled. "Maybe she's hot, Conor. Then the two of you can make computer babies together."

Conor hissed. "She wrecked my computer. The one I built from scratch, bro. Only thing I'm making with her is war. Even if," he tacked on, "I owe her."

Aidan rolled his eyes. "You're the biggest fucking drama queen I know."

"Anyway," Finn grumbled, "before things devolve into a bitching match where both of you prove you're drama queens, what's the solution, Conor?"

"Make friends with the Rossis, kill Fieri, pave the way for a power exchange. Fieri's insane anyway. He's waging war out there like he has nothing else to lose. He must have pissed people off in the ranks."

"You say that like killing Fieri would be easy," I remarked.

"Why wouldn't it be? We're always exposed, and don't we have the Whistler on our side—the best sniper in the country?"

Eoghan heaved a sigh. "I ain't pulling that kind of move without Da's sanction."

"Big baby," Conor rumbled.

"No, I'm just not willing to get my balls cut off when my wife is very much attached to them."

Aidan scrunched up his face at that. "Only attached to them for Inessa's sake, huh? You're all heart."

"Trust me, I know."

Brennan shook his head. "Da's too stubborn to go for this. You know he wants them to kill each other. Sure, we're at war with the *Famiglia* too, but the fighting is between them and the Bratva. He's wanting them to equalize the field and reduce their numbers, so we have more power than ever."

"We got our first shipment of ghost guns in today," I informed them softly. "From Texas?"

Aidan blinked. "Good stuff?"

"The best. Better than expected. But you should see the gear Da ordered." I grimaced as I scraped a hand over my chin. "He's getting ready for battle whether we think he is or not."

"Knowing Da, he'll be two steps ahead anyway," Aidan pointed out.

"We also got a wedding invitation," I commented wryly.

"What? For who?" Aidan demanded.

"Ink and Amaryllis. But it's some kind of new age ceremony or something."

"I think it should be Eoghan who has to go seeing as we had to sit through his wedding already," Conor groused.

"So did I!" he sputtered.

"You got the week off, we just had to deal with the shitty afterparty," was all Conor had to say.

"I haven't even been on a fucking honeymoon yet," he grumbled.

Finn arched a brow. "Ink's alive, at least."

"We have good doctors on the payroll," Aidan said with a laugh.

"Aoife will be all over Inessa. She loves weddings."

"Then you go," Eoghan groused.

"Nah, we're a democracy and we've made the decision that you're going," Finn retorted, his grin widening as Eoghan flipped him the bird. "Aoife will get a kick out of hearing about all the flowers though."

"Christ, that would bore Aela shitless," I replied, grateful as all hell that was the truth.

"Do they have flowers at biker weddings?" Eoghan grumbled.

Aidan snorted. "Look at you, the lot of you pussy-whipped." Then, before he could insult us further, he tipped his head to the side as a thought evidently occurred to him—one that was more interesting than a biker wedding. "Why did Lodestar get in touch with you?"

Conor smiled. "Because I laid the path for her to contact me."

That smile was devious. "What game are you playing?"

"A few days back, I got a hit on her IP address."

"So?"

"It's registered to the Satan's Sinners' compound."

My eyes flared wide in surprise. "She's one of them?"

"Evidently. I sent over the picture of the biker we saw going to Caroline Dunbar's the other day. She knew him."

"Shit, if they have a rat then we need them to kill the fucker," Aidan snapped, sitting upright. It was, I'd admit, the first time he'd looked anything other than stoned in a while.

"Agreed," I stated firmly, and watched as my brothers all confirmed their stance. "I'll get in touch with Sin. Lodestar might sit on the information, so we need to get them to act and fast."

"When are we going to take out Dunbar?" Aidan groused. "She's a thorn in our side."

Eoghan perked up at that. "Any excuse to take out a pig and I'm down."

I shook my head. "There's something going on with her."

"What like?" Eoghan asked, his brow furrowing with disappointment.

"I don't know."

"I do," Conor rasped, his tone darkening. "And that's the solution I was talking about. Lodestar told me that there's a corrupt Fed who acts as the go-between for the *Famiglia* and anyone with beef against the Irish."

My eyes flared wide. "Shit."

"Yeah, shit." He rubbed his chin. "It would be easy to set up too. Haul someone in on fake charges, talk to them, manipulate them, and get them to do what you want so you'll drop the charges... perfect con."

"What do we do?" I asked tiredly. "We kill her, it might unearth a graveyard's worth of bodies."

"Probably would. I think we use the information we have as leverage to get her to stop blackmailing you. We have shit on her, she has shit on us. Maybe that will be enough," Eoghan stated.

"No. This is personal to her. It won't stop until we end her."

"Or maybe we use her and figure out a way to get her to end herself," Conor mused, his tone turning distant.

"We need to tell Da," Aidan murmured. "If we've got traitors in the family because of her, he needs to know."

"He'll just have her killed," I pointed out.

"Then we need to come up with a better strategy," Finn reasoned. "Conor, we need to think about this."

Because the pair of them were our financial strategists, it fit that we'd leave them with this particular 'problem.'

Conor was wrong.

Houston, we *did* have a problem, and it was shaped like a cunt who carried an FBI badge.

"We'll talk about this in the morning," Conor replied. "I need to think."

"Me too," Finn agreed.

"This has long-term repercussions," Brennan argued. "We need to figure out who the rats are before they reveal themselves to us."

"Like with Ryan Hoskins, you mean?" I ground out, referring to the bastard who'd turned on us, killing a Five Pointer in the process—my ma's favorite guard, Rogan—all to help a *Famiglia* goon get into Aela's house to kill my woman and my boy.

He was with the fishes now, but that was less than he deserved.

"Yeah." Aidan frowned. "This is going to create a witch hunt."

"Apparently a much needed one," Eoghan retorted.

"Shit. This is going to make our already paranoid father even more of a psycho," Brennan groused.

Because each of us agreed, we fell silent at that.

Fuck.

I let out a tired sigh. "We can deal with this in the morning. Good job, Conor."

Finn nodded. "Definitely a job well done."

Aidan rasped, "You had feelers out for Lodestar at one point, bro."

"I had someone going to kick the shit out of her," he concurred.

"You calling them off?" Eoghan asked.

His smile was unholy. "Like she said, the enemy of my enemy is my friend. There's more than one way to play war with someone."

"Jesus," Brennan muttered. "I think we found Conor's kryptonite."

"Better than porn," he commented.

I groaned and grumbled, "I got better stuff to do than listen to what gives you a boner, Kid. Now, fuck off, the lot of you. I need my beauty sleep."

I cut the call before they could say another word, then, opening my desk drawer, I pulled out the gift I'd been dithering over whether to give to Aela.

Reasoning this could be my excuse for getting out of bed at this time of night, I slinked out of my office and back into my bedroom where Aela was still snoozing. The sight of her did something to me, filled me with a kind of happiness I hadn't known since she'd left.

Most people sought happiness all their life. Me? I knew happiness wasn't a part of the equation.

It was some lofty goal that people who weren't mobsters could afford to search for. We dealt in reality—cold, hard facts and colder, harder money.

As I moved around to her side of the futon, I set the gifts on the ground before I retreated to my side and slipped into bed, she instantly turned into me, her warmth sinking where that inner chill had festered for over a decade without her.

"Where d'you go?" she mumbled.

I slid my arms around her, wondering how this could feel so fucking good, before I murmured, "Got a present for you."

She rubbed her brow against my chest. "Don't need anything."

I smiled even though I had to shake my head because I knew she meant it. Everyone wanted something from me. Everyone. Apart from her.

Maybe that was what had always made her stand out.

If anything, she didn't ask enough of me. Never had.

"You remember the day you got your tag?"

She tensed. And that was my answer. *She remembered.*

"I hated myself that day."

"I hated you a little bit too."

"Couldn't blame you."

"Loved you more, though, otherwise I wouldn't have had it done."

"I know." I kissed her again. "Funny how that was what brought us to today, no?"

"Funny—haha or funny—strange?"

I laughed. "You're a comedian tonight, huh?"

"Always." She heaved a sigh. "Anyway, what's my gift? Another tag?"

"Nah. Two gifts. Just like that night."

"Christ, that mean I'm not going to like one of them?"

"You should appreciate these ones."

"Promises, promises." She yawned as she sat up. "Where are they then?"

"Beside your bed. I thought you could wake up and see them."

"Instead of waking me up *to* see them, you mean?"

I grinned. "Yup."

I heard rustling, before she found her phone and the light blinked on. Using that as a guide, she found the bulky envelope which, the second it was in her hands, made a clacking noise.

She stilled. "Keys?"

I just hummed.

Knowing she didn't like the apartment, I could sense her excitement as she sat up, leaned over to reach for the light, and switched it on. We both blinked a little as she poured out the contents of the envelope.

When she handled the bunch of keys, tossing them in her palm, she asked, "The brownstone you talked about before?"

"Yeah. You don't like it here, plus paper walls don't matter so much when you don't have a kid," I said wryly.

Her eyes twinkled. "Want to fuck me whenever you get a boner, huh?"

I grinned at her as I stacked my hand behind my head to prop myself up. "There might be ulterior motives behind the move."

"I'll bet." Her brow arched, but she grinned at me, and the grin was magnetic. Enough that it made both my heart and dick take a leap. "What's the other gift?" she asked, but mostly to herself. It was a wad of papers, and her arched brow surged ever higher. "You hired The Cloisters for the day?"

I nodded.

"Why?"

"Because I want to fuck you in the Cuxa Courtyard."

She blinked, but fire burned in her eyes a second later. "You do?"

"Wanted it when I was a kid, couldn't afford it. Now? I can afford anything."

"Pays to be rich, huh?"

"Without a doubt." I tapped the paper. "They're getting a nice donation out of it."

"Looks like it." She pursed her lips. "They're going to turn off the cameras, right?"

"There's no art out there, so I think we can arrange for that. Especially if it's a quickie."

She laughed, then launched herself at me. As her lips met mine, she mumbled, "I love it!"

Her joy bubbled through me. "Good."

This was my way of wooing her. Marriage was at the end of the road, and I knew Da would only wait so long before things were made official, but I wasn't going to push it. I wanted her to know I wanted her for *her*. So I'd show her that every which way I could.

She slipped her tongue into my mouth, and I let her. I let her fuck me, loving that she took charge, loving how she writhed against me, her tits bumping into my chest, the tight peaks dragging against my flesh.

She felt like heaven and hell. The best kind of sin.

I groaned into her mouth as she reached between us, her hand shaping my dick. She squeezed before she started jacking me off a second before she lifted the sheets up, baring my dick to the millions of dollars' worth of art I'd exposed to the night air before we'd gotten into bed earlier.

That the paintings fired her up made them the most expensive porn imaginable, but because she got it, because *I* got it, it just made everything that much fucking hotter.

As her thumb carefully burrowed into the tip of my cock where pre-cum had gathered, she bit my bottom lip and rasped, "Declan?"

"Yeah," I breathed. "I love you too."

She sighed and melted into me, absolutely merged with me like water into water.

Her body turned into silk, and I was more than happy to be covered by her.

I grabbed her wrist when she started for my balls, and I twisted us over, not stopping until she was under me and I was looming over her. I grabbed both her hands, pinned them over her head, then rasped, "I wanna fuck you on your knees, *mo ghrá*, but if you utter a single sound, I'm gonna stop."

Her eyes flared wide before they narrowed with suspicion. "You wouldn't dare."

"Try me," I rumbled, pressing a kiss to her mouth and letting my tongue flicker over the ripe curve of her Cupid's bow.

She stopped wriggling against the mussed sheets, and I moved down, down and down, until my lips could whisper over her nipples. I sucked on them, lathing them with my tongue, flicking the tips until she was squirming against me even more. Smirking against the nub, I bit down a little harder than she expected, which had a guttural squeak escaping her that was quickly cut off.

Letting my mouth trace along her curves, I found the faint indents on her belly. The stretch marks, the scar, and I kissed them all. Tasting the flesh with my tongue, thanking her, silently, with each caress.

When she started wriggling again, evidently wanting me to head further south, I arched up, bounding away from her, and she sat up in surprise, her hand reaching for my arm as she hugged me to her, not letting me move away.

"What did I say about making noise?"

She pressed her forehead into my arm then whispered, "You make me feel too much."

The despondent words shot through me like a shockwave.

There wasn't anything she could have said that could have messed with me more, and I was on her again, faster than lightning followed thunder as I pushed her into the sheets. I grabbed her legs, spread them wide and high, then took a hold of my dick and rubbed it against her bare pussy.

As I nudged her clit, her back arched against the bed, and as I slipped inside her, she hissed as her muscles grew tense with the abrupt penetration.

Slowly, I fucked her. Moving further down, leaning into her deeper and deeper so her muscles could get used to the stretch and I could get farther into her pussy.

I swore, if I could crawl inside her, I totally fucking would.

Groaning as she took all of me, I cut off the noise, well aware my kid was apparently in the know about our bedroom games, so I tried to keep things on the down low. But fuck, the feel of her, the heat, the goddamn pressure, and just knowing it was Aela. At. Long. Fucking. Last. I began to slam inside her. I had no choice. No alternative. My dick tunneled into her, filling her all the way, keeping her full.

I reached between us, my thumb on her clit as I made sure she soared as high and as hard as I was.

Letting her take my weight, I leaned over and covered her mouth with my hand as I pounded into her hard enough for the bed to shake, and when she bit down on the fleshy part of my palm, I hissed as the rapture broke through me like a million fucking fireworks that were sent from above in a glorious light show that proved just how much she was it for me.

As her pussy pulsed around me, I spread her legs, hooked them high around my waist, then collapsed on her. Within seconds, her arms came around me, and she held me close.

And before I slumped totally into her hold, I reached for the tag that signified way too much—and none of it good—and kissed it.

She sighed as my tongue traced the letters, and her mouth brushed my temple as she whispered, "I love it when you fill me with your cum."

I groaned and rumbled, "I love filling you with it." Letting her arm relax against the sheets, I pressed a kiss to her throat before I managed to twist us over so she was on top of me, and holding her close, I whispered, "Now go to sleep."

"Like I was the one who kept us up," she teased drowsily, but seconds later, she drifted away.

And so did I.

Some parts of my world might be up in the air, but that was how it worked in this life. Somehow, at the end of the day, knowing she was here to come home to, that Seamus was seated at the kitchen table doing his home-work, made it all a helluva lot more bearable.

It was everything I never thought I'd have, and everything I'd always wanted.

This life... well, it wasn't all bad, was it?

TWENTY-SEVEN

DECLAN

"YOU'RE SHITTING ME." I scrubbed a hand over my face as I dealt with the news I'd just been handed—it was just one of those fucking weeks.

"I wish I was." Sin, the Satan's Sinners' MC Enforcer, broke into a burst of heavy coughs.

Not that I could fucking blame him.

"Why the fuck would anyone bomb your compound?"

"I don't know, but we're not going to be able to make things right for the run next week."

I blinked at that, wincing at the amount of work it would take, but hell, what was I supposed to say? Hop to it? When half their compound had been destroyed, the Prez's father was in some kind of coma with an arm and a fucking leg lost to the blast, and with a couple of brothers having passed away to the inferno?

Rubbing my eyes, I rumbled, "Don't worry about it. I'll sort it out."

"We just need a week."

"I get it. I'll handle it."

"Thanks, man."

"Want me to put some feelers out?"

"We have people working on it, but any help is appreciated."

I blinked as I stared out at my office, with the windows that overlooked a field of crates that were loaded with all kinds of gear which was waiting to cross the borders. "I'll bet. I'm sorry, man. Send Rex my condolences."

"Bear's a stubborn old fuck. He won't die without a fight."

"I didn't even think he was a part of the MC anymore."

"Technically, he isn't. But it's not like we're going to kick him out. He ain't been the same since his Old Lady passed on."

"Can't blame him."

Sin blew out a breath. "Nah. Shit changes when you find your own. Before, you just feel sorry for 'em. But when you've met yours? Everything suddenly makes sense."

Because I knew exactly what he meant, I reached up and tugged on my bottom lip. "MaryCat wasn't hurt, was she?"

"No. Thank fuck. She and Digger were upstairs, away from the blast. She gets tired now that she's pregnant."

"That was some dumb luck on the attacker's part that you were all on the compound," I murmured, commiseration in my voice.

"Yeah. Either that or someone fucking told them."

I tensed at that. "Seriously?"

"Fuck knows, man. All I *do* know is that our place has no windows, half of the front end is torn to shreds, and we're lucky that the clubhouse bar is in the middle, toward the back so there weren't many injuries. There are only three windows that look out onto the front. Most of our injuries came from the glass that shattered during the explosion."

Jesus.

Weary, I rubbed my eyes again, and even though I knew I'd set Conor onto the investigation so that we could keep appraised of the situation, I rumbled, "Brennan said he told you about our ties."

"He told me my ma wasn't just a cumslut. She was a fancy cumslut."

I arched a brow. "Well, I wouldn't disagree. I know Leanne too well for my own liking."

"Huh? Why would you?"

"You guys really didn't look too deeply into our links, did you?" I asked, amused as all hell. "Didn't MaryCat explain?" I tacked on, talking about his half-sister who'd started the business operation between the Satan's Sinners' MC and us.

"She doesn't talk about the Five Points. At least, not to us. Maybe to Digger, but he's never said anything in church."

Though I cocked a brow at that, I tipped an imaginary hat to her.

Even knowing we trained our girls well, it suited me to hear that MaryCat knew to keep her mouth shut. Even so far as to the extent that she didn't tell her half-brother about his familial links with us.

"Well, she's my second cousin. On your mother's side. Which makes you my second cousin too."

Silence fell at that. "Christ."

Pretty much summed it up. "Anyway, I'll let that sink in, and the fact that you ain't just a Sinner, but a Five Pointer by birth. If you need us, we're here. You got me?"

He cleared his throat. "I got you."

"Any of the women hurt?"

"No. Thank fuck. Got one man with goddamn amnesia of all things."

"Legit?" I had to laugh. "Fuck, it's like an episode of *Days of our Lives*."

"Trust me, I know." He blew out a breath. "We're going to do the best we can to get back to a regular schedule ASAP. I appreciate you cutting us some slack, and I know Rex will too."

I hummed. "Keep me in the loop, yeah?"

"Will do. Thanks... cuz."

My lips twitched. "You're welcome, Padraig."

When I cut the call, I instantly hit Conor's number as I rocked back in my seat. "Got news."

"Good news?"

"Nope. The Sinners' compound was hit with heavy duty explosives."

"Jesus." The line throbbed with his tension. "Anyone hurt?"

"Yeah." Because I knew him well enough to know where his mind was running, I asked, "You really think Lodestar is living with them?"

"I've believed it for a while."

"Well, Padraig said that none of the women were harmed, so you should be okay."

"Like I give a fuck," he grumbled.

I snorted. "Yeah, yeah. Save it for Brennan. We both know he gives you more shit than I do."

"That's why you're my favorite brother."

"I'm sure."

"Naw, it's true. You are."

"I am today."

"I have news for you too."

"Better than mine?"

"Nope. Well, maybe. Cillian Donahue is alive and well and living in Astoria. He *is* in WITSEC."

Fuck.

"Witness protection for what?"

"Must have ratted us out."

"To whom? I mean, shit. What he knew would be enough for Da to slaughter me."

"Whatever he gave them must have helped a case that wasn't related."

"We'd have heard about it, surely? With the court case? We've had no major players sent down for a long time."

He hummed. "I'm still looking into it."

"That means that bitch really is the blackmailer."

"I'm looking forward to her wearing a body bag."

"Me too." I scraped a hand over my jaw. "Any other news?"

"Nope, but I'll put some feelers out, try and see if there are any whispers about who's behind the blast at the Sinners' compound."

"It's like you read my mind."

"I did. It's a skill I picked up a long time ago."

I rolled my eyes. "Sell that to Seamus... and even he's too old to believe you."

"Speaking of, how's he doing?"

"He's okay. We had a good talk the other day. I told him he didn't have to come into the life if he didn't want to."

"Does he?"

"Nope."

"Not surprising. It's not for everyone."

"You mean working on a Saturday ain't for everyone? I'd never have guessed."

He snickered. "Where are they?"

"Dunno. I don't keep trackers on them. Their guards know to get in touch if there's an issue."

Even as the words slipped from my lips, I regretted them.

Especially when my phone buzzed, indicating there was an incoming call.

I cleared my throat as I pulled it away, and when I saw Liam's name flash on the screen, I cursed under my breath.

"What is it?"

"Liam, one of their guards, is calling. I gotta go."

"Keep me updated."

"Yeah."

I switched over to Liam's call, and what I heard had my heart fucking sinking.

Screams.

And gunshots.

Fuck.

TWENTY-EIGHT

SEAMUS

I'D NEVER BEEN to Coney Island before, and after today, I knew I'd never go again.

Ever.

Again.

The place was tainted. Absolutely wrecked. And not just for my memory banks.

At first, I hadn't known what was happening.

We'd been walking on the boardwalk while Mom and I were eating ice cream that melted down our hands. It had been like any other day out. I'd been with her to the beach so many times, eaten ice cream with her so many times, but it was cool to be here.

New York City was my place.

My home.

I wasn't sure why I felt that way, not when I'd visited all over and had spent most of my life in Europe. But it was. Maybe because Declan was here, and the family. They were all insane, but it was a good kind of insane, you know?

They were killers. The lot of them.

But I knew they had honor.

I'd seen dishonorable things in my time. Had seen things I wished I could unsee, and today was one such event.

Just another to add to the tally.

The boardwalk was stained with blood, and bodies strewn here and there. It was like something from Grand Theft Auto—a nightmare.

People, innocent people, were on the ground, crawling toward safety, but where did you find safety on a boardwalk where there was nothing between the ocean and you but the sand?

There was no coverage, that was what made it a thousand times worse, and Mom and I had been lucky. I'd wanted to go into the Aquarium, so we'd been heading through the entrance just when we'd heard shooting.

On either side of the walkway, there was a kind of grassy knoll, and Liam had shoved us down there while George covered us. Mom had hit her head, and though I kept pressing my ear to her mouth, just to hear her breathing, I knew she was okay. She'd just fallen wrong.

I was almost glad she wasn't going through this. Almost glad because I needed her, and she was unconscious.

A flurry of bullets had me clenching my fists to the point of pain because they were close. Closer than before.

I could hear a mixture of accents—Bronx competed with Russian—and I knew this was a turf war.

A turf war in a seaside resort.

What the hell was happening?

I wanted to cling to Mom, wanted to hug her to me, but I knew I could hurt her even more. I needed to stay still, needed not to move her.

It was hard.

So hard.

I wanted to move her out of the way, tuck her into safety—

A dozen screams rang out around me, and I jerked in surprise when a body tumbled over the sidewalk and into the underpass where we were.

When I saw it was George, my eyes widened because...

His head.

It was...

Where was his face?

The mass of blood and flesh sent me back to *that* day. A day I'd tried to forget. A day I'd tried to delete from my brain, but I wasn't a computer, and no matter how hard I tried, there was no deleting files from there.

My great-grandparents had died like this. But it was *her* I could see like it was yesterday. The blood draining from her chest, sputtering from her mouth as she lay on the ground, staring up at nothing.

George didn't even have any eyes to stare with.

He was a mass of pulpy flesh that made me want to puke.

My eyes prickled with tears, though, because I knew that if George was dead, Liam was nowhere to be seen which made me think he'd been hit too, and Jerry was back in the car, I was alone.

I was the only one who could keep Mom safe.

There was blood everywhere, and in the heat of the day, somehow, the metallic scent was all the more powerful.

I knew I'd never forget it. How could I?

This wasn't the first time I'd seen something like this, and that was before Declan had come into our lives.

I'd told him that my great-grandparents had died in a home invasion that had gone wrong—I'd lied.

Well, not about the home invasion. But I'd only known *how* they died because I'd seen it. Great-Grandma had shoved me in a closet a few seconds before the doors had burst open and masked gunmen had stormed in.

I'd watched them shove guns under their chins and blow their brains out.

That had happened when I was five.

I still remembered it.

Like it was yesterday.

I'd asked Declan to look into it, to see if it was murder, and Conor had told me it was just a run of the mill home invasion that had gone wrong... I knew it wasn't.

Sure, on paper it was, but I'd been there.

I'd seen it. I knew otherwise.

Then there was the time when Mom had a job in West Orange.

People died around me.

Gruesome deaths.

Nasty deaths.

It was why I kept checking on Mom. She couldn't leave me. She just couldn't.

I heard some footsteps on the boardwalk above me, and though the prospect of touching George was horrendous, I knew I had no choice. His gun was in his hand, and I could see from the bulk in his jacket that he probably had another weapon holstered there.

As I moved over to his side, my knees burning as they scraped on a stone in the grass as I grazed it, I managed to take the gun from the holster as well as the one in his hands.

Soon, I knew his body would grow stiff with death. Rigor mortis, they called it. I'd read about it on Wikipedia, but reading about it had only made the memories worse.

Mom didn't know the extent of what I'd seen. If she had, she'd have made me see that kid shrink even more. That was when I'd known I had to lie to her.

Even if it was for my own good.

Talking about that stuff while some idiot tried to get me to talk about my feelings over Play-Doh was not how my brain worked.

The gun was warm in my hands, and I clasped it tightly as I checked it over. It was loaded, heavy with bullets, and the safety was off.

I skidded away from George once more, and making sure I covered Mom, I leaned my elbows on my knees to rest them there, then pointed toward the walkway. Just in case.

A shower of Russian voices came and went, then there was Italian. I heard it. And my heart surged up and out of my chest, almost like I was in a cartoon.

"Where's the Westie boy?" I translated, grateful and ungrateful for the fact that I understood Italian thanks to eight months there when I was seven.

I didn't know why they called the Irish 'Westies,' but I'd picked up on it when a kid at school had called me it. I'd broken his nose for the insult, but the term had stuck with me.

It was how I knew the men were looking for me.

It was happening.

Somehow, I'd known they'd come for me. Where the guy I'd seen on the TV finally realized I'd seen what I had.

When he knew I was a liability.

Declan's world was rife with danger, but I'd been born outside of it. Yet, somehow, I'd been fated to walk this path.

To take this path. One where peril and death were a part of my every day.

I tried to calm myself down, tried to stop the shake in my hands.

I'd practiced for this.

I'd practiced so much just in case they ever came for me.

Footsteps tapped on the boardwalk above our heads, but I didn't move, I just stayed focused on the one field of vision I had—the sidewalk that led to the Aquarium.

Even as I prayed that they'd leave me alone, that they'd think we'd gone elsewhere, I knew that wasn't in my future.

My future was blood red.

In the near distance, above the roar of the ocean and the sporadic flood of screams as bullets cascaded into the sand, I heard brakes squealing.

The cops?

They were too late to save me from myself though.

A guy walked down the sidewalk. He paused, looked over the underpass to the left, then, he twisted to the right. The second he did?

I pressed the trigger.

And my soul was awash with blood for the fourth time in my life.

AELA

WHEN I WOKE UP, I was in bed.

The only trouble was, I had no idea how that had happened.

I remembered being in Coney Island. Remembered eating ice cream with Shay, and I remembered—

Huh.

Bupkis.

Stretching a little, and wondering if I'd had too much wine with dinner last night, I encountered someone. That wasn't too unusual now, considering Dec and I slept together every night—with Shay's approval according to Dec—but this was different.

This one smelled of sweat, and even though he was technically not a little boy anymore, he had that odd scent that was unique to him. Like when he was dirty and grubby and it had this sweaty smell that was kinda gross, but his basic essence, and I loved it.

Sue me, I knew it was weird, and I knew he'd prefer his signature scent to be frickin' Calvin Klein, what with how he kept spraying it on himself before school, but nope. Puppy dog's tails and snails was how he smelled to me.

The old nursery rhyme made me laugh, but I wasn't altogether sure why Shay was sleeping with me. In Dec's bed. Not that I minded, *at all*, it was just... he'd definitely think he was too old for this.

Blinking, I squeezed him a little, and whispered, "Morning, kiddo."

He tensed, then peered up at me, and the agony in his eyes had me wondering what I'd missed.

Cupping his cheek, I asked, "Did you have another nightmare?" We'd gotten them under control a couple of years ago, but I'd only seen him like this when he had bad dreams. Dreams so terrible he'd scream the house down.

I knew this was technically an impossibility, but my kid's will was like no other—I was sure he'd stopped the dreams so he didn't have to see a shrink anymore.

"What is it? What's wrong?" I rasped.

"Don't you remember?" he whispered, his eyes bright pink and blood-shot, tears flooding them...

Why?

Then it hit me.

Shit.

The shoot-out.

I blew out a breath. "Did I hit my head?"

"You were out of it for so long." He closed his eyes. "Mom, I did something real bad."

All I could do was hold him, hold him so damn tight he knew I'd never let him go, and I did just that as I whispered in his ear. "Whatever it is, we can fix it."

His head shook from side to side. "You can't fix death."

I tensed. "What are you talking about, sweetheart?"

"I-I killed someone."

Inside, I sagged. On the outside, I had no choice but to say, "It was self-defense."

"You don't know that. You were unconscious."

"I know you."

He peered up at me, biting his lip as he did so. I knew he wanted me to believe him, and I would.

Always.

I cupped his cheek, wiping the tear tracks away with my thumb as I told him, "You know this world isn't like the one we lived in before, sweetheart. Life and death are a part of it. Your dad will fix things. Just you see."

He gulped, but when he nodded, I sensed how badly he wanted to believe me.

Shay burrowed his face under my chin, reminding me that, no matter how old he thought he was, he was still young. So young. Just a baby.

It didn't matter to me that at his age I was just about to meet Dec. That a few years later I was giving birth to Shay. He'd always be my baby. Always. And I wanted something different for him.

I wanted the best.

Running my hand over his head in an attempt to soothe him, I asked, "Where's your dad?" Funny how I didn't even think to call him Declan.

"Him and the uncles are in the living room."

My brows rose at that. Seemed like we were on the same page—claiming the O'Donnelly clan as ours.

"Why?"

"They're talking about what happened."

That had me frowning.

Why were they using the living room?

"Is your grandfather here?"

"No."

After what had just gone down, that Aidan Sr. wasn't here was telling.

"Mom?"

"Yes, sweetheart?" I questioned, even though my brain was whirring with a million questions.

"You know the night when I hid in the safe room?"

Hard to forget.

"Yes, love, I do."

"You remember before you came home, Caro was babysitting me?"

I hummed my agreement.

"I saw something on the news."

"What was it?" The kid was just throwing stuff at me today, and hell, my brain wasn't ready to function. Not without coffee. And an Ibuprofen.

"It was weird. It was about a funeral."

"What about it?"

"I just happened to see it because Caro was watching the news, but it was this man called Benito Fieri. The news was saying how he was an alleged mob boss, and his son had just died in prison."

"Okay," I intoned slowly, wondering where this was going and why my son was talking about a mafia Don.

It wasn't like everyone in the Five Points didn't know exactly who Benito Fieri was.

"I knew him."

"That's not possible, sweetheart."

"It is." He gulped. "You remember when we were in West Orange? You were making that big chandelier."

For a human trafficker.

God help me.

I really needed to run some kind of tracing service on my potential clients.

"Yeah, I remember."

"Well, I know I wasn't supposed to, but I used to play in the big house. When you weren't looking, I'd go inside and mess around with some of the sand and stuff. The builders never seemed to mind."

I tensed up, and though I was annoyed because I'd worked on Donovan Lancaster's chandelier back when the property was still a construction site, what was the point in getting mad about old news when my kid was evidently going through something here?

"I didn't tell you because I knew you'd be mad."

"Yeah, I would have been. What's going on, Shay? What else are you trying to tell me?"

He pulled back to look at me, and his eyes were bright with tears. "I saw something I shouldn't have."

The horror in his voice had me squeezing him. "What was it?"

"The man on the TV, him and this other guy, they were sitting down in one of the rooms that was finished." He bit his bottom lip. "There was another man, he was like a guard, and he had a gun pointed at this woman." He clenched his eyes shut. "The man, the guard, I mean, he shot the lady. But before that, they hurt her. Badly."

I stiffened. "What?"

"I know you won't believe me, but I swear it's true."

I shook him a little. "Seamus, you saw somebody get killed?" And *tortured?*

"I did," he whispered miserably, and I knew he was on the brink of bawling. Jesus, I couldn't blame him. I felt like bawling too.

"Did they see you?"

"N-No."

Relief filled me. "Okay, so that's good. It's all good." I squeezed him. "You should have told me sooner—"

"I told Caro, Mom." He gulped. "I trusted her. I-I thought she was your friend. I thought she was safe. That night, I had a bad dream again, and she came in and asked me if I wanted to talk about it. I was stupid, because I did. I never said a word to anyone, not even the shrink, but seeing that guy on the TV just messed with me.

"H-He was so mean. He just smiled and barked stuff at the guard, and whenever the woman cried out, he'd grin, like he was enjoying it."

Everyone knew Benito Fieri was a sadist.

He *would* have enjoyed it.

"It was like I was watching it all over again. It was stuck on repeat in my head, so I told her."

My jaw clenched as reality hit.

Caroline hadn't just lied to me for years, pretending to be my friend... she was also a *Famiglia* informant. That was why, when I got back from Manhattan, the hitman had sneaked into our house... They weren't after us because we were tied to Declan. But because of what Seamus had seen.

And whoever the woman was, it was bad. Bad enough to need to kill a small kid.

The murder charge wouldn't matter. No, *she,* their victim, was the reason for the hit.

Before nausea could strike, Seamus's shaky voice continued, "Today, at the boardwalk, I heard one of the guys who killed George—" Wait! George was dead? "I-I heard him ask for the Westie boy."

They'd known we were there?

Oh, sweet fuck. That meant either Jerry or Liam worked for the *Famiglia* too? Only they and George had known where we were going today. And if George was dead, then...

A shaken breath escaped me as I tried to process a million things all at once. I hadn't woken up with a headache, just stiff and sore everywhere else, but I sure as hell had one now. Unable to compute what he was saying, a little dumbly, I asked, "Did you tell your father?"

He tucked his face into my throat again. "I did."

Though he wasn't as creative as me, I knew how his brain worked, and I knew what he'd seen had been torturing him for a long time, so I did what I always did—I tried to soothe him in the only way I knew how. "Describe the lady to me."

When he did, it was like I'd cut open a festering wound that gushed its poison all over me. As I rubbed his back, as he talked, relief hit me, and I realized I was thankful. So fucking thankful that Declan was at my side, and that the harsh realities of his life were tangling with mine.

Because the threat against Seamus would be taken out immediately.

Caroline Dunbar, did she but know it, had just signed her death warrant, and call me a cold bitch, but I'd be the first to dance on her grave when Declan protected our boy and shoved a bullet in that pig's skull.

And when Benito Fieri, who dared to think he could take out my son who'd witnessed his sins, went for a swim with concrete boots, I'd piss on *his* grave after and I'd laugh as I did it.

TWENTY-NINE

AIDAN JR.

WHEN DA STROLLED IN, his brow furrowed, his eyes loaded with the wildness that overtook him when he was involved in wet work, I threw him a towel.

"What's so important that you disturbed me?" he growled, wiping his bloody hands on the fabric as I leaned back in my seat.

Ever since we'd learned the extent of the holes in our organization, we'd been getting deeper down the rabbit hole as we struggled to find out who we could trust.

And who we couldn't.

The poor bastard at the end of my father's wrath tonight was Jerry, an old Five Pointer who'd been close to retirement. All he'd had to do was drive Aela, my brother's woman, and their kid around the city. Nothing more, nothing less. But he'd turned traitor.

With George dead, and Liam *half* dead in the ICU, we knew it was Jerry who'd given the Italians Aela and Shay's location, and now my father was currently squeezing details out of him like juice from a lemon.

"I called this meeting tonight because it's time we discussed the next steps we're going to take."

Da frowned as he peered around the council room. It was inside a safe room, the air controlled, the sound proofed. It was like being in an iron lung. I fucking hated it, even if I understood the necessity.

The urge for an Oxycontin was like a mosquito bite I needed to scratch. This was just the start too. It'd work its way up to chickenpox that would make skinning myself just to alleviate the inflammation a wonderful prospect.

At the moment, it was manageable

Barely.

"Where are Tony, Mark, and Paul?" he grumbled, referring to the men he considered his advisors. "They should be here for this."

"How do we know they haven't gotten to them too?"

"We don't even know who *they* are," Da snapped.

"Yeah, so while shit's up in the air, we need to keep things nice and tight, don't we, Da?" Eoghan pointed out, and because, for some weird fucking reason, our father always listened to his youngest before he listened to his goddamn eldest, Da simmered down.

The council room was simple, chairs and a table, not much else. But there was a very fine drinks tray, and uncaring that his fingers were stained with Jerry's blood, he strolled over to it, lifted the bottle, and poured himself a shot.

His hackles were up, even though Eoghan had calmed him down. I knew why too.

We prided ourselves on loyalty.

We weren't a brotherhood, but a family.

Da looked after people. They did right by us, we did right by them.

They didn't, we ended them.

But to learn that someone, *some-fucking-how*, had managed to get to my da's grandson had tipped him over the edge. Jerry wasn't going to last much longer than a night, and that was without Declan getting his hands on him.

By rights, Dec should be the one doling out the punishment, but where Da was concerned, and when he had that look in his eye, you never said no to him.

I didn't even think Ma did in those circumstances, and she had more control over him than any of us.

"What the fuck is going on?" he rumbled. "Got men turning tail who've been like family to us. Men getting killed who're loyal. I don't like it." He took a deep sip. "I don't like it at all."

Declan cleared his throat, and I knew he was nervous. We'd all decided that there was no need for any light to be shone on the fact that Caroline Dunbar had been blackmailing Dec for years. We were focusing on shit that needed attention, not old news.

Sure, that old news was incendiary, but we didn't need to split Da's attention. Killing Dec for past indiscretions when he'd been nothing but a kid wasn't going to get us anywhere.

"Caroline Dunbar's been a thorn in our side since Jimmy D died. It fits that she'd try to get us to betray one another."

"True. I never understood it. He was a fucking snitch. What kind of father is that to be proud of?"

We all looked at each other, a rueful resignation in our eyes. Da couldn't see the forest for the trees sometimes. He'd never think that he wasn't much to look up to either. That would simply never occur to him.

"Well, either way, she loved him, and she's been trying to get back at us for years," Declan replied. "I'm just surprised she has the Italian's ear."

Da spun around at that. "This war's been going on too long."

"We've been thinking about that. We know Domenico Rossi is the next in line after Fieri. If we take him, use him as leverage, get them to stop the war—"

Da raised a hand to stop me. "Fuck that."

"Da, we can't afford to be fighting a war on all fronts," I argued.

But he shook his head. "We don't go in there like pussies. It's time that fucker was taken out. Fieri thinks he can target *my* grandson?" he raged. "Then he'll learn the price that comes with that." He pointed at Eoghan with a hand that was stained with another man's blood. "He'll be well protected. You figure out a way to get to him, take him out without putting yourself at risk, and do it fast."

"It'll take time. You know I need to learn his routine," Eoghan said simply, unaffected by the prospect of killing the Italian Don.

Not that I blamed him. We were all too at ease with killing. It was shameful really.

"That's not a problem. Learn it, learn it well, but take him out. I want no mistakes," Da rumbled as he slammed his whiskey back. "As for that bitch, kill her too."

"No. We need to know what she knows," Finn argued. "She's a fountain of information that we can twist to our own benefit."

"You'd let her live after the stunt she pulled?" Da challenged, his eyes flaring wide. "Impossible."

"There's a wider game at play, Aidan. You have to see that," Finn reasoned. "People are pulling strings, and the only way to know who's at the top is to get close to someone who's a part of the organization. Caroline Dunbar's been playing games throughout her entire career. We need to make her scared. We need to turn her to our side. We need the information she has."

Da's jaw ground down so hard it was a wonder his teeth didn't turn to dust, but even though he was half feral, I knew Finn's cold logic had gotten through to him.

"What if she turns on us?"

"We have leverage on her," I confirmed, casting a glance at Conor who nodded.

Not just how she'd been blackmailing Declan for a decade or more which none of us wanted to use considering it would implicate Dec in a cover-up, but ever since Brennan had picked Dunbar up last night and stored her at the warehouse for processing, Conor had been burrowing into her life. It was a lot easier when you had the key to her house.

"We do. There's a safe as well. She must keep a lot of information in there. I'm sure that will help tie her to us."

Da's shoulders bunched up. "I don't like it. She'll try to betray us."

"So we have to outsmart her," Finn countered. "I think Conor and I are more than capable of doing that."

Because the pair of them had proven themselves time and time again, Da grunted. "The second she tries something, you slice her throat. You got me?"

"We got you." We all said it in one voice, incidentally, but it seemed to pack a punch.

He grunted again, then made for the door. "You find out if Tony, Mark, and Paul are dirty. Let me know, because I'm in the mood for slicing some throats myself tonight."

As he walked out, Conor muttered, "I might plant some evidence against them myself. I hate those fuckers."

"You're not the only one," I said dryly, but I turned to Declan whose fists were strained as he curled them about his seat. "You doing okay, dearthár?"

His mouth tightened. "I should be at home. Either that, or I should be killing Dunbar."

Finn shook his head. "I get it, I do. But you know why we're doing this."

He gritted his teeth, and at that moment, he looked so like Da it was uncanny. "Just because I understand something doesn't mean I like it." He slammed his hand into his fist. "Da's going to have to share his spoils."

When he stormed off, following Da, I watched him go.

"This is a clusterfuck," Eoghan rasped.

"I can't believe they tried to target one of our kids," Finn concurred, and I saw, deep in his eyes, how that infuriated him. With Jacob still so young, I got it.

How couldn't I?

"We'll show them," I replied, my voice as soothing as it could be when I was furious too.

"That a promise?" Finn asked, his gaze on mine.

"It's a fucking vow."

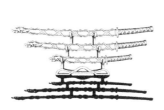

DECLAN
Three weeks later

AS I GRABBED the leg of the stool with my foot, I dragged it over the rough concrete floor. When the bitch flinched at the admittedly annoying noise, her head whipping from side to side as she tried to process what was happening, I carried on. Not stopping until the stool was directly in front of her.

She dangled.

There was no nicer way to phrase it.

Her arms were behind her back, cuffed with her own handcuffs, her feet were tied together, and her graying ponytail was hanging on a meat hook. Just high enough that she had to stand on her tiptoes. It was a delicate kind of torture, but the strain was wearing on her.

I was kind of hoping she'd make herself bald.

The fucker deserved it.

Before I took a seat, I reached up and quickly tore off the duct tape from her mouth. As she screamed, she swayed, and as she swayed, she screamed even more as her hair pulled at the roots.

"Who the fuck are you?" Caroline Dunbar hollered.

"I think you know who I am," I rumbled, watching as she tensed. Her head tilted to the side like she was trying to process all the information I gave up with that one sentence. For three weeks, we'd held her, and that she was starting to crack up was only a bonus to what I had planned tonight.

"D Declan O'Donnelly."

"Give that girl a coconut," Brennan called out.

"I'll give her something," I growled, leaning forward to shove her.

Her scream, her pain shouldn't have been a delight to behold, but it was.

If this cunt had her way, my kid would be dead.

She'd put him in the crosshairs.

And though it was painful, though it fucking hurt, I was doing this for Seamus.

I was going to let her live for him.

Someone was going to die tonight, but it wouldn't be her. Eoghan was out, seeing to that particular job, and here I was, allowed to let loose on the woman who'd nearly torn my family from me before I had a chance to start living for the first time in my fucking life.

But I had a choice.

I could think smart or I could think vengeance, and in the days ahead, I knew we had to think smart.

Jerry, a Five Pointer who'd been with us for forty-four years, had been turned. *Fucking turned.* The Italians had used their little battle as a cover-up to get to my boy, all because Jerry had told them where he was taking them to. Now George was dead, Liam would never be the same again, my son was screaming the fucking house down at night whenever he managed to get to sleep, and we had, only fuck knew, how many rats and snitches just waiting to sell us out.

While I wanted to slice her throat from one side to the other, I knew I couldn't. I knew, in the long run, we'd be safer if she still walked around, and I had to take my need for vengeance out on one person—Benito Fieri.

Tonight, the war with the *Famiglia* would be over because the infighting would begin. The second Eoghan slaughtered Fieri, things would get real messy with the Italians. Though the Rossis were second in line to the *Famiglia* throne, I'd bet my life savings that the Genovicos weren't going to let them ascend without a fight. They'd start brawling and battling over who'd lead them, which would give us time to regroup.

Time we badly needed.

"What do you want?" she sobbed, breaking into my thoughts.

"Typical. Low pain threshold. What the fuck do they teach Feds at Quantico?" I grumbled.

"Apparently not how to be good at their jobs. If she was, she wouldn't have been found out, after all."

"I dunno, bro. What's that old saying? About tangled webs and deceiving?"

Brennan grunted, but his boots echoed around the warehouse as he moved toward me.

The place was empty except for me and him, but that was because we did the wet work. Eoghan too, but his was from a distance. Someone had to take out the trash, and we were fucking good at it. Unfortunately for me, Caroline would end up in the ER tonight, not the city morgue like she deserved.

He flashed me his cellphone, and we shared a smile as I saw the picture Eoghan had sent over.

Benito's corpse with a bullet between his eyes and my brother's boot between his shoulders as he kicked him into the water.

Per Da's rules, Eoghan wasn't supposed to get that close to the fucker. Was supposed to shoot from a distance. It figured he had to get nearer, that he needed to make the bastard know who was taking him out.

This was personal.

The second Da had learned that Seamus was the intended target, he'd gone on a little rampage that not even Ma had been able to contain. There were a lot fewer Italians roaming around, let's just put it that way. But he was out of sorts, and I couldn't blame him.

Not knowing who to trust, who to lean on was wearing on us all.

While Fieri *was* dead now—the plan for the assassination had taken three weeks of solid organization—there was no real justice in this world. Still, I breathed a little easier knowing that cunt was out of the picture.

Which let this one take front and center.

"W-What d-do y-you w-want?" she sobbed again.

"How is it you've been blackmailing me all these years?"

Her sudden stillness told me she hadn't expected me to veer down that route.

"I-I haven't."

My fist sailed through the air before she could finish the sentence. She howled as her head flung back with the force of my punch. The move pulled at her roots and she hopped up and down, trying to find her balance once more.

"You think you can fucking lie to me?" I snarled, my hand coming to her throat which I squeezed. I squeezed so hard I knew I could drain her of oxygen without a shadow of a doubt.

"N-No! N-No! S-Sorry, promise I won't," she sputtered.

A calming hand was laid on my shoulder.

I cut Brennan a look. He stood there, utterly understanding, but it was still a wet fish to the face as I took a step back.

As she gasped for air, I got myself under control.

She could die tonight.

Or she could pay for her sins for the rest of her life.

I was too Catholic not to appreciate the latter.

When she was still sputtering, just not as much, I rasped, "How did you arrange it?"

"I brought Cillian Donahue in," she whispered miserably, but she said it fast. Her words tripping over themselves as she hurried to give me what I wanted. "Told him I needed dirt on you. If he didn't give it to me, I had a nice little cop murder I could pin on him. So he did. Easily. He wasn't happy with you after his sister died, so I made arrangements for him.

"He went into WITSEC after we figured out a way to make him look like he was dead. He sang like a canary."

"About what? There's no way your superiors would put him through WITSEC unless he gave them something good." When she fell quiet, I reached for the corner of the duct tape I'd rolled over her eyes and yanked it good and hard.

She howled as I took off a few eyelashes and half her left eyebrow.

When she screeched some more as it ruptured her balance, I folded my arms, just waiting for her to find her new equilibrium.

"They'll kill me if I tell you," she whispered, blinking at me through pain-dazed eyes.

"I'll kill you *tonight* if you don't."

"They have eyes and ears everywhere." Her mouth trembled, and she cut Brennan a beseeching glance. "I'm a Fed. There are repercussions for doing this. If you let me go now, I'll tell them I was mugged."

Brennan snorted. "Muggers don't wax half your eyebrows off." His smirk turned deadly. "We don't make deals with pork byproducts. You ain't good enough to even be called bacon, bitch. You *will* talk."

She started trembling, but I sensed that whomever she was scared of, she was more terrified of them than us.

Well, we couldn't have that, could we?

I strolled off, leaving her with Brennan, and I headed over to the table that was just out of the light, hidden in the shadows. Finding the wire cutters, I hefted them in my hand, tossing them slightly as I returned to her.

With each step, tension filled her, especially when I approached from behind.

She started to twist, then she'd stop as it pulled on her hair, but each time, I sensed her growing panic, and I let it build and build until I snapped out my hand, grabbed hers, slotted the cutters onto her pointer finger, and let it chomp through her bone.

She didn't even scream, just passed out.

I moved around her with the finger in my hand which I wrapped up in a napkin, and tossing it at Brennan, murmured, "Go and see what she has in her safe."

"Can't believe Conor couldn't hack it open," he grumbled.

"Whatever's in there must be worth hiding."

"What if it needs a retina scan?" he joked. "Gonna plop out her eye with a melon baller?"

"A major component of every torturer's bag of tools," I replied wryly, watching as he strolled out of my warehouse, leaving me alone with this bitch.

I was covered in blood, but before the night was out, I'd be covered in plenty more.

Taking a seat on the stool in front of her, I grabbed my cell and dialed my woman.

"Hey, baby," she greeted, and because she knew more than she ought, she asked, "Is it done?"

"Part one, sure. That's over. Part two, not so much."

"Having fun?" she asked dryly.

"Plenty. Not my usual scene. Do it for the job. This is different."

"I expect no less."

"My bloodthirsty wench," I replied with a grin, but it tapered off as I inquired, "How's the kid?"

"Better. Hasn't screamed yet." She let out a breath. "First time in three weeks. You know who the woman is yet? The woman he saw get killed?"

"No. It's on the to-do list. She just doesn't realize she needs to be more scared of me than whomever she's working for."

"Do me proud?"

"Always."

She smiled, I heard it in her voice, and that smile cleansed me somehow. Better than confession. It made *all* of this right. All of it acceptable.

I was doing this for my woman, for my boy. What other purpose was there for a man like me other than to defend his family? Other than to make the enemies of that family pay?

"I'm sorry you're spending the first night in the brownstone alone." I'd been looking forward to fucking her in the big four-poster in the master bedroom.

"I'm sorry too, but I'd prefer you to be doing what you're doing." When I started to smile, she murmured, "Guess what I found."

Wasn't hard to guess.

A little sheepishly—which was ridiculous because she couldn't see me—I ducked my head. "What did you find?"

"*Master of Dawn.*"

My nose crinkled. "You know how long it took my broker to find that?"

"My first work of art? Christ, I don't even know. It's good to see it again."

"I should have realized you'd immortalized me in art a long time ago."

"My way of trying to get closure."

"How's that working out for you?" I joked.

"Badly," she teased. "I like having it back home."

"I paid for it."

She laughed. "Good to know, cat burglar."

I could feel my eyes twinkling. "You going to be all right?"

"Of course I am. Make her pay, sweetheart."

"Don't worry, I will, *laoch.*"

A sigh drifted from her lips. "I love that you call me that. I don't always feel like a warrior, but when I'm with you, I do."

"You were born to reign at my side, sweetheart."

She fell silent at that, and I let her. I let her process how much I meant that, and then she sealed the deal perfectly by whispering, "I love you, Declan."

"I love you too, Aela. This is the first night of the rest of our lives, okay?"

"Without destruction, there is no creation," she murmured.

And while I could have joked about her turning all poetical on me, I didn't.

Couldn't.

Instead, feeling a little choked, I murmured, "Aela? Does that mean what I think it means?"

Her laughter tinkled down the line, but at that exact moment, Dunbar began to moan.

"Shit, I have to go. We'll talk later."

"Oh, I'm sure we will. I'll wait up for you," she teased, before her tone hardened, darkened, enough to make my cock twitch. "Now, make the bitch pay."

She cut the call for me, and when I stared into the pig's terrified eyes, I smiled.

I had my orders, and like any good foot soldier, even one as high-ranking as me, I knew to always obey.

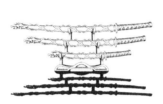

AELA

I STAYED up for him like I promised.

Didn't matter that it was past four AM and I was exhausted. Didn't matter that I wanted my bed more than I wanted my next breath.

I told him I'd stay up for him, so stay up I would.

That was how we were going to work from now on.

No more secrets, lies, half-truths, or broken promises.

Just the truth. Nothing but.

I couldn't cope with anything else, because I needed him more now than I ever had before, and that was really saying something.

The world was in chaos, and Seamus had been in danger long before he'd even entered the Five Points' hemisphere. That told me something—some people were born to violence, and that was us.

That tied us together as well as blood.

I rested my head against the armchair's wing and closed my eyes. I loved the brownstone. It was what I'd needed—solid and not paper screen walls—but it was in dire need of being spruced to my specifications. At the moment, it was a house and not a home.

If this was where we were going to put down roots, then I was going to make it that for us. Our nest. Our haven amid the insanity outside these walls.

The room had a fireplace, complete with mantelpiece, and atop it, there was a carriage clock that ticked and ticked, endlessly ticking. It was soothing, though, and it lulled me into a half-sleep until I jerked awake when Declan murmured, "Oh, *laoch*, you didn't have to stay up this late."

My eyes popped open, and I almost jumped back at the sight of him.

He was covered in blood.

Jesus.

He stared at me, and I knew what he was doing.

Letting me see the real him. Letting me see the monster who hid inside the love of my life's soul.

As he leaned down, I reached out and touched his blood-stained cheek. I didn't need to know what he'd done to see it was gruesome. No one bled this much from a nosebleed, after all.

His skin was crispy with it, and the prospect of him driving home like this had me shaking my head at him. "You have a death wish? Driving around looking like something from a horror movie?"

His lips didn't even twitch, which told me his mind was elsewhere. "Needed to come home," he rasped.

My throat was thick, because I knew why.

He'd heard filth, and he needed to be clean.

He'd heard things that made him think we weren't safe, and he wanted to protect us.

"I love you, Declan," I whispered.

He blinked, and for the first time, his features were less wooden. "I love you too."

My feet were numb from being cooped up in the armchair, but I lowered them to the ground and surged to a standing position.

"Let's get you clean," I told him, holding out my hand for him to take as he also moved to stand.

He was still wooden. Still a little robotic. And even though I worried for him, I knew this was a part of the job.

You couldn't tear into someone without a part of you being affected too.

That wasn't how the soul worked.

We were quiet as we crept through the house, not wanting to disturb Seamus who was on the third floor, and I moved us straight into the bathroom.

I didn't turn the light on, just began to undress him, working the expensive leather jacket off his shoulders, removing the wifebeater, and then the boots, followed by the grimy jeans.

When he was naked, I stripped too, and though he touched his hand to my belly, I merely smiled up at him.

"I'm ready," I told him, my tone strangely serene. And I was. I'd never thought about getting pregnant, but I'd made no move to prevent it from happening either.

I wasn't getting any younger, Seamus was too old for babies around the house to be anything other than annoying, but mostly? I just wanted his kids. More of them. I wouldn't say I was a natural mother, but this felt right.

Perfect.

As perfect as this imperfect world was capable of being.

Sure, I knew what I was bringing this baby into, but Declan wasn't the man he'd been before. He knew who Seamus was. What our kids could be like. I knew he'd do his best to keep them untainted from the life. And me? I'd never be like my mom or Lena. I'd fight for my kids. I'd fight for their futures.

"Thought you had an IUD," he admitted.

"Had it taken out a couple of months before everything went down," I told him, my lips quirking. "Fate has a funny way of working out, doesn't it?"

He hummed. "I hope it's a girl. Hope she looks like you."

"Only fair considering Seamus is your twin," I teased, but I prompted him into action, and he let me guide him into the shower.

Declan's soul housed a monster. One that was cultivated from his father's dictates. But he was still my man.

Mine.

My protector.

My children's defender.

I was careful with the water temperature, then I prodded him until he stood underneath the fall. He let me soap him up, let me tend to him, and when I reached up and cleaned his face, he tilted his head back and bent his knees so I didn't have to lean up on my tiptoes.

When he was clean, I pressed a kiss to his lips, and when he curled his arms around my waist and hugged me to him, I let him. I gave him what he needed in silent thanks for what he gave me.

Tonight, and every other night since this disaster had begun, he'd put his soul on the line for Seamus and me.

That went deeper than love.

I hugged him back, showed him that my need for him was just as fierce, and when the water ran cold, I switched it off, and we drifted, soaking wet, to the bed.

We didn't make love.

We just lay in each other's arms.

The monster was tucked away for another night, until he'd have to rear his head once more to defend those he loved the most.

Me and his son. And now this baby too.

Forever.

AELA

SIX MONTHS LATER

SCOWLING, I OPENED THE DOOR. "WHAT?"

Lena's brows surged to her hairline. "I told you I was coming."

A little dazed because I was knee-deep in my work, I rubbed my forehead, shoving a few strands of black hair away. The blue dye had long since disappeared.

"Sorry, Lena. I was busy. Didn't remember you were coming."

Her laugh was wry as she looked me up and down. "I can tell." Rubbing her hands together, she asked, "How long until I get my first painting?"

"A few more days, *if Declan will just sit still,*" I hollered up the staircase.

"I sit still," he growled back, loud enough to trickle downstairs.

"Not still enough."

Another laugh tinkled from Lena, and she slipped her arm through mine even as she went to tap my belly before instantly freezing. "Oops."

I sighed. "It's okay. You can touch it just this once." Why everyone insisted on wanting to touch my bloated belly, I'd never know.

I'd already made it a point of telling Lena not to do it, and though she was pretty good about it, she sometimes forgot.

My belly was my belly. The only person who could touch it was Declan, and that was if he was going downtown to Oralsville. I didn't even like Seamus touching it, for fuck's sake.

Though I gave her permission, she moved away from me with a

sheepish smile and instead opened her arms to me so we could hug. I liked that we were closer now. It made things easier for Declan. Even though I knew Lena had failed a *lot* as a mother, she loved Dec and that love was returned.

It was nice, as well, to get two different perspectives on things.

Mom and I, well, I didn't think we'd ever be super close. When she'd chosen Dad over me, when she wouldn't come to Ireland with me, she'd really let me down. We had a lot to overcome before we could ever really be close. But I was trying. So was she. For Seamus's sake, at any rate.

But, along the way, as we went out for coffee together, and she'd helped me decorate this place too, she gave me insight into things, and it was so easy to see how Lena and I were on the same wavelength.

Mine would give me trite advice on marriage that made me feel like I was back in the seventies or something.

Lena?

She regularly told me that men deserved a slap upside the head from time to time to make them see sense.

Of course, I didn't always agree unless Declan really goddamn deserved it.

I wanted to be friends with both my mom and Lena, though, so I was trying. Sometimes it was easier than others because opening up was hard, but I knew Seamus needed outside help, and Lena, in particular, with her past, could give him what I couldn't.

Hugging her back, I told her, "He's in the living room."

Lena had been helping Seamus get through what he'd seen. She'd gone through it herself, gone through worse, in fact, and together, they were working on giving him some peace. I never interrupted their time together, I let them be, but I liked to check in with Shay before and after. Make sure he was doing okay. As okay as a kid could be when he'd seen a woman being raped and murdered...

At least we knew who that woman was now. That had given him some closure. Not much, but some. Putting a face to the name had helped him, if not the Satan's Sinners' MC—the Five Points' allies.

As I neared the living room though, which was at the back of the brownstone, I heard the shooting and growled under my breath.

Storming into the room, I snapped, "Seamus O'Neill O'Donnelly! What the hell are you watching?"

His head whipped around, and I saw the guilt on his face as he quickly turned the channel over. But even as I glowered at him, something on the TV caught my attention.

"*Breaking News: Three lost classics have been miraculously returned to the* Isabella Stewart Gardner Museum, *where two of the returned paintings were originally stolen. Vermeer's* The Concert *has been named as one of the works of art. Considered the most expensive missing painting in the world, its return has stunned museum workers—*"

"Now, what's your mother told you about watching that kind of thing?"

Lena's voice was a dash of cold water on my face as I gaped at the screen where *our* paintings—that I'd thought were still in the safe back at the apartment, just waiting on a climate-controlled vault to be installed here —were suddenly being broadcast to the world as they were placed onto a wall in the museum, surrounded by happy faces all around as excited staff and what looked like a few local politicians applauded their return.

In a daze, I twisted away and shuffled back up the stairs to where my studio was.

When I moved inside, I saw Declan was peering down at the street, and I threw myself at him.

My mouth connected with his the second he'd twisted around, and I fucked his mouth, fucked him even as my hand scrabbled at his fly, even as I pulled out his cock and jacked him off. Like always, he was ready to rock in seconds, and I groaned, my panties wet, my pussy molten with heat and the need to have him inside me.

"Like your gift?" he rumbled, evidently understanding where my sudden need had come from, as he jerked away from me and started to lift up the skirt of my dress. When he hauled it overhead, he groaned as my tits spilled free. He buried his face in them, making me moan as he bit the tips of the nipples a little rougher than I could bear when they were so sensitive.

I arched up on tiptoe, my hands sliding through his hair as I hauled him closer, needing to be cleaved to him. Skin to fucking skin.

His hands moved to my panties, and he dragged them down a little before his fingers slipped between my legs. The second he touched my clit, my entire body lit up like the Eiffel Tower. I hissed even as I rocked into him, but it wasn't enough.

Never would be where he was concerned.

He groaned as he felt how wet I was, then he moved me away from the easel that housed a portrait he'd been patiently sitting for over the past three months as I worked on perfection, and shuffled me over to the sofa that was a new item in here.

Before, there'd only been worktables and closet space for my gear, but now, he insisted I take naps.

It was surreal having him around for this pregnancy. Surreal but wonderful. A burden shared was a burden halved. I'd never have known that if it wasn't for this time together.

Carefully, he lowered me onto the sofa, and he slipped between my thighs. When his cock brushed against my heat, my back arched, and I let out a soft cry as he thrust into me with an ease my body facilitated.

I groaned as he filled me, and then he started to fuck me, his beautiful face looming over me as he gave me what I needed.

Him.

His mouth dropped onto mine, and he rasped, "You remember that day at The Cloisters?"

"How could I forget?" I rumbled, thinking back to the day when we'd made an ancient monastery witness the grandest passion of all time.

Ours.

"Well, tomorrow, we're heading up to Boston. I got us the same deal."

"We can fuck there?"

His smile was filthy. Just like him. "We can fuck there."

My pussy clenched down around him, tight to the point of pain as he tunneled through willing tissues that wanted him, but wanted to orgasm more.

As he leaned down and nipped my bottom lip, I dug my hands into his suit-covered back, and rumbled, "I love you."

"And I love you, *laoch*."

When I came, it should have come as no surprise. This man got to me like no other, better than the best BOB. I shoved my palm into my mouth to cover up the sounds I was making, biting down on the soft flesh as I was shoved through an orgasm that beat the many thousands of orgasms he'd given me in our time together.

When he came, he buried his face in my throat, and the heat of him, his breath on my skin, it was perfect.

Just perfect.

I clung to him with my arms and legs, needing to hold him even as I tried to assimilate what was actually happening.

When he peered at me, his eyes softened. "I didn't notice you were wearing this again." He reached up, touched the stick in my hair—the very first gift he'd given me—and murmured, "It suits you." Then he reached for my wrist, turned it over, and kissed my tag.

I'd gotten the hair stick and the tattoo on the same day, after all.

I'd buried the tiny jade ornament in my jewelry box a long time ago, but with us back together again, it hit me in the feels to wear it on the regular.

Because he was looking at me in a way that kind of made me want to cry—stupid hormones—I muttered thickly, "I thought you were building a safe for them and leaving them at the penthouse until it was ready?"

He shrugged. "It's time the world got to see them again." He instantly groaned when my pussy clenched down on him. "Like that, huh?"

"I do," I whispered. "But..."

"But?"

"I missed them. I liked fucking in front of them."

He snorted and reared back. I loved that he wanted to let go of me as little as I wanted to let go of him, and he helped haul me upright so that I was still impaled on him, and his hands were on my butt as he carried me from my studio to our bedroom.

"The safe was finished before we moved in," he told me.

I gaped at him, then slapped him on the back. "You lied!"

He grumbled, "No, but an empty safe is a boring safe."

My eyes twinkled at that. "You didn't?"

He grinned at me. "Gift number two."

The bedroom was a lot more normal than the old one. A regular-sized bed, nice and high so that I didn't have to crawl on hands and knees onto it, with lovely and solid four posts that gleamed with an antique patina that couldn't be replicated.

Amid the curtains that swayed in the breeze when the window was open on a beautiful spring day, was a scarlet and cream Persian rug that was three hundred years old, stolen, of course, and worth a couple of hundred grand.

The nightstands had small bronze pieces on them, two idols that had been stolen from a temple in Tibet back in the fifties. As much as I loved the warriors that were armed with swords and shields, I was working on getting him to return those ones too.

My pack rat of a husband had these little gems tucked in all corners of the house. His jade collection and the kintsugi pieces were on recessed shelves around the room, backlit to show their true beauty for all to behold.

Above the bed was *Master of Dawn*, the portrait of him that was my first piece of art and depicted him in profile, covered in shadows and light—just how I saw him.

But I knew the safe was in front of the bed where the TV was hooked up.

I genuinely thought it was still being made and was going to be installed when it was, but to learn he was fibbing?

I'd have to make him pay later.

Although, he was the one about to walk around with the wet spot on the front of his pants...

"What's in there?" I breathed, unable to deny my excitement.

As much as I wanted the stolen pieces to be back in the museums that housed them, I couldn't deny the adrenaline buzz it gave me to have them here.

He moved the TV away, revealing the stand that hooked it onto the wall. I frowned though, because he looked at me expectantly. "What is it?"

"Press your finger here."

I did as he asked, pressing it to the TV stand, and when some mechanism whirred to life, a giddy excitement whirled through me.

He stepped back as a part of the wall opened up beside the TV, a retractable shelf making another appearance as two portraits were revealed to me.

I gaped at them, then at him.

"You didn't."

His eyes sparkled. "I did."

And then, I had no choice but to kiss him.

And work hard on making that wet spot even wetter.

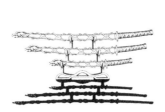

DECLAN
THE FOLLOWING DAY

AS I LED her into the stateroom where our paintings were sitting, a part of me felt a pang of remorse at their loss, but it couldn't be compared to having this woman at my side as we walked down the path of art that led to our personal Mecca.

When she saw the Vermeer, she stopped in her tracks, her hand grabbing mine as she twisted to look up at me with tears of joy in her eyes.

I'd done that.

My woman was a complicated mixture.

As much as she loved the thrill of owning things no one should own, she liked them to be where they belonged too.

I got it. I wouldn't be able to stop, but I could shuffle my personal collection around, give us both what we needed, while slowly returning the pieces to their rightful owners, and picking up others that satisfied my artist's soul.

I mean, I wasn't turning into a saint, and I'd do this until the day I died, but if it pleased her, I'd let some of my treasures go.

As we made it to the Vermeer, I watched the joy on her face and felt it inside my soul.

It made this feel right.

So perfect.

The world was changing, and we were with it. Allies were being torn apart and being forced to rebuild, we had rats inside rats inside rats, and though Dunbar was on our side now, feeding us information that kept us safe, that kept the wolves from the door, that didn't mean the damage wasn't done.

But just because violence was a part of our world, that didn't mean beauty wasn't too.

It was there. In front of us. Timeless.

And as we stood there, appreciating the view, as Conor had arranged, people drifted out from behind us, and she was so floored by what she was looking at, by the breathlessness of the moment, she didn't even notice.

Until she did.

Her head whipped around, and her eyes flared wide as she saw her parents and mine. Shay, my brothers, their wives...

She blinked up at me, but I shushed her, pressing one of my fingers to her lips as I slipped her engagement ring onto her left hand.

Some questions didn't need to be asked.

Some answers didn't need to be given.

She didn't need a ring.

I didn't need a piece of paper.

However... we were still Five Points.

That crotchety old bastard, Father Doyle, who Conor—the organizer of this little event—had to bribe to agree to this, slipped out from the shadows too, and rumbled, "We are gathered here tonight..." and I made her my wife as I stepped up to the plate for the best job in the world.

Being her husband.

AFTERWORD

o.O

Y'all, I sobbed when I wrote that ending.

Just FYI.

I hope you loved Declan's story just as much as I adored writing it.

Thank you for reading, thank you for your support, and thank you for frickin' ROCKING.

Much love,

Serena

xoxo

P.S

Brennan's book is next.

And you can grab it on preorder here: Filthy Sex

Can you guess who his woman is going to be? ;)

If you want to read the whole universe, even though you don't have to as each series is stands alone, here you go...

Bound
All Sinner No Saint
Filthy
Nyx
Link
Filthy Rich

Sin
Steel
Filthy Dark
Cruz
Unannounced Sinners' Novel
Filthy Sex

FREE EBOOK ALERT!!

Don't forget to grab your free e-Book!
Secrets & Lies is now free!

Meg's love life was missing a spark until she discovered her need to be dominated. When her fiancé shared the same kink, she thought all her birthdays had come at once, and then she came to learn their relationship was one big fat lie.

Gabe has loved Meg for years, watching her from afar, and always wishing he'd been the one to date her first and not his brother. When he has the chance to have Meg in his bed—even better, tied to it—it's an opportunity he can't refuse.

With disastrous consequences.

Can Gabe make Meg realize she's the one woman he's always wanted? But once secrets and lies have wormed their way into a relationship, is it impossible to establish the firm base of trust needed between lovers, and more importantly, between sub and Sir...?

This story features orgasm control in a BDSM setting.

Secrets & Lies is now free!

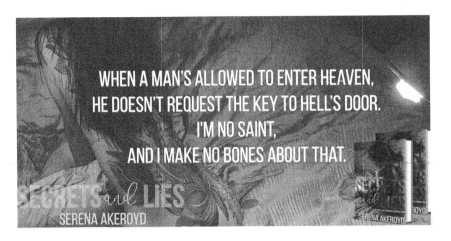

CONNECT WITH SERENA

For the latest updates, be sure to check out my website!

But, if you'd like to hang out with me and get to know me better, then I'd love to see you in my Diva reader's group where you can find out all the gossip on new releases as and when they happen. You can join here: www.-facebook.com/groups/SerenaAkeroydsDivas. Or, you can always PM or email me. I love to hear from you guys: serenaakeroyd@gmail.com.

ABOUT THE AUTHOR

I'm a romance novelaholic and I won't touch a book unless I know there's a happy ending. This addiction is what made me craft stories that suit my voracious need for raunchy romance. I love twists and unexpected turns, and my novels all contain sexy guys, dark humor, and hot AF love scenes.

I write MF, Menage, and Reverse Harem (also known as Why Choose romance,) in both contemporary and paranormal. Some of my stories are darker than others, but I can promise you one thing, you will always get the happy ending your heart needs!

facebook.com/SerenaAkeroyd

twitter.com/SerenaAkeroyd

instagram.com/Serena_Akeroyd

Made in the USA
Coppell, TX
09 March 2021

51530346R00193